A BITTER LEGACY

A BITTER LEGACY

Margaret Graham

BANTAM BOOKS

LONDON · NEW YORK · TORONTO · SYDNEY · AUCKLAND

A BITTER LEGACY
A BANTAM BOOK : 0 553 40819 4

Originally published in Great Britain by Doubleday,
a division of Transworld Publishers Ltd

PRINTING HISTORY
Doubleday edition published 1996
Bantam edition published 1997

Set in 10/11pt Linotype Century Old Style by
Kestrel Data, Exeter, Devon.

Bantam Books are published by Transworld Publishers Ltd,
61–63 Uxbridge Road, London W5 5SA,
in Australia by Transworld (Australia) Pty Ltd,
15–25 Helles Avenue, Moorebank, NSW 2170,
and in New Zealand by Transworld Publishers (NZ) Ltd,
3 William Pickering Drive, Albany, Auckland.

Reproduced, printed and bound in Great Britain by
Cox & Wyman Ltd, Reading, Berks.

For Barbara and Peter Pain

Acknowledgements

My thanks as always to Bath Travel, and to Martock Librarian, Sue Bramble, and her staff. To Sylvia Fortnum for her help in the fashion arena and to Daphne Temple of Artisan's Gallery, Rue Lavaud, Akaroa, New Zealand, who not only alerted me to the existence of women on whaling ships, but guided me towards information. My thanks also to my father-in-law Sir Peter Pain who helped with some of the finer points of property and land 'way back when'. I must also mention our local theme park, Cricket St. Thomas, which I kept in mind when writing Part Three.

I have quoted a line from 'Stopping by Woods on a Snowy Evening' by Robert Frost, published by Collins, on p. 415.

PROLOGUE

Greenwich Village, New York, 1995

Jane Prior sat at the highly polished mahogany dining table smiling at her grandmother who was all clinking necklaces and bracelets as usual; and now Sarah Prior laughed as she held up the list they had been fiddling with. 'Janey, doll, I think we've finished. Asparagus soup, salmon, and hazelnut pavlova. Quite a send off for you, hey?'

Jane's smile faded and she looked around the room, her dark-grey eyes thoughtful as she drank in the family photographs on top of the piano, the ethnic rugs scattered on the woodblock floors, the fire-irons glinting in the grate, all set against soft cream walls which were hung generously with paintings her grandmother had produced over the last few years. They were great wild daubs, full of life and energy. She said, 'I'll miss it all, you all. A year seems a real long time.'

Her grandmother laughed more gently now, the light from the long windows of the Wandle Court brownstone catching her large gold-hooped earrings, and her strident hair, red this week. 'It'll fly past. Time always does when you're enjoying yourself. A year at an English university – hey, that sounds pretty good to me. Now come on, what we haven't done is make a decision on the wine. Chablis or Chardonnay?'

Jane laid her hands flat on the polished surface of the table. 'Dad likes Chablis.'

'But what does Jane Prior like?' her grandmother asked, her eyes shrewd, her face serious.

Jane lifted her hands from the table. A moist impression remained. She rose, restless suddenly.

'Chablis too, I guess. Look, I've got to go finish packing and Mom will be wanting to check the bags and everything. I'll run out to the store for you, then get on home.'

Her sneakers squeaked on the floor, and then on the tiles of the hall. She opened the front door and the August light and heat burst on her, lighting up the wood panelling, falling on the old painting of the whaler forging through stormy seas which hung on the left-hand wall. Her grandmother came up behind her, 'Tell Ivor at the store I'll settle up later.'

Jane nodded, staring at the picture, tracing the shape of the sails with her finger. 'Great blubber boat,' she whispered. 'I don't tell my friends that's how the Priors made their money. It makes me feel dirty. Poor darn creatures. A fortune built out of blood and guts.'

Sarah Prior slipped her arm through her grand-daughter's and together they stared at the painting. 'The *Cachalot* isn't it? Jack Prior's main ship before he converted to steam?' breathed Jane, her brown hair catching the sunshine, and glinting faintly red.

Her grandmother nodded. 'You know, sometimes when it's wet, or cold, or kind of rough outside and I come through that front door and see that picture I almost feel I'm there, being sucked into that world. So I get through into the sitting room just as fast as I can. Four years, maybe five they'd spend in those ships, hunting, killing, rendering down the oil, tracking food sources and therefore the whales. No wonder it bred the Jack Priors of this world. Tough, just such a tough life.'

Jane nodded. 'I'd fight against whaling now, if it was still as big as it was. I don't care what Dad would say.'

Sarah Prior squeezed her arm. 'As you fight against everything you feel is wrong.'

Jane let her hand drop from the picture, but her eyes still clung to the sails, the high-breaking seas. 'I have to, something just makes me.'

12

Her grandmother shook her arm slightly. 'I know, and I admire you for it, but life'd be so much easier for you if you didn't. Your father sees it as "being crossed". The Priors don't like that, they don't like it at all, my darling Janey. They never have, not since Jack Prior's day. I've never known such a driven family, nor one so obsessed with winning. That's Jack Prior's legacy. There could have been better ones.' Her voice was bitter.

Now they both fell silent, and even with the sun and light pouring over them a chill had descended. At last Sarah Prior, moved, sighed and patted her grand-daughter. 'Perhaps when you're in England you'll see Wendham House, Jack's wife's family home. If you do, write and tell me. I want to know if it's worth all that's happened, and if it's worth all that the Priors have become, d'you hear me, darling Janey? I sure would like to know that.'

PART ONE

Wendham House, England 1855

CHAPTER ONE

'It's unseemly,' her godfather called as he approached Irene across the lawn. 'I repeat, it's unseemly. Grubbing about in the earth, on your knees, like any common gardener's boy, and without gloves, and today of all days, when we are about to celebrate your twenty-first birthday. Are you mad?'

Irene continued to plant the Brompton Stock, her crinoline hampering her. Almost, she thought, I am almost mad but it's with rage. She breathed in deeply. One two, one two, slow deep breaths, as her father had taught her when fear or anger threatened. Father!

Her pale, finely boned face sombre, she fixed her grey eyes on the terrace her father had designed and which rose from the lawn via stone steps.

On the terrace rectangular beds were lush with roses, foxgloves and perennial geraniums. Double poppies drooped in the heat. Delphiniums were staked in the beds butting up to the hamstone walls of her home, Wendham House. It glowed in the June sun, and so too did its lands, ranged behind and all around it; wheat-rich and orchard-covered.

Was there anywhere else as beautiful in the whole of Somerset, or indeed the world? Her father had said not, and she believed him, for there were few places he had not been.

It looked just the same this year, 1855, as it had last year, and like last year the wheat would be harvested, the cider would be produced, but it wasn't the same – and never would be.

Her godfather towered over her, casting her into shade, his stocky body seeming immovable. 'You have staff to do this. Indeed, Irene, you think too little of your status. The duty of our class is to instruct, not . . .' he paused. 'Not grovel amongst them.'

She ignored him, looking down at the bedding plant, firming it in, feeling the warm friable earth beneath her hand. Only when it was secure did she sit back on her heels, moving so that the sun fell on her face again, feeling the breeze lift strands of her copper hair which had escaped from the restrictions of hairpins. She waited, staring up at him, for she knew he was not finished.

Samuel Jeffries's greying side-whiskers were startling against his sallow, lined, coarse-featured face. It was a face alive with anger, but Irene was unmoved. Her eyes merely travelled over his frock coat and top hat which struck her as ridiculous here, in these surroundings. Her father had always been bareheaded in the garden, he said the sun made him feel alive. She smiled slightly.

Her godfather shook his head. 'You are again without your bonnet. You'll be flushed for the dance tonight. It won't do.'

She asked pointedly, 'When did we decide that you and Aunt Mary would return to India?'

He moved so that his shadow again fell on her, his face setting at her tone. 'We will return when I have steered you away from disaster and left you in a secure situation.' He drew out his handkerchief and wiped his brow.

Irene threw down the trowel. 'For pity's sake, there is no disaster. That happened last year – it's name was typhoid.' She leapt to her feet, gripping her black skirt, shaking it at him. 'Or do you forget why I wear mourning, Uncle Samuel?'

Samuel Jeffries stilled his hand, shook his head and said softly, 'Forgive my clumsiness, but it is born of worry. My dear Irene, you must try to understand that I have my duty.'

She strode across the lawn. He followed, almost running until he was able to grip her arm, forcing her to stop, his voice was firm, his brown eyes urgent as he bent close. She smelt tea on his breath, the ever-lasting tea that he and his wife seemed to have drunk unceasingly since their arrival hotfoot from India a month ago. 'I have my duty,' he repeated.

Irene pulled from him, her hands trembling with rage as she counted off on her fingers. 'Ah yes, your duty. What was it you said last night? I am to wear half-mourning from this evening on. And why? So that I am more appealing to Barratt, this city gentleman with new money you have found. A man whom I'm to impress as I prance around at my twenty-first birthday dance. Which incidentally is a celebration I do not want.

'Secondly, the rents of my tenants are to be raised which is something my father pledged would never happen. He rebuilt the village, Godfather, so that his people would have good homes to work and live in. *That*, he felt, was his duty.

'Thirdly, a factory is to be built near Yeovil station for making gloves, something else my father would rail against. The last thing he wanted was to be part of the industrial world that's despoiling our land. Wendham was an image he clung to when he travelled, an unchanging image. Unchanging, Godfather, where families worked on the gloves in their own cottages.'

Samuel Jeffries reached out to her again. She brushed him aside, saying sharply, 'But wait a moment, God-father, here I am, talking of father's travels. Surely you've not missed my father's whaling fleet in your swathe of destruction? You'll no doubt find time to set about that also?'

She waited. He said nothing, merely took out his watch, checked it. The gold chain glinted. She shouted, 'Damn you, Uncle Samuel. Damn you, and don't look so shocked. That's what my father would have said to you if you had dared to insist he stop grubbing in the earth, if you had dared to change everything he's worked and planned for.'

Now it was his turn to shout, replacing his watch, gesturing towards Wendham House. 'If he'd planned things rather better then I wouldn't have had to travel to Somerset. How could he leave any woman all this, with no entailment, no guidance? You must be saved from money-grubbing opportunists. Wendham must be made viable. Your father was a fool. My friend maybe, but a fool.'

'I won't listen to this,' she whispered, ducking beneath the old apple tree her father had insisted must not be felled, then along the cinder path he had designed, towards the terrace. She could hear his beloved voice. 'Fashions and fancies are not for us,' he'd stated, standing beside her and her mother, his face weathered from his travels, his arms flung wide to encompass all he held dear. 'There is no room for landscape gardening at Wendham. There is no need to tease nature into something which does not threaten. Natural abundance is what sets the senses reeling. Vegetables, herbs, and brimming flowers for master and servant alike, a tumbling chaos.' Yes, she could hear him as she rushed along.

As she reached the terrace steps her godfather caught her again, pulling her round. She struggled. His face contorted as he shouted, 'Your mother wrote to me, dying from typhoid, distraught with worry because your father would not revise his will and entail his property, or provide you with a guardian until such time as you were married. I came when I could.'

She panted, 'My mother had no right to interfere. My father always knew best.'

'Your mother had every right. She loved you. She loved Wendham. She knew it would be too much for you – and how did she know? Because it was your sainted mother who put your father's ideas into action whilst he shipped off to far flung places searching for excitement, be it whales or bits of plants – those botanical specimens he liked to boast of.' Impatience was in every syllable. 'I will not leave until I have secured your future and that of Wendham, and I act on behalf of my cousin, your mother.'

He released her. A cuckoo called, the rooks in the elms on the far side of the walled kitchen garden cawed. She said, 'But the Estate Manager is handling the farms and the estate just as he's always done.'

Her godfather shook his head. 'I fear that might just be the case, and Wendham could be so much more.'

Irene looked across the gardens, and then up to the house. The sun's rays flashed across the bow window. 'Wendham is perfect as it is.'

Her godfather said, 'We have talked enough. Now, it is well past five o'clock. Go and prepare yourself. Young Barratt cannot fail to be enchanted by such a beautiful young woman.'

He waited and at last she began to climb the steps, but then stopped, 'And the whaling fleet, what of that? The master, Mr Prior, is due this evening, isn't he? I warn you, my father loved those ships. Tread carefully.'

In her bedroom Irene stood in front of the mirror as Martha, her old nursemaid and now her maid, pulled her corset tighter still. She tried to imagine life here with a man. Perhaps they'd have to share a room. She shuddered. Martha stopped and looked over her shoulder into the mirror, her plump ruddy face concerned. 'Mite tight?'

Irene shook her head, then said, 'He wants me to marry this Barratt, but what about love?'

Martha raised her eyebrows, panting slightly as she heaved again on the laces, 'Love, what's that to do with anything?' Then seeing Irene's face she said gently, 'You're twenty-one, too old for fancies.'

Irene retorted, 'What do you, an old maid, know of anything?' But then immediately regretted her words. 'I'm sorry.'

Martha nodded, her jowls wobbling. 'Forty isn't old, just you remember that when you reach it. And by then it's to be hoped you've a brood of daughters around you who treats you better'n the Queen's jewels, not as Irene Wendham, a flibbertigibbet of a spoiled charge, does.' Her face was fierce but her eyes were laughing. She continued, 'Many's the ones who've married without love and something good has grown. Now, on with that there crinoline,' she sniffed over the rustle of linen, 'and the petticoats, though I thought you was going to help me sew them this morning, t'was what your mother would have wanted.'

Irene felt their weight, and their warmth, and longed to discard them, and run barefoot through the evening dew to the copse beyond the garden. There she'd sit and gaze at the moon as she'd done when her father was on a voyage, taking comfort from the fact that he was somewhere beneath that same moon and would one day be home, and her life could begin again.

Irene said, 'I don't know why you insist on so many petticoats. Three or four would cover the whalebone ridges well enough.'

'I've told you before, and I'll tell you again, that you swish that crinoline around as though 'tis a sheet in the wind, and lord knows what people would get to see if you didn't have them eight on top, keeping things right. Don't think I didn't see you running across the lawn this afternoon, and I thanked the lord t'wasn't a gallery of gentry looking on.'

Now it was time for the muslin gown, pale grey with soft pink embroidered roses. 'You shouldn't have let your cheeks get so like Old Henry's apples,' Martha tutted. 'No wonder your uncle gave you a piece of his mind. He's got his head screwed on and I'm right glad he's here.'

Irene stood in front of the mirror, smoothing the dress with her hands. Grey seemed a betrayal of her grief. Martha said, 'You best make sure you keep your gloves on tonight. There'll be quality there and behaviour that was all right for your father won't be considered all right for you, young miss, and don't you forget it.'

Irene spun round and walked to the window. 'You sound just like Mother.'

Then she stopped, and her voice faltered, 'I miss them. I don't know what's happening any more. I don't know what I should be doing.' She rested her head on the window-frame. Martha came to her, slipped her arm round her waist. 'Your godfather's quite right, you know. You do need someone.'

Irene gripped her hand. 'I've got you. I'll always have you, won't I?'

'Mercy, I dare say you will, on account of you needing a good hiding from time to time.' Martha slapped her lightly on the shoulder.

Irene gazed down at the terrace. Light shone from the sitting room where the carpets had been lifted for the dancing. Sometimes, on long summer evenings, her father had swept her mother out through the doors onto the terrace, dancing her round and around until Irene's head had spun just watching them.

'He was so exciting, so big, so different, so loud. He made even the air move somehow. It was worth the absences just to have him here for a while, boiling up, bringing everything, and everyone alive.' She gripped Martha's hand. 'I want the same. I want to feel alive. Mother was so lucky.'

Martha said dryly, 'I dare say she'd rather have swapped all that "excitement" for a steady husband who stayed behind and saw things through. We'd all be exciting if we could pack our bags and sail away whenever we wanted, leaving real life to others.'

Irene snapped, 'That's enough.'

Martha retorted, 'No, t'isn't. You haven't had your hair done yet, so sit you down and stop being so sharp, or you'll get the flat of my hand across your backside.' She shooed Irene across the room to the dressing table. The polished rosewood glowed, the gas lamps hissed. A maid entered, and scooped up the clothes Irene had discarded.

As she brushed Irene's hair, Martha asked, 'Did Mrs Philips feel better for the calves foot jelly?' Irene flushed and fingered her mother's sapphire necklace and earrings as they glinted in their box. Martha brushed more fiercely, glaring at Irene in the mirror. 'You did take it?'

'The bedding plants needed putting in.'

The brushing became fiercer. Martha grunted, 'You needed to do what you wanted, more like. Your mother would have done what was necessary. Your uncle's right. You're not ready.'

Rage and anguish swept through Irene. 'Then she should still be here. They should both still be here. This isn't fair. None of it is fair.'

After dinner Irene stood at the entrance to the sitting room greeting those guests who hadn't merited an invitation to join them at table prior to the dance. She tried to concentrate but failed, her smile wavering beneath the recollection of young Joseph Barratt Esq guzzling his way through soup, woodcock, and a sickly dessert, whilst doling out an even sicklier diet of flattery and stilted conversation. Joseph Barratt – he of the pale-blue eyes and the well-cut suit which failed completely to disguise the plump body. She snatched a glance into the sitting room. He stood by the unlit fireplace, sipping from his glass. Their eyes met. She turned away.

The vicar was standing before her. 'Felicitations, my dear Irene. Seems only yesterday you were in your mother's arms.'

Loss tore through her. She wanted to break from

them all and run, run, back to the past. Instead she led him to a small table by the dark oak dividing doors which were secured hard back against the deep damask walls. He said, 'Forgive me. How inappropriate to distress you.'

Her eyes were bright with unshed tears. His arm slipped through hers. 'Bear up,' he murmured, nodding towards the paintings on the wall. 'Look, so many happy memories.'

All around the room were hung paintings by little known Somerset artists whose subject matter was the sun, and fields, and exuberant youth. These had replaced her father's earlier Turner favourites, which had been consigned to the attic. He and her mother had promised them to her for her coming of age, together with her mother's sapphire necklace and earrings.

Irene touched the necklace, glad of it, but the Turners could stay in the attic. She smiled at the vicar, calmed and comforted. 'Yes, he had wonderful taste.'

She walked back to the entrance, past sweet smelling spermaceti candles which flickered in her wake. They were made from oil brought back by their own whaling fleet; as her father insisted. Now the fleet was back, but this time he would not be the one to bear the barrel home. Again her composure was threatened.

Mary Jeffries joined her, her lavender water wafting. 'A smile would be pleasant, Irene,' she murmured.

Irene swallowed, anger forcing distress to one side. Mary Jeffries fluttered her fan. Again her lavender scent wafted. Now Irene gazed down the length of the sitting room and saw that the bow windows were closed. She said, 'We usually have a window open. It allows in the scent of real flowers.'

Mary turned from welcoming Sir Michael Edwards, Irene's neighbour. She flicked shut her fan, her face frozen in annoyance, 'You are too rude, Irene. They will remain closed for otherwise the moths will enter, and I do not care for them. Now, let us mingle.'

Irene looked into the hall. Her godfather was hurrying towards the library. 'You don't include Godfather in your orders I see. He presumably has more weighty matters to attend to,' she snapped.

Mary Jeffries slipped her arm through hers. 'Come, my dear. Let us not cross swords.' She steered Irene towards Joseph Barratt, her grip like iron, her tone crisp. 'Your godfather has dealings with the whaling master, and will join us in due course. Talk to Mr Barratt whilst I circulate. He's a good and necessary man and has marked your card for the quadrille. I will instruct the musicians to play that in ten minutes.'

Irene looked at her in amazement, and laughed before saying, 'Good heavens, we don't need an army in India with you there, do we? No wonder Father always called you "The Colonel".' But anger was still present beneath the laughter.

Mary Jeffries tapped her with her fan. 'At last, a laugh. Much more presentable than the long face that has become a fixture.'

She swept off to talk to the local school teacher, who had earlier sent a note saying how much he would appreciate Irene's involvement in the school her mother had instigated, for following her mother's death she had not been once.

The musicians were breaking into a square dance as Irene approached Joseph Barratt who inclined his head. The punch in his glass spilt and his embarrassed flush seemed vivid against his starched dress collar. Surprised at his vulnerability Irene said gently, 'Please don't worry.' She beckoned to Alice, one of the maids, who unobtrusively wiped up the spillage while Irene led him from the scene, asking, 'Do you enjoy dancing, Mr Barratt?'

'I seldom have time, Miss Wendham.'

His hand shook, his other was tucked beneath his coat-tails. She said, 'Yes, our world is getting busier every day. It's changing so much with all this industrialization. It's all such a shame.'

Joseph Barratt placed his glass on the table behind him, and now tucked both hands beneath his coat-tails. 'But is it? Progress is exciting. We can't stand still.'

She watched her guests dancing, their crinolines swaying.

'Some may at this very moment, be wishing that they could,' she smiled, gesturing towards the dancers, their waists scooped in by corsets.

Joseph Barratt didn't understand, though her father's laughter would have pealed across the room. 'Then they are wrong,' Barratt replied his tone flat.

'Of course they are wrong, if you say so.' She longed for this evening to be over.

Aunt Mary caught her eye and frowned. Irene nodded and turned back to Joseph Barratt. 'It's rather hot. Would you mind opening a window for me?' Her smile was glowing and inviting.

He inclined his head again and offered his arm. Aunt Mary looked over her fan and nodded her approval, but, as they approached the windows, and Joseph threw one open, she gasped, lowered her fan, and flicked it shut.

One battle charge to me, my dear Aunt Mary, crowed Irene and for a moment was exultant. She breathed in the scent of honeysuckle, and looked out over the garden. Standing next to her, Joseph Barratt said, before the window which remained shut, 'It is my dream to have a country house. I would create a geometric garden, with a landscaped park behind. Order is so important, isn't it? I have this dream of arbitrating in village disputes, and discussing over dinner the vicar's sermon. I would—'

She interrupted, 'What do you do, and where do you do it, Mr Barratt?'

She was still looking out into the darkness where no geometric garden lay, and only would over her dead body. She glanced at his reflection and it stifled her. 'I am a lawyer handling property transactions for the railways.' His breath clouded the window, removing the image of his face, and she was thankful for small mercies.

'How convenient,' she said, understanding now how her godfather had found Joseph Barratt Esq.

Joseph Barratt spoke again, 'Eighteen fifty-five is a time of industrial opportunity, and the growth of the railways leading to easier distribution will change the face of manufacturing. It will make Britain even more important in the world. I intend to be part of that.'

She turned back into the room. A quadrille was announced. The breeze from the window caused the candles to flicker, a moth was drawn towards a flame. She hurried, caught it in her hands, carried it to the window and watched it soar away. 'Please shut it for me.' He did. Aunt Mary smiled. Irene just looked at her.

She ignored Joseph Barratt's request for her hand for the quadrille. No, not for a dance, not for marriage, not for anything, she thought as she walked from him.

In the library Samuel Jeffries reviewed again the clutch of bills before dropping them back onto the desk. He took up the message which had reached him yesterday from the shipping agent in Bristol. So, the fleet was in, but most of the crew were not signing on again, and were complaining loud and long that the master, Jack Prior, had short-changed them on their lay, and even more vehemently, that he had treated them with a harshness which could, the agent surmised, be called cruelty.

'A lay is . . . ? Let me see?' He checked in his notebook. 'Of course, a seaman's percentage share of the profit of the whaling ship. A tenth of the cargo value for a captain, down to one part per two hundred and fifty for an inexperienced hand,' he said aloud, tapping his finger against the page.

He read on, about the meagre profit, and the deal

which Jack Prior had done directly with the middleman when he should have done it through the agent. Now how could they check the number of barrels Prior purported to have sold?

He moved to the blazing fire, standing with his back to it, lifting his coat-tails. God, but it seemed cold after Lahore. He turned and held out his hands to the flames, looking all the while at the photograph of his friend, and Irene's father, Sir Bartholomew Wendham. 'God, what a mess, Bartie. All this,' he gestured to the bills, 'and Irene too. You could at least have got a suitable husband lined up.' He grimaced. Talking aloud, soon he'd be locked up in Bedlam.

He listened to the hissing of the gas lights. Always full of good ideas weren't you, Bartie, and getting gas on at Wendham was one of the better ones. But why buy a whale fleet – if you can call it a fleet. Two boats is hardly a large concern. He felt as though his head was bursting.

He knew of course the whys and wherefores of the purchase of the whale fleet. Gwen Wendham had written to Mary telling her of the old American whaling captain, Tom Prior, whose ship Bartie had booked passage on nine years ago. It was on that voyage that he found the New Zealand botanical specimens which led to his knighthood.

When Tom Prior couldn't pay his gambling debts, Bartie had taken pity on him and bought up the fleet, keeping Old Prior on as master, letting his son, Jack, take over when he died, four years ago. 'Sentimental twaddle,' he huffed.

Of course, back then whale oil had just about been holding its own, but you didn't keep your finger on the pulse, did you, Bartie? You just didn't watch, and *think*. For God's sake, man, you only had to look at the gas you installed here. 'Coal gas is a far superior illuminant, and rapeseed oil is cheaper than ever now. Why didn't you put two and two together and realize whale oil was bound to come down?' He was talking to himself again, but who cared. It eased his headache. He laughed abruptly. Even when he and Bartie were at Eton together his friend had never been able to count.

He looked in the mirror which hung over the mantelpiece, seeing the bags under his eyes, the lines of strain. God in heaven, after a month at Wendham he looked more tired than after a lifetime in India. He drew his watch from his pocket. Nine-fifteen. Jack Prior should have been here an hour ago. Bristol wasn't the end of the world, for pity's sake.

He paced across to the billiard table, he counted the stags' heads mounted round the room, he counted the wooden panels beneath them, and then heard a knock at the door.

'Enter,' he barked, hurrying back to the desk, picking up the shipping agent's report again, ignoring Jack Prior as he approached, ignoring him as he waited. Finally he lifted his head to snap, 'Jack Prior, I presume.'

The man was dark and tall, with broad shoulders. He carried several bound volumes under his arm. His face was ruddy from years at sea, and deeply lined. Samuel read again the agent's comment, *A man of thirty, who's known nothing but the power of command for the past eight years, first as captain of the second ship, then as master of them both. He has a sense of his own importance and takes care to return to New Bedford, the American seaboard port, to reinforce his Americanness, as his father did before him. Speaks with a faint American drawl, in spite of the family having left some seventy years ago.*

He looked at Jack Prior again. He stood with his legs slightly apart as though he was still on the quarterdeck, his cap stuffed in the pocket of his tweed suit. Their eyes met and in Jack's there was no deference, only – what? Defiance? Arrogance? American upstart, how dare he?

'How do, Mr Jeffries,' Jack Prior said, and yes, there

was the vestige of the drawl. Samuel drew himself up, ignoring Prior's extended hand. The American shrugged, and let his arm drop, saying, 'Jack Prior, you presume? Well, you presume correct. I'm not Jack Sprat, that's for sure.'

His lips were drawn back but he wasn't smiling beneath his moustache, and neither were his hard, dark-brown eyes. Samuel dropped his gaze, placing the agent's report on the blotting pad, lining it up against the edge. 'You have your log, Captain Standing's log, and the ledger?' Samuel's voice was cold.

'I have.' Jack Prior dropped the volumes onto the desk. Ink splashed from the inkwell. Dust rose from the books. Samuel coughed.

Jack Prior looked at the fire. 'Find it inclement after India, do you? Find it stuffy myself.' He ran his finger round his white starched collar.

Samuel tapped the ledger. 'We're not here to discuss the clemency or inclemency of the weather. We're here to discuss this.' He held up the agent's report.

Jack Prior brought a chair to the desk, sat down, waving to Samuel's chair. 'Take the weight off your feet while we discuss whatever it is you want to discuss, and then I can get back to refitting the whalers. You want us to take out convicts this time, right? Strange 'cos I put that to Bartie last time. He wasn't having a bar of it.'

Samuel shuffled the bills, coughed again, looked at his watch. Damn, he hadn't known it was Prior's idea he had found noted in Bartie's diary. It weakened his position. He sat down heavily. Then rose immediately. This was ridiculous. This man was master of a ship whose crew would not sign on again, and he, Samuel Jeffries, must have answers to questions, and while he was doing it, damn it, he must cut this man down to size. He leaned across.

'Mr Prior, it is *Sir* Bartholomew Wendham to you, and I arrived at the idea of transporting convicts independently of any notions you might have had. For now, though, we are discussing the problems which have occurred under your command of the whaling fleet. I wish you to take note that I have grave doubts about your ability to captain one ship, let alone two.'

'I can live with that, 'cos I'm partial who I take note of.'

Samuel breathed deeply. 'Then let me suggest that you become "partial" to listening to me, as you would have listened to Sir Bartholomew, in whose place I stand. I believe you were notified of this situation by my agent the moment you put into port.'

Jack Prior lounged back and raised his eyebrows, then looked around the room. 'So you picked up all of this, and Miss Wendham is out on the street?' His voice was heavy with sarcasm.

Samuel tugged at his white, dress waistcoat, fiddled with his watch-chain. 'Of course not, and furthermore I am not prepared to go into the highways and byways with a hired hand. Suffice it to say that I am the guardian of Miss Wendham's affairs and as such I have to inform you that I am disturbed by A' – he wrote the letter A in the air – 'the treatment of your crew whilst at sea – I have word of unacceptable harshness. Now B,' he wrote B – 'the apparent discrepancy between the expected lay, and the actual lay. And most importantly C' – again he wrote in the air – 'the shortfall in expected profits.'

Samuel now sat, his eyes on Jack Prior who had not responded to the accusations beyond a tightening of the mouth.

For a moment more the only sound was the spitting of the fire and the hissing of the gas, but then Jack Prior stood up, leaned forward, his hands on the desk. His voice was quiet, but his eyes, Jeffries now saw, were bright with rage. 'Firstly, harshness and whaling go hand in hand. We're not out collecting botanical specimens, we're out hunting beasts which we catch, slaughter, boil up, barrel down. I sailed with a green crew, and they needed to be hauled into shape.

'So, they end up not liking it. See if they like the factories you people are building any better. I'll bet you a guinea they don't. And your goddamn facts are wrong. I have two mates remaining on the *Cachalot*, and three harpooners, the cook and the cabin boy. On the *Queen of the Isles* Captain Standing's officers are going out again with him, and some of the crew.' He brandished the ledger.

'In this book you'll see the expenses the men incurred. Clothes, victuals, booze. Four to five years, matey, is a long time at sea, and they forget what they took from the slop chest, or bought in port, all of which goes against the lay.' He thrust the book across, opening it as he did so.

Samuel saw rows of meticulous figures. He scanned the columns, turning page after page, his confusion mounting, because at first sight they seemed impeccable. He looked up at Jack Prior. 'Profits?'

'I did my best. Some ships ain't even broke square, and if you're any sort of an owner and not just someone who knows the first letters of the alphabet, you'd know that. I run a tight ship. Profits are always in me mind. Just as they should be in any master's. The men got a bit of lay, you got more than a bit of profit, and when the price of oil is down, that's a mighty effort. Check the figures.'

Samuel leaned back in his chair. '*You* sold the oil in London then came on to Bristol. Why put into London at all, Mr Prior? You should have waited to sell through the agent, not made your deal.'

Jack Prior laughed, a huge ringing laugh. 'What am I then, a mind-reader? How was I to know things were different? Bartie left it to me to sell the barrels on last time, so how was I to know it was different this time?'

Samuel was on his feet. 'You should have known. A

message was sent via other ships to your supply depots. You must have come across them.'

'Must I? Have you any idea of the size of the world?'

'Don't be presumptuous. I have travelled to and from India for the best part of my adult life, and the agent tells me letters are passed from ship to ship, depot to depot.'

'The agent. Is he God all of a sudden?' Jack Prior strode to the fire with that swaggering gait of his, then across to the billiard table. He picked up the black ball and tossed it in his huge hand. 'I'm not of a mind to put up with being ranted at after a damn long voyage, and then accused of stealing by someone who acts an owner, but isn't.' His voice was quiet, slow but the anger was still obvious. 'I'm telling you I got no letter. I just did my job, as Bartie wanted.'

Samuel slammed his hand on the desk. 'Sir Bartholomew, and you just remember who you are, and who I am, or by God, I'll take these ships from you and sell them now, as my sixth sense tells me to do.'

Jack whirled round, spinning the ball across the cloth. 'No-one takes Prior ships away from a Prior, specially on a trumped up charge.'

Samuel said, 'May I remind you that they were sold to us, and are no longer Prior property.'

Jack's laugh boomed again. 'Us, us. Who's this us?'

Irene's voice rang out from the doorway. 'Exactly, Mr Prior. The ships are mine, bought by my father, loved by my father, but under the captainship of the Priors, men my father respected.'

Irene stood quite still in the silence that followed and drank in this man whose laugh had reached her in the hallway, whose vitality even when he was motionless, as he was now, seemed to make the air move.

She said to Samuel, 'My father found no fault with Mr Prior's handling of his crew, or his ship when he sailed with him. You just have to read his journal of those years.' She looked at her godfather but all she

34

was aware of was Jack Prior. 'And now Aunt Mary wishes to cut my birthday cake.' She turned again to Jack Prior. 'Perhaps you would care to join us?'

Samuel raised his hand. 'My dear, Mr Prior is weary, and he is hardly dressed for a soirée. Besides, we still have business to discuss.'

Jack Prior held her gaze which was full of pleading. She said, 'I hardly think anyone would object to an honoured guest making a brief appearance in inappropriate attire at my birthday party.'

Jack Prior grinned, and inclined his head. 'Sounds mighty fine to me, once our business is concluded. Though I bring no gift.'

'Just come,' she said, as she withdrew.

Samuel called after her, 'Present my compliments to Mr Barratt, and request that he takes my place beside your godmother.'

Crumbs lay around the cake. Her guests were dancing the polka. She stood beside her godmother and Mr Barratt but her thoughts were still within the library, still with Jack Prior.

Had she imagined it? Was Jack Prior really so vibrant, so different, so tall, so broad, so bold, fighting his corner, defending his ships as she was attempting to defend her home? She imagined his face in every detail, heard that voice, that laugh. This was as it had been for her mother and father. This was love, this stirring of the air, and the senses.

She looked at her reflection in the mirror, touching her hair, her mother's sapphire necklace. A pulse was beating in her throat. She wanted to pace the room, to wring her hands. Would he come?

He came as the first polka ended, and another began. He came, striding into the room, forcing his way through the guests, walking as not even her father had walked; boldly, loosely, his head held up, looking neither to left nor to right, looking only at her, holding her gaze, stopping so close. 'One dance, Miss Wendham. And then I must leave.'

She could smell the scent of his hair oil, see the shine of it where his hair touched his collar. She laid her hand on one that was broad and strong, and warm, so warm. She slipped in amongst the dancers and it was as though her hand was on fire, even through the satin of her glove.

He pulled her close, too close, closer than the crinoline should permit, and she gloried in it and all the time the music rose and fell, and now they were dancing and she looked only into his eyes, nowhere else. Her feet flew, her dress spun, and she would have flown to touch the stars, if he had led the way.

His eyes were boring into hers and neither spoke. There was no need. Round and round they went and she longed for the music never to stop as the pressure of his hand on her waist seared into her body.

He lowered his head and said, 'You're the most beautiful woman in this room and I'm not going to forget this moment as long as I live.'

On they danced and there was excitement in every breath she drew, and it was as though she'd not been truly alive until this moment, it was as though her father had paled into insignificance, as though she was breathing different air to the rest of humanity.

On and on they danced and his strength was such that at times she was lifted from the floor, and soon the other dancers were forced back to the walls, and she was exultant, because love had come, at last it had come. 'I'm so happy,' she said.

Jack laughed then, that loud, different, bold laugh and she knew that she had been born for this man who had entered her life when she thought that all was lost. At last the music stopped. He released her. Her guests stood shocked and unsure in the silence.

Her godmother came, white-faced and thin-lipped.

She hissed, 'Mr Prior has to take his leave. His carriage has arrived. Mr Barratt wishes the next dance.'

Jack Prior bowed, and walked from her, across the empty dance floor. Her godmother said loudly, 'These Americans – they are so casual, so rash. What is a hostess to do, but humour them? Your courtesy does you credit, my dear Irene.' But her face was still white, still furious.

Jack Prior stopped in the doorway, turned, looked at her for a long moment, bowed. Irene started forward. Her aunt dragged her back. Irene stretched out her hand towards Jack Prior, but he turned, and was gone.

CHAPTER TWO

The next morning Irene watered the wilting bedding plants in the glasshouse. Soon she would bed out the marigolds and fill the gaps left by the overblown forget-me-nots. Beneath the glass dome the hot humid air was thick with the scent of compost and flowers.

She brushed back her hair and looked around the garden, then over to the house and the fields beyond. No breeze stirred, and no Jack Prior strode into view. But why should he?

He'd be travelling back to Bristol, with never a backward thought for Irene Wendham, and she dropped the empty watering can, wanting to weep, forcing herself not to for she must not let her godfather see red-rimmed eyes on her return to the house or he would think that his homily on modesty, decency and the rightness of behaviour had brought repentance.

She dawdled into the vinery, she touched the leaves of the exotics. Oh Father, why didn't you just obtain your plants from Kew, then you would never have travelled, never have bought the fleet, never have brought Jack Prior into my world?

She tore a leaf from an orange tree, folding and unfolding it until it broke. Love couldn't come like that, then just stride out into the night. But it had, and it was not fair.

A voice said, 'Guess your father wouldn't take kindly to that treatment for his plant.'

She spun round, dropping the leaf, forcing herself to stand quite still. Jack Prior stood at the entrance to this towering section of the glasshouse, in the same tweed suit, smiling the same slow smile, looking at her with the same piercing eyes.

'Mr Prior,' she whispered. 'Jack.'

'I guess it is.' His gaze never wavered from hers, and his eyes were so dark and deep, and his face so strong, and now he walked towards her, took her hand, bowed over it. His lips brushed her skin. No gloves, thank heavens she had worn no gloves.

He stood close, and now it was as though a breeze rustled amongst the vines, and the palms, and the orange trees, and into her, though she knew the air had not moved.

She found words, and they were calm, with never a tremble. She said formally, 'I thought you would be halfway to Bristol?'

'You have been thinking of me then?' His eyes still held hers.

In the harsh light of the glasshouse she could see the scar above his eyebrow, the shot of grey at his temples, the deep lines from his eyes, and the deeper ones to his mouth, the mouth that had just touched her hand.

Again she spoke, again she was calm, though her breath was shallow and fast. 'Indeed I thought of you. After all, it is the duty of a hostess to be concerned about the well-being of guests who have far to travel.' But she wanted to whisper, Don't leave. I love you. Never leave me.

'You elevate me, I can't claim to have been a guest.' The mellow scent of pipe tobacco mingled with the scent of his hair oil as he dug deep into his pocket.

'But you became my guest.' Their eyes met, locked. A bird beat its wings against the glass high above them, trying to find the skylight through which it had entered. She tore her glance from Jack Prior and watched the finch, but knew his eyes were still on her.

'And I surely thank the gods that I did become your guest.' His voice was low.

She watched only the finch. Could this strong, in-dependent man feel as she did? Could this man, this buccaneer, as her uncle had called him this morning, feel anything for a country girl? Please say he could.

Now she said, as the finch found the skylight, 'Father wouldn't have a cast-iron framework for the glasshouse. He insisted on wood.' She wanted to ask, Were you using me, as my uncle said this morning, to challenge his authority, to insult him before the guests, to make him appear a fool? There, the bird was out, free, soaring.

Jack said, 'You must miss your father? I know I do. He was the finest man who ever walked the quarterdeck with me, apart from my own father that is.'

She turned back to him. 'Tell me what it's like, out there on the ocean. Tell me what you did, you and my father?' She must not let herself ask, Were you using me? Do you love me?

He told her of the sighting of the whale, the lowering of the boats, the arching through the seas, man against beast. He told her of tracks he had walked in New Zealand with her father, the specimens they had packed into bottles. He told her of the storms which had roared round the Cape, and the gentle air near Java.

She drank in the images he wove, he told her of the transparent blue mornings of the Tropics, the scented air, the kelp-heavy seas, the creaking of the rigging, the flapping of the mainsail. 'And at night, the stars are so close and clear that it makes you feel you could stretch up and snatch one.' His lips were perfect, full. His breath was on her face.

They stood, silent. Now tell me that is why you are here. Now tell me that you were not using me. A door opened, a breeze carried in the sound of the gardener's boy as he opened another skylight with the window pole.

She pulled Jack Prior behind the palms, her finger to her mouth. His jacket was coarse beneath her fingers.

He stood close, gloriously close, and her heart was pounding as Young Matt, the gardener's boy, clomped by, whistling, his farm boots muddy, his corduroy trousers tied under the knees with a thick rope of straw. She smelt hay and sour milk, but all the time it was as though she was on fire.

Young Matt propped open the end skylight, before leaving through the west door. Irene forced herself to return to the aisle, her legs weak, but Jack remained by the palm. She turned, smiled, held out her hand. He stood erect, distant. 'I'm not to be seen, is that it?' His tone was terse, and it slashed her as though it were a knife.

Irene clutched at her skirt, feeling as though it were a fleeing love she was grasping.

'I'm not to come unbidden, is that it? I'm not to come bearing a birthday gift from the master of the fleet to the owner, as I would have done to her father?'

Irene gripped her skirt tighter. Was that all she was to him – an owner, when in Jack Prior she had found heaven? He started to leave. She couldn't bear it. She held out her hand. 'Don't. No. Forgive me. It's just that . . .' She stopped, rubbing her forehead. The magic had fled, the heat of the glasshouse was back, the leaves of the exotics were well defined, the disappointment was too sharp to endure.

She held a pillar for support. 'Oh, I don't know. I meant no offence – of course you were right to come. You have no idea how right. But . . .' She gestured to the house. 'My godfather . . .' She trailed off. 'Don't go. Forgive me.' She would beg if she had to.

Jack Prior came to her then. 'No, it is me who should apologize. Goddamn, as though it weren't enough to break into your party, dance like a wild man, I set about you now. I don't know what's got into me. I did last night though. Last night I was just plain mad with anger and it went to my head, to begin with anyway. But then it wasn't anger, any more. Anger got chased right away.'

He hesitated, then stumbled on. 'I left feeling something else. It sort of got in the way of thinking about anything else.' He broke off, and shrugged. 'I lied just now. I wouldn't have brought this if the owner was anyone but you.'

The magic was back, and he was close to her, his eyes intent, looking deep into hers, and her breathing was shallow, and again there were only the two of them in the world.

He placed a package wrapped in white linen into her hands, before bowing and walking away. She shouted urgently, 'No, please wait. Let me unwrap it, so that I may thank you properly.'

Her hands were trembling. Would he stop? He did, and turned. The gift was heavy. She removed the linen. Jack said, 'It's scrimshaw. A whale's tooth which I carved myself on the voyage with your father. It's no great shakes but it's all I had. Last night, after I left, I felt it might kind of comfort you to have something your father saw being made.'

Irene could barely speak. All she could think was that her uncle was so very wrong. This man was no buccaneer. He was a true, strong, exciting man who was good, honest, thoughtful. He was someone her father had sailed with. A man who brought unshed tears to her eyes at the thought that he had worked on this, in her father's sight. A man whom she could not bear to see leave. A man who had transported her to another world.

She said, her voice unsure, breaking, 'I love it. I'll keep it for ever. You are so kind.'

'It's you who're kind to accept it. I'll think of it, near you.'

She held the scrimshaw, and wanted to press her lips to the hand that had made it, to press her face against Jack Prior's chest, to tell him that he set her on fire, he made the air move, made her alive again. She said nothing, did nothing.

He laughed gently. 'I ought to go.'

'You are so kind,' she repeated, though what she wanted to say was, stay with me, never leave me, Wendham needs you. I need you. I need you just to live, and she gloried that in less than twenty-four hours her life had changed so totally.

He said, stepping back, 'I have business to attend to. I must take my leave of you.'

She shouted, 'No,' but her voice was too sharp, and sounded like an order, and this man would never be ordered to do anything, as her father would not. She repeated calmly, 'No, you have not yet told me of yourself, only of your voyages. You have the advantage of me. You knew my father, but I know nothing of your family, and after all they were the originators of *my* fleet. *Mine*, not my godfather's.' She wanted to say, Tell me you love me too.

Jack Prior looked at her, his face still, his eyes blank, his shoulders stiff and she could not understand the tension that had suddenly chilled the air, but then it was gone as Jack smiled. 'Well, what can I tell you, a Wendham, about the Priors? Not a lot, 'cept my grandfather whaled out of New Bedford. Good harbour that, better than Nantucket, no bar to traverse, but then came the Independence War with Britain. Guess it had to be fought. Independence is everything, if you know what I mean.'

Irene looked towards the house. Oh yes, she knew what he meant. Jack Prior continued, 'OK, we won but you Britishers sailed into New Bedford and fired the place. The Priors were lucky, 'cause my grandfather's fleet were out in the Japan Grounds, doubly lucky 'cause no Britishers sank us on the high seas either. After the war the American whaling industry was in trouble. So, my grandfather moved his ships and whaled out of Britain. But we did, and still do, put into New Bedford on the cruise. Keep up with my roots, you understand.'

Irene said slowly, not understanding, 'But how could

your grandfather have come to the land of his enemy? How could he bear it?'

She was examining his face with her eyes; his mouth, his broad jaw, the way his muscles moved beneath his skin when he talked, 'Responsibilities, Miss Wendham. Mouths to feed, livings to be earned.'

'But why didn't you go back?'

'A mother to be found, and when she was found we seemed to have lost the ships.' His voice was a hiss, his shoulders rigid.

She moved closer, clutching the scrimshaw, brushing against an orange tree, wanting to stroke away the pain she saw. 'A mother to be found?' she queried.

He turned to look at Wendham. 'Ain't that the truth.' He laughed gently but there was no mirth in it.

'Please, Jack, tell me.' Her hand was on his arm.

'Well, seems like Mother couldn't wait for Father to come home one trip when we were living near Lerwick. Took herself off with another man. A Britisher, a soldier boy. I was ten. We spent our leaves looking for them. I went to sea when I was fourteen. Kept looking. Now I don't. She's dead.'

She pulled at him. He wouldn't turn. So she stood in front of him. His face was empty, careful, controlled. He said, 'So we might have different roots, Miss Wendham, but in some ways we're pretty much the same. We haven't any folks.'

Her mind was whirling. Her parents had died, but she knew they'd always loved her, whilst poor Jack Prior had been left by his mother.

'I'd be right happy if you'd tell no-one. I've never said anything to anyone before.'

She continued to look at Wendham, her birthright. She thought of the Prior fleet, which was now the Wendhams'. 'Your father?' she murmured. 'He sold your birthright. On top of everything else, you lost your ships.' But she was thinking, He's told me something he's never told anyone else, and she moved closer.

Jack laughed out loud. It was a harsh sound. 'Sure did, because he was an honourable man, my old Pap. Gambled wrong, trusted a refitting agent, had a poor whaling season, and couldn't meet his debts. Sold it, to a Britisher.' His tone was ironic. Then he shifted and looked away from the garden, up to the house, then down at her. 'To your father, who's as fine a man as I've ever known. He kept me on as master when the old man died.'

She was standing so close she could have reached up and kissed his mouth. She smiled, words coming, though her lips felt too full for speech, 'Father knew the importance of home, of belonging, of independence. That's why he trusts me with all this.'

Jack Prior stepped back, away from her. He said, his tone almost formal, 'That's why I almost didn't come. Makes it awkward, me standing here, with nothing, talking to you, someone with everything. I think I've been presumptuous.'

She shook her head. 'You could never be that.'

Young Matt came out of the kitchen garden pushing the wheelbarrow. Jack Prior gripped her elbow, and pulled her back behind the palms, and she blessed the boy as she felt Jack's hand remain on her arm, felt his grip tighten, saw him lower his head towards hers. Then he hesitated.

Young Matt disappeared into the potting shed. Jack Prior checked his watch, staring at it, then at her, distancing himself from her, dropping her arm, saying slowly, as though the words were being dragged from him, 'I must leave you, Miss Wendham. I have ships to refit suitable for taking convicts. I bid you a happy birthday.' He ushered her before him into the aisle, bowed, walked from her.

She called, 'You'll come again? You've been wonderful, not presumptuous.'

On the point of stepping out into the sun, he stopped, tapped his leg. He looked across at Wendham, then at her. 'I'd like very much to come, but maybe I shouldn't. I'm not after anything and I don't want you to ever think that I am. Don't care what anyone else thinks. It's you that's important. Do you believe I'm not after anything?' His eyes were full of pleading.

She smiled, her heart in her eyes and voice, 'I insist you come. I believe you.'

He stared and it seemed as though he was exploring her soul. He nodded, then left.

Joseph Barratt had been invited to dine on the Friday of the next fortnight and while he and Uncle Samuel discussed Samuel's recent business journey, Irene played with her dessert. Her aunt frowned at her, 'You appear to have lost all appetite these past two weeks.'

'It's the heat,' Irene replied, placing her dessert fork down and leaning back in her chair. The sun had faded the dark red patterned wallpaper, but that was how her parents had liked it. 'Reminds us of the hot summer sun, when winter's upon us,' her father had boomed.

Since her aunt had been at Wendham the curtains had remained shut in the day, so that too had changed. Irene fanned herself. 'It's too hot.'

'Nonsense, dear. Any cooler and your godfather and I would catch our death.'

I must pray for snow, Irene thought, then pushed the thought away. She must do and think nothing wrong even in jest, for Jack Prior had not returned, and he must.

She spoke to her godfather. 'How is the refitting progressing, Uncle Samuel?'

He patted the napkin on his knee, chewing while he looked at her. Twenty for every mouthful. Irene waited, counting. At last he swallowed, then took a sip of champagne. She had been allowed half a glass, and even that had made her head swim, unused to it as she was. He dabbed his mouth with his napkin. 'The refit goes well, and is on schedule.'

'You have spent time with the ships, with Mr Prior? He will be reporting here shortly?' She kept her voice calm, uninterested.

Joseph Barratt and Uncle Samuel exchanged glances. 'We've spent a little time with the ships, and with our agent, and believe me, Mr Prior will be too busy to leave his post to report, unless I specifically request it.' His laugh was brief and without humour.

Her aunt leaned forward. 'The matter of the lay? You've sorted that out?'

Her uncle shook his head. 'Not to my satisfaction. Can't get to the bottom of it, though that Prior's a damned cheat, that much I do know. Told him to his face, too, when he presented his figures.'

Irene stared at her plate as her aunt talked to her of the needlework she had expected Irene to have finished, and her archery score last week. As her voice droned on Irene caught snatches of conversation between the men, but never enough, until she could stand it no longer.

She asked loudly, 'What do you mean about the lay?'

Her godfather sucked his teeth, patting his napkin again. 'It is poor form to discuss business whilst dining.'

'Then you and Mr Barratt are guilty of a breach of manners, and may I remind you that I am the owner of the fleet and must surely be included in your conversation.'

Joseph Barratt lifted his glass, sipped, keeping his glance on the painting above the fireplace, pretending not to have heard, whilst her uncle flushed with annoyance.

'I am the owner,' Irene insisted.

At last Samuel Jeffries explained that the lay distributed to the crew had been inadequate, and that the profits from the trip were suspect, that they felt sure a fraudulent deal had been struck between Jack Prior and the middleman.

'You have proof?' she snapped.

47

Her uncle shook his head. 'That's what we've been trying to uncover but Jack Prior's too clever for us. However, I know a thief when I meet one. Jumped up ruffian.'

She clasped her hands in her lap and breathed deeply. One, two. One, two. At last the anger was under control sufficiently for her to speak. She said, almost spitting out the words, 'And you, Mr Barratt? What progress are you making with the factory site? What progress towards back to backs, drunkenness, costly machinery and a labour force of underpaid men, women and children? Or have you been too busy hanging on my godfather's coat-tails while he runs a mythical demon to earth?'

'Irene!' barked her godfather. Aunt Mary held up her hand to him, leaning towards Irene, her lips tight, 'My dear, I know that you still suffer grief, and that it manifests itself in outbursts, but remember your mother's dying instructions to your godfather, and your manners.' She smiled reassuringly at Mr Barratt.

The candles were casting their flickering light on the exuberant oil paintings that hung around the room as Irene nearly choked on her frustration. Where are you, Jack?

Joseph Barratt was talking to her, his face intent, his sandy hair dry and lustreless. 'I have been drawing up plans which I would be delighted to discuss with you, Irene.'

She dragged her attention back. 'Plans?'

'For a geometric garden. I have included angular, circular and serpentine forms for the beds, which will form a satisfactory whole. You see, not only will order be created but each bed will be handsome in itself *and* harmonize with the others, therefore precluding any disagreeable impression on the mind.'

Irene looked at her godfather who was still chewing, and her aunt who was drawing her shawl tighter around her shoulders. She said dryly, 'You are quite sure, are you?'

Barratt looked puzzled.

She said, emphasizing each syllable, 'You are quite sure that this will preclude any disagreeable impression on the mind?' She was gripping her shawl tighter and tighter. Her godfather said hastily, 'Cigars and port in the billiard room, Barratt. Squire'll be along shortly.'

Her aunt nodded, 'Whilst Irene, Mrs Turner and I play cribbage. Nice little woman, if a little unintelligent. You must draw her out, Irene. See if you can coax her to hasten her game a little.'

Her uncle and Joseph Barratt were leaving the room. There was a burst of laughter. She thought she heard her godfather say, 'Good one, dear boy. The day will most certainly come when he'll be blubbing over his blubber boat.'

She rose, wanting clarification of the remark, but at that moment Mrs Turner was announced. Her aunt said, 'Please show Mrs Turner into the sitting room, Alice. We will be along directly.'

Three days later Irene received a message via Young Matt. The note was in strong firm handwriting and was from Jack Prior. *I will be in the copse early evening, at the fallen tree. Jack.*

The afternoon seemed interminable and Irene ignored Martha's instructions to remain inside and attend to her correspondence once afternoon tea was cleared and the crumbs swept from the small mahogany table by the undermaid, Rose. 'No, I must water the kitchen garden.'

Martha admonished, 'The midges will torment you something chronic, and that kitchen garden is not for ladies. You best leave it to Young Matt. I don't knows what your aunt would think.' Martha peered at the clock on the mantelpiece. 'She'll be back soon, you mark my words. That Mrs Turner chucks out about this time, likes a nap in between meals, and what meals they are. She'll be as big as Wendham by Christmas, you mark my words. Can't think why your aunt calls her a nice little woman.'

Irene laughed with her, and stopped by her chair, leaning down to kiss Martha's cheek. 'I love you. You never change.'

Martha looked up in surprise, then beamed with pleasure. 'Don't knows about that. Sweet nineteen I was when you was born, and now look at me, a bird's nest of grey hair, and all due to you.' She shook her head. 'Go on then, just come in the side door, and pretend you've been reading your Bible in the shade of the cedar.' She raised her eyebrows. Irene laughed and said, as she swept out onto the terrace, 'Do you really think they'll believe that?'

Martha's laughter followed her down the steps, and then she was on the lawn, hurrying to the walled kitchen garden, pushing back the guilt of her deception. Guilt which cast a shadow over the excitement that was roaring, and it was a guilt she owed to Martha, not her aunt and godfather.

She filled the watering can from the water-butt, and drenched the radishes, lettuce, and the leeks which she had just planted out. Refilling the can, she glanced at the clock tower and hurried to the tomatoes which grew against the south-facing wall, slopping water down her skirt, peering through the open gate across the lawn, towards the copse. Was he there, watching her? Was he? Was he?

She could bear it no longer and threw down the can, picking up her skirt and running along the cinder path, out through the gate, into the shade of the young elms which grew at the end of the lawn, keeping in the shadow near the laurels and then into the dark, cool copse.

Her footsteps were deadened by the fallen beech leaves as she ran to the fallen trunk at the centre. It was a place she had visited when the moon was bright, and her father was away, and now she would love it even more.

He was there, sitting with one leg up on the trunk, whittling a stick. She stopped and could hear her rapid breathing, and the sound of his knife on the stick, and his soft whistling.

He turned, and smiled, threw the stick away, pocketed the knife, bowed, 'Jack Prior, at your service.' His voice was low, his eyes lingered on hers, and they were full of pleasure.

'I received your note.' Her voice too was quiet. She stood quite still, unsure suddenly. What was she doing here, in this copse, alone with this man? A man who made her blood race, a man who had kept sleep from her, a man her godfather called a rogue and a deceiver. Love vied with doubt and she hated herself for letting her godfather's words lodge in her mind.

He said, 'I don't like creeping around like this. I like to come to the front door but if this is the only way I can see you again, then I have to accept it. Why don't you take a seat?' He looked closely at her. She avoided his eyes. He gestured to the fallen tree, but stepped back himself.

She sat on the trunk, holding her crinoline down, brushing at her grey skirt splashed and darkened from her watering. He said, 'I trust you are well?'

She said, 'I am, and you?' The late afternoon sun filtered through the beech leaves, midges danced. He nodded, standing motionless, still watching her, and she felt as though she were exposed to him, that he had seen her love, and her uncle's words gnawing at that love. Again she hated herself.

She picked at her skirt, then heard herself say, 'Please, I must ask you what it is that has happened with the lay, and the profit?' She was then appalled, wanting to snatch the question back. She half rose, her hand out. 'Forget those words. Please, forget them.' For his face had darkened, his lips had thinned. He turned from her.

There was silence, broken at last by Jack tearing off a young beech twig, and snapping it, again and again. Only when it was in small pieces at his feet did he look at her, and now she saw his sadness, his disappointment. 'I didn't mean it,' she stammered.

Jack began to speak, and somehow his drawl seemed more pronounced. He told her of the lay, and the expenses which had to come out of it, of the figures he had presented to her uncle at the end of the voyage. 'Check them.' His voice was abrupt, but not loud, not harsh, not anything, but his eyes said something different. They spoke of a searing affront, of a deep distress, of frustration.

She nodded, dropping her eyes, feeling her heart pounding at his stillness. She whispered unsteadily, 'Forgive me.'

'Have I passed the test?' Emotion had reached his voice now. His hands were clenched, his knuckles white. 'There's not many I'd allow to question me, Miss Wendham. I'm my own man, with my own code, though I own I'm not an English gentleman. But now I've answered I must leave, I can't stay where I'm not trusted.'

The sun was filtering onto his jet-black hair, onto his face and his strong jaw, his firm mouth.

She whispered, 'I had to understand. I'm trying to hold out against my uncle. I'm trying to cling to my future. Please . . .' She came to him, reached for his hand. 'Please, try and understand.' Her desperation was clear in her voice.

He was so close. He raised her hand to his lips, holding it there, looking at her, and she at him, while the midges danced in the air, and the gentle sun flickered through the leaves.

He pulled her to him. She let him, for so too had her father clasped her mother, and how could such contact be wrong? She leaned against him, and felt his arms around her, strong, firm. She whispered into his neck, 'Please do not leave me to fight alone.' He replied, 'Whenever you need me, I'll come.'

All that summer they met in the copse, sometimes once a week, with Jack travelling overnight by horseback if necessary. They talked and whilst they did so their hands touched, their eyes held one another, and gently he would kiss her lips, and she barely heard his words as he told her of the four oceans he sailed, of the fogs he had drifted in, the iceberg he had scraped, of the cook who had drunk too much and had to be locked in the aft-cabin, where there was no porthole, no light, no comfort, and which served as the ship's lockup.

She barely heard the words, but she drank in his voice and his hands as he shaped the 'blubber boat' he loved, and the light in his eyes as he called, 'She's bl-o-o-w-s', the signal that a whale was sighted.

He in his turn listened to her tales of Wendham, and she told him in a torrent of indignation of Barratt's plans, and answered his questions as to the current profitability, and the capital she held, and the outlay, and with each visit she felt more sure of her need for him in her life, and in Wendham's life.

In the company of her godfather and Barratt she no longer objected to their foolish plans, for once Jack Prior proclaimed his love, and they could walk out into the full view of everyone, Barratt would be as nothing, and her godfather alongside him.

One August day, as the afternoon sun baked the earth, she brought a white linen tablecloth to the copse and laid it on the ground. She unpacked sandwiches and scones, and poured tea into bone china cups, and told Jack Prior that it was what her mother had done for her father, beneath the cedar tree on the lawn. 'This is our place though,' she said, reaching for his hand, raising it to her lips. Surely it was time. Surely he would speak of marriage, of love.

He smiled on this warm still afternoon, and there was only the humming of bees in the distance as he took the cup from her, placed it down, and kissed her, his mouth moving on hers, opening. She arched her back, the heat seared through her, he kissed her mouth again and again, and then her cheek, and her neck.

For the first time he undid the button at her throat, kissed her, ran his tongue across her skin. She moaned, and wanted more. She wanted to grip his hair, press him to her, hold his face, kiss his eyes, cheeks, lips. For how could passion such as this be wrong between two people who felt such love?

But then he drew away, his breathing rapid, his eyes half closed. She clung to him, but he pushed her away. 'Forgive me. I should not have presumed. Forgive me,' he begged. 'I just was driven mad by your nearness. Forgive me. I have no right.'

Tell me you love me, ask me to marry you, then you would have every right, she wanted to plead. Ask me, for soon the ships will sail, and I can't bear for you to go. But he didn't, and that night she lay in bed, touching her throat, confusion tearing her apart, and Martha's admonishment ringing in her ears, 'You've not taken the flowers to old Mrs Greaves. You've not visited the Endersby children, and your skirt is dirty again. You should not be mooning about on that old tree in the copse, reading. Since when have you read in the summer? And do up your button, are you a hussy to open your throat to the sun?'

Irene had replied, 'They're gardening books. I've got to keep up with Barratt.'

'So you're coming round to the idea then.'

Irene had cried, 'I don't know about anything any more.' But she did. She wanted Jack Prior to have every right to kiss her throat, to run his hands over her body, to kiss her face, her neck, her belly, she wanted him to be by her side, to be master of Wendham, master of her, master of the captains they would send out in the ships, while they stayed here, at Wendham, for ever.

She went to the window. The moon was huge, the stars faint in its glow, the scent of roses and honeysuckle were strong. She imagined Jack Prior dancing with her on the terrace, crushing the thyme and camomile beneath their feet, the scent of it rising to their children.

As August became September they continued to meet, and his lips caressed hers, and still she wanted more, and still he said nothing. When the harvest was in, and the wheat dust no longer clouded the air, she received a note from Jack, who said he was staying at a nearby inn in Yeovil that night, because the refit was completed and he had been called to a meeting with her godfather the next morning.

He couldn't meet her that evening because he had a report to prepare, but would meet her in the copse immediately after breakfast.

The next day she rushed through breakfast, then hurried to the copse. He wasn't there. She waited, forcing herself to sit still, to appear calm, beautiful, irresistible. Ask me, Jack, or it will be too late, for the ships will sail for Portsmouth and once cleared by the inspectors, the convicts will be loaded and the fleet will sail and you will be gone for at least four years, perhaps five, and this summer has been leading me closer to heaven each day, or is it to hell? For that is what it would be if you left me. Ask me.

She waited, and while she did so she thought of the estate staff who would pull their carriage back to Wendham after the wedding, of her godfather's face as he was forced to see his factory plans disappear, of Barratt's geometrical designs that she would tear up, of all their faces as she said slowly and clearly, 'My mother wanted me to have guidance. I have found my guide. I have found Jack Prior.' That's what must happen. It must. Ask me, Jack, for if you do not, I must ask you.

But it was Young Matt who came then, running through the woods, not Jack. She stepped behind a tree. He called, 'Miss Wendham, ma'am.' She emerged, explaining, 'I was planning a painting.'

He looked confused, and panted, 'Mr Prior has to see Mr Jeffries earlier than he had thought. He will be here directly. He said to say he has a question to ask you.' Matt was squinting, concentrating. He paused, 'That's all. He'll be here directly. Just wait.'

He ran off. She waited.

In the library Samuel Jeffries stood with his back to the fire, eternal goddamn fire Jack Prior thought, as he stood on the Indian carpet beneath the chandelier watching the older man, who, now that the greetings had been dispensed with, cleared his throat, and held up an envelope.

Samuel Jeffries said, 'In this envelope is money. It is more than you deserve but it is a pay-off fee. I have found another master for the Wendham fleet. You will not set foot on either ship again. The ships are at this moment being sailed to Portsmouth for inspection and loading, whilst your belongings are still at Bristol. Take them, and go back to your damned New Bedford, and cheat someone else.' He flung the envelope down on the desk. 'And do not even think of violence, for I have the gamekeeper within call.' He crossed his arms, his face grim.

Jack took a step forward, smiling. Samuel Jeffries sidestepped and reached for the bell-pull. Jack shook his head, 'There's no need for that. You are in no danger, writhing worm that you are. You think you are so clever but did you really believe you could do something like that without me hearing in a port the size of Bristol? I've known since you started sounding people out, you crazy damn fool. You, with your gentleman's code, you with your blinkered stupid ideas. You talk of cheats – but what are you?'

Samuel Jeffries reached for the bell-pull again.

Jack knocked his hand away, 'I said you were in no danger. You are not, but understand this. Those ships you think are being sailed round by another master are not. The *Cachalot* is being sailed under the command of my first mate because those ships are Prior ships, every last plank of them.'

Samuel paled with shock, then roused himself, groping to understand, spluttering, finally shouting. 'They are not yours, not any more, are you insane? You've cheated, and lied, and stolen, I know you have, and one day I'll prove it. From now on the Wendham "blubber boats" are to be someone else's concern, and let's see how much better they prosper from this day on.' He scattered papers on the desk, finding a letter, shoving it at Jack. 'Here, this is the letter from the new fleet master. I tell you the ships are on their way to Portsmouth.'

Jack read it, threw it on the fire, and laughed, his head thrown back, but rage was in every movement he made. He roared at Jeffries, 'You tried to cheat me, to take what was mine, and my father's before me, but first you thought to work my bootstraps off. Well damn you to hell, Samuel Jeffries. Damn you.'

He saw the fear in Samuel Jeffries' eyes, he smelt it oozing from every pore of the man's skin, and now Jack backed off. 'Damn you,' he repeated, turning on his heel, striding for the door, returning, taking the envelope full of money and tearing it in two, before throwing it back at the man. 'I don't need this for, as long as you've been making your plans, and even earlier than that, I've been making mine.'

He wrenched the door open, then looked back into the room, with its curtains shut against the evening sun, the fire in the grate, the stag heads on the wall, the billiard table down the end, the dull panels. 'Enjoy it while you can,' he said, slamming the door as he left, grabbing his coat from the maid, leaping down the steps leading onto the drive, and into the carriage he had hired.

He whipped the horse, not looking back at Wendham, pulling the horse up by the back of the copse, leaping from the carriage.

In the copse the light was fading as clouds banked in the west, bringing a cool breeze. Irene pulled her shawl around her. Where was he? How long did a refit report take? She walked to the edge of the copse and looked across at Wendham. She would be called in for embroidery soon. Where was he?

What was the question he wished to ask her? It must be marriage. They would appoint a captain to take the *Cachalot*, and in the years the fleet was away they'd grow together, love, she'd bear children. But then she pressed her hand to her mouth. Where was he? Was it marriage he wanted? She swung round. It must be. But no, it might not.

She heard him running into the copse from the other side, where the track lay. He was calling her, and the urgency in his voice caught and held her. She lifted her skirts and ran towards him, heedless of the branches that caught at her, ripping her dress, snagging her hair. He was in the clearing, his hands on his hips, looking round, torment on his face. When he saw her he came to her, taking her hands, trying to speak, but he could not.

'What is it? Tell me what has happened?' She shook free of his hands, and held his face, forcing him to look at her. 'What has happened?' she demanded.

He told her then, in a voice so full of agony she barely recognized it. 'He's taken the fleet from me. Put in a new master. I'm nothing. I've nothing to offer you, not even my expertise, not even the world I wanted to show you.' Then he added, 'I wanted to ask for your hand, but now how can I?'

She tried to take in her godfather's cruelty and arrogance. 'Tell me again,' she almost wept, kissing his cheek, his lips. He did.

She said, harsh anger in her voice, 'Wait here. I won't have this. For heaven's sake, I own the fleet, I'll stop it. How dare he? I'll tell him I love you, that we will marry, then, my love, you will become the owner. He'll go back to India. I'll tell him at last that he must leave.'

He caught her, held her. 'D'you love me? Just tell me that you do, and I'll be happy, and then I guess I'll go.' His grip was hard, he was hurting her shoulders, a cool breeze was building up, Martha was calling.

She said, against his lips, and now she was weeping, 'Yes, I love you, and no, you won't go. You mustn't go. I would die. No, he'll go. You'll stay here, with me. We'll marry. Yes, they'll go. I have my partner, my husband.' Oh God, why had she not spoken sooner?

He pushed her from him, shaking his head. 'No, don't you see? They'll stop it. Somehow they'll stop it. An adventurer, they'll say. And I couldn't let you throw yourself away on someone like me. I've nothing, I've just told you. Nothing. I can't ask that of you. I just wanted to hold the thought of your words, your love, to me.' He backed from her.

Martha was calling. She was coming towards the copse. Irene whispered, 'Don't go, don't leave me. Come with me, to the house.'

He shook his head. 'No, I told you, they'd give you cause to doubt me if we stayed here, they'd stop us somehow. It's best that I go.' He was still backing away. 'Remember I love you.'

Martha was closer. He was gone, in amongst the trees, moving away from her. She held her head in her hands, trying to think, trying to get everything to slow down, trying to stop the world while she thought.

He was almost gone. 'Wait,' she screamed.

He called back, 'Go to Barratt, go to your English gentleman. Be happy. Accept his garden, his factory, his fat body, his children. They'll destroy us if we stay here.'

Martha was closer. Jack was gone. Irene snatched a look at Wendham, bathed in sun which had broken through the cloud, and then she picked up her skirts. 'Wait,' she screamed again.

CHAPTER THREE

Irene opened her eyes and stared without recognition at a small attic window, where floral curtains wafted in a sun-filled breeze. She heard gulls, the roll of barrels, the raucous cries of street vendors, the clatter of horses' hooves, the rattle of carts and at last she remembered.

She was in lodgings that Jack Prior had found in Portsmouth, following their flight yesterday. He had taken two rooms; his was next to hers.

She moved. Her arms stung. She remembered the scratches from the branches which had whipped and broken as she rushed through the copse, calling to him to wait. He had. She had insisted that he take her, that she could not go on without him, desperately looking round all the time, fearful that Martha would catch up and beseech her to stay.

Irene turned her face into the pillow. What had she done?

There was a knock at the door. She froze. It opened. Was it her godfather, or Jack? The landlady entered with a tray, her mop cap sparkling clean, her smile wide. She was plump, like Martha, but older. 'Brought you tea, as 'ow the gentleman instructed me before he left at dawn. Said as 'ow you'd be parched for a cup. Nice piece of bread and butter on there too.'

Irene pushed herself up, took the tray. 'How kind.' But her voice trembled.

Did this woman know that she was bringing tea to an eloping girl, a girl her godfather would say had no shame, a girl her Martha would say . . . ? But no, she couldn't think of Martha or the tearing within her would start again, because now she knew that she would not be returning to Wendham for at least another four years.

The landlady nodded towards the window. 'Fine day, though I don't doubt that's not what them convicts will be saying. Gawd almighty, you'd think that after months in prisons or on them hulks they'd want to be going out to somewhere the sun shines instead of moaning so. Good riddance, if you ask me. Don't want them sort staying here, best to ship 'em out, away from decent folks.'

Irene sipped at her tea, wanting the woman gone, not wanting to think about sailing away, leaving Wendham, England, Martha. But perhaps it was best that she was 'away from decent folks' too.

The landlady moved to the door. 'Your gentleman's come back once, then gone again but he'll be back any minute, he said to tell you.' She smiled, then sighed, 'Ain't no business of mine, I suppose, but seems a mightily queer do. You and 'im. Must be some mother crying about it somewhere.'

Irene slammed her cup down. It cracked the saucer. 'That's all. You may leave me, and take the tray. I'm no longer thirsty.'

She waited, leaping from bed the moment she was alone, unable to remain still for any longer. Backwards and forwards she paced, before starting to dress, but there was no-one who could lace up her corset. She stood in front of the mirror, turning it so that the laces were at the front but that was no good, it would be too tight to heave round once it was done up.

She left it loose and stared at herself in the mirror, her hair awry, her face red from effort and had never felt so alone and now she cried, 'Martha, I need you. Martha, what have I done?'

She had written a message to Martha from the railway station, telling her that she and Jack would return as man and wife, and then to her godfather telling him the same.

She stared at herself, making the tears stop. She wiped her face with the back of her hand, lifting her chin defiantly. She'd had no choice. It was their fault. It was her godfather, Aunt Mary and Martha who were to blame, endlessly harping on, making plans, taking over control of her life. Well, now it was she who had taken over, just as her father would have wanted, just as he would have done.

It was when they arrived at the lodging house late in the evening that Jack Prior had talked to her gently, in the dull light of the oil lamp set on the small table in the centre of this room, 'You have told your Martha that we will be returning as man and wife, and sure we shall. But it ain't going to be immediately.'

She had protested. He had held up his hand, put his fingers to her lips. 'Hush. You must realize that this runnin' off will cause a storm. I've had a bit of time to think. We'll duck out of it for a while, give the dust time to settle. We'll take the fleet and bring in a fine ole oil harvest, and the voyage'll be my weddin' gift to you. You see, I've not got much 'cept my knowledge, and so's I aim to show you my world, and the world that was your father's. It'll satisfy my sense of honour, my code, so you got to allow me to do that.'

She had kissed the fingers which were still against her lips. How she loved this man, and how she thrilled at his words, and the love which saturated every one. How could she refuse? How could she want to?

But she did, now in the bright light of morning she did. But she must not. He was to be her husband, and on their return her beloved Wendham would be waiting, and they would never again leave – he had promised her that. 'Squire and Mrs Prior,' he had said softly.

She had whispered, 'And the men can stay and work with their families in their cottages, not in a factory, and there will be no geometrical garden.' She had moved towards him, but he had shaken his head. 'No, we are not married. I want to give you every chance to send me on my way, until the very last moment. I'll not arrange the wedding until a few hours before we sail, just for that reason. Though even then it's not much time.'

She looked again at her reflection, and ran her hands across her breasts. How wonderful he was, and how pure and good not to realize that she was already compromised, damaged too deeply for society to ever accept her return unless it was as a married woman.

'A married woman,' she said aloud, thrilling to the thought. 'Soon . . .' Quick footsteps on the stairs broke across her thoughts. There was a light tap on the door. Jack called, 'Irene?'

He opened the door and stood there smiling, his dark jacket open, his jersey high to his neck, his trousers tucked in his boots. His smile froze, and only then did Irene remember her half-naked state. She tried to cover herself with her hands.

He strode to the bed, swept off the counterpane, handed it to her without looking at her, saying, 'Forgive me, you should have forbidden me entry.' His tone was awkward, formal, almost English. He looked up at the ceiling in his embarrassment.

She laughed gently, suddenly feeling bold in the face of his discomfort, feeling suffused with love, and compassion, feeling an adult. 'We are to be man and wife, and there is no-one else to lace me, so, my dear, would you, please?'

She turned her back, holding the counterpane up to her breasts, looking at the reflection of them both in the mirror as he loomed large behind her. He hesitantly took hold of the laces, his forehead creasing in concentration. He tugged, and all the while his fingers brushed her skin, and it was as though she was scorched.

She watched his furrowing brow in the mirror, the

tightening of his lips beneath his moustache, his heavy lids. He looked up, met her eyes. His hands grew still. 'All done,' he breathed.

He traced her shoulders with his fingers. Her legs grew weak. She leaned back against him, her eyes half shut as he kissed her hair, her neck, her shoulder, and his grip was hard on her skin, and his breathing rapid, as was hers.

She lifted her arm and touched his cheek, then his hair, the nape of his neck. His lips travelled to her back, his hands were on her arms, around her waist and she turned to him. His mouth found hers. He kissed her lips gently, then her cheeks, her eyes, and her mouth again, and again, and now there was urgency and neither heard the pounding feet on the stairs and it was only when the door burst open that they reeled apart. 'God damn you, Jack Prior,' her godfather shouted, standing in the doorway, his chest heaving. He lunged across the room, reaching for Irene.

Jack thrust her to one side, stepping in front of Samuel Jeffries. 'Have a care, sir,' Jack said, his hand up to ward off Samuel Jeffries' stick, which was raised against him.

'Godfather,' Irene screamed.

There was the sound of other feet on the stairs. The landlady ran into the room, holding her skirt up with one hand, her face red and angry. 'I'm not having this. Take your quarrels elsewhere. This is a good clean house.'

Jack pushed Samuel Jeffries to one side, turned the landlady around, marched her to the landing, shouting, 'This is no quarrel, this is business, and you'll mind your goddamn manners, and your tongue, d'you hear me?'

Irene backed from her godfather, her eyes flicking from him to Jack who was insisting that the landlady return downstairs. Her godfather kept coming, his sallow face flushed with anger. He was closer, closer, almost touching. She saw the redness of his skin, the drawn tiredness round his mouth.

She was against the bed. She sank onto it, gripping the counterpane so tightly that her arms shook. Samuel Jeffries stood in front of her, shaking his head. He was trembling. 'Irene,' he almost sobbed. 'Oh, Irene, how could you do this?'

Suddenly he paled, reached for the chair by the chest of drawers and sat down as though exhausted. Jack returned, closed the door behind him, and leaned against it, his hands deep in his pockets.

Irene looked at her godfather and wanted to reach out, take his hand, comfort him, comfort herself. She said, 'Why did you come? I wish you hadn't come.' For Wendham was crowding in, Martha, her parents too. 'Why did you come?' she almost screamed, hating him for stirring up questions, doubts, for that's what he had done, just by being here, just by looking so drained, so damaged. 'Why?' she whispered, conscious suddenly of her undressed state, embarrassed, ashamed.

He reared up, standing over her again. 'Come home. We can stall, we can pretend it never happened. I'll pay this bastard off. I'll sort it out with Barratt. He knows nothing yet, he need never know and if he does, I'll pay him off. I'll pay this damnable thief off, too, for it's gain he's after, not you. Come home with me, Irene. Come to your senses, remember who you are, what responsibilities you have. Come along. It's not too late. It mustn't be too late. There has been no marriage, so therefore it is still recoverable. Somehow we'll save your name.'

Jack walked towards Irene. She held up her hand to him for with every word which had fallen from her godfather's lips she had seen what she had fled from, and now fury cleansed her of all remaining doubt. 'You dare to call Jack Prior a bastard. You dare to burst in here and insult the man I love, the man I have chosen. You dare to continue to make plans, to disregard my love, my hopes. You dare too much.'

She could hardly breathe, her rage was so great. 'It *is* too late, Godfather. I could be bearing his child. Do you feel Barratt would like the idea of that? A Prior bastard brought up under the Barratt name?'

In the deadly silence that followed Jack shot her a look. She ignored him, ignored the hand that her godfather stretched towards her, his mouth opening, shutting, his lips trembling as at last he said, 'Don't say that. Please don't say that.' His voice was suddenly that of a man ten years older.

'I've just said it, Godfather,' she repeated, forming the words clearly, her rage still feeding her, the lie coming easily. 'I hope for a son.'

Outside a cart-load slipped, gulls wheeling above the roof, but inside this room no-one spoke. She looked at neither man, only at the oil lamp, then the sideboard, then the brass bedstead, then the trunk which Jack had brought in late last night.

She felt quite calm, in control. It was over, the authority of this man was over. It should never have been there in the first place. She was Irene Wendham, Bartie Wendham's daughter, and authority would pass to Jack Prior, a natural successor to her father. Today she would buy clothes for the voyage. Everything must be new. Everything. Everything.

Her godfather sat down again, resting both hands on his walking stick. He said to Jack, though he looked only at Irene, 'May I have just a few moments with my goddaughter alone?'

Irene stared at him with an icy rage, a rage she recognized as that which her father had used to exert his control, one she had never felt before. She drew herself up. 'Will you never listen? No, we have nothing more to say to one another.'

Jack returned to the door, saying to Irene, his face wounded, 'I'll go, if you wish.'

'No,' she insisted, rising. Again she recognized her father's tone, and gloried in it. At last she was the daughter he had hoped for. At last her life could begin again.

'The lady says no,' Jack told Jeffries, closing the door, leaning back on it.

She turned to her godfather. 'You see what sort of a man Jack Prior is. A man who would leave if I wished. A man who respects my decisions.' She still gripped the counterpane, but there was no embarrassment any more.

Her godfather just looked at her, sadness in his face. 'A clever and a cruel man.' He paused, began again. 'He needed a new crew, doesn't that tell you anything?'

Contempt joined her rage. 'It tells me more about you than it does about him. My father sailed with him, and liked him, bought his fleet. That should tell *you* something. Jack only needs new crew because he's shipping convicts. Crews don't like that, isn't that so?' she queried Jack.

He nodded, his face sombre, his eyes watchful. She continued, 'But the same cannot be said of you, my dear Godfather, for it is you who decided on transportation to enhance profits. So who exactly is the cruel one?' Now her icy face was close to her godfather's.

'It was initially Jack Prior's idea. But of course, he didn't tell you that.' Jeffries reached for Irene's hand. Jack shook his head in disbelief. Irene pulled from her godfather's grasp. 'I would prefer that you didn't touch me,' her voice tight with controlled rage. 'And I would also prefer to hear nothing more from you.'

But Samuel Jeffries shouted over her words, 'What he's told you is rubbish. Ships' crews are happy on transports because there are rules governing the handling of convicts and crew. There are officers and soldiers on board who temper a captain's misuse of power. Abused seamen feel they will be safer.' He was beating his fist on his knee. His cuffs were dust-spattered. There were age spots on his hands which she hadn't noticed before. It occurred to her that he wore no gloves. 'Are things so very serious?' she said slowly and contemptuously.

He didn't understand.

She said, 'When you intruded so often on my life at Wendham it was frequently connected with gloves. You wear no gloves.'

Jack laughed, Samuel Jeffries howled in his anguish and frustration, 'Don't be stupid and arrogant. This is your life we are talking about. And yes, your life is far more important than gloves. Think of Wendham, of the garden which needs you, the tenants, the . . .'

Jack's laugh ceased. He stood upright, alert, his eyes fixed on Irene. There was shouting in the street, blows over the stricken cart, and she lifted her voice to rise above that, 'Enough. Crews object to shipping convicts who are of the same class as they, Jack has told me. It's no good, Godfather, you can't poison my mind against Jack. I love him, I have loved him from the moment we met. I have loved him more at every meeting. You talk of Wendham – well rest assured that I have Wendham's best interests at heart and therefore none of your improvements will be carried out.'

Jack relaxed.

'Meeting secretly, shamefully,' her godfather whispered, his head in his hands.

She objected, 'Always at my behest.' Her uncle looked up at her, and the torment in his eyes killed her anger. She said, gently, 'Jack is an honourable man, and the person I intend to live with for the rest of my life. It is I who forced him to take me, not he who cajoled. Together we will travel the route my father took, then we will return to Wendham, take up our place there. In the meantime I will give instructions to the Estate Manager that he is to proceed as before.' She turned, his distress touching her, his disintegration too much to bear. 'Believe me, I'm grateful for your good intentions.'

Her godfather leaned closer, his voice low, 'You mean

Jack Prior will give instructions. On your marriage you become his, your property becomes his. Your rents and the management of the land becomes his, but, thankfully, not the land itself which is secure from any threat of sale by him by virtue of being crown land.'

She pressed her fingers to her mouth, struggling for patience. 'Both Jack and I realize the difference in our fortunes. It was one thing that held him back, wasn't it, my dear?' Jack had moved closer, poised to come to her aid. She said, 'Give me your blessing, Godfather. Please.'

Samuel Jeffries continued as though she had not spoken, speaking rapidly, twisting, so that his back was to Jack, his face close to hers. 'No, listen to me, Irene. He doesn't want you, can't you see that? It's the use you are to him.'

'You're doing it again. You're maligning Jack.' Rage flared again.

He hurried on, 'You must understand your position absolutely.' Jack was closing in on them. Her godfather pushed on, 'If the unthinkable happens and he takes over Wendham, and excludes you, for that is just what I fear he will do, remember he is obliged to provide you with equivalent accommodation.'

'Godfather, stop.'

'No, you must know all this. He has no money. His sort longs for the prestige of an estate, longs for the money it can bring. They'll hold onto it with one hand, and make money out of it with the other. Remember, you foolish child, that as your husband he can lease out Wendham's lands for twenty-one years, but only *with* your concurrence.' He dropped his voice to a low whisper. 'Whatever you do, always think to protect yourself, Irene. Bear this in mind at all times. Do not trust this man, I beg of you.'

She recoiled. Jack was closer still, concern in his eyes. 'Don't you go upsetting her,' he shouted. She pushed past her godfather, coming to Jack's side, sheltering against him. 'This is pointless. Make him stop, Jack.'

Her godfather followed her, desperation in his voice. 'It is anything but pointless. You must remember.' He put up his arm to ward off Jack, who was dragging him away, towards the door. 'Remember it all, Irene. Remember, or you will lose Wendham more completely than you could ever imagine. Give him the fleet, pay him off. Give him what money you have, but save yourself and your home. Do not marry him. Do not let him have the rights that marriage will bring.'

'Oh God,' she buried her face in her hands. 'Stop it. Stop it,' her voice was a scream. Her uncle shouted as Jack hurled him onto the landing, 'Irene, come with me. For the love of God, come.'

'I hate you, I hate you,' she moaned. 'I hate you for coming, for taking every vestige of kind thoughts I had for you away from me.'

Jack slammed the door shut, came to her, held her. She wept. He soothed. Saying into her hair, 'You can go with him, it's not too late. You can go to Barratt, and cosy gardens, and British manners. I can find a fleet anywhere. I'll go back to my country. I'll leave you in peace. Don't cry. I can't put you through this.'

The door burst open again. Her godfather stood there, dragging a package out of his pocket, throwing it across the room. It fell on the bed. 'Keep this. Hide it from him somehow. One day you will need it.'

'Get out,' she screamed. 'Get out. All I wanted was your blessing, not your poison, your cruelty.'

Her godfather stood, fragile in the face of her anguish. 'Never contact me again,' he said. 'Never, you are soiled, despoiled, not worthy to bear your family name.'

The wardroom lamp swung with the motion of the ship as it ploughed on through the swell on the evening of their departure from Portsmouth. 'There's little wind

71

tonight, but more than enough to send us on our way,' Captain Meldrew, the Army officer-in-charge of the convicts, declared lifting his glass. 'And I'd like to toast our master and his bride and wish them well for their own journey – life's journey, eh, m'dear?' He nodded at his wife then at Irene and Jack.

The four army officers, two of whom travelled with wives, lifted their glasses to Irene. She smiled at Jack, who sat at the other end of the table. He held her gaze, leaning back in his chair, resting his arms on the raised ledge of the table, and there was deep satisfaction in his eyes, a contentment that she had not seen until this moment.

Talk around the table resumed, food was brought, goose with a gooseberry sauce. Mrs Meldrew turned to Jack, amazement on her face, 'Somehow I had not expected such fine food.'

'Enjoy it while you can, for the livestock we carry'll not last long. Soon be onto salt beef as we've a ways to go before we put in again, and three months before we arrive in Fremantle. So, as I say, enjoy it while you can.' His eyes fell on Irene, and he smiled.

Three months with Jack, three months as the master's wife, holding court in the wardroom, deferred to by these women, or strolling on deck with the sea breeze in her hair. Why, life would be little different to that at Wendham, only now she had her partner, a man with strength, a man in whose hands their fate depended, a man of honour and competence.

The man who she had married this morning, the man who had stayed with her all night after her godfather left, holding her in his arms as she wept. A man who painted pictures of the life they would have on their return, of the plans they would leave in the meantime for the estate manager, of the son they would one day have. Of the letter of reconciliation they would write to Samuel Jeffries who would, with time, admit his error.

Not once had he forced himself on her. Not once had

he more than kissed her brow, and her heart had become more firmly his with every second that passed, and her trust even more implicit.

She gazed at him, fingering the sapphire necklace, which is what the package had contained, along with the earrings. She had wanted to return it to Wendham to await her return, not wanting anything to remind her of her godfather but Jack had said, 'No, you are to be the master's wife. It is yours. Wear it with pride.'

She glowed with it as her husband leaned forward, saying firmly to Lt. Carstairs, 'No, there's no luck when you go seeking whales. It's to do with knowing the set of all tides and currents, and understanding the drifting of their food.'

Mrs Meldrew said, 'But, Captain, surely there is a wee bit of luck?'

He tapped his finger on the polished table as the gently swinging lamp bathed his face in its undulating shadow. Irene wanted to reach out and stroke his cheek. 'Luck figures in nothing. Everything is down to planning, to second-guessing, to leaving nothing to chance.' His voice was still low, but there was an edge to it, and now he glanced at Irene.

She smiled and suddenly he threw back his head and laughed. Talk ceased around the table. Captain Meldrew looked askance at his lieutenant, who shook his head slightly in reply. 'Best to leave nothing to chance,' Jack repeated, his eyes on Irene. Eyes that held something, but she did not know what. Eyes that were cool and matched the hardness of the laugh.

Jack raised his hand, 'Forgive me, I just can't believe my good fortune today, still shocked I got such a prize. It all just explodes out of me, stupid of me.' He still looked at Irene as he spoke and his eyes were alive, and his laughter gentle now, and she knew that anything else had been a mere trick of the light.

She murmured, 'No, anything but stupid.' For joy had exploded out of her as he had handed her into the carriage after the marriage ceremony, saying, 'Let me help, Mrs Prior.' It hadn't mattered that there had been no-one she knew as a witness. Her parents were dead, her godfather was gone from her life, Martha also for the next few years. But Jack was here, to take care of her, and one day Mr and Mrs Jack Prior would return to Wendham.

Yes, she thought as she heard Jack telling of the work involved in converting the whaling ships into prisons, it hadn't mattered, for here was a man who had assumed his role as her partner in life with joy and with intelligence.

Yes, a joy which had shone from him when he poured champagne in the lodging house dining room after their wedding, kissing her between each mouthful so that they tasted the champagne on one another's lips. How many glasses had they drunk? It seemed like hundreds, but no, that had been the kisses. It was a bottle they had drunk together, more, much more than she had ever drunk before.

'But it is not every day that you wed the prize you've dreamed of,' Jack had laughed as she protested. Yes, he had thrown back his head and laughed as he had laughed tonight. She looked up at the low wardroom ceiling, the walls which seemed to crowd in upon them. It was this confined space which had made it sound so harsh.

She forced herself to listen as Mrs Meldrew questioned Jack on the route they would take though she wanted to drag him to their cabin and make him kiss her as he had done this afternoon. She nodded with the others as he said, 'We sail through the Bay of Biscay, down round the Cape and then run on to Australia, and a sure relief it'll be to arrive, but not as great a one as it was to weigh anchor this afternoon. Goddamn refit rules.'

Dr Evans, the medical officer employed by the authorities, pursed his lips. 'Rules that are to be obeyed.

Too many convicts' lives are lost otherwise. Western Australia needs a labour force, remember, not corpses.'

'There'll be no more than the usual lives lost on this ship, or on the *Queen of the Isles*.' Jack's voice was cool. 'And I'll remind you that it is the master's authority that holds sway on a vessel, particularly mine.'

The medical officer inclined his head. 'I need no reminding of that, Captain Prior, but I trust you will allow that it is my duty to supervise convict health and correct any abusive conduct by the ship's officers.'

Jack tapped his fingers on the table, drawling, 'I trust that isn't an accusation?'

An awkward puzzled silence fell. Irene heard the creaking of the ship, the patter of feet above them. She put down her knife and fork. Dr Evans said quickly, 'Certainly not, a mere comment.'

Jack nodded slowly, his eyes flicking round the table. His drawl seemed very pronounced as he said, 'Just so long as we all understand one another.' His eyes came to rest on Irene, and the light sapped all warmth from them again.

Jack spoke again, 'Damn it, it isn't as though I'm unaware of the need for ventilation, the need for swabbing heads, the need for disinfecting with lime and oil of tar, of fumigation and exercise.' He was stabbing the table. 'I'm not unaware of the two logs I have to fill in, one of which is for "the authorities". I'm not unaware of any one of the rules I've had to supply and refit by.' He grinned and pointed to his head. 'It's carved into this brain, just as deep as the carving on the scrimshaw, over there.'

Irene snatched a look at the scrimshaw he had given her, to replace that which she had left at Wendham, then looked back at Jack. He met her eyes, and there was joy in his again.

Mrs Meldrew said, 'Your crew all appear to be American, but you sailed from Portsmouth?'

Jack nodded. 'I sail with my own kind. I pick 'em from visiting ships.'

Irene smiled. She was truly blessed for she, a Britisher, had been admitted into his kind. She sat back, as the men listened to his tales of the Tropics and the women too, and on their faces was admiration. Pride swelled at his firmness, his knowledge, his leadership, as it had done at the lodging house.

What other man would have said during the hours leading right up to their marriage that she must consider herself free to leave, that she must return to Somerset if she felt any doubts? That if she stayed she must understand that they had to offer the estate manager a nominal four-year lease to secure any moves on her property by her godfather in his well meant but mistaken concerns on her behalf. That if this disturbed her in any way he would understand and provide transport back to Wendham.

She had been suffused with love then, as she was now, for how could her godfather have doubted such a man?

He had given her more champagne as they waited for the lawyer, and she had watched the glint of her wedding ring, loving it, loving him. 'We must leave nothing to chance,' he had insisted, holding the champagne glass to her lips. 'We must think of your heritage.'

She had drunk deep, again and again, for it was his strong tanned hands which held the fragile glass as tenderly as he was holding his wife's well-being. Again he poured, again he held the glass, and as she drank her head felt so heavy, her lips strangely clumsy.

'I love you,' she had murmured, her words indistinct but her meaning clear, for he had smiled, and sunk his mouth onto hers. She had said against his lips, 'My godfather is right. Everything I have is yours. All that I have is yours. I am yours, and glad of it.'

The lawyer had arrived, with two witnesses from the

street. Jack had opened another bottle of champagne. She could drink no more though, indeed she could barely move her hand to sign the document. 'Read it, you must read it,' Jack insisted, pouring another glass, raising it to her mouth.

'I have,' she had said, though her lips wouldn't form the words clearly and she could read nothing with her head swimming as it did.

She had lain down in the lodging house as the lawyer and Jack concluded their business. She had clung to a bed which already seemed to be on a whirling sea. Beth, whom Jack had employed to travel with them as Irene's maid, packed her trunk with new clothes, though the dresses were still grey. 'My parents died, you see,' Irene had murmured.

'You and me both. That's why I'm going with me man to Australia,' Beth had said, coming to her, bringing a bowl of water, bathing her head. 'He's in chains, but so's I, in a manner of speaking. I love him, can't go nowhere he isn't, so if he's transported to Fremantle – I goes to. God bless your man for the job.'

In chains, Irene had thought, and now she thought it again as she looked down the wardroom table at Jack. He caught her eye and said, 'Perhaps you would take the ladies to the transom cabin, Irene. We'll just play a hand, and pass the port, then the mates must take their turn at the table, they need their victuals too.' Yes, she was in chains, to Jack, and he to her and now it was she who laughed aloud, with pure happiness.

The ladies sat gingerly on the horsehair sofa, feeling confined in the narrow cabin, which was a mere six feet by eight feet, and lined with drawers, as was the sleeping cabin, and the wardroom. 'It's all so strange,' Mrs Carstairs sighed, and the other two nodded. 'Everywhere so cramped, and such a long time before we land, and then what?'

77

The women fell silent. The whole of my life, Irene thought.

'I must retire, I'm just so exhausted,' Mrs Carstairs said, rising. Mrs Meldrew remained behind. The lamp was swinging, they could hear the running of feet on the deck above, the creaking of the boards, flapping sails, the slap of water against the side, a shout, the ringing of a bell.

'The watch is changing,' Mrs Meldrew said, walking to the door, turning, steadying herself, one hand on the master's chart table, the other on the door-frame, her forty years showing in the lines of her face, and the greying of her hair. 'And it feels as though the wind has freshened a little.'

The narrow companionway led up to the quarterdeck, and the noise of the wind was louder.

Irene nodded, 'There's so much to get used to.' She felt alone suddenly.

Mrs Meldrew nodded towards the master's sleeping cabin, which led off from the transom cabin. The door was open and the bed clearly visible. It was little more than an extended berth – a mattress laid within a box. It was secured to the floor, as everything was, or if it wasn't it hung from chains.

Mrs Meldrew hesitated, then said, 'My dear, this is your wedding night. You are to experience the most intimate of a wife's duties. As I told my daughter on the eve of her wedding, sometimes women are fortunate, sometimes they are not. I use the term wifely duty advisedly. It *is* our duty to offer our bodies to our husbands. Indeed we must by law. I find it helps to look at a spot on the ceiling, and comfort oneself with the thought that it will soon be over, and will not happen too often, once the first flush is passed.'

All the time she had been speaking she had looked at the lamp, following its swaying. Irene blinked in astonishment. This woman was mad to think that kisses such as Jack's were something to be endured, in fact, she was impertinent to refer to it in any way. She said stiffly, 'Goodnight, Mrs Meldrew.'

Beth came once Mrs Meldrew had departed. She held out the crisp linen nightgown and Irene took it. She brushed her hair, and all Irene wanted was for her to go, and Jack to come.

On and on the girl brushed. 'Still got some shine, but you wait, the salt'll get into it tomorrow. Good thing it ain't got it yet though. Good thing 'cos it's your first night with your man.'

She packed away the brush, and folded back the bed linen, patting it. ''Op in then, and don't you worry about what that old bag said. Just you wait and see.'

Irene clambered into bed, saying, 'I'm not at all sure that this subject is entirely suitable, Beth. Neither is listening at doors.'

She leaned back and shut her eyes. At least when this bed moved it was because the ship moved also. She opened them again and now she grinned at Beth, and then began to laugh, and the girl laughed with her, tossing her head as she left the cabin, carefully closing the door.

Still Irene laughed, sinking into the pillow, feeling as though she was being rocked by the movement of the ship, and sung to by the creaking and flapping, and slapping, longing for Jack to come, longing to feel again the shaft of longing that his kisses had brought to her this morning. How could Mrs Meldrew talk of such closeness as a legal duty?

He came soon, stepping into the cabin, ducking beneath the lamp, coming to stand by the bed in his jacket, his sweater, his trousers and boots. He sat and the mattress sank with his weight. Her hair was spread on the pillow. He reached across and wound a strand round his fingers, his eyes on that, not her. She waited for the tender touch of his lips.

He unwound her hair from his hand, took hold of the sheet and stripped it from her, silently. She lay in her nightgown. He unbuttoned her bodice and then, one by one the buttons that carried on to the hem, his fingers whispering across her flesh, and she shivered. She lifted her arms to him.

'Lie still,' he said, his voice low. She did.

He flipped open her nightdress and stared at her body, while she locked her eyes on his face. 'I love you,' she murmured, feeling exposed, embarrassed. 'I love you.' Still he didn't meet her eyes.

He rose from the bed, and removed his jacket, his jumper and hurled them away. In the dim light from the swinging oil lamp his skin gleamed, and beneath his skin his muscles rippled. He kicked off his boots, and undid his belt. She looked away, up at the ceiling. This was wrong. This was not the closeness of their earlier loving.

She looked back at him, and he was naked and so close to the bed, and she shrank from him, from the ugliness, from the size of him, from this man who still hadn't spoken tenderly. He loomed over her, the lamp cast a giant moving shadow. 'I love you,' she whispered again, lifting her hand towards him.

His eyes were on her breasts. The mattress sank as he climbed onto the bed, and lay beside her. 'I love you,' she again whispered and he touched her breast. She lifted his hand to her mouth and kissed it. He pulled away, back to her breast, rubbing it, pulling it, too roughly. She kissed him, tasting port. He thrust his tongue into her mouth, she gagged, recoiled.

He moved his hand from her body, and gripped her hair, holding her immobile with pain, his mouth grinding on hers, his eyes closed, his tongue probing. She fought for breath, pushing at his shoulders, pushing his face from her, squirming from him. 'No. No,' she panted.

He lifted his head and his eyes were glazed, his breathing heavy, rapid. He ran his tongue down her neck to her breasts. His hand was on her belly, moving

80

down, down. It was between her legs, his fingers were probing, pushing, hurting.

She caught at his arm. 'No,' she groaned again. He brushed her off, pushed apart her legs. She clamped them shut. He tore his hand from her hair, the pain whipped at her. He pinioned her arms above her head. 'No, Jack, no. Jack, Jack.'

His leg was forcing itself between hers. He raised himself over her, forcing her legs apart with his other leg. All she could hear was his rapid, loud, heavy breathing.

She struggled from his grip, 'Jack, Jack.' She held his head, kissed his face, his lips, searching for the longing, for the love, and his mouth opened over her, warm and wet, and he gripped her hair, and his kisses were now on her eyes, her cheeks, her mouth, edging her lips, and it was coming, the longing was coming, gently, it was coming.

But now he thrust his tongue into her mouth again, grinding down on her, panting into her mouth. He lowered himself onto her body. She could feel the stiff hugeness of his organ on her belly, the wetness. He was too heavy, his mouth was on hers. She couldn't breathe, and now there was no love, no longing, only fear.

She pushed at his shoulders, tore at his hair. He rolled to his side, taking her with him, lifting his mouth from hers, looking at her uncomprehendingly. She wept, 'Jack?'

He said, 'This is how it is, between men and women.' His voice was hoarse, breathless.

It couldn't be. This couldn't be what loving was.

'No, no, this isn't right. This can't be right,' she wept. His breathing slowed, his eyes focused and it was as though there was a stranger staring at her, with dark, empty eyes, and then he ground down onto her mouth, hard, urgent, and his eyes clouded, and then they closed, and he rolled her onto her back, looming over

81

her. His hands were beneath her buttocks, he was raising her to him.

She gripped his shoulders, her mouth working. She saw him in the lamplight, huge, dark, his eyes empty. 'No, you mustn't. You can't. You mustn't.'

She shook him, then gripped his head between her hands. 'Jack, you can't.' He opened his eyes, sweat rolling down his forehead. He said, 'At last you are my wife.'

With that, he thrust into her, and the pain slashed and throbbed, and took all the breath from her. Her scream was buried in his flesh, and the next, and the next as he moved his body on her, and in her, and though her eyes were open wide, and staring at the ceiling she could see nothing, nor hear the flapping of the sails, nor his gasps, as he heaved and thrust, harder, and harder, quicker, and quicker. Then he groaned, and rolled out of her, off her. But his arm lay on her breasts, and his head on her hair.

She lay trembling. The trembling grew into a shaking. She pulled the sheet and blankets up and around them both, and lay looking at the ceiling, feeling the throbbing pain where he had been, and not understanding this thing called love.

CHAPTER FOUR

As the voyage progressed the days assumed a pattern, much as they had at Wendham, though here the bell sounded for watches not for meals, and the wind sang in the rigging, not in the trees and around the eaves.

The sounds which had seemed so strange, like the patter of feet on the deck above the transom cabin, became familiar to the point where Irene no longer noticed, and so too the creak and strain of the timbers.

Soon it was as though she and the other two women had never lived anywhere but in the dark small cabins, had paced nothing but the deck, had avoided coiled ropes all their lives, and geese, hens and pigs, even the two sheep, for one had been slain last week for food when they were one month out.

Now, as they strolled in the warmth of the Tropics, basking in the subtle breeze, relaxing to the sound of waves slapping against the hull, Mrs Meldrew complained, not for the first time, 'I still feel that these animals should be penned.' A breeze caught the topsail, the rigging sang, the women held down their crinoline skirts, almost without noticing.

Irene said calmly, 'As I have already said, my husband prefers that they have the run of the deck, for they live longer that way. There are plenty of convicts to clear up after them.' Her tone implied that the matter should not be raised again.

She looked at Jack as he stood on the quarterdeck. My husband. The words still gave her a thrill. He was master in charge of all this, so clever, so strong and it was not his fault that men and women were so different, and that, when the sun went down, she trembled at the assault she feared might come again, though so far it had not done so.

Mrs Meldrew had said, when Irene confided in her recently about her wedding night, that if it was only that one night then in Jack Prior she had a considerate husband, one who would spare his wife the worst of his lusts, and she should be thankful. My husband, she thought again, full of gratitude, trust and love.

She left the women to return to the wardroom where the steward should be waiting. She gathered her skirt close to her and squeezed down the companionway. Tomorrow she would discard the crinoline, she thought with irritation. But knew that she would not, because she was the master's wife, and must set an example.

The steward was waiting in the wardroom. She said, 'The man I put to fish off the prow has had a good catch. We shall eat fish this evening, baked. Fish chowder first. Apple pie to finish. We do still have some apples in store? I want no dirty knives, Sinclair, is that clear?'

The wardroom steward, a stooped grizzled forty-year-old American from San Francisco grunted, his thin face reflecting his resentment of her interference. She took no notice, for she was merely fulfilling her role as the master's wife, but as he turned to go he sniffed his disapproval.

She snapped, 'If you keep up this attitude, Sinclair, you might well find yourself in the deck galley, cooking for the hands.'

'Aye, ma'am,' he grunted, heading back to the wardroom galley.

She sighed, as Jack hurried down the companionway, brushing past her into the transom cabin. 'Sinclair is so ill-tempered,' she complained, following him in, watching as he pored over the chart.

He grunted, not looking up at her. 'He's a whaleman. Whalemen work hard, and eat to keep strong, not for enjoyment. Victuals are scarce. Women do not earn their rations.'

'You're not whaling now.'

He raised his head, his eyes flashing. 'And more's the pity.'

He hurried out. She gripped his sleeve. 'I'll earn my keep. I'll always earn my keep.'

He laughed harshly, shaking free of her. 'We'll see, damn it,' he grunted, taking the stairs two at a time. 'Yes, we'll see.'

She stared after him. They were too cooped up, he was too busy to be pleasant but she loved him, and he loved her. It would be different when they arrived.

That afternoon she accompanied Dr Evans into the stifling hold for the first time. 'It would be appreciated,' he had said after luncheon, when she had approached him within Sinclair's hearing.

Below decks the stench of unwashed bodies, rancid food, and foul water made her gag. She put her handkerchief to her mouth, peering into the gloom, staying close to Dr Evans as he walked around the prison quarters which had been formed by running a bulkhead across the width of the ship. At intervals the guards stood on watch, their muskets protruding through the bulkhead.

She stooped to avoid the low beams of the deckhead. There was a low murmuring all around them. See Martha, here I am, visiting the poor. I'm fulfilling my duty. Sinclair, you can stop your sighing. Jack, oh Jack you will hear of me earning my place, and be pleased. She felt proud as she breathed even more shallowly through her handkerchief.

'God in heaven,' the medical officer ground out. 'If pigs get the run of the deck, these men should too.'

She turned on him, lowered the handkerchief. 'The pigs have done nothing wrong. These men have, or they wouldn't be there. Besides, you know very well they are taken on deck regularly.'

Dr Evans didn't pause to answer but stooped down to an elderly man, peering into his mouth, feeling his throat. 'To work, you mean, to swab the decks and release the seamen for other duties. These men need more air, and lime juice, or we'll have scurvy before we're halfway through the voyage.' He didn't turn to her as he spoke, but moved on to the next man, saying, 'See the halo round the lamp. Fetid air.' She looked.

'We need wind-sails rigged over the hatches to get a breeze down here and they should have more than their two pints of water a day in this heat.' Dr Evans called to the guard accompanying them, 'See to it.'

'Not sure if the capt'n like that, sir.'

'D'you mean Captain Meldrew?'

'No, Captain Prior, sir.'

Dr Evans grunted, 'If it's that or lose one, he'll do it, never you fear.'

Irene smiled in spite of the heat and stench. There, godfather, the medical officer is talking so confidently about the man you called cruel.

Dr Evans pointed to another man's arms. 'See that, Mrs Prior.' She peered through the gloom and could see blisters on the man's arms. She recoiled.

Dr Evans laughed grimly. 'Don't worry, nothing contagious, just the pitch which has melted in the heat and dropped from the seams. Yes, we certainly need wind-sails.' She looked up, the sweat clinging to her back, soaking into her undergarments. Soon it would stain her muslin.

That evening, over dinner, the medical officer raised the question of the wind-sails, the increased water ration. When Jack hesitated he said, 'You'll lose lives if you don't, or let me put it another way, the head count will be down, if you don't.'

Jack agreed to the extra requirements immediately. Irene then said, 'I accompanied the medical officer to the prisoners' quarters, my dear. Lime juice is now necessary to avoid scurvy, and increased exercise would also aid their well-being. I have instructed lime juice to be made available, and strongly endorse the need for deck time. I told Dr Evans that I was sure you would accede to his request.'

'Did you indeed?' His voice was quiet.

She said, 'I've arranged to dispense the lime juice to the prisoners during their spell on deck, after their chores.'

The medical officer nodded. She looked beyond him to the steward, then to Jack, her smile triumphant.

Jack questioned the medical officer. 'Scurvy?'

'Indeed.'

'Then by all means, my dear, add this duty to your daily round.' His voice was still quiet.

That evening, as she waited in bed for Jack, she smoothed her nightgown, feeling satisfied, even victorious. Today she had proved herself worthy to be wife of Jack Prior. She smiled as he entered.

He stood with his back to the door, looking at her, tapping his leg. At last he said, 'A master's wife does not intrude into conversations that do not concern her. I am the authority on this ship. I make the decisions. Tonight, my dear, you overreached yourself. Take care. Take great care never to displease me again.' His face was dark with anger, his eyes so blank and cold, his voice like ice.

With that, he turned on his heel and left. Irene lay in stunned silence, then turned into her pillow, her fist pressed against her mouth, his words repeating in her head, the blankness of his eyes always there, the coldness of his voice, and she cursed herself for her rashness, cursed herself for causing him difficulties, cursed herself for the fool she was, and wept because marriage was so strange.

When Beth came to dress her as morning came, Irene whispered, 'Hurry.'

Beth looked startled, and laced her quickly. Irene snatched the hairbrush, dragged it through her hair, seeing in the mirror that her eyes were red and swollen. 'Pin it,' she whispered, snatching up her bonnet as the girl did so. She hurried into the transom. He was there, poring over his charts. She stopped, 'Forgive me, Jack. I would never do anything you didn't want. I would never do anything you disapproved of. I love you. I thought I was helping, doing my duty, earning my keep, making it easier for you.'

He kept his finger on the chart, whilst he turned to stare at her. Some hair hung by the side of her pale face, there were dark circles under her eyes. She came to the table. She was trembling. 'Forgive me. I love you. I couldn't bear to think I'd caused you any difficulties. I am your wife. I have been put on this earth to help you, I will do anything for you, anything.'

For a moment their eyes held one another's, then he turned back to the chart. 'Just as long as you understand, for there can only be one master.' His eyes flickered to her face once more, and she saw confusion. She bent and kissed him. He drew back. 'I have work to do.'

That evening, as the flying fish soared and dipped, she went to him on the forward deck. As the fish glinted in the moon's limpid glow she leaned into him, hardly daring to breathe, fearing his withdrawal into harshness. He stood motionless, not moving away, but not holding her either.

The wind sang in the sails, and the *Cachalot* drove through the seas, leaving fluorescence in its wake. 'I love you,' she breathed. 'All this is so magical. We're in our own world here. No-one can reach us.' There was a long moment of silence.

He said, 'Come with me.'

He led her along the deck, beneath rigging and beams, and around coiled ropes, and past the matt blackness of the four whale boats which hung from davits.

He steered her up the steps onto the quarterdeck, then down the companionway, into the sleeping cabin, jerking his head at Beth, 'Leave us.' His voice was low, gruff. Beth curtsied and hurried out.

Jack turned Irene around, and unbuttoned her bodice, bending to kiss the rise of her breasts, and she beat down disappointment. She wanted words of love, not this. He removed her dress, unlaced her, discarded her crinoline, not speaking until she was naked. He led her to the bed, and with each step she tensed, fixing her eyes on something, anything.

He undressed, then lay with her, kissing her roughly. She whispered, 'I love you.' He opened his eyes, and again she saw confusion. He buried his face in the crook of her shoulder. She held him, stroking his hair, not understanding but grateful for a reprieve.

For a moment he lay like that, and then his mouth was on hers, hard again, demanding, and she stared at a spot on the ceiling as his breathing quickened, but there was not the violence of before, there was almost a stumbling, and then a cessation, as, uncompleted, he lifted himself from her, lying with his face on her spread hair. She turned and saw his drawn face, his tears. She tasted the salt as she kissed them. 'Oh my love, you're tired. I'll take care of you. I'll love you. I'll do everything to make you happy.'

He looked at her and there was that confusion again, and then he turned over onto his side. 'I'm not tired,' he shouted. 'It's this damned wind, sets up a chill, that's all,' but she heard the thickness in his voice and, reaching out a hand, stroked his back.

'I know,' she said. 'I know.' But it wasn't the wind, it was vulnerability, and this man, Jack Prior, had shared it with her. Mrs Meldrew was wrong, this act wasn't lust, it was a man's form of closeness and her love grew even deeper.

*   *   *

In the days that followed Irene and Dr Evans dispensed lime juice to the convicts, and at the end of the next week she heard the ring of steel as their shackles were removed. As they shambled about the deck their unshackled legs lifted involuntarily. Dr Evans said, 'It's always the case. They'll adjust. It just takes time.'

She'd looked to Jack on the quarterdeck. It was two weeks since that night of closeness, and it was true, one did adjust, for though it had never been repeated it had happened, and at night she was beginning to sleep, adjusting, as her husband was.

After they left the Cape the weather deteriorated. They steered due south, nearing the Antarctic Circle, then took passage to the east. Storms swamped the deck, waves broke inboard, drenching the convicts' quarters, pouring down the companionway.

A cast of ships' biscuits was found to be crawling with bugs. There were cockroaches and rats in the galley, and bed bugs in the cabins, but none of it touched her.

A convict died of dysentery, and they stood in sheeting rain as Jack Prior read the service, and the body was consigned to the deep. She stood beside him and it was as though she was at her parents' funeral again. She told him. He said, 'You were fortunate to have both parents to grieve over.'

She cursed herself for her thoughtlessness. 'I'm so sorry,' she said.

He turned from her and for the rest of the day she sought to make amends and was grateful when a storm raged, and Jack dashed to the quarterdeck, roaring up to the rigger at the masthead, while the first mate, Mr Osborne, yelled to the men down the hatchways.

'Get below,' Captain Meldrew ordered the women, as the guards herded the convicts back to their quarters.

'Will it never end?' murmured Mrs Meldrew. 'And

when it does, what sort of a life shall we have in Australia?'

The weather cleared and Jack, who had been sleeping in the hurricane cabin on the quarterdeck returned to the cabin, taking her roughly, but she stared at the ceiling and this time it didn't seem so bad, or such a violation, or cause her such pain, and she smiled as he finished. 'I love you,' she murmured, for by coming to her he had shown that he had forgiven her thoughtlessness, he had wanted to be close.

As they approached Western Australia they basked in a dry clean heat, and Fremantle shone as she stood with the medical officer on the deck, while the pilot came aboard and guided them into harbour. Beth came to her placing a shawl around Irene's shoulders. 'You'll have to make sure you keep this on when you're sailing about that nasty great ocean, 'cos I won't be here to run after you.'

Irene laughed, for that nasty great ocean was going to be privy to the greatest happiness that the world had seen, and she longed for her godfather to see how wrong he had been about Jack Prior.

She murmured, 'I'll take care of myself, and Jack, and our dreams.'

Beth raised her eyes at the doctor, who shook his head, his eyebrows raised, 'She'll be seeing cupids sitting on the clouds next.'

When the convicts marched onto the quay, Beth came to her, carrying her belongings in her knotted shawl. She waited while Irene waved ashore the Meldrews and the Carstairs, then touched her arm, saying, 'You're going to be lonely. New Zealand, did he say?' She nodded towards Jack who was checking figures with the medical officer.

'Yes,' Irene said. 'New Zealand, to build the deck try-works, and replace the crew who've just jumped ship. They, like you, feel Australia's a land of opportunity.' She laughed ruefully. 'Mr Prior says that in New Zealand there will be escaped convicts he can take on. They make good crew for they've no future other than on the ship. But, Beth, I'll not be lonely, I'll have Jack.' She stopped, hugged the girl. 'Be happy.' She dragged her shawl from her shoulders and handed it to Beth. 'Take this, you seem to have another use for yours.'

The two young women laughed together as Beth patted her shawl-wrapped bundle. 'The first mate tells me other wives sail with their whalemen husbands. You'll meet up with them.' She walked down the gangway.

Irene watched her reach the quay, followed by the medical officer, Dr Evans. She lifted her hand in farewell, but was glad they were all gone at last, not caring whether she met up with other wives or not. She cleaned the transom cabin, and the sleeping cabin, singing to herself, smoothing down the blanket, touching the pillow where his head had lain. Now would be their time as the whaler idled on the cruising ground. Now he would show her his world, as he had shown her father.

She looked around her sleeping quarters, at the bare wooden shelves and drawers, at the bed, so dull and austere, at the pewter lamp which for once was not swaying, and she remembered her room at Wendham, and there was no pang of homesickness, there was just enthusiasm.

She threw down the cloth and hurried on deck, telling Mr Osborne she would be back in a few hours. She walked into the town, her legs uncertain with this earthbound stability. Her hat shielded her eyes from the searing heat and her skin from its harshness. She wore gloves for she must remain beautiful for her husband.

She searched until she found a small shop that sold material. She bought yards of a bright poppy-

and cornflower-splashed cotton, and returned to the *Cachalot*, whose sails were furled, and whose dark stained prow gleamed in the sun. 'You are the most beautiful "blubber boat" in the world,' she crooned as she hurried up the gangplank, laughing.

For the rest of the day she sewed at the wardroom table, oblivious of the heat, and of the first and second mate who came and went, until she heard their curses. 'Damn bugger of a third mate – he's jumped ship. What's the matter with him?'

She looked up then. Poor Jack, she thought. She cleared away her material, and waved back the steward who brought her the menu for this evening. 'No, I leave it entirely to you. Our guests have gone, and therefore my interference is at an end. Perhaps it should never have begun. Forgive me.'

She carried the material through into the sleeping cabin and draped it over the covers. She stepped back. Yes, now she had poppies and cornflowers which were the essence of Somerset, in this, her other home. No, in this *their* other home. A home in which she would sail to New Zealand, a home in which convicts had been brought safely to harbour. See, godfather, there has been no cruelty. How wrong you have been.

As they sailed they would walk the decks beneath the stars, sit together in the transom, draw closer, and when they reached New Zealand she would tread the same paths as her father.

They remained in Fremantle for only two days, by which time the *Queen of the Isles* had arrived, and offloaded her convicts. To avoid losing any more crew, the officers stood their watches at the head of the gangway of each ship, whilst Jack worked the seamen night and day loading supplies.

Shortly after breakfast, on the morning of their departure, a knock on the transom door startled her. Sinclair called, 'Captain's compliment, Mrs Prior. Best come on deck right away. The constables are coming aboard for the stowaway search. Quick now, for we don't want you swallowing any sulphur.'

He held the door open for her. 'Sulphur?' she asked.

The steward nodded. 'They'll be searching the ships, and letting off their sulphur bombs in the hold.'

Now she could hear banging, and hurried up the companionway, onto the quarterdeck. Constables swarmed over the ship, banging on casks, rampaging through the fo'c's'le, the crew's quarters, and the aft-cabins.

One constable bayoneted flour not yet lowered into the hold. Jack roared from the centre of the quarterdeck, 'You be careful there.' He roared even louder at the crew standing in the waist, 'Remember what I said. If any escaped convict's found, then you'll all pay.'

She asked Sinclair who stood with her by the hurricane cabin, to the right of the companionway, 'Pay what?'

Sinclair grimaced. 'The captain'll be fined a month's wages for every officer and seaman on board, which he'll have to cough up afore we leave. Then the crew'll start paying.'

She stared at the constables, then at the men who were murmuring together in the waist, then at Jack who was pacing the quarterdeck in front of her. He stopped, pulled out his watch, checked the wind, turned on his heel, resumed his pacing.

She said to Sinclair, 'He'll set it against the lay, you mean, do you?'

Sinclair just stared ahead as he said, 'That'll be part of it, the best part of it.' His mouth was working, he ran his fingers through his beard. His hair was long and drawn back in a pigtail.

The constables were recalled to the deck, and stood over the hatches. Sulphur bombs were released. Smoke billowed from the hatches.

Everyone watched and waited. No-one spoke. Then

they heard coughing, and a man stumbled from the forward hold. A groan went up from the men. The steward shifted his weight, and exchanged a glance with Irene.

She stood motionless, sensing the rage rise in Jack, feeling the anger rising in herself. Someone had spoilt it for her. Someone had ruined what was to be the first day of their proper lives together.

The officer in charge of the constables came to Jack, and together they conferred, and she heard Jack's protests, but it was to no avail. The fine had to be paid.

That night when they were at sea, she and Jack ate alone, since the first mate was on watch, and the second mate was in the fo'c's'le questioning the men. 'I'll get the devil who helped him,' Jack said. 'And when I do, God help him.' He toyed with his chicken.

'Are you sure someone helped? Could he not just have come on board himself?' she ventured.

He looked at her, his eyes blank. 'Do you really have the gall to question me, still?'

She put down her knife and fork, her fingers trembling. 'Did you and my father go to Fremantle?' She must keep him talking, she must reclaim him. So they talked of the voyage Jack and Bartie had made, and he grew expansive and leaned back in his chair, sipping brandy, while she drank coffee, and later, when they retired to the sleeping cabin, he forbade her to remove the coverlet, but stripped her nightgown from her, and took her on the poppies and the cornflowers, and her heart cried for a softer closeness but she stared at the ceiling and knew she would willingly suffer far worse if that also was an expression of his love.

In February the *Cachalot* sailed in between the many islets of the magnificent New Zealand Bay of Islands towards Port Russell and Irene stared across the almost primeval waters. At last they were here. At last they would drop anchor, and at last there would be a cessation of the first mate's raucous bullying, Jack's anger, the men's exhaustion.

At last there would be no more thuds of the rope across the sailors' backs, no more groans as the decks were scrubbed, the brass polished, no men fainting from weariness. Or would it cease, for no-one had yet confessed?

She held herself erect, staring at the small township. Here they would find more crew. Here they would refit. Here Jack would stop peering through that telescope as he was doing now, sweeping it across the horizon. Here everything might be made mellow.

She said to him again, as she climbed the quarterdeck steps, 'But what are you looking for?'

Now, for the first time he told her. 'A ship.'

'What ship?' For the *Queen of the Isles* had been within sight for the whole voyage.

His voice was cool as he lowered the telescope. 'All in good time.'

She turned again to the harbour, seeing the four other whale ships with their straight-standing masts. There was no pier, just a beach and a small collection of houses. Sinclair brought two coffees. She held hers between both hands. Jack said, 'This was intended to be the capital of New Zealand. Once it was overrun with fleets, and your father called it a hell house of bawdiness, but that was before the South Sea fishery dwindled. Now it's on the slippery slope. Ain't got no manufacturing, only a few coal mines. Pathetic. Helpless.' He was staring at her, through her. 'Helpless,' he repeated.

She looked across at the township, hearing him call out order after order, solid, strong, in control. Her father had been here, with Jack. She glowed.

At last the anchor was down, and already boats were being lowered from the other ships, bringing their captains to the *Cachalot*. She knew that they would immediately closet themselves in the wardroom with Jack, eager for news, and any mail that the *Cachalot* might be carrying for them.

The steward said to her, on his way from the quarter-deck to the galley, 'Ain't no captain's wives on these ships, ma'am, but don't you fret, there's some around and we'll cross their path.'

She stayed aboard for the next week as Jack was rowed backwards and forwards to Port Russell, and all around her sails were repaired, new sails were brought on board, and bolts and canvas, coils of rigging. There were spare lines and harpoons, a spare boat, spare spars. And there were Maoris, tattooed and huge, selling peaches, pears and honey from canoes beneath their bows.

Beef, bread, and stays were stowed. The cooper tapped throughout the day, making new casks, and she watched as they were roped together, end to end, and floated high on the water to shore, then towed back, heavy from the drinking water they contained.

There were no beatings, no grated orders, no kicks. There was no need, Irene thought, her spirits soaring, for Sinclair had come with a deputation from the fo'c's'le who declared that the aft-oarsman had slipped the convict on board, and then jumped ship.

The try-works were built amidships in the space of two days. First a frame of brickwork was erected, then the two gigantic pots were set up side by side over the furnaces. It was here that the whale blubber would be rendered down, and each day she pictured how her father would have watched, learned and breathed in the balmy air as she was doing.

It was finished on the evening of Thursday, when the light had gone, and cressets lit the deck, and lanterns hung from the rigging. Jack walked past. Sounds of laughter and singing wafted from the grog shop on shore. She called after him, 'I'm so happy that the crew have told you about the events of the convict. So happy that I am here with you, as my father was before me. So happy that we can begin our life at last.'

He strode on. She shrugged. He had clearly not heard her.

The replacement crew arrived the next day, including a replacement third mate; an escaped convict with some experience before the mast, having sailed to the Japan Grounds with several whalers.

Jack went ashore at midday, after staring through his telescope and searching the sea. Before he left she said, 'What is this ship you are waiting for?'

He said, 'Something to make my life complete.'

He came back just before dinner, stumbling from the boat as it was winched up, his voice slurred from the brandy he had drunk.

He came to the wardroom where they waited dinner. He stood, swaying, looking from one to the other. He came back to Irene. 'Wear your jewels,' he ordered, his voice curt. 'Wear 'em as your mother would have worn 'em for your father.'

She left the wardroom, took them from the box in the sleeping cabin, holding them against her skin, doing up the clasp, her hands trembling, for his mouth had been cruel, his voice harsh and he had spoken of her mother and father as though he could not bear the taste of their names.

She returned to the wardroom and seated herself. The first mate shoved bread into his mouth. A piece fell to the table. She shook out her napkin. Jack leaned towards the new third mate who sat at his side and said, his voice slurred, 'Little jewel, ain't she, Travers, but not as bright as those gems?'

The young man looked at his plate, his thin face colouring, his long lashes casting a shadow on his cheek-bones. 'Eh?' repeated Jack, jabbing the man with his elbow. 'Eh, Mr Harry Travers?'

Irene sat quite still, stunned. Then pleaded, 'Jack.'

Jack poured more brandy. He held up the glass to

the lamplight, called to the first mate, 'Still no sign. You've a man in the crow's nest?'

The man nodded, 'Aye, Capt'n.'

Jack cursed, downed the brandy in one gulp and slammed the glass on the table. It cracked, cut his hand. He laughed, sucking the blood. It ran down his chin. She rushed to him, and bound his hand with her napkin. 'Jack,' she whispered. 'You are overtired. Please, lie down for a moment.'

He gripped her arm. 'Take your seat.' His voice was savage. He pushed her towards her chair.

She sat, smoothing her skirt, looking at the meat which Sinclair doled onto her plate. 'That's enough,' she whispered, shock making her feel cold, freezing her mind.

Jack leaned towards Mr Travers again. 'You and she's the same. Two Britishers with nowhere to go.' She stared at Jack, his words penetrating the cold. 'What d'you mean?'

'Here you both are, stranded, can't go nowhere but to sea, can't go running off, 'cos there's nowhere for you to go.'

She looked down at her plate. The lamb fat was congealing. She raised her eyes in the silence. The third mate was looking at her, confused. Jack said, 'That's right, isn't it, Harry Travers? You can't go nowhere, you're in thrall to me, else you'd be picked up by the British, the ever-powerful British. You're mine, can't go nowhere. Just like she's in thrall, she's mine, and can't go nowhere else, unless I say so. Helpless, without power, the pair of you.'

The third mate dropped his gaze to his plate. Irene rose, and swept from the wardroom. She stumbled up the companionway. The evening air was still, and heavy. The deckboards still threw up the daytime heat. They must leave for the open sea. Jack must get away from this endless work, the strain of it all. That's what it was. It was natural for a man to drink, to say such things when he carried such responsibility. But she banged her fist onto the ship's rail, wanting to pummel him for comparing her to a criminal when she was wearing her mother's jewels, for comparing her to a criminal at any time. Rage and pain vied for supremacy. 'Why? Why?'

The steward brought her a mug of coffee as she stared at the lights of the town, her mind still racing. 'Best get this inside you, ma'am.'

He cut through her panic. She snapped, 'It would be better being poured down throats in the wardroom.'

He nodded gravely. 'Some's going down right now. That Harry Travers is gulping it as though his life depended on it.'

'My husband?' The stars were vivid and it was these she stared at.

'The captain too.'

Her cheeks were still burning. She had to get off this boat. In thrall indeed. A Wendham in thrall. She touched her necklace as rage triumphed. 'Tomorrow I go ashore. Make sure there's room for me on the liberty boat.'

The next day she was rowed to shore in a boat crewed by the third mate's team, and with her sat Jack, contrite, a basket beside him, packed by the steward. 'A picnic,' Jack had said over breakfast. 'I'll take you on a picnic, to eat crow. I allowed my mouth to take over last night.'

She stared straight ahead now as the boat dipped and rose, forging through the waves, avoiding the third mate, who stood in the prow, issuing orders to his men in a West Country voice which fuelled her anger and hurt. Yes, she was a Wendham, and it was this she clung to, not his cruel stupid words. How dare he compare her to that criminal, how dare he?

Jack moved beside her. She stiffened. He brought his telescope to his eye and swept the bay. 'What is so important about this ship?' she demanded, too angry to care, too upset to mind her tongue.

Again he said, 'You'll see, or I hope to God you will.' He sounded tired. She looked at him and saw the anxiety on his face, and she felt shame at her tone, and the rage dissipated, as her mother's had always dissipated in the face of her father's worry.

She touched his arm. 'A few hours away from all this will do us both good.'

The waves of the bay they walked to crashed onto the sand and were much bigger than those that rolled ashore at Lyme Regis, where her father had taken her in summers gone by, and the noise of it drummed all around them.

She sat close to Jack on one of the many rocks. This one was large and flat, and hot from the sun. She shaded her eyes against the glare, wafting away the flies as she envisaged the lane down which they had just walked; its honeysuckle, its cow parsley. She said, 'At Wendham March is cool still, though spring will be breaking out.'

'Well then, I guess you should be happy to be here in this heat.' His tone was lazy. He sank down onto his back, flinging his arm across his face.

'I am. I'm happy. I have you to myself, and there is our whole life before us. Oh Jack, *you* are happy too, aren't you?'

He said nothing. She stared out at the waves, up at the sky, out to the horizon. She saw sails. She shaded her eyes. Was this the one he'd been waiting for? Would his anxiety ease?

She shook him, 'A ship, Jack.'

He hurled himself to his feet, kicking over the picnic basket, snatching up the telescope, focusing. The breeze caught up the red and white tablecloth which spilled from the basket, and tumbled it along the beach. She started after it. He ran after her, kicking up sand, laughing that laugh. He grabbed her, thrust the telescope at her. 'You have a look too. Just you have a goddamn look.'

'The picnic . . .' she repeated.

His grip tightened, and he shouted right into her face, 'Look at the ship, you damn woman.'

She froze.

'Take it, I said.' Slowly she took the telescope, lifted it, and held it to her eye. He still gripped her arm. 'I can't see anything but sea.' Her voice shook. He jerked her arm. 'You're hurting,' she whispered, lowering the telescope.

'Focus on the horizon, for God's sake.' His voice was hard.

She found the ship, steadied the telescope. 'It's a whaler,' she said. 'It's just a whaler.'

'Keep looking. Find the name,' he commanded.

She steadied the telescope, her eye aching, her arms too. She found the name. '*Wendham*,' she read aloud.

She lowered the telescope and turned to him. '*Wendham*?' she queried.

Jack had moved away and was staring out at the ship, his face exultant.

She dropped the telescope. '*Wendham*?' she demanded, a terrible uncertainty gripping her. '*Wendham*, why is it called *Wendham*? I insist you tell me. I insist, do you hear?' She ran at him, pulling at his sleeve.

He brushed her hand from his arm. She looked again at the ship which was bearing, full-sailed, towards Port Russell. *Wendham, Wendham*. The name echoed in her mind. 'Tell me,' she whispered.

'It's called *Wendham* because it pleased me to name her that.' He turned right round to face her, and again there was that harsh loud laugh.

The waves were pounding and dragging at the sand, the tablecloth was caught on rocks hundreds of yards along the beach, the picnic was half buried in sand which whipped in clouds across the beach.

She said, 'We haven't enough money for another ship.

You have nothing. There are only a few shares. All my wealth is in Wendham . . .' She trailed to a stop.

'You forget, madam, what's yours is mine.'

She tried to push him to one side, tried to see the ship. 'What have you done?' she screamed.

He grabbed her, pulled her close, shouted into her face, 'I've taught you that you've nothing 'cept what I give you. Cast your stupid little mind back to Jeffries spouting his damned words of wisdom to you in the lodging house. I could have told you all he said. I made it my business to ask the right questions the day I heard of your crazy father's death. I just had to sort how I could get the most out of marrying you.' He laughed again and it was as though he was mad, as though the world was mad.

She struggled to free herself. He held her tight. 'Look at that ship, feast your eyes on it.' He pulled her round to face the sea with him. 'That is what Wendham's land and house bought. A twenty-one year lease to Barratt, not a four-year lease to the estate manager. He can do what he likes; sack the staff, build the factory if he wants – it ain't Wendham land after all, so it's his to own. And there are your workers to feed it. Then come 1876 and I'll lease it again. Let me see now – March – he'll be starting on those flower beds he was talking about.'

She screamed and screamed, throwing her head back, unable to stop.

He slapped her. She spun, fell to the ground. Sand was in her mouth, and blood. Her head was exploding. No, it wasn't true. He hadn't said those things. No. She pushed herself up a few inches, turned her head. Saw his boots just a yard away. She bit on sand, spat red spittle. She struggled to her feet. He watched, he laughed. She shouted over the sound of the waves and the wind, 'I signed a four-year lease, that's all.'

'You should have read it, and you should listen better when I talk to you. I've said, you've signed for twenty-one years.' He was laughing again, this man she loved was laughing, and the waves were pounding and the ship was getting ever closer, as it ran before the wind.

She ran at him, shaking him, 'You're drunk. You love me. I know you love me, you were adjusting, you were considerate, Mrs Meldrew said you were. I don't believe this, any of this.'

He hurled her down onto the sand again. 'Collect the picnic, fetch the cloth, get back on board. Believe it, Mrs Prior. Believe also that I enjoyed planning it, and carrying it out.'

He strode off, back up the beach, then into the lane, his jacket flapping.

She lay on the beach until the shadows grew long, beyond thought, but not beyond feeling, repeating his words, grappling, fighting them, changing them. It had to be the drink. It could not be true. After all, he had not imposed himself on her in the lodging house, he had contained his lust. No, it could not be true. Her father would not do this, and Jack Prior was like her father.

At last, frantically, as the insects bit with increasing vigour in the dropping wind and the fading sun, she gathered up the picnic, ran along the beach, clambered up the rocks, the breeze catching her hoops but what did she care. She reached the trapped tablecloth, pulled it. It tore. A corner remained trapped. What would he say? He would be cross. His words might turn into the truth.

She climbed higher, higher, slipped, gashed her leg. She climbed again and eased the red and white cloth from the teeth of the crevice, scrambling down, folding it neatly. It must be neat, to please him. She hurried down the beach, down the lane in the light of the moon, passed the grog shops, the few houses, the stores and reached the liberty boat.

The third mate was there, pacing the beach, looking first one way, and then the other. The crew were resting on their oars. He spun round as she ran up. She clutched his arm, 'Jack, where's Jack?' She could hear herself screaming the words, but it was as though it was a long way off, and that's where they should be, far away from here, together, just the two of them because none of this would have happened. She must find him, sail away with him.

Harry Travers shot a look at the crew, who were craning to hear. He pulled her up the beach. 'Calm yourself, Mrs Prior. Your husband is in the town. We expected you long ago.'

She shook herself free. 'Where in the town?' She dropped the picnic basket. 'He'll be waiting for me. I must go to him.'

Harry Travers shook his head. 'He said we were to take you back aboard.'

She slapped him now, hard across the face. 'Tell me where he is. Just do as you're damn well told. He'd want me to go to him. He wanted the picnic basket.'

She stooped, picked it up. Harry Travers stood quite still, looking at her. She screamed at him again, 'Where is he?'

He told her. She ran back down the beach, to the grog shop. She stumbled up the steps and shoved open the door. The room was thick with tobacco smoke, and laughter, and male voices. The breath heaved in her chest as she stood in the entrance, searching the room.

He was there, in the corner, drinking at a table with Captain Standing, and another man, bluff, black-haired, lined. But no, he wouldn't be the captain of the *Wendham* because a Wendham with sails couldn't exist.

She pushed her way through the crowded room, with each step she took the room grew quieter until she reached his table, by then it was silent.

Jack cursed when he saw her. She dropped the picnic box on the table, scattering the glasses, spilling the drinks, knocking over a candle stuck in a bottle. He roared, 'What the hell are you doing here? I told you to get back on board.' He swept the picnic basket off the table, the glasses too.

A woman laughed, and sauntered over towards him. Her bodice was unbuttoned and revealed sagging dirty breasts. She lolled against Jack, putting her arm around his shoulders. 'You got troubles, sweetheart?'

Jack stared at Irene. 'Not any more,' he said, slowly and clearly. 'I got me three ships, I got me a wife and the use of her body, boring though it is, and I've got everything she used to own. No, can't say I've a trouble in the world.'

The two men he sat with looked at one another, then down at the table. There was a stirring around the room, an embarrassed murmuring. The woman stroked his hair, 'So Black Jack's made it big, has he?'

'Sure has. Planning, that's what it's all about. Plan and you can just about get anything you want but sometimes you have to have something you don't want in the parcel, or someone. Then you's just have to use 'em as you see fit,' Jack said, taking tobacco from his pocket, cutting off a piece, sliding it into his mouth, his eyes on Irene. He chewed, fifteen times, no sixteen. She continued to count. Nineteen.

He stopped, leaned to the side and spat at her feet, staining her shoes.

At that she moved, coming to him. 'Why?' she said. 'Why have you done all this. Why? Why, when I know you loved me, when you were kind, brought me scrimshaw in the glasshouse, wept in my arms in the cabin.'

He shoved the whore from him, hauling Irene almost off her feet, dragging her to the door, through ranks of men who avoided his eye. Someone sniggered.

He dragged her down the steps. 'You whore, you damned lying whore. I never wept, and be certain I never loved you. I took you, not out of pleasure but out of contempt, out of triumph.'

She struggled from him, kicking him, slapping him. 'You wept. I saw you. You're the liar, and the thief, and the cheat. You're a bastard. My uncle was right. A damned bastard.'

The word sounded foreign in her mouth. What was she doing, spewing abuse, shrieking in the street? She didn't know any more, all she knew was rage and pain, and humiliation, but over it all was disbelief. 'I hate you. I'm leaving. I'm going home.'

'You have no home 'cept where I am,' he roared at her, standing with his hands on his hips. 'Barratt's at Wendham and will be for twenty-one years. What'll you do – turn up on the doorstep? Think of the scandal if you do. You're finished 'cos you ran off with your fleet's master. You can't go home, you can't go to your uncle, you can't go nowhere, you've not a penny to your name, all you've got is "equivalent accommodation" – my ship, a "blubber boat" that you should be proud to call home – all the legalities observed, hey?'

'Why?' she sobbed.

'Why? 'Cos your damned father took my fleet. He could have lent the money, but no, he had to own us. Well, I've got it back, and everything he owned too. Just like I promised myself I would. You see, you don't cross the Priors. If you do, we destroy you.'

Curious people were coming onto the street from the houses. They carried lamps. A woman clutched her shawl around her. Suddenly it was as though the world had stopped. As though her mind was clear.

She said quietly, 'My father bought your fleet because your father lost his money. He kept you on as master. He was a fine man. Just as you could be. Think, Jack. It was me who ran away with you. You didn't compromise me. You wouldn't wed me in haste, you gave me time to change my mind. Jack, you're drunk. This isn't true. This is all a stupid game.'

Jack took a pace towards her. She stood firm, lifted her head, put her shoulders back. He stopped. 'A game, eh? I played it well then, didn't I? I knew I had you dangling that first night, just as I knew you'd take to me, 'cos you'd think I was like your father. There was never any need to push it, 'cos you was panting for me from the start. I gave you time before we wed because I couldn't get the damn licence any sooner. I didn't lie with you, because you made me sick. You're a Britisher see, like your father, like the bastards who drove the whalers out of New Bedford, like the man who took my mother, that bitch who never loved me.'

She laughed now, and it was as harsh as his had been. 'No-one *took* your mother. She left, and who could blame her, if your father was anything like you. You are nothing. You are scum, from scum stock who ran away when the British burned them out, who drive women to hate and despise them.'

He lashed out. The blow caught her face. She staggered. He said, 'Get to the ship. Now.'

'I'd rather die.'

'Why not?' He moved towards her.

The whore called from the top step of the grog house, 'Sweetheart, I'm missing you.'

Jack stopped. He looked at Irene. 'Get back to the ship.'

She stared at him, and saw the truth. She backed from him, out of the pool of light from the grog-house lantern, then turned and ran.

Jack watched until he could see and hear her no longer, awash with black anger and hatred as he had been from the start, though it was deeper than ever now, for his mother had not been driven from them. She was a harlot who had run from her home, enticed by a Britisher who mewled and puked about love and tenderness when he, Jack Prior, had found them.

The whore called to him again, 'Come on, sugar.'

He went, putting his mouth on hers, pushing away the memory of Irene's whispered words on the deck as he stood watching the flying fish. They had been the same as his mother's on her only voyage with them, when he had been ten years old. She had stood with him watching the fish. 'It's all so magical,' she had said, her hand on his shoulder. 'Remember I love you, Jack. Whatever happens I love you. Don't become like your father. Don't ever strike a woman.'

The memory had flared, he had used Irene's body to wipe it away, but it had come back, turning him cold, bringing that stupid goddamn tear, bringing that awful pain, because his mother was a lying whoring bitch who would never have left if she'd loved him.

He shouted at the whore, 'My mother deserved to die. I told her that, when I found her. I told her.'

CHAPTER FIVE

Irene huddled on the bed in the sleeping cabin. It was midnight and still Jack hadn't returned from the grog shop. She stared at the empty jewel box on the bed, the one which had contained her mother's sapphire necklace and earrings – *had* contained, damn you, Jack Prior. When she'd found the necklace gone she'd rushed to the safe, but it was locked and she had no idea where he kept the key.

She'd raised the steward from the galley, but he had professed ignorance. Again she looked through all the drawers, before throwing herself onto the bed, wanting to hit out at something, anything, because the necklace had been her only hope of purchasing a passage on the one whale ship that she knew was returning home.

Once home Barratt would surely let her have Wendham back, beloved Wendham. Martha would look after her, the estate manager would take over, everything would be all right again. Everything, and nothing. Her mind was going round. She tried to hold on but tears were coming.

She gripped the coverlet, hating its poppies, its cornflowers, hating its mocking memories and tore it again and again until the air was thick with lint. Father – what shall I do?

As the lint settled she lifted her head and heard as though for the first time the patter of feet above her, the coughing from the mates' quarters, just the other side of this cabin, the creak and groan of the ship, the slap of the water and remembered her godfather's words, and Mrs Meldrew's. There was nothing she

110

could do. Jack Prior owned her, he was right and she sank to the floor, past crying, past groaning.

Jack found her like that when he returned at two a.m., slamming open the door, the smell of brandy wafting from him, and cheap perfume, the whore's perfume. He strode through the remnants of the coverlet and stood above her, legs apart, hands on hips and he laughed that harsh loud laugh. 'The poppies not to your fancy then?'

She stared up at him, her eyes red-rimmed. 'Jack, please. This isn't fair. You can't hate me this much, I know you can't. It's the drink isn't it?' She clung to his legs. 'Jack, we can love one another, I know we can. Somehow we can forget all this. I can pretend you never said and did such things. I know I can.'

She gagged at the stench of the perfume, at the image of that whore with him. She cried, 'Don't do this to me. If you don't love me, send me back to Wendham. I beg you – there, I've said it. I beg you.'

He sent her sprawling. 'Get up. Go on, get up. Get on deck. It's your watch. From now on, you're to earn your victuals like every other person on board this ship.'

She lay there, seeing the lint clinging to his trousers, hearing the lapping water, and his words, feeling his boot prod her. 'Get up, Goddamn you. You'll share the watch with your soul mate, Travers. Two paupers together, two Britishers, two hands with no option, both at the bottom of the barrel. D'you understand?'

She staggered to her feet, struggling to take in more air, gasping, stumbling, but there wasn't enough. She clutched her throat. 'I'm your wife,' she whispered at last, hoarse with shock. 'I'm your wife and you can't treat me like this. How dare you send me on deck, like a common seaman? I'm a Wendham.'

He pushed her towards the door. 'It's because you're a damned Wendham that you need to be taught your place, alongside that other piece of scum.'

She gripped the door, sobbing. 'This is the rum

talking. You didn't do this to me when we left Sydney, this isn't how you really feel, it's all a dreadful mistake. I'll go into the transom. I'll keep out of your way, anything. But don't send me up there, don't humiliate me. Tomorrow when you're sober, you'll deeply regret it.'

He laughed. 'It's not the drink. It's planning. This is the *real* me. Before I had to think what would happen if something had gone wrong, if the solicitor had turned into a gossip. What if that jackass godfather had tried to scupper me? I had to keep you sweet so's you'd defend me. Now there's no need.' He sat on the bed and tugged his boot off. 'So just get the hell up on deck.' He threw her cloak out after her.

As she stood with Mr Travers on the quarterdeck, out of earshot of the helmsman, she said, still shuddering from the shock, still trying to stop her mind from spinning and her voice from breaking, 'My husband jests you know. He says things that sound serious but are not. I am not really to be treated as a hand. I am Irene Wendham of Wendham House.' Mr Travers looked quickly at her, his hazel eyes full of compassion. He said, gently, 'If you say so, Mrs Prior.'

'I do say so.' She stopped abruptly, staring out to sea.

He turned to watch the crew passing buckets from the scuttlebutts in the waist to those near the taffrail. He lifted his hand to push back his hat. She saw pitch scars on his arms and remembered the stench and crimes of the convicts in the hold.

She repeated, her tone high pitched, out of control, 'I do say so, because it's true, and I am not to be given orders by a convict, do you understand, and neither do I need your pity. I am Irene Wendham of Wendham House and you and I may be the only British on board but we have nothing in common. Is that clear? I have a beautiful home. I do not have nothing. I am not nothing.'

She bunched her fist against her mouth. Be quiet, she told herself. Be quiet. But the words kept coming, in a stuttering stream like the gusting rain that had begun, almost obliterating the stern and forward lanterns. 'He's drunk. He will change. We sail tomorrow. With the wind in the sails he will mellow, this madness will pass.'

She panted for breath, her chest tight. 'He'll raise whales, lots of them. He has the knowledge, he knows the drift of the tides. We will earn enough to buy back the lease. He couldn't mean it.'

Mr Travers was silent.

She stood the midnight watch with Mr Travers, and crawled to the transom sofa, in clothes drenched with spray and thick with salt, to sleep for an hour. At six she rose, to eat breakfast in a wardroom presided over by Jack, where no-one spoke or looked at her, only at their plates. In her turn she fixed her gaze on her mug. This nightmare would stop, it must stop, she told herself, just as surely as the effects of the rum would stop.

But though Jack appeared quite sober he ordered her to take the windlass handle opposite the cooper at noon, and under her husband's gaze she strained to raise the dripping anchor, still shuddering in shock, barely hearing his barked complaints.

They headed out past the islets and took course for the Japan Grounds, keeping the *Queen of the Isles* and the *Wendham* in sight. Now, it would stop, out here where the wind was blowing fair, where the seas were breaking over the prow. Instead with each hour the nightmare deepened and her hands grew blistered as she was ordered to polish the try-pots, alongside the aft-oarsman, until Jack could see his face in them.

By the next day her knees were swollen as she scrubbed the deck alongside the men. 'I am eager to experience all facets of life on board ship,' she told them. 'It is my way. I gardened too, you know, at Wendham. It is my way, the Wendham way. Anyone who knew my father would know that.' Too often she said it, and none ever replied, just averted their eyes. But it helped her to stay sane.

All the time she counted her breaths, or dredged up memories of the passage over, and the good survival rate of the convicts. She knew all this must pass, that if it wasn't the rum it was a temporary madness born of guilt at his fraudulent dealings. In the face of her acquiescence Jack would relent. He must. No-one could be this cruel, no-one.

Day after day the pattern was repeated with the addition, after a week, of the harpooners cutting out their irons, and practising their throwing through a hooped wire on the rail.

After a fortnight Jack and the officers whetstoned their lances to a fine edge and took over the hoops from the harpooners.

Three weeks out Jack ordered the lowering of the four boats, and Irene watched as together they surged through the waves, the sails of the small boats hoisted, the harpooner standing tall at the prow. 'A practice,' Mr Travers had said as he ran past her to his boat. 'God help us if we get it wrong.'

She had turned from him, and now stumbled to the transom cabin. He was a convict with whom she might have to share a watch, but how dare he assume familiarity. There was nothing familiar between them, nothing in common, nothing. Nothing. Nothing.

She fell exhausted onto the sofa, having been forbidden the bed by Jack, sleeping until Sinclair shook her, bringing her tea. 'Boats returning, Mrs Prior.' She had been dreaming of the copse at Wendham, of the white tablecloth, the porcelain cups, his kiss, the sun, the peace.

Clutching his sleeve, she said to Sinclair, 'All this will pass. He will become as he was. He's a good man. He kept more convicts alive than was usual, he's not a cruel man. This isn't the real him. This can't be him.'

The steward said, 'This sure is him, Mrs Prior. He's a mean crazy man who went a mite crazier when his father sold the fleet, so it's said. But something happened before that, who cares what, though 'tis said it's to do with his mother. No, he kept them convicts alive 'cos you gets more money that way – corpses don't make good workers. None of this ain't going to pass, Mrs Prior, so don't set your sights on nothing foolish like that.'

His sleeve was coarse in her grip. It rubbed her blisters. 'This will pass,' she insisted.

'It ain't going to pass, Mrs Prior,' Sinclair repeated, his wizened face tense. She stared at her rough and swollen hand on his jacket, she stared around the cabin at the charts on the table, Jack's brandy by the sofa, the endless drawers, her trunk bought in Portsmouth, at her dresses, bought in Portsmouth. 'Then I have nothing,' she whispered. 'I really have nothing. I really am no-one.'

Day after day the wind drove them on and, though the sun blazed down, it was as though the day never dawned as she worked beside the men, silently now. In the fifth week she removed her hoops as Jack ordered. He was right, it was easier to work. She took up the hem, as he ordered. He was right, she didn't trip on them. She mended the clothes the officers brought her, as Jack ordered. He was right, she was honing her skills. She cleaned the transom and the sleeping cabin because Jack ordered that Sinclair must not, and Irene must. He was right.

She forced herself to adjust, for adjust was everything. He was right, he was training her. She was to be an owner's wife. That was it. It was her duty to know things in depth.

In the evening she sat with Jack and the officers for

meals. She was silent, but erect. She was Irene Wendham, of Wendham House, and a whaling fleet. She was exploring the world of her staff as her duty dictated. Again and again she said it to herself, and so she survived each day.

It was only each night, when she took the watch with Mr Travers that she gave way, forcing herself to put aside her distaste at his past, confiding her fear, her pain, her confusion, opening her heart. For only an Englishman, however base, could understand the level of torment a woman of her breeding was enduring.

As the ship bore on towards the cruising grounds, she told him of her life in Somerset, of her garden, of her parents, of Jack's trickery, of Martha, of the tenants, of Jack's trickery. Of her godfather who had been correct about Jack, of Barratt, of Jack's trickery.

'Will Barratt change everything? Will he destroy the kitchen garden? Will he cavalierly take my memories from me? How could he accept such a lease from Jack? He must have known it was something that I would not want. It is dishonourable, but what else can one expect from new money? Surely even someone with your background can understand honour, Mr Travers. I say again, how could Jack do it? How could he use me so? How could he take me away from Martha, who's just like a mother?'

He merely nodded but that was correct, for how could people of his class offer constructive comments? Each night, weeping as she left to take over the aft lookout position as Jack had ordered, she would say, 'But it's so unfair, I've done nothing to deserve any of this and I don't know what to do. I want to go home, I need to go home. I must go home to Wendham.'

Day after day they sailed nearer to the Japan Grounds, and there was a five pound tobacco bounty promised by Jack to the lookout who raised the first whale. Competition was keen in both the main and foremast crow's-nest day and night. Bets were taken, tension rose.

At the end of the sixth week Irene was allowed to regulate the slop chest with the steward, debiting the cost of each article against the lay. She handed out soap, matches and tobacco to the men, and jackets to the new crew, including one to Mr Travers.

She marked in the book the cost of the items against their lay. She needed soap. Jack charged it against her lay. 'Just like the other crew,' he said. 'Now get this to rights, and get back on deck.'

That night she leaned against the hurricane house on the quarterdeck, while the crew squatted about the waist, and told Mr Travers what had happened, adding, 'How absurd that as a wife I'm entitled to nothing, but as a crewman I'll get something, and when I do, I'll buy passage home.' But then she remembered the charges her godfather had levied against Jack and the huge deductions from the previous lay.

'But if he cheats again, what's to become of me?' she whispered.

Mr Travers just stared out over the deck. But then, what could a convict say to comfort her? she thought. What could anyone say?

The next morning over breakfast, after a night of gentle breezes, Jack scythed through the air with his hand. 'Quiet,' he barked. The wardroom fell silent and in the hush a lookout's voice was heard, 'Bl-o-o-w'. There came a hurricane of noise overhead, and shouted orders. Jack grabbed his hat, and was onto the companionway at a run with the others behind him.

She followed and stood at the rail as the boats were lowered by winches, splashing onto the sea. Sinclair, the steward, breathed in her ear, 'All boats'd better give way to the captain. He'll lead the chase or want to know the reason why. Most captains stay on board, but not Black Jack. He needs to be in at the kill.'

117

'Needs?' she queried. From the boats bobbing on the waves she heard, 'Break out your oars, darn you.' There was a clatter as oars were set. The crews were straining, pulling, digging their oars into the rolling seas again and again.

Sinclair nodded, pointing as the lookout yelled again, 'Thar she blows.' She saw the spout of vapour now, way over to the east. Oars were shipped, boat sails hoisted. The officers were steering from the stern, the harpooners poised in the prow.

The whale dived beneath the waves. 'He's sounded, gone deep,' Sinclair said quietly. 'He'll breach to blow, cain't say when, cain't say where.'

Jack's boat swung up into the wind, the others followed, lying hove to, rocking on the swell, the centre boards lowered. At last the steward breathed, 'Bl-o-o-w,' and she brought up the telescope, and there it was, off to the west. 'The *Wendham* and the *Queen of the Isles* are after their own bulls.' He pointed.

The fourth mate yelled from the quarterdeck to the seaman standing ready to hoist the signal flags which guided the boats, 'Three points abaft starboard beam.'

The flags were raised and fluttered in the breeze. The boats veered west, surging towards the whale, Jack's in the lead, closer and closer, until they were within striking distance. Irene held the telescope steady. The halyards were loosed, the sail and mast downed in all boats. Jack's harpooner stood at the prow, his arm drawn back, steadying, aiming, and then hurling, and she could almost hear the attached line sing round the loggerhead, and on, into the whale.

As the whale surged another harpoon was hurled from the first mate's boat, and now the great creature was away, dragging the two boats through the water, its tail slapping, pounding. She swung the telescope to the east. The second mate and Travers stood off, waiting.

In the attacking boats the harpooners scrabbled to

the stern, and the lancers headed for the prow. For an hour they fought the whale, with the wind rising every minute, and the whale tiring. The *Cachalot*, under the command of the fourth mate, sailed in closer. Jack stood poised at the prow, hatless, his shirt streaming out behind him. His arm came back, his body twisted, his lance glinted, and then he lunged at the whale.

Irene held the telescope steady on his face. It was grim, harsh, cruel. She lowered the telescope and watched as the boat's crew hauled in the main sheet and crawled up into the wind, and all the time the whale was convulsing, raising his gigantic tail, threshing the water, rolling until the sea was white with foam.

The first mate drew alongside and thrust his lance into the whale also.

The sails on both boats were down and fleeted aft, oars were out, the whale sounded again. The line span out, oars were shipped, the boats flew. On board, beside her, the men lined the rail, silent, intent, chewing tobacco, spitting on her clean deck.

The whale breached, slowly surging from the foam. The boats were almost on it, and now Jack sank another lance. She snatched up the telescope and kept it to her eye as the whale spouted bloodstained vapour. On board, alongside Irene, the men cheered, danced, slapped one another's backs. Beside her the kanaka lookout was crowing for he had won the tobacco bounty.

But Irene was not cheering, she was lowering the telescope as though in a dream, for she had seen the naked lust, the exultation on Jack's face as he saw the blood, and knew that Sinclair had been right. Jack Prior had a need to kill, and now fear clamoured loud. She had seen that same lust on his face before, and it had been when he struck her outside the grog shop.

By evening the boats had towed the whale back to the ship where its black bulk was secured by great clanking chains – its head to the stern and its tail to the bows, and the sea lapping at it. A series of planks was lowered around and above the whale to form the cutting-out platform. 'We'll work through the night, Mr Osborne,' ordered Jack, his shirt-tails gusting in the wind. 'But get the men fed first, for we ain't stopping for six hours, then half can go off watch.'

He shouldered through the seamen, to the companionway hatch, roaring at the steward to get the damn food on the table.

The first, second and fourth mates hurried down, but Mr Travers came to stand beside Irene as she stood gazing at the sharks which were twisting and turning and gorging around the whale.

'You should eat,' he said.

She shook her head and whispered, 'I can't.'

She turned back to stare down at the sharks, who were tearing at the flesh. The sea was becoming redder and redder, and against it, it seemed that she could see Jack's face.

Within half an hour the men and officers were back on deck, rushing to ropes, to the windlass, everyone busy, everyone focused. She gripped the rail, still staring at the sharks.

The head was severed and held secure, over the stern, by cables. Still she stared.

Behind her the block of the cutting tackle was hoisted and lashed to the lower masthead, and the tackle swung over the whale. A great blubber hook was attached to the hawser by Mr Travers and Mr Smith, the second mate, as they balanced on the cutting-out platform. All the while the waves rose and fell, and the moon and the lanterns cast eerie shadows and Irene watched the glint and gleam of the sharks.

'Start cutting in the hook, Mr Smith. You too, Travers,' roared Jack.

The two mates began to hack out a strip from just above the two side fins, cutting a hole within that strip, shoving the hook through. Behind Irene the crew rushed to heave at the windlass, shouting in unison whilst the first mate flayed them with a tarred rope. Still she watched the sharks.

The mates slashed. The ship quivered. The men forced the windlass, but the strip wouldn't part from the whale. Again they turned. The *Cachalot* tipped, going over to the whale instead of the strip coming to it.

The men strained again. The ship lurched. The angle of the deck increased. Irene stared from the sharks now, up to the masts which quivered. The deck dropped again. She slipped and at last jerked from one nightmare to another, screaming, clinging to the rail, looked back at the whale, the men, but then down at the sharks again, splashing, threshing, there, below her. Waiting. Waiting.

There was a snap. The blubber tore from the whale, the two mates slashed wildly at the strip as it was dragged upwards by the windlass, rolling the whale over and over as it did so. The ship heaved up and back and settled in the ocean.

The blubber rose higher and higher, dangling leaden from the hook. Water and grease drained into the blood-streaked ocean.

The sharks lashed, sliced, danced in the blood and the grease.

She backed from the rail, turned, began to run, anywhere, everywhere, but he was there, Jack, the one who lashed and killed and lusted just as the sharks were lusting. He was there, in front of her, straddle-legged, his laugh scorching from him, his eyes dark with hate. He was reaching for her, with those huge hands. She screamed. The first mate swung round, the winch halted. The second mate swore. Mr Travers stared.

Jack grabbed her. 'Not so damn fast, and stop that goddamn noise. You'll be needed.' She beat at him. 'Let me go.' He laughed again, that laugh. He dragged her back to the rail. 'Watch the flensing, Irene Wendham, the lady who likes to learn how things are goddamn done.'

In the light of the slung lanterns and the deck cressets and the dim moon she stared, blank-eyed, as the long spades sliced. Mr Travers slipped, caught himself. The sharks threshed, slamming into the ship, tumbling over one another. Irene flinched. Jack hissed, 'Look, just like peeling an orange.'

She shut her eyes. Jack shook her. 'Watch, darn you, or I'll break your damn neck.'

She opened her eyes. The blubber was spiralling, peeling, and the image of Christmas oranges, pithy and sticky, kept repeating in her head, alongside carols, and chestnuts roasting in glowing hearths, and smiling parents and Martha, and it was all a charade, the past was a charade, a dream world, a nothingness, a trick, and she was laughing, but there was no mirth, and she couldn't stop. The first mate called to Jack to join him. Jack yelled to her, 'Shut up, and watch.'

The men heaved again and again on the windlass and now Jack sent a seaman to the cutting platform, bellowing, 'Travers, get up here on deck, and cut loose the strip from the whale.'

Travers handed over his spade and clambered on board as the heavy oozing blubber strip swung high above her, a bloody dripping mass. Mr Travers pushed past her, panting. 'Make way, Mrs Prior.'

He sliced a hole in dangling blubber, hooked in and held it while he slashed the strip. At last it swung free, but it splashed the deck, the sails, the men, and Irene with its greasy gore, and now she laughed again, a wild mad sound, which went on and on.

Rain mingled with the grease and blood, and the wind tore at her hair, and the spray from the frenzied sea hurled over the deck. Still she laughed again, smelling Christmas oranges, hearing her parents' soothing tones, seeing Martha's smile.

She clenched her fists against her mouth but the

laughter wouldn't stop as the try-pot fires were started. It wouldn't stop as the men on the forward windlass peeled and hoisted another strip. It wouldn't stop whilst the other windlass slackened away and lowered blubber through the main hatchway into the blubber-room.

It wouldn't stop as the raising and lowering continued, and as the blubber was cut down in the blubber room, and the men at the mincer removed the slimy black skin, and hung it from the rigging, and the men at the try-pots boiled, boiled, boiled the fat.

It wouldn't stop as dense clouds of smoke curled up, up into the rigging, and the sails, and billowed across the deck.

Still she laughed as Mr Travers came towards her, saying, 'We're to skim the skin and tissue from the try-pots. Captain Prior's orders. We're to keep the furnace supplied with the waste from the blubber.'

She looked at him, then at the try-works, the men, the smoke, the blood and grease, the dipper. As the smoke rose and the rain fell she backed from him, and her laughter stopped.

She shook her head. 'So, we've to skim their tissue from the try-pots. So the poor damn creatures even burn themselves. He must love it. How he must love it.' She heard her own voice. It was almost a scream. She saw Jack watching. He shouted, 'You and the damn convict'll work together. You and him, soul mates, the dregs. See where the Wendhams are now, see where the Brits are.'

Still she backed. Travers shouted, 'Take the dipper.' He thrust it at her. 'For God's sake take the dipper, or he'll have us both.'

The men's faces shone red in the glare from the fire as they turned to stare. The cooper raked up the fires. The *Cachalot* was pitching, blubber was dripping. She looked down at her clothes, and then back at the ship, and the men – all covered in blood and grease.

She backed towards the offside rail, then stopped. 'It's a nightmare,' she screamed at Travers. 'It's a nightmare I've done nothing to deserve.' She said it again, and then again, and the laughter was back, forcing its way out of her distended mouth, alongside the words which wouldn't stop, 'Oranges should be sweet-scented, not big black creatures sucked dry by sharks – sharks which thresh and plunge and stand there.' She pointed at Jack, then dropped her arm to her side, and wailed, 'Martha gave me oranges. I want to go home to her. None of this is fair.'

Travers yelled right in her face, 'Shut up, you whining fool.' He reached for her hand, closed her fingers round a dipper. 'Take it, Mrs Prior, or Irene Wendham or whoever you damn well think you are. Take it, and remember that this is what you left Wendham for – your own satisfaction, your own wants.' He flung out his arm. 'Night after night I've listened to you complaining, and have you ever expressed regret for your actions?'

The laughter fled. The red glare faded, the wind seemed dulled and the rain gone as the shock of Travers's rage penetrated. 'Me,' she moaned. 'Me, what have I done? It's him, it's what he's done to me. Are you mad?'

'No, it's what you've done to yourself, and to your tenants at Wendham. When have you ever thought of them in all this? You talk of responsibilities, embarrass the crew, insult me, whine on night after night, but what thought did you give to real duty? None, when you thought you wanted something different. No, Mrs Prior, you walked away from them, heedless of the consequences, and left behind in ruins your people, your home, your parents' hopes.'

She dropped the dipper, shouting against the wind, 'I did not. I thought I was leaving for just four years.' Her lips seemed stiff, the wind so very cold.

Travers shouted at her, his face still contorted with anger, 'You say you thought, but that's just it, you didn't think. If you had thought you'd have read the lease properly. No, I'll warrant you never have thought, never have taken responsibility for anything, ever. You'll just have done what you damn well wanted. You need your Martha, do you? Well, you've never once wondered what she needs. Does she need a roof over her head? Where is she? You need Barratt to keep your memories as they were? Well, what about the tenants? Damn your needs Mrs Prior, now pick up the dipper.'

The wind had shifted and the black oily smoke from the try-works was rolling over them. She coughed, covered her eyes. He took her arm, began to pull her to the clear air. She struggled, 'Let go. How dare you touch me? How dare you say all these things, you who deserve everything that's happened to you?'

The wind shifted again, the smoke rolled away.

Jack was laughing over at the windlass, laughing because he had heard this convict speak to her as though she was nothing. She jerked from Travers, strode forward, slipped, fell, down into a deck awash with grease, blood, water. Jack roared with laughter, the rain and wind howled. She screamed to Travers, who was rescuing the dippers, 'Help me.'

He looked at her, and shook his head, 'Help yourself. Take hold, or you will not survive. You will be lost.' There was no anger in his face any more, just exhaustion, just shock. He turned and walked to the try-pots.

Irene clawed at the deck as the ship lurched and rolled. Water splashed into her face, she tasted blood, grease, salt and retched, coughed, wept.

'Help me, please,' she sobbed. Then she felt a hand beneath her elbow, steadying her, pulling her to her feet. It was Sinclair, and behind him she saw Jack stop laughing, and his face grow dark.

She pulled away from Sinclair. 'Thank you,' she whispered, and walked to the try-works, her skirt dragging at her legs, the cold knifing through her. She took the proffered dipper from Mr Travers and neither spoke nor looked at him as the smoke billowed and the cressets burned. She just fed the fires with the whale's waste, until dawn broke.

At midnight half the crew were sent below to sleep, though not Mr Travers and Irene. As dawn broke, and the watch changed once more, she and Mr Travers were again denied rest, and ordered to remain at the try-pots by Jack, who said, his voice dark with anger, 'Like stays with like.'

She hissed at Travers, 'You are not worthy to walk beneath even a steward's feet.'

When the carcass was peeled the head was raised onto the deck, the spermaceti was ladled from the skull, rendered, and barrelled as fast as the cooper could bang up barrels. At last, at noon, the oil had been stowed in the hold, the deck and rigging cleaned, but still the try-pots remained to be scoured, and this she was made to do alone, while Mr Travers rested.

All the time the whale carcass drifted further and further from them, and the air became a cacophony of birds, and the sea a ferment of sharks.

For two hours everyone except those on watch were allowed to sleep, even Irene.

At length she woke, aching in every limb. She rolled onto her side and looked at the heap of clothes on the floor. Jack's were on top of hers. He'd said, 'Only way to get rid of the grease is to soak 'em in urine. Use the piss barrel. You'll do the officers' clothes too. Then wash them in lye.' He'd then stripped her clothes from her and taken her on the floor of the transom.

She shuddered and rolled onto her back, forcing the image from her mind, letting the sounds of the day take over, breathing, counting, hearing the creaking of the ship, the rattling of the rigging, hearing the watch bell, realizing suddenly that she had slept for four hours, not two.

She threw on clothes, fearing discovery, and hurried

to the dirty laundry then stopped. It was so quiet. There were no orders, no sound of running feet. Had they gone? Had he left her here, to drift alone, taken the food? No, he'd never leave his ship. She dropped the laundry, and crept up the companionway, and then stopped before stepping out onto the quarterdeck.

The crew were gathered in the waist and she heard Jack begin to speak from just in front of the helmsman on the quarterdeck, to her right. His legs were braced against the slight swell, his hands were on his hips, his voice was strangely quiet but satisfied. She stood still, expecting to hear how many barrels they had harvested from the whale but then his words penetrated.

'. . . two dozen lashes and demotion from galley to fo'c's'le cook. Seaman Menson'll take over as galley steward. This is what comes of interfering in things which don't concern you. This is what comes of not sticking to your own business. This sort of attitude lets escaped convicts on board in Fremantle and gets us all damn well fined. Let it be a warning to everyone.'

As he stared at the men she slipped off the quarter-deck, moving through the crew, slipping in between them, hearing the lash slap into flesh, hearing the groan forced from Sinclair, hearing a fore-oarsman whisper to his mate, 'All he did was help that half-mad woman, that's all.' His mate nodded, chewing tobacco, spitting, saying out of the corner of his mouth, as Irene paused, 'First mate said it was different when old Wendham was here. Black Jack kinda knew his place then. He's just gone back to his old ways now, the bastard.'

His friend grunted and said bitterly, 'I'm off this ship, soon as we put in anywhere.'

She pushed through to the front and saw the first mate lift the lash again, saw Sinclair tied to the mast, saw his bare back scored and broken open where the lash had landed. Down it came again. Sinclair jerked, shuddered, moaned, blood ran down his back. For a moment she couldn't move, then her eyes met Travers's

127

and for a moment their eyes held, but then his gaze slid from hers, becoming blank.

Why wasn't he doing anything? Damn it, he was quick enough to tell her what she should be doing, thinking, and feeling, wasn't he? The lash came down again. Sinclair sobbed.

She started forward, unable to bear it. Travers shook his head. She looked at Sinclair. The lash came down again. She looked again at Travers. Was this the man who had dared insult her last night, who had dared lecture her on responsibility, on duty?

She heard Sinclair moan, and now guilt and righteous anger swept her along and she darted forward, standing between Sinclair and the first mate, as the whip was drawn back. Osborne stayed his arm, she could hear his breathing, hear Sinclair's whimpering.

She glared at Osborne, imagining her father, drawing on his image, remembering who she was, standing erect as he would have done, commanding the first mate to, 'Stand aside. Lower your whip.' The men muttered. She shouted up at Jack, 'This isn't fair. He was only helping me. Take it out on me, not him, if you must take it out on anyone. You must reconsider.'

At the sight of his face darkening, at his hands gripping the rail, fear swept aside the anger, but then she clenched her hands. No, they must all see that she was her father's daughter, that a Wendham had a sense of duty, and the courage to go with it. Jack Prior must see, then he would know his place, they would all know their place, Mr Travers especially, and at last it would all be over.

She shouted to Osborne, 'If you bring that whip down again, you'll bring it down on me.' The first mate hesitated. She stared up at Jack. 'The man a Wendham would marry would not allow his wife to be beaten and the name of Prior to be humiliated. Think carefully now, Jack Prior.'

Jack leaned on the rail, chewing on his tobacco,

staring at her, his eyes like flint. At last he drawled, 'Mr Travers, kindly escort my wife to the transom cabin, while I issue fresh orders.'

For a moment she couldn't believe the words she had just heard, then, as Mr Travers moved towards her, she looked up at Jack. 'Thank you,' she said quietly, hearing her voice shake and for a moment she thought she saw the man who had given her a birthday gift. The man who had appeared to love her and hope sprang within her.

Mr Travers took her by the arm. She recoiled at his touch, and forged ahead of him. The seamen looked away. She approached the quarterdeck, climbed the stairs, drawing closer and closer to Jack. His eyes were alight, there was a faint smile around his mouth. She wanted to stop, to speak words of forgiveness, of understanding, of her acceptance of the strains of command, but she continued to walk, because there would be time for that this evening. She lifted her face to the softness of the sun, and the brightness of its light, and felt weak with relief that it was at last all over, and that, in the end, it had come so easily.

She left the quarterdeck, and began to descend the companionway and as she did so she heard Jack say, 'Fresh orders for you, Mr Osborne. Just add another half-dozen lashes, on account of being so disturbed. I shall personally attend to Mrs Prior.'

CHAPTER SIX

The next morning, once the boats had pulled out after another whale, Irene crept into the fo'c's'le, stooping beneath the beams, gagging on the foul air, seeing the halo round the lantern.

She stumbled over a sea chest, and groaned. Sinclair called faintly, 'Who's that?'

'Shh,' she breathed. 'Be quiet, Mr Sinclair. It's Mrs Prior.'

She searched the gloom, and saw him on the starboard side. She picked a way through the scattering of men's clothes, boots, pipes, a book or two, steadying the bowl of hot water she carried, and the strips of petticoat she had boiled. She knelt on the floor by his bunk where he lay facing the hull. She bathed the raw and bloodied welts. As Sinclair whimpered she murmured, 'I'm being as gentle as I can.'

He protested, gasping between each word. 'You shouldn't be here, ma'am.'

'Don't worry, I won't make it worse for you this time, Mr Sinclair. No-one saw me come down.' Her voice shook. 'Forgive me,' she breathed, squeezing the cloth, letting the water run over the wounds. 'There, is that less painful?'

'Sure is, ma'am.'

She brought out the bottle she carried in the string bag slung over her shoulder. 'This'll hurt, really hurt. I've boiled up water and mixed it with salt. A good healer, but brace yourself. My mother taught me this. I thought I'd forgotten, just as I'd forgotten so much of what she did. It's amazing how things come back to you, in the dark night hours, after . . .' She stopped, squeezed the salt water over his back. He stiffened, moaned.

She reached for an upright and hauled herself up. She said, 'You need fresh air. Fresh air and good food, that's what my mother always said, and my mother was a wonderful woman. But I never realized.'

She turned, staggered, clenched the mug, hung her head, unable to move. She couldn't go on, but she must. So she did, walking slowly to the galley, bringing back gruel which he ate, but so very slowly. Hurry, hurry, she wanted to say, but did not. She heard cheering from on deck and relaxed. They'd be out for a while yet. She said calmly, 'They've killed another, Mr Sinclair.'

'Sure have.'

'I'll get something done about the air in here, Mr Sinclair.'

'Best not, Mrs Prior.' He closed his eyes and shook his head at the last spoonful. 'Cain't eat no more.'

'Yes, you can, just as I can do something about the air, but I will be careful, Mr Sinclair. Believe me, from now on I will be very careful.'

She left him then, and found her way to the fo'c's'le galley, and prepared salt beef and biscuits for the men, because Jack had told her that she had to do fo'c's'le duty until Sinclair was upright and could take over.

She put the food onto the table when the men filed down, then left because the dislike and resentment and embarrassment at her bruises was tangible. Why should it not be? she thought as she stood on the deck looking at the secured whale, which was old and dried out. Not many barrels from that, not much lay. Yes, why not resentment? After all, I added to Sinclair's punishment.

She moved to the bow when she had finished her chores and looked down at the sharks, and the blood-streaked sea. She made herself watch them until the sails were shortened at sunset, and she remained watching them as the moon rose. 'You can't touch me, if I'm careful,' she said at last. 'And I'll be careful because I'm learning to think, just as my mother did, and finally, as I at last realize, my father did not. Again my godfather was right.'

She heard Jack's shouted order, 'Make doubly secure the whale. We'll flense at dawn, no need to get the men exhausted over this one, there'll be richer pickings all season.' She heard the first mate's orders, heard the men scurry to obey, and as the cressets cast their light she looked once more at the sharks before heading for the transom.

Once there she lay unable to sleep but resting. At two a.m. she joined Mr Travers on watch, as usual. She took the aft lookout platform, as usual. He came to her, and said awkwardly, 'Sinclair is better today. That was good of you.' He looked past her, to the sea.

She said, equally awkwardly, 'It was my duty, as you so recently pointed out, and, after all, I am greatly to blame for his punishment.' As she spoke he turned to her, his eyes tracing her wounded face and there was no contempt, only pity in his eyes. She repeated, 'It was my duty.' She swung from him, scanning the horizon, unable to speak again, unable to apologize for her nights of selfish reverie for if she spoke again, she would weep, and that she had sworn she would never do again.

No more words passed between them until six a.m. when every bone ached as though it was on fire, and her head threatened to burst, and her cut lip split wider every second in the salt-laden wind. Then, as the four bells sounded, and all around her the crew took stations for flensing, she said, 'Mr Travers, the fo'c's'le air is foul. I would be obliged if you would present the idea of a wind-sail over the hatches to Mr Prior.'

He hesitated, his eyes on the blood that trickled from her lips and the bruises that were livid around her eyes and cheek. She said, forcing her lips around the words, ignoring the sharp pain, 'Please, accept my apology. Accept that I am trying to make amends to you all. This request cannot come from me if it is to succeed.' She broke off, seeing Jack emerge from the companionway, then whispered hurriedly, 'Please broach it in my presence now. I will then . . .' The ship lurched into a trough. Her voice faltered, her eyes filled and it was the wind, not the pain, she insisted to herself. She swept her arm across her eyes. Jack moved towards them.

Mr Travers stared at her, and she couldn't read his eyes. She tried to say, 'You see . . .' But Jack was too close and there was no time to explain her intentions, to excuse herself in advance. 'Trust me,' she whispered, her lips not moving, her eyes flickering to Jack.

He nodded and accosted Jack as he passed by. 'Beg pardon, sir. Air's foul in the fo'c's'le. Men's health'll go downhill and threaten the work. Permission to set up wind-sail, sir.' Travers stood rigid.

Jack Prior shoved him to one side. 'Goin' soft are you, Mr Travers? Lost leave of your senses to ask such a thing, have you? Permission refused. Now get down on deck, and I guess you need more time on watch to sort yourself out and stop yourself taking on such a fool notion again.'

He was taking a sighting from the sun. Travers glanced at Irene, suspicion of her flaring.

She shook her head slightly, her eyes pleading for understanding, even as she said, her voice mocking and bitter, 'For once I agree with you, Jack. Mr Travers seldom has a good idea, but what can you expect from a common criminal?'

Now Travers's suspicion turned to anger, and his contempt was back, and she wanted to put up her hand, stop him, tell him she was thinking as he had said, that she was doing it for the men, that she would explain but then Mr Travers shouldered his way past her, jolting her, hissing. 'Satisfied, Mrs Prior? Revenge has made your aches better, has it? Trust you? Never.'

She stared after him as waves of pain washed over her, knowing he had barged her deliberately. She swept from the quarterdeck, and as she passed beneath the windlass she heard Jack say, 'Set up wind-sails, Mr Travers, and tonight Mrs Prior'll take an extra watch, not you.'

She reached the scuttle, passed into the shelter of the try-works, and only now did she allow herself to stop and lean against the brickworks. Only now did she allow herself to hold her ribs, breathe in short sharp gasps, groan softly and give in to the agony, an agony which drowned the hiss of Travers's words, but not his actions for no suspicion he harboured warranted that and she knew that her fellow Britisher was as brutal as Jack Prior for hadn't he also watched as she floundered on the deck.

That night, when the ship was clean after the flensing she took her watch at midnight with the second mate and then with Mr Travers, who said, 'Forgive me, I did not jolt you intentionally. You were right to approach the captain in that way. I was wrong. Forgive me. Believe me . . .'

Irene interrupted, taking up her station, throwing over her shoulder, 'I believe no-one any more. I know nothing.'

The next day, when the boats were out again she wrote a letter to Barratt, one that she would hand to the next home-going captain. In the letter she pleaded with him, *as a gentleman to help my tenants, Martha especially must be kept on, and one day I will reimburse, but in the meantime you have my full permission to sell the Turners in the attic, which were a personal gift from my mother to me. Only Martha knows where they are, so if she has gone, there is every reason for you to find her. Please use the money to make good the difference in any increased rent you may feel obliged to levy on the cottagers. I beg of you, please reconsider the construction of the factory and allow work to continue in the village. I also beg you to relinquish the lease at the end of this trip, in four years' time, for a commensurate sum.*

For by then she had promised herself that somehow she would take her full lay, and flee to Wendham, no matter what the scandal, for she had work to do there, and her self-respect to redeem, and her duty to perform, and everything else to leave behind. *Write to me, care of the* Cachalot *in confidence. Please* in confidence. *New Bedford.* For that is where Jack had said he would end this voyage, and damn England.

She hid the letter beneath her drawer lining, unwilling to disclose to Barratt at this stage her stupidity in signing the lease, wanting to tell him face to face, wanting to explain Jack Prior to him, and tell him that once she was reinstalled Jack Prior could not move her unless he found her suitable alternative accommodation, accommodation she would refuse.

Barratt would tell her that Jack could legally force her to return to him, but she would throw herself on his mercy, tell him that she would resist Jack somehow, anyhow.

Before the boats returned she tended Sinclair's back; now he could sit and her own pain was less, they talked in the fresher air as he spooned his gruel, he told her of San Francisco and she told him of her home, and they both fell silent.

As she left he said, 'Good to have the clean air, Mrs Prior, though I didn't mind too much. It'd have been bad for Harry Travers though if he hadn't got a berth in the mate's cabin. Reckon it'd have killed him, cain't stand dark places since them hulks, and the transport hold. Kinda crazy when all he did was take a sheep to feed his mother and brothers. Kinda crazy like I sez, when we're out taking these great monsters every day. Was on the way to being a teacher, was Harry. Taught to read by his mother from the Bible. Father was a bargee before he took to farm labouring in Devon. Died of the flux. He's a good man, he wouldn't hurt anyone, not deliberately. Honest he wouldn't.'

She nodded, not saying, as she wanted to, that she did not believe in anything or anyone any more. She touched her ribcage.

All morning they flensed the whale that had been caught and as the thick dark smoke billowed, and the heat from the furnace broke out the sweat all over her body as she wielded the dipper, she knew that Jack was watching her every move, and that Sinclair must be parched for he had had no fluids for hours. But as she scooped out the fibres she saw Travers slipping into the fo'c's'le shortly before midday with a half-hidden mug of water, and as he did so, his eyes met hers and she thought she saw confusion, regret, and pleading. But she turned from him.

All this could no longer be a nightmare to Irene Wendham, the daughter of a mother who had known what duty was, and of a father who had not. It was not a nightmare because she could no longer afford such luxuries if she was to survive, and survive she would, just to spite Jack Prior, and everyone else. D'you hear me, Mr Travers? she called silently.

As she worked she concentrated on the mincer slicing the blubber into thin leaves, the cooper who rolled along the barrels. She must miss nothing, for when she escaped she would need to know as much as any captain.

She stood straight, scanned the horizon and saw smoke and the raw red light of the fire billowing from the other two ships. Which was the *Wendham*? She heard Jack shout, 'Get working, blast ya.'

She did so, heedless of the heat, or the oil which surged up the sides of the pots as the ship rolled, staring out towards the *Wendham*, for it was to there she had decided she must flee. It was there she must impose her authority if she was to protect her lay, and herself until she was free of all of this.

*   *   *

The next day the *Cachalot* sailed idly until two bulls were sighted, and all four boats were lowered, as they were from the *Wendham*, and the *Queen of the Isles*. Irene looked westward where the bulls lazed. There was a gentle north-east wind blowing and the sky was a deep cloudless blue.

The boats danced on the gentle swell, the sun glinted off the sea. All twelve boats were drawing closer. She saw Jack in the stern, waving back the *Wendham* boats but they came on. The cooper beside her groaned to himself, and started muttering into his beard. She strained to hear. 'They ain't seen. He's wanting the kill for the *Cachalot*. I knew he'd start this. God, sometimes I wish the bugger would come face to face with another squid. It's the one thing that'd keep him off the sea, or so it goes. Mark you, he'd kill any man who'd say that. Got tangled up with one when he was a boy, out with his father, came up with the whale it did. Near paralysed him with fear.'

'What's that you say?' she asked.

The cooper started, and stared at her, 'Not me. I ain't said nothing, just talking about the ways of the sea, that's all. That's all, you hear?'

She looked at him, but he shuffled off, and now the whales were sounding, the boats swung up into the wind, laying hove to, almost stationary. She shrugged. What importance was an old man's prattle? Again Jack waved the boats back. Two made their way to the *Wendham*, but two remained. She looked at Jack again. He was watching the sea ahead of him.

She snatched the telescope from the fourth mate. Jack was looking towards the *Wendham* boats now, nodding that the two could remain, but waving back a couple from the *Queen of the Isles*.

The whales broke water, and the chase was on again. The boats surged through the swell, closer and closer. The harpoons were thrown, the lines sang, the whales threshed, the sea churned and heaved, the boats ripped through the swell.

The men on deck cheered and whistled, and Irene lifted her head to the sun, closing her eyes, breathing deeply, thinking of the soft green gardens of home, conjuring up the peace of it all, but then there was a loud groan from one of those beside her, and curses from the cooper. She stared out to sea and saw a *Wendham* boat smashed, men in the water, a whale rolling from side to side, its fluke raised, then slapping down onto the boat again.

She heard the cries carried on the wind, she saw the splintered remains of the boat. She saw a *Cachalot* boat turn to the wreck, oars digging deep, men's backs straining.

Again she snatched up the telescope, and saw it was Travers's boat. He stood in the prow, his lance still in his hand, a lance he dropped into the bottom of the boat as he cupped his mouth and shouted to the *Wendham* men, some of whom were clinging to wreckage.

'Damn fool,' the cooper groaned. 'Look at the captain.'

She swung the telescope round. Jack had hurled his lance into his bull, but even as it blew red he turned to shake his fist at Travers. He gestured with his other hand to the whale the *Wendham* boat had been going for.

Travers continued to haul in the *Wendham* men as the bull sounded, only to rise in triumph far off to the west. The fourth mate said quietly, into the appalled silence, 'Best be getting to them.'

Tension showed on every face while the bull was secured to the *Cachalot*. There was no speech, no laughter, just rigid backs and eyes that looked at no-one else as the first mate yelled, his face set in a rage, 'Flensing in six-hour watches.'

As Travers's boat returned from the *Wendham*, and was winched to its davits, none of the crew looked as the third mate leapt to the deck, nor as he approached the captain. Nor did Irene look, she just thrust fuel beneath the try-pots.

But as the cooper brought up the barrels, and the sails flapped hollowly against the rigging, she looked up as Jack lowered his head and bellowed into Travers's face.

'D'ya know what the damage is, Mr Travers?'

'*Wendham*'s second mate dead, plus three crew. Four bad, one with a busted leg. Captain Baines will be busy with the saw tonight.'

Jack gripped Travers's shirt. He twisted it in his huge fists. It tore. Travers kept his gaze on his captain, no emotion visible.

'Mr Travers, the damage is a bull lost.' Jack jerked his head towards the cooper. 'A bull lost that would have filled up one hundred barrels, that would have given them, your shipmates, more of a lay. That is the damage, and it is damage I don't care for, because you have hurt my purse too, Mr Travers, as well as crossing me.'

The head had been cut free. Irene watched it rise above the deck, dripping. The sharks would be circling, the water would be red . . . No, not that. She bent to her task.

Jack's voice was harsher still, as it had been when he had beaten her. And she mouthed silently, See what it's like, Mr Travers. See what it's damn well like and tell me that I am a whining woman. See what it's like to be held, raged at, as you did to me, as he does to me. See what it's like to be hit, because he will hit you, and later, because of his rage, he will probably hit me. Will you jolt me again and add to my pain? She stared across to the *Wendham*. She must get away. She must.

The cooper dropped a barrel, it rolled, cracked, split. Jack pushed Harry from him. 'Get down into the blubber room, then when the flensing is over, just take the whole damn day to show us all how good a shine you can get on that pot.'

He turned to point, and saw her. She caught sight of the *Wendham* over his shoulders, its sails billowing in the evening breeze, its masts stark against the sunset. She met Jack's gaze, saw Travers's pale face out of the corner of her eye, heard in her head Sinclair telling her of the hulks, but she threw the memory aside, as though it was waste, clinging instead to the memory of Travers shouldering into her as he passed, telling herself she owed him nothing, that duty had been done, apologies had been made. She summoned his contempt, and his hissed words, hugging them to her as the moment dragged on.

But now she was seeing Travers take the cup to the fo'c's'le, seeing the confusion, the regret and pleading in his eyes, but these images she beat back, drawing his harshness to her again, and all the time Jack's eyes held hers and it was *his* cruelty that in the end she could not turn from.

Cursing Travers, she scrabbled desperately for inspiration, almost smiling with relief when it came, but then as she called out the words the relief was thrust aside by fear, 'Again I agree with you, Jack,' she said, 'for you should treat that criminal worse than you do me.'

She glared at Harry, and then laughed, hearing the tremble in her voice, praying that her husband could not.

Jack stared, took a step towards her, stopped, yanked Harry forward. 'You, ma'am, get below into that blubber room. You, third mate, get fryin'.' His voice was like ice, then he laughed that laugh.

Once the whale was flensed, and the carcass cast adrift, Harry holystoned the pots all day, whilst Irene used the ashes she had taken from the try-pots to make lye to wash her clothes, and to rub her skin and hair. Anything to get the stench of the blubber from her, anything to rid herself of the memory of squeezing in the fetid darkness between the great greasy mass of fat, cutting it up into pieces, trying to keep a footing on the oily floor as the vessel rolled, gasping with pain, retching and vomiting.

On watch that night she took her place on the aft lookout platform under Travers's command, as usual, but this was not a night like any other, was it? Was it, Mr Travers? she ground out.

She waited as he paced the quarterdeck, then moved amongst the men in the waist, then back to the quarterdeck. She waited, and while she waited she looked at the fluorescent waves, at the dark night. When would he speak? For speak he must, after today. She looked to the east. The *Wendham* was there, she could see the light burning in the cresset.

Travers cleared his throat behind her. 'Mrs Prior, I'd like to thank you for what you did. I know Sinclair told you I can't stand the hold. It was good of you, far better than I deserved, and clever of you to do it as you did. It shows a great sense of duty, of responsibility, and I crave your pardon for ever thinking any different, and for behaving in a way that shames me.' As he spoke he twisted his hat round and round in his hands.

She felt the breeze lift her hair, then said, her voice mirroring her distaste for this man, 'I am uninterested in anything you crave. All I want, indeed, insist on from you in recompense is for you to find out all you can about Captain Baines, the *Wendham* master.'

She kept her eyes on her ship. Her ship, d'you hear, all of you?

Travers spoke at last, his voice cold and empty as she turned to him. 'I'd have done that for you, without feeling I must. I still can't forget that I jolted you, or forgive myself. Yes, I'd have done that for you, without all this.'

He walked away. She turned again, to gaze across the water to the *Wendham* as her anger drained from her, and shame took its place, and she felt as though

141

her head would never clear, as though nothing would ever be simple again.

As dawn broke a whale was spotted and Mr Travers manned a boat before his watch was complete. Irene was glad to be rid of him, glad that it would not be his hand aiding her from the platform.

By mid-morning the crew had hauled the bull fast by the fluke when the wind veered to the north-east, howling through the rigging whipping up the sea to a frenzy. The sails were made snug, the boats hoisted to the top notch of the cranes.

'Damn it,' raged Jack. 'Can't cut out for now. We need a shift in the wind.'

The wind didn't shift and as the day wore on and the sea battered the fleet they were forced to run before the wind. Bracing herself in the transom cabin Irene listened as the huge carcass alongside tore and strained, and the ship creaked and groaned, pitched and rolled.

All the time she was memorizing and repeating the orders that had been given as the storm came up because she must focus only on the *Wendham* and her escape. Again and again she repeated the procedures in her mind until a lull fell. She rose, bracing herself on the drawers which lined the cabin, pulling out one, taking the journal she had begun, noting down the orders and the day's events for when she took control of her ship. She replaced the journal beneath the clothes in the drawer. 'Wendham,' she whispered.

That night on watch the wind tore and the rain beat too much to speak to, or even look at, Mr Travers as he ordered her to the shelter of the hurricane cabin.

All the next day the wind howled and the rain sheeted, and Irene fought against the wind to reach the rail to stare at the everdistending carcass, mentally making a note of the consequences of a delayed flensing.

She then searched through the weather for the fleet. She found the *Queen of the Isles* to leeward, prow down in a trough, then rising. She looked for the *Wendham*. It wasn't there. Anxiety tugged at her, and she staggered across the deck, and stared to windward. Not there either.

Sinclair struggled past her, taking coffee to Prior. She grabbed him, the rain lashing as the weather closed again, the wind snatching her words as she shouted, 'Where's the *Wendham*?'

He shrugged, and continued on.

Above her the rigging and the sails whipped and strained. She felt a hand on her arm, and spun round. Travers stood before her, the rain beating into his face, running off his chin, his hazel eyes half closed against it. She shrugged free of his hold. He shouted, his hand cupping his mouth, 'It'll be running before the wind. It hasn't a whale to act as a drag. Don't worry, your ship will be safe, ready for you.'

He pulled his hat further down, rain streamed from the brim. Then he was gone, struggling along to the main mast.

Of course. Why hadn't she thought of that? No whale, of course it had no whale. It was in her journal – stupid fool. Then she paused. Travers had said, 'ready for her'. He must know, oh God, he must know what she wanted to do.

She gripped the rail, searching the deck, pulling down the brim of her own hat, protecting her eyes with her hand, searching for Travers. The wind was howling louder than before, buffeting her as she stood.

She found him by the main mast, and hauled herself along the rail. She stumbled, recovered, gripped the stanchion, set off across the deck, fumbling from one support to the other. She reached Harry Travers, grabbed at him, was forced to cling on. Her fingers were almost numb, water ran off her sleeve, down her arm.

The wind battered them. The *Cachalot* hulled down

into a trough. She slid, wincing as she twisted her ribs. He grabbed her arm. She shouted, 'How did you know? Will you tell him?'

He snatched a look at the quarterdeck. She could see that Jack was in the hurricane house, beside the helmsman, scanning the clouds. Travers dragged her to the shelter of the windlass tackle, and she almost fell over in the still air, though above and around them the storm still raged. He steadied her, saying, 'I guessed when you asked me for information about Captain Baines, but I didn't *know*, until now. No, I won't tell, as long as you take Sinclair and me with you. We've both crossed him, so we're marked men. Take us, or . . .' He nodded to the quarterdeck.

Then he was gone, out into the storm again, the wind tearing and snatching at his jacket, and she stared after him, anger coming again, darker and deeper and it thrust aside all shame, all guilt, all regret until her mind was clear. 'Damn you all,' she whispered.

Hour after hour went by with little change in the weather, though putrid gases distended the whale beyond belief and, as it did so, Irene paced in the wind and the rain until she accepted that she must acquiesce, telling Travers as she passed him, 'I'll take you both, though I would have taken Sinclair without the blackmail. Not you, however, never you.'

As she walked on, the whale at last exploded and hurled its foul detritus and Jack's fury knew no bounds. That night in the cabin he beat her again but in the morning, as she stumbled on deck, she saw the *Wendham* back in place, and it was this that held her erect, this that gave her the courage to go on.

As the season at the Japanese Ground drew on Jack Prior kept the crews working at a furious pace, frequently bringing back two whales at once, flensing until the men could barely stand. Twice Captain Baines of the *Wendham* sent him an appeal for some men, just a few, to replenish his crew, for they had rebuilt the fourth boat.

Each time, Jack refused, slamming his hand on the table at dinner, laughing, gloating over his increasingly loaded hold, a hold that was fast outstripping either sister whaler.

Each time Irene's fear became further muted by contempt for this brute who had to beat anyone, and anything, even though as owner, he took the profits of all three ships.

Again and again they sighted whales, and although the weather was breaking and the small boats bucked and pitched in the unstable seas, they caught and killed until the waves ran red, and now Jack drank less brandy at night, but instead dragged her from the sofa, through into the sleeping cabin, falling onto her as she lay inert. It was nothing. None of it meant anything because she would leave. Somehow she would leave and Captain Baines would not have to wait until a supply depot for his replacement crew.

Slowly she stored away the information that Travers gleaned from the crews of the visiting captains when they came to play poker with Jack. Apparently Captain Baines had sailed a merchant ship out of New Bedford to Bristol, where he had ended up heavily in debt to Prior. Baines, a whaling master of many years' standing, was sailing the *Wendham* to pay off the debt. 'In other words,' Mr Travers had said last night, as the moon passed behind cloud, 'he could be Jack's man, or he could not.' His voice was neutral, his eyes were fixed on the helmsman in the hurricane house.

'How very helpful that remark is, Mr Travers,' she had replied, her voice scathing.

Day after day they raised and killed whales and there was still no plan in Irene's head, until one Thursday when the harpooners hurled their irons into yet another whale, and the lines sang out as Jack's whale charged away, drawing out the length of the line.

From the deck of the *Cachalot* Irene watched as another line was attached, as the whale dragged the boat through the water slamming it down on the waves again and again, as Jack fell backwards into the boat, as an oar flew skywards, as men were thrown about in disarray.

She snatched the telescope from Sinclair. 'Can it be he will die?' she whispered, forcing back the hope into a containable size, peering through the telescope.

Sinclair shielded his eyes from the glare. 'Can I?' He reached out for the telescope. Irene passed it to him.

Jack's boat hoisted sail and drew near again, only for the whale to raise its great fluke, its tail, and beat the water, rolling from side to side, heaving its bulk out of the water, up and up, huge, fearsome, then down onto the boat, and now hope soared again, roared, almost sang in her.

She couldn't breathe, couldn't move. Sinclair breathed, 'It's a squid, it's a goddamn squid.' She snatched back the telescope, groping in the recesses of her mind. What did she know about squids? What? What?

She couldn't think, then dismissed it – for what did it matter? – for as she trained her glass the whale disappeared, leaving turbulence in his wake, leaving a smashed boat, floating spars, oars, men. She counted. One short. Please let it be Jack. Please, if there is a God, let it be Jack, drowned, dead, gone. She'd be free to go home. Free of them all.

Boats were converging on the area. Behind her the fourth mate galvanized the *Cachalot*'s crew, sails were hoisted. 'Hurry, for heaven's sake, hurry,' she called.

Sinclair looked at her in surprise. She rushed to the bow-sprit, leaving him in the waist. Who was missing? Please let it be Jack. Please let her go home. Leave

Sinclair, leave Travers. Let her just go home, to her real people.

The *Cachalot*'s other boats were hauling in the men as the fourth mate bore the ship down to them. She studied the faces in the telescope. No, that wasn't Jack, nor that one, nor that one. Her breathing was shallow, fast, her hands were unsteady. Nor that one. She swung round to Travers's boat which contained survivors. Nor that one.

Then she saw her husband, slumped aft in Travers's boat and she lowered her arms, her hands icy, her mouth dry and tears were running down her cheeks, her shoulders were shaking, but no sound came.

The *Cachalot* was ploughing through the waves towards the boats which were swinging back into line, one after the other, Travers in the lead. The *Cachalot* furled sail. Travers's boat rowed up. He hailed the fourth mate, 'Send down a chair.'

Irene walked slowly to the waist, her tears wiped away. She peered over the side, gazing into the over-crowded boat as the crew tried to attach a line. Jack was slumped against the aft-oarsman. She willed him to be injured, a flicker away from death, for a flicker would soon whither to nothingness.

He was winched over the side, with Mr Travers standing on the back of the chair, calling, 'Winch the boat up. Get the injured aboard.'

She approached the chair. Travers was saying quietly, 'Get out of the chair, Captain Prior. Come on, get out.' She clenched her arms across her body, wanting to pummel him, to shriek like a banshee for bringing her husband back.

Travers tried to prize Jack's fingers free, but he clung to the chair. 'Come on, Captain.' There, he'd done it.

She watched as Harry hoisted him over his shoulder. Again she hugged herself as the chair was sent back for the injured crewmen.

She followed Travers into the transom cabin, watched

as he eased Jack Prior into a chair, where Prior clenched the arms again, and just stared.

She came to Travers, pulled him round, whispering fiercely, 'Tell me he's injured, damn you. Tell me he's near death.'

Travers looked at her, his face drawn, answering also in a whisper, 'I'm sorry, I wish I could. He's just petrified with fear. I don't understand it . . .'

She heard the boats knocking against the hull. Travers was loosening Jack's collar. She pulled him away, shaking him, slapping his face again and again, hissing, 'Why didn't you kill him? Why did you save him?'

Travers's cheeks were red from her blows. She slapped him again. He snatched at her hands, held them. 'Why?' she shouted. 'Why?'

He backed her towards the wall, brought his face close to hers. 'Shh. Be quiet,' he whispered. 'Be quiet. I wanted to. I couldn't. In spite of all my hate, I couldn't. In spite of what it would mean to you, I couldn't.'

She struggled. Travers held on, his hands and arms strong, his lip bleeding from her blows. She looked away, his words ringing in her head, his eyes sympathetic, and at last she allowed herself to believe in him as he said, 'Forgive me.' He murmured, 'Not even for you . . .'

'What have I become?' she murmured, all fight leaving her.

Travers still held her wrists, still kept his face close, still spoke in a whisper, 'You're trying to survive. D'you understand me? You're just trying to survive, as I am. Now think. Can we use this to get away? I feel we can. I just don't know how.'

Behind them, Jack muttered and groaned.

Travers turned back to him, stooping, loosening his collar, saying, 'It was when he saw the squid, damn great thing, it flew off into the boat. Thought he was going to hack it to smithereens and the boat with it.'

Irene looked from Travers to Jack, who was staring at her with no recognition, naked fear stark in his eyes and now she remembered the cooper. Of course, the squid, Jack's great fear of squid.

Yes, they could use this. Yes. Just then Jack shoved Travers from him, cursing him; she saw blood on Jack's arm.

Jack shoved again, and now he saw the scratch, for that's what it was. He clutched his arm, groaned, 'I'm hurt, damn you. I'm hurt. I've a cut, a deep cut, to the bone. Tell the men I'm hurt. That's it, tell the men.'

Irene looked at the scratch, then at Travers who stared at it. 'But sir, it's only a . . .'

She shouted, 'Be quiet.' Her mind was racing. She rushed from the room. 'I'll get bandages.'

She rushed up on deck, and down into the fo'c's'le galley, calling to Sinclair who was opening a barrel of biscuits. 'Come with me,' she snapped. 'This is our chance. Get brandy from the galley, and bandages, bring them into the transom.'

Sinclair pushed his surprise aside, and hurried after her, his questions unspoken. At the door to the cabin she waited, clutching her forehead, making her mind slow down, making it think. Sinclair came to her. She said, 'Come, but keep your mouth shut. Let me do the talking. But tell me again that you want to come to the *Wendham*.' He said, 'Sure I do.'

She pushed at the shiny wooden door, and went in.

Jack was less pale, but his hands were trembling. She came to one side, motioned Travers to the other. Jack pushed her aside. 'Give me that,' he snarled at Sinclair, grabbing the bottle.

Irene passed a glass. Jack knocked it from her hand as she'd known he would, hitting out at her body again and again. She let him, warning Travers with her eyes not to interfere. He shook his head at Sinclair. Jack drank from the bottle, his head thrown back, his throat moving. While he did so, she took the bandages from

149

Sinclair and said, quite clearly, and loudly, 'Jack, fear is normal, no-one noticed but us. And what would it matter if they had? I'm sure other captains have collapsed when their men haven't. There can't be more than a few thousand squid in the sea. It's just a shame that the big one that landed in the boat got away, is still out there, waiting.'

He hurled the bottle at her, striking her head a glancing blow. She saw the scratch on the arm that he had thrown it with. Travers started towards her. She said, 'No.' He stopped. The pain made her want to groan. She smelt the spilt brandy on her dress. Jack snarled, thrusting out his arm, 'I am hurt, that's all. Just hurt. Patch me up.'

She swabbed, bandaged, saying nothing. He glared at Mr Travers and Sinclair as though he'd only just remembered they were there. 'Get out,' he roared. 'Get on with your business.'

She went to the fo'c's'le and tended the other men. She went on deck and walked round, motioning away Travers, until she was sure that everyone had seen her wounded head, and only then did she return to the sleeping cabin and bathe it.

On watch that night Travers insisted she sat in the hurricane room. She did, resting her throbbing head on the wooden upright, whilst she explained that the time would come when Jack would want them gone from the ship because they had seen his fear, a fear that wouldn't die quickly. Travers nodded, asking, 'But when, Mrs Prior?'

She said softly, 'I don't have a crystal ball, Travers, but soon, hopefully before he kills us, or before I strike you again. Forgive me for that, for everything. I know you didn't jolt me deliberately. I know the blackmail was born of desperation. I should have offered before you spoke.' Her smile was rueful.

He shook his head. 'We both have regrets, mine are intense. Let's leave it behind us now.'

'Do you think we can?' Her voice was tense.

'We can leave it all behind, if your plan works.'

'It will be when he really is convinced we are a threat. I'll have to make sure that it happens.' They both stared out across the ship, deep in thought, but at least they were working together now, and to Irene the knowledge that she was no longer alone brought a comfort that was sweeter than anything she had experienced before.

The next morning at breakfast Jack ate in the transom cabin, and when the lookout called bl-o-o-w he called in the first mate. 'Put the fourth mate in my boat. I cain't make it. Cain't lift my throwing arm, deep cut, damn it.'

All week he nursed his arm by day, and drank by night, and at the end of it the other crewmen were recovered, but Jack Prior was not. He stayed on the ship when the boats went out, sitting on a chair he insisted was brought to the quarterdeck. 'I might be ill with an infected arm, but I won't be kept from my quarterdeck,' he'd yelled at her for all to hear.

She'd just stared, for there was no infection, only fear and though she knew all about fear she could spare no pity for this brute. She would only use it.

At the end of the next day she watched him carefully as the boats neared a whale. She saw him begin to shake again, and search through his telescope. It was then that she fetched Sinclair, because Captain Baines had sent another messenger that morning, pleading for at least two crew members, one who could act as second mate. 'Watch me, and make sure Jack sees you.' She climbed onto the quarterdeck and stood next to him, making sure she was to the lee of his bandaged arm.

'Jack, fear is natural. There is no shame in that, but it must be conquered by a man such as you – a bully and a braggart. It must in particular be conquered on a whaler or the men will flee at the next supply port, or beg to go to Baines, over there to that ship. A ship which is a constant running sore to me, an insult to the memory of Wendham House. Your crew's confidence will be gone. They'll not call you Black Jack, but Yella' Jack. You'll be a laughing stock, once they know.' She mimicked his drawl and braced herself for the blow she knew would come.

He backhanded her with his bandaged arm, knocking her to her knees. Her shoulder ached where he had caught her.

She clambered to her feet, pointed to Sinclair, 'Sinclair was with that damned third mate and me in the cabin. You shoved Travers with your scratched arm. You used it to throw the bottle at me. All the crew saw the scratch. You've just hit me with it again, your "infected" arm, and Sinclair's just seen that too. You'll have to be careful Jack, we could be driven beyond our own fear of you one day, and reveal everything.'

Jack wheeled on her, half rising, his face contorted. 'Get out of my sight.'

She left. Sinclair melted into the fo'c's'le. She stayed by the rail, watching the kill, feeling his eyes drilling into her back, his hatred an almost physical force. She watched carefully as the lances were thrown, listening to the orders that Jack bellowed. She would write them down in her journal, her hand would be steady, the letters clear. She must think of that, not of what might happen to her tonight in the cabin, if her plan failed.

But all the time she stood her fear was welling, it was too great to be contained, and though she tried to draw breath it was as though she were drowning.

'Get up here, Mrs Prior.' It was Jack, his voice deadly. She walked slowly towards him, clenching and unclenching her hands, for the man staring at her had death in his eyes. She climbed the steps to the quarterdeck. She stood in front of him, within reach. He said, 'You bitch. You'll never get the chance to spread your poison on my ship, any of you. I'll see you all dead first, I'll see you fathoms down where I don't have to keep on seeing you about my ship. That's what I'm going to do, and you've brought it on yourself.'

She said, 'Even you cannot get away with the murder of your wife and two crewmen. No, there's no way you can rid yourself of us in the middle of the ocean, my dear Jack. Rest assured I look forward to haunting you with my presence day and night, and for the first time for a very long while, I shall feel happy.' She smiled and had the courage not to tremble as she walked away again.

When the boats returned and, even before the whale was flensed, the first mate was told to sail his boat across to the *Wendham*, taking Sinclair, Mr Travers, and Irene. As she clambered down the ropes, after her trunk, Jack hissed, 'No way, eh? You wanted Wendham, you have the *Wendham*, that ship that is a running sore to you. You can wake up to her every day and know that she was bought by your house, and you will suffer for every second you are there. Along with you will be the convict you hate, and the steward you had whipped, and whose hatred of you must run in every fibre of his being. Now see how you fare with those two for company, and remember Mrs Prior, one word out of turn and I'll get you back, just like that.' He clicked his fingers in her face.

She said clearly, 'And then what, the bottom of the sea?'

'No, a living death.'

Jack watched her leave, his hands itching to break the neck of this woman who had seen him weep, who had just pushed him too far. Let the *Wendham* have her, for now, but he knew that one day he would probably kill her.

CHAPTER SEVEN

As the boat reached the *Wendham* a chair was lowered from the waist. Irene ignored it, standing up, bracing herself as the boat pitched and rolled. 'I'll use the ropes,' she proclaimed. Mr Travers glanced at her, insisting, 'It would be better to use the chair.'

She shouted to the fourth mate, 'Bring the boat in alongside. I'll take the ropes.'

Mr Travers tried to stop her. She grinned, 'You really must try to mind your own business, Mr Travers. The *Wendham* is my ship, one for which I have worked, and studied, and suffered. Now, stand aside, for I start as I mean to go on, showing that I am as capable as any man, and well able to take over my responsibilities.'

The fourth mate eased the boat tight alongside the vessel. The sweat broke out as she judged the distance to the ropes which had been knotted into a vast strong net and thrown down the side. The boat shuddered as it slammed into the hull, waves burst over the prow, her wet skirt clung to her. 'Now,' yelled Mr Travers.

She jumped, grabbed the ropes, clambered up, spray in her eyes, the waves snatching at her, the noise of their pounding almost drowning Mr Travers's shout from below. 'Not you yet, Sinclair. Wait till she's reached the deck or you'll jerk her off.'

Irene panted, lifting one leg, one hand, then the other. 'Let him come, Mr Travers, no-one will jerk me off my ship. No-one.' It seemed as though she was climbing a mountain, but it didn't matter. She was free of Jack, she was here on the *Wendham*. It was the start of her return journey.

Hands were reaching for her. She looked up, her hair streaming in the wind. 'Leave me,' she shouted. 'Just leave me be.' The bearded faces withdrew. She forced herself on. Her strength was almost gone, her gloves were ripping. She gasped, took a deep breath, lunged over the side, onto the deck. Somehow she kept her feet, somehow she stilled the trembling, and held herself erect as the first mate came to her.

She said, 'I am surprised that the captain did not see fit to greet me. Please take me to him.'

The seamen were standing in groups, sliding glances at her, muttering. She stared at them. Let them see their new owner. Let them know that she was to be respected, that she was to be in authority, that she was to be as an owner should be, clearly visible.

Mr Travers jumped down onto the deck, following Sinclair. He came to her, his face suffused with concern. 'You should have taken the chair, Mrs Prior.'

She said, 'Thank you for your concern.' Her voice softened. 'Try and understand, I must prove I am not a burden, a useless mouth to feed. I must earn my place, and their respect.'

He hesitated, started to speak, saying, 'But forgive me . . .'

She held up her hand. 'We're here,' she whispered. 'At last we're here, but I don't know what's going to happen now. Think of me, I'll do my best for us all. He must be Jack's man, for he chose not to greet me.' Her face was drawn with anxiety as she lifted her skirts and turned from him. 'The captain,' she repeated to the first mate.

He led the way to the quarterdeck, then down the companionway. Mr Travers and Sinclair followed.

The first mate knocked on the sleeping-cabin door. 'Enter,' a deep American voice drawled.

Irene paused, demanding courage from herself. She must be careful and strong. She must fight for them all. She swept into the dark cabin, shutting the door behind

155

her. Maps were rolled up on the table, the lamp swung gently.

Captain Baines looked from under brows as thick and dark as Jack's. His eyes were deep-set, almost black, like Jack's. His hands were powerful as they snapped shut the log, the hairs on the back of his fingers were coarse, like Jack's.

She heard the orders being issued on deck, heard the pounding of feet, felt the change of motion as the sails filled, and felt suddenly tired, aware of her torn gloves, aware of the blisters that had formed on the palm of her hand.

Captain Baines stood up, looming above her. Her mouth was as dry as Captain Baines's smile, and there was no humour in his watchful eyes, just the same sort of simmering rage that was always in Jack's.

He motioned to the chair opposite him. 'Good-day to ya, ma'am. I kinda felt you'd like the aft-cabin.' His voice was expressionless. 'I hope ya agree.'

She sat clenching her hands, drawing strength from God knew where. 'Then you hope wrong, Captain Baines. In the aft-cabin on the *Cachalot* we store trunks, or hold transgressors. There is no porthole, it's only suitable for rats, nothing more. Neither do I find it agreeable that you were not on deck to greet me. I am the owner. I must be seen to be the owner. I will take *your* cabin, Captain Baines, but before I do so, I will acquaint you with some facts.' She ticked them off, 'A, *Wendham* is my ship, bought with my money. B, It is to be run as I would run my estate, with humanity towards its crew, and that includes my two men, and with respect shown to its moral owner – me.'

He began to speak. She held up her hand, leaning forward as she shouted at this man who sat down heavily in his chair, staring at her, his eyes wide with surprise, 'D'you hear me, its moral owner, if not its legal owner.'

She slammed her hand down on the table. The

inkwell shuddered, her blisters burst. He leapt to his feet. She shouted even louder, 'Sit down, I say.' He hesitated. 'Sit down, I tell you, and believe me, I have every right to tell you, order you, so understand that well, Captain Baines.'

He sat, picked up a ruler, turning it over and over in his brutish hands. She felt her own trembling. She was winning, wasn't she, or was he going to rise and strike her? She swallowed, then continued. 'You see,' her voice broke. She swallowed again, and forced herself to speak slowly and clearly. 'You see, I know of your debts. I know that you are owned by Jack Prior. Well, my dear Captain,' her voice was under control, and now she made it contemptuous, 'everything my husband owns was originally mine. If he should die, as he almost did just recently, all would revert to me. I would be your owner. You'd do well to think of that before you try your tricks, before you cross or abuse me or my people in any way. And you'd do well to think of it before you run to my husband with tales.'

The captain flushed and now he surged to his feet, leaned forwards, his face just a foot from hers. She did not flinch, though she longed to. She said again, 'Sit down, I haven't finished.'

'Ya have, Mrs Prior. Indeed ya have.' His voice shook with rage. His eyes were half closed. She saw the scar on his cheek, his large pores, and now the streaks of grey in his hair, just like Jack, and her courage broke. She backed a pace. He continued, ticking off against his fingers, 'A, I guess I have every sympathy for anyone who has to stick with that monster, Black Jack. I *had* every sympathy for you. I was sitting at his table in the grog shop in Port Russell. I have heard tales of your life on board. B, But, Mrs Prior, you're in mortal danger of allowing him to twist ya into his image, to destroy you, just as surely as if he had killed you, for you're an offensive, aggressive woman.'

In the aftermath of his words it was as though the

feet no longer pounded, as though the lamp no longer swung, there was just a sense of shock, of incomprehension. There were just his eyes, full of anger. But then the anger seemed to fade and now his voice was gentler, slower.

'I had kinda first thought to offer you my cabin, but then, hearing about the raw dislike on the *Cachalot* after the whipping, I feared that if you were seen to take a cabin you would draw resentment here. For if you took mine, I'd have to take the first mate's, he'd have to shove into the officers' quarters, and so it goes on. I jest kinda thought we should start on a better footing – that you'd want to be seen to be kinda accommodating. I also thought that your husband, on account of him sending you here as a punishment, might take more kindly to leaving ya here, if you was in the aft-cabin. Thought he might see it as consoling. Maybe I was wrong, maybe I should have put it to you better. Anyways, I apologize and offer you, belatedly, this cabin.'

He walked from the table to the drawers lining the cabin, standing with his back to her, tapping his fingers on the top as Jack always had.

She felt weak, trying to grasp at something, slow things down. Her mind was racing, in turmoil. She said, 'But you weren't on deck?'

Captain Baines shook his head. 'I was, but then I heard you override Harry Travers over the chair. Kinda wanted to kick your backside. Felt I'd get on out of it for a while, simmer down. You could have lost a man his life if you'd gone into the sea and we'd had to send someone in after ya. And I fear you're wrong. Prior won't die. His sort never seem to die.'

She looked down at her gloves, torn and old. She smoothed them, then said weakly, 'I am the moral owner. I must be seen to be in authority. I must be seen to be in control. I've learned so much. I'm ready.'

'You will not be seen to be in control.' His voice was low and calm.

She insisted, her voice strained, near to breaking, 'But I have every right, Captain. I must have that right.'

'Enough.' It was as though the air reverberated. He continued, his voice low and calm again, 'A seaman will clear out this cabin, or take your trunk through to the aft-cabin. Please decide which.'

He waited. She slapped her hand on the desk again, desperation forcing caution into the distance. 'I will be in control. I will not be at anyone's mercy ever again. I insist I am in control.'

He stared at her. 'Get up on deck, get some air, and find some of this darned "control" you talk of. When you have, I guess we can pick up this conversation again, if ya approach me as a grown woman, not a rude child.'

He stood. She walked to the door. Opened it. Sinclair and Mr Travers leaned against the wall. She stared at them and they at her, concern in their eyes. She reached out a hand. Sinclair took it. She whispered, 'I don't know what to do.'

Travers mouthed, 'Mr Andrews, the first mate, says he's a good man.' Sinclair nodded, gripping her hand tighter.

She looked at the floor, then at Travers. 'Which cabin?'

He whispered, 'You know which cabin.'

She turned back into the room and resumed her seat, looking across at Captain Baines as he eyed her warily. 'I do not need to go to the deck, Captain. The aft-cabin will suit, thank you.'

He smiled, then reached forward and turned the two photograph frames on the table towards her. In one was a stout woman standing next to Captain Baines – both faces were alight with laughter. In the next were a boy and girl, replicas of their parents.

Captain Baines took up his pipe, tamped it, sucked

it, though he did not light it in her presence. He said, 'I guess I was a fool. I played cards in Bristol with Jack Prior in the summer of 1855. It was when he was travelling to Wendham House,' he glanced away from her. 'I cain't never prove he cheated, but he did, just as surely as he cheated you.'

They sat in silence for a moment, and slowly her body relaxed.

Captain Baines continued, 'You're right, he owns me, just as he owns you and in spite of that I've to captain this ship to the best of my ability. I've to raise whales and bring the crew as much of a lay as possible, though your husband makes sure it ain't easy – only two of our boats allowed out, if there ain't a pod to share.' He laughed, looked back at her. 'But I've no need to tell you that, you've seen it all for yourself.'

Irene said nothing.

Captain Baines said, 'You are indeed the *moral owner* of this ship, but I am the only one capable of bringing the *Wendham* home, and home I will most certainly bring her, to my wife and my children – there she is, in that photograph. A Parisian seamstress, my little lady.' He smiled, then sobered. 'You must understand what I'm saying, Mrs Prior. You really must grasp that I will tolerate no interference on *your* ship. There can only be one captain, one person in control.' There was steel in his voice now, but he had said she was the moral owner, he had said 'your' ship.

She sat back staring at him, then at his hands which were not brutish after all as they held the pipe, and his fingers which were slow and gentle but held great strength, looking into his dark eyes which were calm, wise and understanding.

Captain Baines put down his pipe. 'Now looka hear. I want ya to be visible. I want you to have the respect of the crew. I want you to have some peace, so that you can wipe out of ya mind that man, then I can wipe out of my mind that scene in the grog house, where I did nothin' to help a lady in distress.' His tone was kind, regretful.

She tried to speak but couldn't, and as she struggled for control her shoulders shook, her hand clenched. He reached across, gripped one of them, saying nothing.

At length she relaxed, but still he held her hand, and now she returned his clasp, raising her eyes to his. 'Forgive me,' she murmured.

He said, 'What's a few words between friends?'

She shook her head. 'No, forgive me for everything.'

He patted her hand before withdrawing, sitting back, laughing softly. 'It's him, over the water, who should ask that of us all. Now, we made the aft-cabin nice, homely. Found some cloth, hung it to pretend it's curtains at a porthole. Cooper did it, so it ain't perfect. Now, you cain't give no orders, for no owner should, but I want ya to sit at the wardroom table where the owner should sit. I want ya to deal with the slop chest. I want ya to heal my crew when they're sick. I want ya to heal yourself. I don't want ya scrubbing the decks, flensing the whale like you've been doing. That ain't woman's work, it ain't owner's work. Is that clear?'

She nodded, and that night she slept as she had not slept since before her parents had died and in the morning she sat with the officers at breakfast, whilst the galley steward who was not Sinclair served them.

Mr Travers saw her face and said, 'Sinclair is to be in my boat crew. I'll train him well, never fear.'

She nodded, somehow she knew he would. She smiled, and he nodded, his eyes at peace, just as hers were, and now, in front of the captain, and all the officers she said, 'Forgive me, Mr Travers, for ignoring your advice on taking the chair. I will attempt to listen in future.'

Mr Travers replied, 'And I will attempt to mind my own business, unless it is strictly necessary, Mrs Prior.'

*　　*　　*

Later in the day she visited the fo'c's'le and there was a halo round the lantern. That evening in the transom cabin, as she and Captain Baines sat relaxing before dinner, she asked if wind-sails might be set, searching for the right tone, realizing that she had almost forgotten how to make a request normally. Captain Baines looked over his log at her, 'Good idea. I'll set Mr Andrews onto it.'

She sat back. It was so easy, suddenly it was so easy. She took up one of Captain Baines's torn shirts, threaded a needle, and smiled.

The next day she wrote up the ledger for the slop chest, doing a copy as Captain Baines had instructed. 'I've been keeping it separate, but handy, just in case there's a query in New Bedford,' he said. The wardroom fell silent.

It became a habit for her to sew in the transom cabin in the evenings, whilst Captain Baines read his newspaper, which was six months old, and faded and fragile from its nightly handling. 'Bit of civilization,' he had murmured the first evening, and gone on to talk of his daughter who was inheriting her mother's needle skills and sense of style, of his son who was a great strapping boy, of his wife who still worked as a seamstress in New Bedford, but who only took commissions that interested her.

She had thought of her father whose newspaper had been ironed by the housekeeper. She told Captain Baines who looked at her and shook his head, then laughed, asking her questions about her family, about Wendham.

Each day she walked the decks, regaining her strength, talking to the crew not on watch, sharing their hopes, their fears, their loves, as her mother had shared those of the staff, the tenants, the villagers. Increasingly she could put names to faces, and by the end of the first week she talked to Dave of the love he had left behind in Bristol, and to Tom of the small farm he had left near Nantucket, and to Derek of the mother he had left in the Central Park shanty town in New York.

Increasingly she heard her own laugh ring out, felt a spring in her step as her strength returned, but it was more than that, it was her sanity which blossomed also. A sanity which bathed her in a great calm as she sat at the end of the first week on the quarterdeck beneath a parasol, made by the cooper, of sailcloth and whale-bone, hugging to herself the knowledge that Captain Baines would run before the next squall and leave the fleet behind until the designated meeting time at Port Russell in October.

But now a shadow chilled her pleasure and she turned to Captain Baines who stood beside the helms-man.

'But won't he come after us?' she asked appre-hensively.

Captain Baines shook his head. 'Did he last time? No, he won't come after us, fleets don't stick together, specially Prior fleets. We'll put into Port Russell come October, meet up there, as he's arranged.'

She asked Captain Baines, 'But then why did you come back last time?'

Mr Andrews, the first mate, pointed at Mr Travers who was in the waist, standing by Sinclair as he dished water to the hands. Captain Baines nodded, saying, 'For him. We kinda figured he'd be in trouble for breaking off from the whale and rescuing our boat crew. Thought maybe he'd be sent over if I kept requesting a second mate. We would have asked for a spare owner, if we'd thought.'

He and Mr Andrews laughed softly. Irene murmured, 'Mrs Baines is a very lucky woman,' and wouldn't think of her own husband, over there, in the three-masted whaler. But that night she tossed and turned in the stifling aft-cabin, and at midnight she clambered up onto the deck, walking in the soft air, moving to the waist where Mr Travers stood, watching as she approached.

She said awkwardly, 'It seems a long while since we took a watch together.'

He nodded and dug his hands into his pockets.

She said, 'We've come a long way.'

'Thanks to you, Mrs Prior.'

She leaned back against the hurricane cabin. 'No, I find it is thanks to you. The *Wendham* stayed for your sake, but then you know that but never thought to crow about it. Thank you, Mr Travers.'

The wind was flapping in the shortened sails, the lanterns swung lazily. A porpoise broke the surface in a leap. They both watched together. He said, 'Nothing to crow about. We're even, for I feel it is thanks to your courage, and the quickness of your mind that we arrived here.' They smiled at one another again.

She said, 'We've been through a nightmare together, and only the three of us can understand what it was like. That's a bond nothing can break.' She held out her hand, 'Hallo, Mr Travers, and thank you.'

He took it. 'My pleasure, Irene Wendham, and it's an honour to meet you.' They laughed together, then turned back to the sea which was bathed in the light of the stars.

The next day, as the seamen on lookout on the main and mizzen mastheads drowsed, clouds rolled in from the east, rushing towards them, darkening the sky, churning the sea with their accompanying wind. Irene who sat in the hurricane house, sewing Arnie, the cabin boy's, trousers, leapt up at Captain Baines's shout, and heard the helmsman laugh. Mr Andrews called into the cabin, 'Squall, Mrs Prior. Just what we needed.'

The rain and hail came, the seamen scrambled into the rigging which was whipping and creaking. The topgallant halyards were let go, but while the sails were being clewed up, the fierce wind that followed rain rent and tore them. The ship tipped, lurched and rolled with its force.

Irene stood in the doorway, bracing herself against the wind, the trousers still in her hand. As the mainmast pitched, tipped and swung she gloried in it, and in the flapping of the sails and the howling of the wind.

As Captain Baines ran before the storm, saving what canvas he could, she stood and stared through the rain. 'Goodbye, you damned man,' she shouted.

That afternoon, in the transom cabin, she tended the sailors who had been pitched from the rigging, splinting the broken arm, binding the ugly gash, pouring brandy down one boy's throat, soothing the other, sitting up with them both throughout the night, feeling no tiredness, laughing at Captain Baines's suggestion that she should rest.

'He's gone, that devil's gone,' she said to him.

'Until New Zealand,' he warned, his eyes sad.

'It doesn't matter, for now he's gone,' she insisted, and slowly Captain Baines smiled, touched her cheek. 'Aye, you're right, for now he's gone.'

CHAPTER EIGHT

In October, with their hold a quarter full, they returned to Port Russell and as they sailed in Irene stood at the prow staring until her eyes ached, searching the port, then staring behind. The *Cachalot* wasn't here, and her heart soared.

Captain Baines called her to the quarterdeck. 'Made sure we got here a good bit before we was expected, missy. Just you try to stop fretting so.'

'I wasn't,' she snapped, then shook her head. 'Forgive me. I was. I couldn't bear to have to go back.' Her voice shook.

The muscles of Captain Baines's jaw were working under his skin. He said, 'Cain't say I rightly blame ya. Just remember not to look too happy when he does come in, else he's sure to snatch ya back, and there's not one of us on board who'd want to see that happen. So remember what I tells ya.'

He ordered the dropping of the anchor. Behind her Mr Travers ordered the furling of the mainsail. She looked out across Port Russell again, then removed her gloves, lifted her hands to her face, and breathed in the scent of the spermaceti oil Mr Travers had insisted she rubbed into them, and felt their smoothness. Happy? Yes, and why not, for she was progressing towards her freedom, towards her home, but still the dread was with her and as she stared at the straggling houses she clenched her fists.

The boats were lowered once the ship was safely anchored, and only a skeleton crew was left on watch under the command of Mr Andrews as Captain

Baines accompanied Irene and the crew ashore.

Irene walked with him and Mr Travers to the store with the crew, and ordered a stock of provisions to be made up by the end of the day. Whilst the men bought tobacco and beer, with Mr Travers writing down the purchases against their lay, Sinclair and Irene bought tea, sugar, milk and a kettle. They bought bread, butter and biscuits. They bought apples. They put them all in a basket Sinclair had brought from the ship at Irene's insistence because, as she had stood on the deck, she had determined to visit the beach again, *that* beach.

The cabin boy stood watching them. 'Looks like a picnic to me,' he said.

Irene laughed, though it was an effort. 'That's because it is. Are you coming? I'm going to lay a ghost.'

Arnie shivered, and shook his head, hopping from one foot to the other. 'Nah, don't hold with them things.'

Sinclair ruffled his hair. 'Ghosts or picnics?'

Arnie ducked away, 'I ain't a kid, you wouldn't ruffle her hair.' His tone was belligerent. The crew who were milling around them, staring at the picnic, laughed. Mr Travers called from beside the flour sacks, 'I doubt that we would.' But his eyes were on Irene, for he had heard the tension in her voice.

She felt his gaze and looked up. He looked so young, so puzzled, so anxious. She caught sight of herself in the glass front of the soda cupboard. She looked young also. Even Sinclair looked younger, even Captain Baines. She grinned suddenly. She was here with her friends, she was strong, young. She grinned and she nodded and now Mr Travers smiled and turned away. She crouched before Arnie. 'Come with us. Picnics are fun. Have you ever been on one?'

'Lived in Bristol, miss. Don't have picnics in Bristol.'

'I'll come,' Mr Justine, the third mate called. There was a clamour of voices and only a third of the crew went to the grog shop with Mr Travers, and Captain Baines. The rest walked with Irene, Sinclair and Arnie through the town, and while they walked and kicked up dust she told Arnie of her home, of the haying, the harvest teas.

He told her of the mean streets and of his mother, gasping at the brightness of the spring flowers in the hedgerows and the heady scents but somehow, for Irene, the colours didn't feel as bright as she felt they should, or the perfume as intense, and she knew that it was because of their destination, of her task.

They passed a hawthorn laden with blossom, and she heard Mr Travers's voice hailing them, hoarse from running, 'Thought we'd best come. Got to make sure young Arnie doesn't get his hair ruffled again.' Suddenly the hawthorn scent seemed to billow around her like a cloud.

She laughed now, lifting her head to the deep blue sky, pulling Arnie to her, keeping her arm round his shoulders as they walked, drinking in the beauty of the land, easily pushing away the memories of last time, daring them to hurt her, because this time she was not alone. She glanced across at Sinclair, looked back at Mr Travers, and Captain Baines, and back to Mr Travers.

Nonetheless as they approached the dazzling white beach sloping gently down to the sea, she felt deeply chilled.

Arnie broke free from her and ran down onto the sand, flinging off his shoes, whirling round and round. Sinclair and Jacko groaned as they watched him and grumbled about the heavy wicker basket they carried between them. 'Once I was young like that too,' Sinclair muttered.

The group hurried onto the sand, and Irene searched the beach.

'This'll do,' Sinclair urged, pointing haphazardly to one of the many flat rocks.

Irene held onto her hat as the wind whipped up the sand. 'No, further on, there, that rock.' She pointed.

Yes, that's where she had climbed to retrieve the table cloth.

As they approached the men ran on, with even Sinclair and Jacko galvanizing themselves, while Captain Baines kicked up the sand in their wake. Irene clenched her hands, repeating silently, I'm not afraid of him any more. I'm not . . .

The sweat broke out on her forehead and she knew that she was.

She stopped. 'Oh God,' she whispered.

She felt a hand on her arm, and swung round. Mr Travers said, 'You're amongst friends, Mrs Prior.'

'I had to come. It was on this beach that he told me. It was here I discovered what he was like,' she murmured. His hand was still on her arm. She needed it, she needed the warmth of someone else who understood to help her make the last few steps.

He let go of her arm. She longed to plead, 'Help me.' But Mr Travers was a friend, not a mind-reader, not someone like Martha who loved her. She took a deep breath, 'You carry on, Mr Travers. I will be along directly.'

He hesitated, the sun lighting up his eyes, glancing off his brown hair where it rested on his collar. She said again, 'Carry on, Mr Travers. I am quite able to proceed alone.' Her voice was detached, firm, cold even as she struggled to contain the past.

He turned away, striding off, not looking back. She forced herself on. One pace, another, and she heard Jack's voice sending her for the tablecloth, she felt again her disbelief, her pain, her hope. Another pace. She looked at the rock. Fear was here again, deep and dark as though it had never left her.

Another pace. Mr Travers had stopped, had turned again, his hand was out towards her. Arnie was kicking sand at Sinclair who growled, lunged, laughed. Arnie darted from his grasp, out past Mr Travers, rushing up to Irene, pulling at her skirt. 'Come on, missus. There's

169

oysters. We can build a fire. Sinclair says we should eat 'em raw, but that's disgusting.'

He was pulling her along. She reached out, ruffled his hair, laughed at last, called to Mr Travers, 'You're right. I'm amongst friends.'

He dropped his hand, smiled, and walked on towards Sinclair.

The *Queen of the Isles* came into Port Russell two days later. Just a day later the *Cachalot* dropped anchor. Irene remained in her cabin as Captain Baines was rowed by Mr Travers's boat crew to a meeting with Jack Prior aboard the *Cachalot*. On the way they were passed by the first mates of the *Cachalot* and the *Queen of the Isles*, heading for the *Wendham*.

As the first mates were entertained in the wardroom, Irene lay on her bunk, and Mr Harry Travers waited in the boat alongside the *Cachalot*, watching the surging tide, the lapping waves, the light dancing on the surface, and in the *Wendham* fo'c's'le Sinclair sat hunched over on his bunk, and they all wondered if they would be recalled, or if the letter Irene had sent with Captain Baines would work. A letter in which she complained of life aboard the *Wendham*, expressing her misery and fury at the continued presence of Sinclair and Travers.

As the sun was setting Captain Baines returned. Still Irene lay on her bunk, waiting, waiting. Still Sinclair sat. Only Travers held in his head the decision as his boat was winched aboard. There was a knock on Irene's door, at the same time that Travers called Sinclair.

Stiffly, Irene rose, opened the door.

Captain Baines stood there, a note in his hand, she reached out, took it, opened it, read. *I glory in your misery. I jest love to think you find yourself poorly done by. I have told Captain Baines that he has carried out my orders to my complete satisfaction, and that he may continue to do so for the next three years. Until New Bedford. Jack.*

She handed Captain Baines the note. He waved it away. 'I know what's in it, he read it to the whole wardroom.' She screwed it up. 'We'll consign it to the deep, Captain Baines,' she ordered, her voice triumphant.

'That jest happens to be an order I'll allow you to give, missy,' Captain Baines replied, holding his arms out. She walked into the warmth of the embrace of this man, who was a father to her. A wise, solid father, unlike her own had been.

On the deck above, Sinclair and Travers stood side by side, staring out at the *Cachalot*, and relief deepened the bond between them.

Over the next months they cruised north, fading from the fleet within two days and penetrating far beyond the routes taken by ordinary trading vessels as all whalers did. She wrote in her journal, and at least once a week she joined Mr Travers on deck, sharing the watch, talking, drawing the comfort of his recollections of the West Country and later sleeping loose and deep.

In the 'horse latitudes' the rain came down in frequent torrents, permitting the whole crew to wash well and often and each evening Irene wrote up her journal, and one day described the glare and roar of rain so heavy that the ship's deck became full of pure water, a day on which Arnie had flung himself into the flood, heedless of the fact that he could not swim.

She had rushed from the hurricane house, plunged in, stroking as her father had taught her, dipping down beneath the surface, groping for the submerged boy, forcing her eyes to remain open, seeing Mr Travers there, opposite, doing the same.

Together they had brought him coughing and spluttering to the surface, before handing him over to Sinclair, who cuffed his ear, then fed him coffee. Sinclair had also thrust some at Irene, telling her to go and change, telling Mr Travers also, while Captain Baines looked in the doorway saying, 'If I'd known there was a coffee in it, I'd have dived down myself, danged if I wouldn't.'

As an addendum to her journal that night she wrote, *Slowly I see that, though my mother had great strengths, my father did much for me, also. I also see how blessed I am to have friends such as these.*

Day after day they drifted, almost idling, with the weather fine now, and never a fleck of white in the sky and just a few solitary whales, which they caught, and which added to their total. There were flying fish, another bonito, a shoal of dolphins which rose in a great wave of silver, then skimmed through the air, rising and falling for perhaps a hundred yards before slicing away. There was still some fruit left, consequently there were few boils.

On Sundays they sometimes ate fowl that they had taken on in New Zealand. Daily she wrote up the crews' expenses in the book and nursed any who fell sick. In the evenings she joined Mr Travers on deck and sometimes they talked of the soft sweet hills, sometimes of the fragrant meadows each seemed to have run through, of the harvest scent and bright red sun, and the cool cider supped beneath spreading oaks. But at other times they just stood side by side, silently sharing the soft night, silently sharing the end of the nightmare.

As day followed day and boredom set in, Irene took Arnie through his letters and they sat together near the prow as she drew an apple on the slate, and an ugly bat, and a cat and he repeated his letters, and smiled at her pleasure. But by the next morning he had forgotten them again, slumping down, his eyes glancing across the sea, seeking whales, or judging the wind. Progress was slow all week.

The next week she laboured over his sums, asking him to take away seven apples from Farmer Giles's basket of twenty but it was no good, the boy grew increasingly restless, uninterested. Other crew joined them, but soon they were as distracted. She said, 'Look at Mr Travers, his mother taught him and see how well he's done.'

They tried but progress was still slow.

Over dinner one night she said, 'It worked well in the village school where mother would go to help.' She paused, then said in a lower voice, 'Where I should also have helped, but seldom did.'

'Enough of that,' Captain Baines said, leaning to one side as Sinclair dished fish stew onto his plate. The steam rose, to join the thick tropical heat. Mr Andrews nodded, 'Yes, enough of that. You's tending the crew right well, so I reckon all that's cancelled out. Stone me, you're mending a few clothes too, or so's I hear now.'

Mr Travers leaned forward, reaching for the salt. 'Arnie loves whaling, try making it A for Arctic.'

Captain Baines interrupted, 'Arctic's no place to be, you can tell him that from me. Been up there catching bowheads for them corsets you lassies wear. It's the baleen you know. Sort of like teeth, but they're filters really, back of the mouth. We had to get it out of the head, hang it to dry, then them workers at home cut it suitable for corsets, ain't whale*bone* at all.'

'B for bonito,' the fourth mate interrupted.

Captain Baines leaned forward. 'Trouble is the ice can trap you, smash your boat, kill ya, if the frost-bite or the icebergs don't get ya first. Terrible place to be, specially when the owners won't pay to have hulls reinforced or for proper clothing. Get in and out before the cold comes, they say. I sez, some-times you can't. I know, I've been trapped,' he shuddered.

The first mate said, 'W for the *Wendham*.'

The third mate said, 'Q for *Queen of the Isles*.'

There was an awkward pause. Irene said, 'C for Cape Horn.' Her voice was quite calm, though inside her there was a bleak darkness, as dark as the Arctic memory that had plunged Captain Baines into gloom.

That night she did not go up on deck.

The next day she sat again with Arnie at the bow-sprit, feeling the heat on them and around them, and on the slate wrote A for Arctic, B for barrel, C for Cape Horn, and instead of his gaze flickering from the crow's-nest to the expanse of sea he concentrated. At the end of an hour he was able to recite the alphabet, and tell her how many barrels of oil there would be if Mr Travers took six from a pile of twenty, or how much lay there would be after certain subtractions. The crew joined in again, and did almost as well.

As she passed Mr Travers at the fo'c's'le scuttle she murmured, smiling, 'A good idea of yours, Mr Travers.'

'That's what comes of not minding your own business,' he said quietly, his eyes full of humour.

Later that day they changed course for the Philippines as Captain Prior had ordered. They sailed, aware that out beyond the horizon was the *Queen of the Isles*, and the *Cachalot*, but confident that they would not all meet up again until the Seychelles. As they progressed the weather darkened, the fowls on board left their food and moped. They made little headway that day, or night. The barometer fell at dawn, the sea got up. Extra gaskets were put on the sails, everything movable about the deck was made secure. Only the two close-reefed topsails and two storm stay-sails were carried.

Captain Baines said, as Irene stood next to him on the quarterdeck, 'Put in your journal that we're in excellent trim for fighting what's about to come.'

She pulled her cloak close about her against the force of the wind which moaned in the rigging, flinching at the waves growling, rolling, crashing. 'But what's about to come?'

Captain Baines had no time to answer and strode to the waist as glimmering lightning nudged the eastern horizon. The hatches were battened down, the stove too. Sinclair hurried past, 'Cold victuals from now on.'

The air seemed alive with static. The men were on their hunkers near the hatches. The officers were pacing the decks. Captain Baines was back on the quarterdeck, standing behind her with the helmsman. Where was Mr Travers? She searched with her eyes, found him checking the davits. He looked up as though he felt her eyes and smiled. She felt calmer.

She saw Arnie near the forward scuttle and hurried down to him, taking him through multiplication as the ship lurched, rolled, and the seas roared. 'I've never been in a storm,' he shouted, the wind almost whipping his words away. 'Not like this one. Mr Travers says I'm to go below when he gives me the order. I ain't going to.'

She gripped his hand. 'Oh yes, you are, if that's what he's said. Besides, I'll need company. Storms frighten me, and I'll need a man to give me strength.'

The clouds were black and purple, now split by lightning, now racing on. The seas were whipping, changing. 'Furl the topsail and fore stay-sail,' Captain Baines bellowed.

The crew rushed to obey. Irene and Arnie stood staring, clinging together. The clouds were rolling nearer, now they were over them. Rain torrented down, water whipped off the sea. Noise filled every fragment of space left in the world. 'Haul down the stay-sail,' Baines bellowed.

Remember this, write it in the journal, she told herself again and again, trying to still the panic, her eyes seeking Mr Travers, needing her friend. The roar of the wind grew even louder. They rose, fell, careering into troughs, and now the deck sloped off thirty-five degrees. She and Arnie cowered but still she searched for her friend through the sheeting rain and now she saw him, battling the wind, his crew behind him, securing the last of the boats.

She peered up at Captain Baines but Arnie turned to her, pulling at her arm. 'This ain't a storm, this is a cyclone. C for cyclone.'

She hugged him. 'Yes, C for cyclone, clever boy. B for brave boy.' For she had seen the fear in his eyes, seen his lips which he had clamped together, felt the trembling in his body. 'We should go below. Come and calm me,' she said.

He shook his head, burying his face in her breast. 'We can't move. We'll be blown overboard. He hasn't given the order.' She had to bend her head to hear and then whispered, 'Then we'll stay until we're ordered.'

The noise was worse. How could it be?

At noon the wind suddenly fell to a calm, and the noise with it, but as she and Arnie stared at the sea, terror took hold, for before their eyes a mountain of water rose, climbing higher and higher, rushing towards them, cresting, tumbling at the peak, then turning in on itself, smashing into another crest which came from the east, rolling on, smashing onto the deck. Washing over and through the waist.

The moon emerged through cloud. Another wall of water reared up, cresting, breaking, coming on, smashing down. The *Wendham* tossed and twisted, in the madness of the sea, the decks boiled with water.

Mr Travers forced his way towards them, waving his arm. 'Get below. For God's sake, get below now. I'll batten down again behind you.'

She stared past him, gripping Arnie, backing, backing, pointing. Travers turned. Mr Andrews yelled from the steps of the quarterdeck, 'Hold on for your lives. Hold on.'

Higher and higher the wall of water rose, towered, hung level with their lower yards. Arnie was screaming, clawing at her. Irene held him, stretching out a hand to Mr Travers as she did so, screaming, 'Be careful.' He ran towards them, reached them, snatched Arnie from her, held the boy's arm, held her with the other, tightly, round the waist, dragging her towards the quarterdeck.

The water broke above them, crashing down with a great roar, engulfing them, driving the breath from their lungs, tumbling them, tearing at them. Mr Travers's arm was still round her waist. She clung to his neck, his face was against hers, his eyes open as hers were but then she felt Arnie dragged and pulled by the force of the water. She clutched at him, seeing Mr Travers reaching for him, even as she was doing. Arnie. Arnie.

She caught the lad's arm, saw his hair streaming. The water tore at their flesh, forced her grip to weaken, forced Travers's arm to slacken around her waist, tore Arnie from her. Arnie. Arnie.

They were tumbling over and over, and now Mr Travers was gone. Arnie was gone. The weight of the water was pounding her. She couldn't see, couldn't shout, mustn't breathe. Arnie mustn't breathe. She was turning, turning. Don't breathe, Arnie. Don't breathe, Mr Travers. Harry. Harry.

Her lungs were bursting. She was slammed up against the scuttle, clung to it, a body swept into her. She grabbed at it, held it, cloth tore, hands tried to hold on to hers, but were snatched away. She mustn't breathe. She mustn't breathe. There was a roaring, her lungs were bursting. Harry. Arnie.

The torrent was sliding from her, draining from her, from the deck. She gulped air. She tore at her collar, breathing, coughing, choking. She dragged herself free of the scuttle, crawled amongst the men who were retching, spluttering. Arnie, Harry, her mind screamed.

She felt hands on her, pulling at her, holding her, forcing her to rise, dragging her to her feet. The ship was still shuddering, plunging, then rising, battling. It was Harry, keeping her safe. There was blood from a cut pouring down over his eye. He pushed his face close to her. Her legs gave way. His arm came round her again, held her close. 'Thank God. Thank God. Arnie, Arnie?' she repeated.

He said, 'Be quiet. Be quiet. I have him. But you must get below. For God's sake you must be safe.'

He dragged them back to the quarterdeck as men scrambled to their posts. He helped them up the steps. She could hear his breathing, Arnie's too, see the water running down his hair, his neck. She could feel his arm, and the strength of him.

At the helm he paused. Captain Baines touched her cheek. She smiled weakly, 'We've survived, it's an omen, you see. It must be an omen, for us all. We'll be free to go home.' Her voice was shaking, her body was too.

Mr Travers exchanged a glance with Captain Baines, then eased her to the companionway. He released his hold. She almost fell. He caught her. 'No, take Arnie,' she whispered. He eased Arnie gently down the companionway, then came back for her, slipping his arm around her, holding her so tightly, leading her down the steps, his head close to hers.

'It's an omen,' she repeated again, not wanting this man to leave her here in the cabin as he was doing, not wanting his hands to push hers to her sides as he was doing. Not wanting him to say what his eyes were telling her. He said, 'It's not over. We're in the eye. Now stay here and pray to God to help us.'

The wind came back with a roar, and the noise in the cabin was worse than on deck, with the timbers groaning and creaking. Arnie ran for the door. She pulled him back. He said, 'I want to go up. I don't want to stay here. I want to go to Mr Travers.'

She said, 'What we want doesn't matter. We're in the way. Mr Travers saved us, but he had to bring us here, it was all extra work, all extra worry. Do as you're told. It's something I've had to learn and I don't want you to learn as I had to. You're too sensible for that.'

As the storm roared she talked the boy through her

life, and his, and heard of his dreams to be the captain of a ship, and a man like Mr Travers or Captain Baines, and all the while she pleaded with God to help them survive, and felt again the arm that had held her and Arnie, the face that had been so close to hers, the voice that had said, 'You must be safe.'

At dawn the cyclone moved on and as she held the sleeping boy in her arms, she stared at Sinclair, Captain Baines, and Mr Travers as they stood in the doorway, dishevelled but alive. She kissed Arnie's hair, stroked his face, her eyes searching out Mr Travers, but he was looking at the boy, only the boy, and saying in a voice dead with weariness, 'You're right, it's an omen, Mrs Prior. One day you'll be free, and will return to Wendham House.'

As Harry Travers stepped out onto the quarterdeck behind Sinclair he breathed in deeply, trying to still the trembling, trying to remove from his mind the feel of her body against his, the memory of her eyes locked onto his, the reality which her words had thrust at him. 'It's an omen. We'll all be free to go home.'

Mrs Prior, oh God, she was *Mrs* Prior and for a moment he had forgotten.

179

CHAPTER NINE

'April 1860 – I'm nearly twenty-six and somehow it doesn't seem as though I've been whaling for five years,' Irene murmured as she stood on the *Wendham*'s deck, looking out over the sea, straining to see New Bedford, the whaling port on the east coast of America, but it was still not in sight. 'I've been most fortunate. I've been all over the world. I've seen so much.'

At her side Mr Travers nodded, ''Cepting the Arctic, and Antarctic.'

They both said, 'Which Captain Baines would say, for as long as anyone of us allow him to, "Is worth missing, jest let me tell you." ' Their laughter rang out, and why shouldn't there be laughter between such old friends she thought, and fell silent because, for a moment during that storm . . . But no, she was Mrs Prior who had need of friends, a right to friends, but nothing more.

So after that night she had not shared the night watch with Mr Travers ever again, and he had never queried her absence, and their eyes had seldom met, and when they did they were carefully cloaked, empty, and when her dreams had played tricks and brought back the feel of his arm holding her, protecting her, guarding her, she had stirred from sleep and filled the aching void with Wendham and her plans, and sometimes it had worked.

From the quarterdeck she heard Captain Baines order the whale bones to be run up the rigging. 'It's nearly over,' she said.

'Indeed it is, ma'am.' After the storm she had forbidden anyone to call her Mrs Prior. Mr Travers continued, 'Though it's sad that we're without Mr Andrews and ten of the crew. That damn storm took a lot of good men.'

They stared across the sea, never at one another. No, never at one another. She said, 'Indeed it did, but left a lot of good ones alive also.'

Mr Travers stirred himself. 'You'll be leaving then, once we reach the port? Are you so sure that Mr Barratt will give up the lease?'

There was a smudge of smoke on the horizon. 'There she be,' called Captain Baines from the quarterdeck. 'There be New Bedford. There's that dratted smoke. Still burning the oil, still making the candles, praise be to God.'

Irene stood on her toes. How stupid, she'd see nothing more by doing that. She stood full square again, dredging up a reply, whilst her mind thought, It's nearly over, it's nearly over. She wondered how she could survive without the knowledge that Harry Travers would be near her for another day. She said, 'Oh yes, I'm sure. It would be the act of a gentleman to do so, and all he aspires to is that reputation. Jack would not dare to dispute it openly, drag me back as I know he is legally entitled to, for at last I have dredged up some protection for myself, Mr Travers.

'You see, I would charge him somehow with foul dealing over my signature, I would drive my metaphorical lance up to the hilt in any plans to repossess me. Yes, I'll be leaving, I have work to do, amends to make. And yes, Mr Barratt will relinquish the lease.' As she spoke she felt determination stir and her doubts were subdued at the thought of her duty and the home she loved, for what else was there in reality? She added, 'But what of you?'

She shaded her eyes with her gloved hand and wouldn't turn to look at him. Mr Travers stared towards the black smudge which was more clearly etched with every minute that passed. 'The crew will disperse, eager to take their lay and be free of the man who purports to be owner.' His tone was wry. 'So I too will make my escape.'

She scanned the deck which was pristine, the try-works which gleamed in their idleness. She felt the *Wendham* roll sluggishly in the water because she was so heavily laden. She said, 'Will you still head towards San Francisco?' She glanced in his direction, but not at his face, his eyes, his lips.

He smiled gently, and with his eyes still fixed beyond her, said, 'Yes, since I can't go home. Sinclair and I will take passage on a ship bound for there. Arnie's coming too. There'll be a trio again.' They fell silent.

She fixed her eyes on the quarterdeck where Captain Baines stood, his eyes alight, his thoughts clearly on his family, and the settling of his debt, and his release from Prior. She looked at Timmy from Maine, Arnie from Bristol and nodded, 'I'll miss everyone,' she whispered, fixing her gaze on Bedford which was emerging with more clarity by the league.

Mr Travers's voice was firm, 'But you're going where you'll be safe. You're going home. Once you're there he won't risk a scandal. Just fix on that.' He left her then, striding to the quarterdeck.

She gripped the rail and conjured up honeysuckle, the garden, the village, clinging to the vision as above her the sails flapped, the ship creaked, the officers shouted orders to which the crew responded and as she did so she forced herself to re-examine her plans. She would make a solitary life for herself, assume her responsibilities safe in the knowledge that Mr Travers had made her capable of her role. Why, she might even find one or two friends again, and now she broke, and pressed her hand to her mouth.

Arnie clutched her arm. 'It won't be long before you're there, before you've got your lay and can get back to where you belong, ma'am. Don't fret. Just have to hope we've got there before that devil so's we can arrange a good price. Captain Baines has made it back two weeks before he was expected, so it should be all right. You sorted out the ledgers, did you, just in case he's there?'

She forced a laugh. 'Indeed I did. I've duplicated them neatly. Captain Baines will present one to Mr Prior. I will keep the other in the aft-cabin, just in case.'

At the thought of her husband the anxiety and anger drove all other emotion from her and she basked in the relief it brought, and her sense of purpose was hardened beyond any doubt.

As they tied up at one of the many wharves, alongside whaler upon whaler, Captain Baines called her to the quarterdeck, put his hand on her shoulder, his face tense, 'He's here already.' He gestured with his head. She swung round and searched the whalers and barques. 'Two wharves down, and there's the first mate, over there.'

The *Cachalot*'s first mate, Mr Osborne, was standing by the rows of seaweed-covered casks at the head of the wharf. His hands were on his hips, the smile on his face was broad. He marched towards the *Wendham*. The gangplank was lowered.

She looked above him to the hill overlooking the harbour, and the grand mansions owned by the whale fleet owners. Her voice rose as she said, 'I'll get the ledger. He'll have sold the oil, but he can't dispute the ledger.' Panic was roaring. Jack Prior was here. He shouldn't be, he should be out there, in the vast ocean. Would he take what was theirs from them, would he cheat her people?

She rushed below and brought up the ledger, seeing Captain Baines at the head of the gangplank taking the mail from Mr Osborne, handing it to Arnie for distribution.

She passed over the ledger to Captain Baines, her voice terse, full of dislike, for this was the pretence they

183

had all maintained whenever the fleet combined. She watched as Captain Baines walked down the gangplank alone, clutching his log, and ledger, his hat firmly on his head, but she had seen his eyes.

Behind her Mr Travers said, for he was now first mate and had been since Mr Andrews's death, 'Come below for a dram, Mr Osborne.'

She murmured, 'I hope it chokes you, Mr Travers.' Then swept towards Arnie, looking over her shoulder, following Captain Baines's passage down the quay. He turned, she wanted to wave but could not, for in public eyes he was no friend of hers.

She waited near the stanchion, as Arnie gave out the letters, content that the men should have theirs first, confident at the nature of Barratt's reply which should be amongst the letters Arnie was doling out. While she waited she let her mind play over the ledger figures. Prior wouldn't be able to fault them. He couldn't, they were perfect, and she had a copy, and they'd kept the dead seaman's name down in case he rescinded her lay, which they all knew was probable. It was a man that they knew had no dependants and so no need of his money.

The men were laughing as they grouped themselves round Arnie, who called out their names.

What if he'd sold the oil cheap? What if he lied about the price? He'd done that before. Suddenly the image of Wendham's library came into her mind, and the tobacco smoke, and the dust motes, and the stag heads, the billiard table, her first glimpse of Jack, his size, his energy.

She shut her eyes against the image but he was here again, huge as he bore down on her, huge as he beat her, his face exultant, his hatred so tangible she could almost smell and taste it.

She opened her eyes, the panic turning into a rage of eagerness to be away, out of reach of him, and everything else was forgotten as she rushed towards

Arnie, her hand out, shouting, 'Come on, Arnie. If you can't read quicker than that after all the hours I spent, you must be stupid.'

His look of hurt surprise, the murmurs of the men, halted her. 'Forgive me,' she said. 'I . . . oh, just forgive me.'

She turned away, but Arnie called, 'Here you are, ma'am. Two letters. Just two.'

She swung back and took them, peering at the writing. Martha! The other was Barratt. It was this she opened first, tearing at the seal, eating the words, reading them again, and again, as the shock of disappointment took the strength from her legs, and the breath from her chest.

Sinclair, who had been watching, caught her, leading her to rope coiled on the deck, making her sit, taking the letter from her limp hand as she said, 'He's refused. Was I mad? Why did I think he would? Yes, I'm mad.' She looked towards the *Cachalot*, and knew she visibly trembled.

He read it, and said, 'I'm sorry.'

She shook her head, unable to speak.

Sinclair went on, as he scanned the words, 'But he's taken back your Martha, and fixed the rents for as long as the Turner profits last. That's fair, I suppose.'

She put her head in her hands, shutting her eyes against the brightness of the deck, shutting her ears to the whoops and laughter of the men, to the cry of the seagulls, the rattle of barrels being loaded on the wharf, and groaned at the realization that from now on she'd be alone in Jack Prior's world. They'd all be gone, all of them, and Harry Travers too.

But then she looked up at Sinclair. No, she'd flee to San Francisco with them; Sinclair, Harry Travers, Arnie. Yes, that's what she'd do. But then she closed her eyes. No, he'd come after her, find her, find them, find Harry. Her clawing hands found Martha's letter on her lap. And what of her tenants, her duty, her damned duty?

185

She ground her forehead against her hands.

Sinclair crouched beside her. 'Go anyway. Talk to Barratt. He'll not be able to resist you. Take your lay and go.' His voice was urgent. She gripped his hand, stared into his eyes. He was right. Barratt had married and had a small child. She'd appeal to his wife. She'd tell her it was *her* family home. Somehow it would be all right. She'd rekindle the cottage industry. He could keep his factory. Then Mr Travers could leave for San Francisco safely.

The crew waited all day for the return of Captain Baines, checking the wharf as they unloaded the barrels, but it wasn't until the early mist curled in the passageways and over the seaweed-covered barrels that he staggered up the gangplank. Then his face was ugly, and he reeked of liquor and as he reached the deck he hurled the ledger and the log across the waist hard against the scuttle. The crew men melted silently into the shadows.

Irene, Travers and Sinclair stood as though turned to stone, until Harry Travers called, 'Sinclair, to the captain.' He and the steward dragged Captain Baines down the companionway into the sleeping cabin.

Irene followed, in time to hear Captain Baines groan in a voice hoarse and desperate, 'It's the fine he paid in Fremantle, when the convict was found, God damn him. All this time he's been adding interest to the money he paid out. Sez we all owe him for it – so don't matter how perfect the ledger is, we owe him on top. He got a lawyer sat beside him to defend it. Says the *Wendham* was part of the fleet 'cos it was bought in England before that date, so we're liable too. We're goddamn liable, and I'm stuck with the *Wendham*, and he's taking the fleet to the goddamn Arctic after the bowhead, 'cos the price of baleen has gone through the roof.'

Captain Baines beat his fists on the table, saliva ran from the corner of his mouth. 'I cain't tell the men. How can I tell 'em? They trusted me. I let them down, and now I'll be taking them into the ice and that bastard'll not spend money on the hull, he won't spend money on warm clothes.' He sprawled across the table, face down, knocking the photographs of his family flying.

Mr Travers sent Sinclair for coffee, flashed a look at Irene, and this time there was no laughter at the mention of the Arctic, how could there ever have been laughter while Jack Prior lived? Travers said, 'You must still go. Go on, get out, get away. Get to Wendham.' She stood there.

He skidded a fob watch across the table at her, and his eyes held hers and this time there was no careful masking, there was urgency and insistence. 'Take this, sell it. It's a start. It'll get you to England. You can talk Barratt into it, if you set your mind to it. I know you can.'

The watch glinted. She said, 'But how? You have no watch.'

'Correction. I now have, the first mate of the *Cachalot* hasn't. He shouldn't play cards with a convict. Got to be the first rule in the book.'

The watch lay between them. She reached for it, weighing it in her hand. 'And all of you?'

Travers shrugged, hauling Captain Baines up, taking the coffee from Sinclair, making the man drink. Captain Baines coughed, choked, swallowed.

Travers said, 'If I stay maybe some of the crew'll stay, though some'll still jump. If the old man has just a few experienced hands it could mean the difference between getting through drifting ice, or foundering. We'll be back at the start of winter, in September. I'll go then.'

Sinclair said, 'Then I'll stay too. San Francisco's still standing. It'll be there for a bit longer.'

Irene heard the water lapping against the hull though the light barely swayed at all here at the wharf. She righted the photographs as Mr Travers told her that Osborne said Black Jack had been in a rage since they arrived. 'He's heard that something called petroleum has been discovered. It'll be the end in time for whale oil, so he's going all out for baleen, gone to New York to set up a deal with a corset maker – that business is booming. That's where the future lies.'

Captain Baines pushed the coffee mug away. It slopped. The brass handles of the drawers glinted. He slammed his hand on the table again. 'That devil's bought an auxiliary steam engine for the *Cachalot*, but he won't stump up a reinforced hull for us or the *Queen*.' He was stabbing the table. 'That engine'll power him through the ice and leave us behind.'

Mr Travers said, 'We won't get trapped. We'll be out by September, you know that.'

Captain Baines thrust Mr Travers away, and hauled himself to his feet.

'But on the other hand, we jest might not, with that bastard. Out of my way, I'll have to tell the men.' He shrugged and straightened his jacket.

Irene spoke, her voice strained, 'I am the moral owner of the *Wendham*. It is my duty to tell the men.'

Captain Baines stared down at the table. 'Nope, it's my duty, missy, as captain of this blubber boat.' His tone was final, but now he continued gently, 'Mr Travers is right. Get out. Forget us, forget that devil. Make a life.'

She stared again at the watch, then replaced it on the table. 'Barratt won't relinquish the lease, so I'll write again and go at the end of the next trip. I'm not needed, you see. Martha writes to say she's safe, on the top floor again, looking after the new baby. The tenants can wait for a few years. If a woman goes to the Arctic, won't the men feel reassured, especially if we can promise them a lay? Though next time we must deliver that promise.'

Sinclair, Travers and Captain Baines looked at one another. Mr Travers rubbed his forehead. She cut in, her voice insistent. 'Will they come, if I go?'

Captain Baines shook his head, 'Won't make a jot of difference.' But he didn't meet her eyes as he said it.

She turned to Mr Travers, her voice soft. 'You'll tell me the truth.' It wasn't a question and now she stared into his eyes, but he glanced away, rubbing his forehead, until at last he said, 'Yes, ma'am, they'd gain confidence from that.' He raised his eyes to hers, and they insisted, Don't come. Be safe.

She turned to Captain Baines. 'Then that's what we will do. After all, it's only a few months.'

Captain Baines told the crew the news within the next half hour, and all but Arnie stayed, for the men collected together what money they had and sent him on his way. 'For the Arctic is no place for a cabin boy,' Captain Baines growled.

That night she tossed and turned though it wasn't for fear of Jack who was in New York working a baleen deal, or even because of the fierce joy she had allowed herself at the thought that she would be with Mr Travers for a few more precious months. No, it was none of these, it was because of the plan she was trying to formulate to ensure that the Arctic voyage would be as safe for her people as possible. In the early hours she despaired but by dawn she knew what she must do.

She dressed, stepping into her corset, pulling the front-opening laces tighter than they'd been for years.

She stepped into her hoops, lowered the skirt over her head and the bodice. She examined herself in front of the mirror. The skirt was too short. She undressed, drew thread from her needle box, ripped down the hem. It was faded. Never mind. She sewed the new hem. She had aired the satin once a month at Captain Baines's insistence and there was at least no mould.

Again she dressed, smoothing the material, adjusting her hair in the looking glass, seeing the dark shadows beneath her eyes. 'Well, what d'you expect after a sleepless night?' she asked herself, pinching her cheeks to give herself colour.

She appeared on deck, struggling to keep the wind from lifting her skirt, whilst clasping her hat to her head. The men stopped their work, removed their hats. Arnie gaped, Sinclair nodded approvingly. She called him over, murmuring to him. He thought long and hard, then answered her quietly.

She called to Captain Baines, 'I'm going ashore now. I may be a little while. Not that that is any business of yours.'

Captain Baines nodded, recognizing the need to maintain the pretence, though he had to ask, 'But where?'

She ignored him and started down the gangplank. Mr Travers stood on the quay, one foot on the gangplank, his eyes never leaving her, hers never leaving his.

He escorted her into the carriage. He spoke, raising his voice over the sound of the horses' hooves, 'Where are you going, ma'am?'

'Duty. It's called duty, and you must leave me free to do it. We are enemies, remember. Make sure everyone remembers. I am to be treated with obvious dislike when I return.'

'But . . .' He clutched her arm.

She shouted, 'Unhand me this minute.'

Harry recoiled. She wanted to explain but no, it was better this way. 'Drive on,' she shouted to the coachman.

Once in Union Street she found a jeweller and sold her hatpin and Mr Travers's watch, buying one that was much cheaper and a common necklace, with blue glass instead of sapphires. Then took a cab to the *Cachalot*'s wharf.

As she descended from the coach and walked towards her husband's ship Irene slowed, then set her jaw and increased her pace. She strode up the gangplank to be met by Mr Osborne, the first mate, his arms crossed across his chest, barring her entry to the deck.

'Out of my way,' she said, her voice hard and fierce.

'Mr Prior is not here. I'm in charge and ain't received orders to let you on.'

She tapped her foot. 'I've come for the clothes Jack Prior failed to send in the trunk when I was transferred to that damn tub, the *Wendham*. This is my only decent outfit, and while I'm in port I'll need to uphold my position as Mr Prior's wife, or you'll all be even more of a laughing stock.'

He thrust his face into hers, 'What d'ya mean by that?'

'Do you tell the time by the sun now, Mr Osborne?' She dug into her reticule, and brought out a cheap fob watch. 'Here, I don't like that Travers to get anything over on anyone. He's still got yours, this was all I could afford. Now, out of my way.'

He took the watch, and stood to one side. She stormed across the deck, up onto the quarterdeck, down the companionway and into the transom cabin, reaching down into the pocket which had been sewn into the back of the sofa, digging out the key.

Her heart was beating rapidly. She approached the sleeping cabin, opened the door, stared in. She could smell him, his tobacco, his hair oil and her courage fled, but then she breathed deeply. There, the essence of the man was in her lungs. She expelled her breath. But now it was out, and it had not hurt her.

But she shook as she approached the safe and unlocked it. Inside were wooden boxes, his log, letters. She scanned through these, careful not to blow the dust off, careful to note in what order they had been placed.

She dragged out box after box. His pistols were in one, a decanter in another. Hairbrushes in another. Right at the back was her mother's box, the one her uncle had brought to the lodging house.

For a moment her breath caught in her throat. If only . . .

No, no time for that. She heard the sound of seamen above her, muffled curses. She dragged out the box, careful not to disturb the dust on its surface. She opened it, removed the necklace and earrings which she dropped into her reticule before putting those she had bought in the jeweller's in the box. He wouldn't know what a good one looked like. They would do until he tried to trade them in. But she wouldn't think of that, for then he would probably kill her.

She carefully shut the lid, replaced the box exactly where it had been, then the others, then the letters and the log. She tried to ease the safe door shut but the catch clicked loudly. She froze, stared at the ceiling, then at the door. No-one came.

She opened her trunk, heaped clothes onto the floor, choosing a few which she hung over her arm. With shaking hands she replaced the key in the pocket of the sofa, and hurried up the companionway, forcing herself to slow down as she left the steps of the quarterdeck and approached Mr Osborne, who sneered, 'I'd have thought an owner's wife would have crew to carry a trunk, not go along the quay like a washerwoman.'

She wanted to push him into the oil-stained sea. Instead she said, 'Looking like a washerwoman is preferable to any of the *Wendham*'s crew laying hands on my belongings, even a trunk. No, I preferred to come alone.'

She swept past him, down the gangplank, back towards the *Wendham*. It was true, for if Jack ever discovered the loss, he must know it was she alone who had taken it.

Sinclair was waiting at the foot of the gangplank. He asked anxiously, 'Was I right?' She said, 'Yes, it was a good guess. I'll meet you outside the captain's cabin. No-one must see you touch anything of mine.' Sinclair flashed a look down the quay. He said, 'Osborne's watching.'

'I know, follow me up on deck, shake your fist at my back.' Sinclair did so.

Outside the cabin she passed over the clothes, then rushed ashore again. Osborne had gone. She hurried to the refitters.

On deck Harry Travers moved to the gangplank. Sinclair barred his way. 'Leave her. For God's sake, if you care for her, leave her.'

Harry stared at him and murmured, 'You know she's my life.'

'Aye, so leave her be.'

They waited on deck, Travers, Sinclair and Baines, pacing, worrying, with Sinclair the only one to understand. At last she reappeared out of the dusk, pale and exhausted, and walked slowly up the gangplank. Again Travers started towards her. Captain Baines put out his hand. 'Leave her be, lad. Don't spoil nothing for her. She don't want us involved, so respect that wish.'

But his voice was tense, and he was at her side as she reached the top of the gangplank, and it was Captain Baines's hand surreptitiously under her arm, steadying her onto the deck, while Harry Travers wanted to sweep him aside, and lift her, hold her close, brush the hair from her eyes.

She shouted at Captain Baines, 'How dare you touch me?' She swept up the quarterdeck and to the companionway. They saw her stagger, collect herself, begin her descent. Only then did they move, and halfway down the companionway it was Travers who slipped his arm around her, taking her weight, wanting to hold her like this for ever, wanting to protect her, guard her, love her, send her far from here, if it would make her safe.

She told them in the transom cabin, sitting on the sofa, sipping the brandy they gave her, that she had taken the necklace to the refitters. 'In exchange he will reinforce the hulls of both the *Wendham* and *Queen of the Isles*. Not as much as they should be, but some. In

193

addition there will be warm clothes delivered to both ships.'

Mr Travers said into the silence that followed, 'You should have used that money to go to Wendham. It would have bought back the lease.' He could barely speak.

She smiled though there was exhaustion in every line of her face. 'This isn't the time.'

'You could have gone to Wendham,' he shouted again.

Captain Baines gripped his arm. 'Steady, leave her be. She's a mind of her own.' But his voice was tremulous.

Irene rose, handing her glass to Sinclair. 'I'm tired. I'm going to my cabin.'

She left. Mr Travers stared after her, then said to Sinclair and Captain Baines, 'She should have gone to Wendham.'

Sinclair and Captain Baines looked at one another, then Sinclair said, 'She's the woman you made her. She's the woman she was meant to be. We'll just have to try to keep her safe, for if Jack Prior discovers what she's done, God help her.'

CHAPTER TEN

It was early June when the lookout sighted Cape Farewell beyond which the icy wastes of the Arctic beckoned. At noon Captain Baines ordered all the crew, even the lookouts, to the waist and there Sinclair broke out the grog, and after prayers everyone toasted the success of the voyage, though in addition Mr Travers, Captain Baines, Irene and Sinclair silently acknowledged their relief that the theft had not been discovered.

Neither had Jack Prior summoned her to his ship, preferring instead to order her to remain aboard the *Wendham* during the discomfort of the refit. A refit he had stormed about in the cabin of the *Wendham* cursing at Captain Baines and Irene for setting the repairs against the expected lay from the Arctic trip, for that is what she had arranged for the refitter to say.

She had summoned her courage and stormed at Jack. 'Think of the insurance. No chance of that without reinforcement. Think of your standing in New Bedford if you allowed two of your ships to put to sea with no protection when you've modified the *Cachalot* to take an auxiliary and welded iron plates to the hull. We only have wood. It's just too humiliating and I should be allowed back on the *Cachalot*.' She'd flicked a disdainful hand at Captain Baines. 'It's an outrage that I'm to remain with this crew. It's an outrage that I had to beg the refitter to put the cost against lay which included my own.'

Her husband had sneered, snatching open the door.

195

'It's the thought of your outrage that'll keep me warm at night, Mrs Prior.'

Now, as they stood on the deck of the *Wendham*, she edged up to Captain Baines, whose face was still as drawn as it had been for the last two months. 'Everything will be fine. Trust me. I know. I feel it, your wife feels it too.'

Captain Baines smiled gently, 'Yes, I'm glad you came to the chapel with us.'

Irene agreed, 'Your wife is wonderful and just as I imagine a Parisian seamstress to be, such style, such beauty, and I can never thank her enough for sending me the dress she made for me.'

Captain Baines's smile was broad now, 'Mighty clever with her hands. She just kinda guessed your size from looking at ya.'

'I'll wear it on our return, at the meal she promised us before I leave for Wendham. Just think, by then you'll have money coming at you from all ways, because I have a written agreement from the refitter to allow us back the two thousand dollars when Jack delivers it from the lay, and deliver it he will for New Bedford will not forgive him if he doesn't. So pour another rum and let's drink to that as well. We have done everything possible, just think of that, and now we need you. You are the one who will bring us home. Go on, pour.'

He looked at her, as though he could not really see her, then around at his men, and at the *Queen* sailing on the ee, and the *Cachalot* to windward, then back at her, and it was as though he was slowly waking from a long sleep. He stood erect, doffed his hat, smiled and said, 'Now, that's an order I'll allow you to give.'

Once into the mouth of the Davis Strait they ran headlong into the ice draining out of the Arctic, and with it came the cooler wind. Irene pulled her cape around her, tugging the collar up, drawing the shawl close around her head as she briskly paced the decks in an effort to keep warm. 'He's looking better,' she murmured to Mr Travers as their paths crossed.

'Indeed he is, ma'am. It's done his heart good to see that ice come through the Strait. Means the inlets and sounds are breaking up as they should. And it's done him good to think that after this trip he need never sail with Prior again. But most of all it's done him good to hear you say we need him.'

They both smiled, though their eyes didn't meet.

They trailed along in Jack Prior's wake, though he was still only using sail. 'Saving his engine, as he should, as I would, for icing up,' Captain Baines grunted on the quarterdeck, sniffing the air. 'I can smell ice.'

Irene looked at Sinclair, and they both laughed. Irene said, 'You'd be foolish if you didn't, we're sailing through it.'

Captain Baines glowered, then laughed along with them, shrugging, 'Forgive an old man.'

Now they both groaned. 'Get his walking stick, Sinclair, and take over as captain.'

Even the helmsman laughed this time.

They steered for the east side of the Strait, where the warm current had opened a corridor of open water. It was here that the lookout called, 'Bl-o-o-w.'

The boats were lowered, the sails hoisted and the pod approached. It was here that she and Captain Baines watched as Mr Travers and all the *Wendham* boats were made to lie hove to whilst Jack Prior's boats attacked the pod. Only when they had finished and were towing back their whales were the *Wendham* boats waved forward. By then the pod had dispersed, and there was no point in them doing other than return to the whaler.

'God damn him,' breathed Captain Baines, his hands white from gripping his telescope.

Sinclair laughed ironically, 'I guess it's kind of re-assuring – the familiarity, I mean.' He handed out coffee which steamed in the crisp air as the *Wendham*'s boats were winched aboard.

Irene clutched the mug between both hands, sipping the drink which was already losing its warmth. There was no try-works on the decks, for the trip was too brief to allow time for rendering down, so she peered across at the *Cachalot* as the baleen was removed, and the whale 'peeled' and the blubber stored below. 'We are not going to be fragrant at the end of this trip,' she stated as Mr Travers joined them in the waist.

'I think you can rest assured on that,' he replied, laughing. 'But at least it's Jack Prior who'll have to put up with it the longest. Osborne hailed across as we came to the Strait that they're going on to Dundee before putting back to New Bedford. They're selling off the blubber for oil to the jute mills.'

She swung round, 'You mean we'll be making for New Bedford alone?'

Mr Travers nodded, 'Absolutely.' This time his eyes met hers, but broke away as Sinclair brought him coffee.

'So we can sell off our own baleen, our own blubber?' she asked after a pause, as she forced her mind to concentrate on this information, not on his hazel eyes, his long lashes.

'Only blubber,' Captain Baines nodded, handing his mug back to Sinclair, and wiping his mouth on the back of his hand. 'Not the baleen for Prior's set that up in New York but we can off-load the rest and make sure we get our proper lay and make good our losses. Yes, thank the Lord Almighty, we'll be able to do that.'

Now spirits were soaring and the lookouts were instructed by Captain Baines to look for the 'blink', that white reflection low in the sky indicating where the ice lay, for it was here that the bowheads normally were, not out in the current as the first pod had been.

After a week, the *Cachalot* got up a head of steam and drew away from them.

'He's shown who's master, so *he's* heading off, and more's the blessing,' Mr Travers crowed.

'He'll not do that. Not in the Arctic. He'll always be in sight. It's a code, you see. No, he must've seen the blink from up for'ard, and he's getting there first,' Captain Baines was searching the east.

Irene shuddered, and looked away. Always in sight.

As June became July the summer did not arrive as it should. Instead large icebergs drifted past, and fog fell, curtailing the hunt. Captain Baines had a man at the prow calling 'I-c-e,' and as long as the sound did not echo back, tension was light, but when it did, everyone counted as the man at the prow called again, for the shorter the wait, the nearer the iceberg.

Now no-one talked very much in the wardroom or the fo'c's'le. They all just shrank into their clothes, and dined on salt cod, potatoes, cheese, bread and a cup of tea or coffee before clambering into their berths to snatch a few hours' rest before the next watch. But they seldom slept, for they were waiting for the splintering crash as the hull drove into an iceberg.

At last the fog lifted, and with it the tension and the darkness of their mood; they caught whales again, Irene watched the crewmen separate the baleen from the jawbone of the giant heads, staring as the carcasses drifted away and the grey-white fulmars swooped, crying their greed, to feed on the carcass, until, satiated, they drifted lazily on the current, too full to fly, too full to call. Every little thing she noted down in her journal. Every minute, hour, day, brought her nearer to Wendham and the end of all this. And it was only Jack Prior's ship, always in sight, which made her glad.

By September they had drifted up into Melville Bay, at the top of Baffin Bay and the hold was as near full as dammit and each day Captain Baines eyed the *Cachalot* waiting for the signal to leave. 'Damn bay's shallow and ice gathers thickly holding fast to the bottom,' he said ten times a day.

'The channel between the shorefast ice and the middle pack is well open,' she comforted each time, though his anxiety was clawing at her too.

On fifteenth September, she stood beside him as he held his telescope to his eye, shading it against the freezing sunlight, searching the rigging of the *Cachalot* for the signal. There was nothing. He faced the prow, then called to Mr Travers on the quarterdeck, 'Tell me if the wind shifts, specially if it hails from the east.'

He went below. She continued to stare at the *Cachalot*. September. In two weeks it would be October, and they would have left. The *Cachalot* would head for Dundee, they would make for New Bedford. They would all depart.

The next day at dawn she clambered up the companionway, bleary with sleep, looking for Sinclair because the galley was deserted, drawing her cape around her. She had been woken by a cold denser than any she had ever known, and now she hurried, stepping onto the quarterdeck where the cold wind sliced her lungs, and made her cough.

The officers and crew were staring ahead at the dark sky, then up at the rigging, and when she followed their gaze she forgot the stench of the blubber and the galley, for the ice was thick on the glistening sails, and the rigging, and the deck. She followed their stares out to the thickening ice on the shoreside, to the narrowing channel, and she drew close to Mr Travers as Captain Baines ground out, 'He's got to turn. He's got to let us get out, the crazy fool, for the wind's from the east. It's been from the east all night.'

Mr Travers glanced at her, 'Can you get the galley going? We need something warm to drink.' He was shivering. 'Sinclair's got the fever. He's in the transom.'

She made coffee, thinking of the darkening sky, the

200

portent of a storm. Thinking of another storm, and it wasn't fear that made her hands tremble, it was longing. For here a storm would mean the closing of the ice. It would mean the capture of the *Wendham* until the thaw. Then Mr Justine called through the door, 'Damp the stove, ma'am.'

At that moment she heard the second mate call, 'It's the signal, sir. We can turn about. It's the withdrawal.' Irene stood quite still, ashamed that she could have hoped for something else. Ashamed at the disappointment which threatened to overwhelm her.

'Nearly too late, damn it,' Captain Baines groaned, and ordered all hands to the rigging. The sails were unfurled, storm sails rigged, and Irene carried coffee to the hurricane cabin through whipping snow. When she saw his face, so tense, so angry and bitter, she said, 'I'm sorry.'

The second mate nodded towards the sleet and snow which battered the fleet. 'It's your husband who's too late, not you, ma'am. For he surely is too late.' His face was as white as the snow which was piling the decks. But that wasn't what she had meant.

All day they ran before the storm, with the *Cachalot* overtaking them, steaming past, cutting through the rampaging seas which tumbled over the *Wendham*'s decks and rigging to turn into icicles before their eyes. 'We might still do it,' Mr Travers shouted into the wardroom at her.

By nightfall the storm had eased, but the ice was closing fast. Mr Travers said, as she joined them on the quarterdeck, 'There's no way we'll make it. If we're lucky we'll be trapped. If we're not we'll be crushed.'

'I'm sorry,' she murmured, staring blindly at the devastation.

Captain Baines shouted at his officers, 'Prepare to abandon ship. There's tents in the transom, and the fo'c's'le. Get all the supplies ready that you can.'

Irene jerked herself into action, shriven with guilt at

her earlier hopes, working alongside Sinclair, whose fever had subsided. 'Amazing, in't it?' he grinned. 'How death makes you feel better.' Irene couldn't smile.

Within two days the ice closed around the fleet, even round the *Cachalot*, out in front, but although the wind continued to blow, and the ice heaved, buckled, and closed in even tighter, it didn't break the groaning hull.

In all this time Captain Baines didn't sleep, didn't leave the quarterdeck, but his voice was strong as he ploughed across the deck again and again in hail and snow, checking the stations himself, cheering on his men, stooping into the fo'c's'le at the start of the third day, and saying calmly, 'Half rations from this moment. Could be we're stuck for a while.'

It was only Irene and Mr Travers who saw his face as he turned from his men, and it wasn't calm, it was distraught and desperate. As Irene turned away the rage and hatred she felt for her husband consumed her.

The next day the weather cleared, then blew up again, and as it did, the pack around the *Queen of the Isles* heaved, bucked. There was a grinding noise as the ice tore open her side, as the masts broke, and fell, as the sailors, all sixty of them, leapt onto the ice, and now screams were heard above the wind. In ten minutes the *Queen* was crushed, and all that remained were strewn splinters on the deathly white ice.

Irene watched as the men stumbled across to the *Wendham*, some helping others, some with a few clothes in their arms, some without, some with provisions, some not. How could she ever have wanted this? Now some of her hatred was for herself.

The second mate called, 'Look at the *Cachalot*.' They swung round. In the distance they could see the smoke from the steam funnel. They ran to the prow and watched as slowly, so slowly, the *Cachalot* moved away, signalling as it did so its intention to return, when it could, with aid. They stared, and the crew of *Queen of the Isles* stared too, then ran, trying to catch the *Cachalot*, but falling to the ice in exhaustion.

Captain Baines said, 'Get the ropes down, help them on board. Go and get those fools.' He pointed at the men who had collapsed in their headlong flight to catch Jack Prior's ship.

Irene watched until even the smoke could no longer be seen. Captain Baines came up behind her, 'He's right to go for help. He'll forge a path through to us, with a half crew aboard to take the *Queen*'s men, or be waiting for us at Davis Straits when the ice clears with provisions. We're his fleet, he wouldn't leave us.'

Mr Travers nodded, 'Yes, and until then we'll manage.'

'Quarter rations, now we've the *Queen*'s crew too,' Captain Baines barked to the second mate. 'Put a guard on the galley. Send a party to gather the wooden remains of the *Queen*.'

She asked, 'Couldn't he have taken both crews on board?'

Captain Baines said, 'Aye, but maybe he reckoned he could also go down himself, be crushed. Maybe.'

What none of them spoke of was the insurance Jack Prior had taken out on his ships, and insurance that negated any need for a master without human feelings to return.

Ten crewmen from the *Queen of the Isles* would not come on board. They had grabbed liquor from the store before abandoning ship, and all night long they sang, and danced. 'We must get them in,' Irene insisted. 'I'll go.' For guilt still gnawed.

The captain of the *Queen* shook his head, 'They're better dead, and by morning they will be. They're troublemakers.'

By morning they *were* dead, but so was the captain, from a heart attack, which Captain Baines said was due to grief, for the men were his crew, the *Queen* was his ship.

*　　*　　*

That night Irene came on deck, hugging her cloak to her, pacing in the face of the snow until Mr Travers came out of the hurricane shed, dragging her into its shelter, rubbing her hands, staring at them in the dim light of the oil lamp. 'Are you mad?' he asked quietly.

She stared at his hands rubbing hers, then at the light from the hurricane lamp striking his dark-brown hair, then back to his hands, so slim yet strong and now she gripped his fingers, forcing him to remain still. He lifted his head and she stared into his eyes and said, 'Yes, I think I am mad, for when the ice . . .' She stopped as the helmsman swung into the cabin, snatching away her hands as though burned, leaping to her feet, gathering her cloak about her as she stepped out into the wind, fighting her way to the companionway.

He stared after her, his hands still feeling the pressure of hers. The helmsman said, as he slapped his arms against his side, 'She must be fair desperate with fear, but she's sure covering it well. Poor woman.'

Harry Travers looked down at his hands. Yes, that was it. Fear. But in her eyes, for a moment, he thought he'd seen something else. He thought he'd seen love, and he thought he'd seen guilt, and all he wanted to do was to take her in his arms, and keep her safe.

In her cabin Irene lay beneath all the covers she could muster, feeling his hands, saying to herself, Fool, fool. Are you quite mad? Flushing at the memory of her hands gripping his, her words welling up, her need to tell him of her joy at their entrapment, of her guilt, for how could any decent person have prayed for this hell, how could love make you long . . . ?

But now she sat up, gripping her hair. 'No, not that. It can't be that. I am Mrs Prior. It is not love. It can't be love. It would only be death.' She shuddered. 'Yes, I'm Mrs Prior,' she whispered.

For the rest of the night she told herself that all this was a result of the cold, of fear and by dawn she knew that it was. Yes, she knew, she told herself again and again.

By November the cold was more intense and everyone on board was weaker from lack of food, lack of heat, lack of hope for still Jack had not returned. No-one dared to remain on deck for more than a few minutes at a time for fear of frostbite, and now they split the watches into twenty-minute periods. On the second day Irene insisted on taking her turn as fever spread through the ship.

As she stood in the hurricane shed, blowing on her hands, Mr Travers entered, the door swinging from his grasp as the wind took it, his breath white in the freezing air.

She spun round. He grabbed the door and man-handled it shut. 'I would rather be alone,' she insisted.

He shook his head. 'No. No-one takes a watch alone.' For the helmsman had been right, any woman would be frightened.

She sat, staring out into the darkness. He stood by the chart table, looking at the oil lamp, the charts, the ice coating the inside of the shed, the snow falling outside until the silence between them seemed almost tangible. Then he looked at her as she sat still staring out onto the deck and wanted to reach out and hold her, saying, Don't be frightened, I will always keep you safe. But how could he keep anyone safe when the ice was stronger than them all, and when he ached with weariness, with hunger?

He leaned against the wall, staring as she was, his mind searching for words of comfort, for something. But it was she who spoke. 'I remember the first day of snow at Wendham. It was always as though it was a newborn world, untouched except perhaps by the feet of birds, or foxes.'

He said, watching the snow gust across the quarter-deck, 'I remember the ice-hard ground of the farm I laboured on, and the cold snow on my hands, the warm breath of the beasts, and then the bursting into leaf of the trees with the coming of spring.' He turned to her, and she was staring at him, her eyes eager as though she was drinking in his words, and he knew that she was clutching at any image to remove herself from the present. He said, 'Tell me of your springs. Of your summers.'

She did, staring out at the snow again, conjuring up the warmth of a May morning, the gathering of armfuls of cow parsley, the lying down in the sweet-smelling hay, the drowning of the senses, the rustle of insects, the blue of the sky.

Now, as she finished, their eyes met and they smiled with their cracked lips. She said, her eyes on his, 'Tell me of your summers.'

She wanted to suck in every memory he had, everything she didn't yet know about him, for it kept the fear and weakness away, that's all. It just kept them away.

He spoke, his eyes still caught by hers, sucked in by hers, 'I remember going in the wagon. It was a Sunday School treat. They were good, they taught us everything, not just religion. My brothers went too, and my mother. Lots of other children. Lots of other wagons. We went to the meadow where the buttercups were high, where the skylarks were soaring. We drank ginger beer. It was warm. Sticky and warm. We ate pasties. Farmer's wife made them, together with the rector's wife. My mother was happy that day, really happy.' It was as though he couldn't get his breath, as though his blood was roaring in his ears, as though he was drowning in her eyes. Her lips were parted, she was leaning forward. He continued as though driven.

'We sang songs, we played in the long grass. I can remember crawling along, seeing the grass stretching above my head, smelling its sweetness, hearing the insects. Good man that farmer must have been, to let us do that. Must have ruined his haying.'

His voice trailed off, and with the ending of his words their gazes fell. There was a silence. The cold recaptured them.

She said at last, her voice low, correct. 'You really loved your mother?'

'I really loved my mother,' he repeated, his eyes fixed on the oil lamp.

'Tell me of your father.'

Harry Travers dug his hands in his pockets, hearing the howling wind, wanting to look at her again, wanting to say, 'I love you. Do you even know I exist?' He said at last, 'He was a good man too. Great belly laugh. Sometimes he'd laugh when we went under the bridges in the barge. It'd echo, then we'd all do it. "That crazy Travers family," the other bargees would say.'

Now she laughed, and it was as though the sun blazed on him, warming him and he bunched his hands in his pocket. Fool. Enjoy this moment. Forget everything else. Forget reality, and now his laugh rang out too and he folded his arms across his chest.

'Our neighbours would say – "That crazy Wendham family",' she said. Again they laughed, and on and on they talked, weaving sunlight and laughter and peace, until Mr Justine came to take over the watch with the cooper.

That night, though ice at the foot of Irene's bunk was an inch thick, it seemed warmer than it had ever been, and her dreams were full of joy and the taste of a ginger beer, and the scent of long grass, and she had every right to be privy to the past of her old friend. Of course she had.

In the morning the decks were covered with yet more ice. Frozen rigging rattled in the breeze, boards popped and snapped with the cold. Ink froze in the nibs. Lamp oil had to be thawed at the stoves before it would burn.

Captain Baines forbade Irene to go on deck, so she stayed in the transom with him, or nursed the crew, and Mr Travers nodded when he saw this. Yes, this was safer, then he asked himself what he meant – and wouldn't face the answer.

Lookouts continued to peer from the prow daily. No Jack Prior.

As Christmas Day dawned they all crammed into the fo'c's'le and sang carols, crouching over, trying to hug themselves into warmth, into a pretence of strength. Each person had to tell a tale. Tom told of the horses he had ridden, Mr Travers of the stale bread he had been sent to fetch from the baker, asking that it be cut with a hammy knife to give it flavour, Irene of the scent of honeysuckle on a warm summer evening; but as she lay in her berth that night it was not the scent of honeysuckle but of ham which threaded through her dreams and she woke, crying of hunger, and of something else which she pushed away.

January brought a further decrease in rations, and some of the men went down with blotched skin, bleeding gums, and loosening teeth. 'Scurvy,' Mr Travers whispered to Irene and Captain Baines in the privacy of the aft-cabin.

They could do nothing, for they had no fresh food, no fruit, no lime juice. That night Captain Baines collapsed with fever, as it had raged in so many others these past months. 'How could I ever have hoped for this?' she murmured as Mr Travers passed. He thought he had heard incorrectly.

The next day a crewman from the *Queen of the Isles* sought out Mr Travers and told him that they should be eating the blubber, that a Maori had once told him that the skin was as good for the body as a piece of mutton and an apple any day.

Each day they all ate a piece in the fo'c's'le alongside the crew as Captain Baines ordered, saying in his weakened voice, 'You lead by example. You just remember that, Mr Travers.'

For a while the health of everyone grew no worse, except for Captain Baines whose skin became more translucent, and whose body became more fragile until he could no longer leave his berth.

'He's slipping away,' Irene told the officers, but wouldn't look at any of them as she said it, for she couldn't bear the thought, any more than she could bear to see their thin gaunt faces, hear their voices which were faded and exhausted, just as the men's were, just as she was.

In January some of the crew caught a bear. Broth was made and lasted two days. Even Captain Baines took some. The cold became more intense.

The stoves could only be lit each morning, just long enough to cook the day's hot meal for they had so little fuel. Great care was taken every time, for if the ship were burned, they would have no shelter. Each day there were muted arguments between the officers as to whether they should take the stove onto the ice, but the wind was too great, and there was no energy for dissention.

Irene seldom went on deck but would sit in the transom with Captain Baines, who had taken the cabin at the beginning of the week so that the *Queen*'s officers could take his. They, in return, insisted he take all the extra blankets from the wardroom but still he grew weaker, the fever eating into him, the scurvy taking a hold too now, but it was more than that, Irene told herself as January drew to a close. It was the Arctic. It was the ice which she had half wanted.

The next evening she told Captain Baines, who half sat up and said, 'Don't you be so foolish. This weather was on its way, and why shouldn't you want it? You take what love you can, d'you hear? You take it. I'm old and I'm tired of the life, and I've a fever. T'ain't nothing you've done, so absolve yourself, d'you hear?'

'But I never spoke of love,' she protested quietly.

'I'm not a fool,' he said, before falling back on his pillows.

For hour after hour she ministered to him, calling Sinclair to her side and Mr Travers, for Captain Baines had not spoken again, but had burned with fever, his breath rasping, his lungs struggling. They took turn and turn about, insisting that Irene sleep as well. She returned at dawn, trying to hurry to his bedside but there was no strength left. She carried a fresh cloth in her hand. Sinclair looked from her to Mr Travers, then left to stoke the galley. She said, 'He's not dead?'

Mr Travers stared at her, then at Captain Baines, confusion in his eyes. He shook his head as though to clear it, then ran his hand through his hair. He said quietly, 'No, not yet.'

Irene sank on her knees, and felt Captain Baines's pulse. It was so faint, so erratic. She swung round to Mr Travers who was staring at her. She asked, 'Has he come round at all? Are there any good signs? What is the matter with you?' She was panting with the effort of so much speech.

Mr Travers hesitated, 'He spoke, but he's no better.' His eyes never left her face. It was as though he was searching for something, reaching deep into her head, but it was so cold, she was so tired. She turned from him as Captain Baines groaned.

Mr Travers said, 'I have the crew to see to.' She heard the door close.

Irene took Captain Baines's hand, kissed it, saying, 'Come on, don't leave us now. Just think of Antoinette, of your children. Keep fighting.'

He opened his eyes a fraction, squeezed her hand weakly, muttering, 'D'ya hear me? D'ya hear me?'

She said, 'Yes, I hear you.' Though she didn't understand. She repeated, 'Yes, my dear, I hear you.' He closed his eyes. All around the ship she knew there would be muffled voices, the rattle of the rigging, the howling wind, but in here there was just the struggle for breath, a great brave struggle for breath, for life, a struggle that was waning, even as she looked. Within the hour Captain Baines was dead, but still she sat holding his hand to her face until her calls brought Sinclair to her.

She didn't weep then, nor when they wrapped his body in canvas and stored it in the hold, alongside the stinking blubber, to await burial when the ice melted, for she was too numb, too sad, too tired, too cold, too dead.

Neither did she weep that night, as she lay alone in her aft-cabin wearing the layers of clothing they all wore day and night, feeling the weight of blankets on the top. Blankets which increasingly failed to keep the cold from her body. Blankets which seemed heavier each day as her strength depleted.

She listened to the creaking, the snapping, knowing that again tonight the temperature was further down than ever, feeling glad suddenly that Captain Baines was out of it. Hour after hour she shivered, wanting to grieve but still she was too numb, too tired, too alone.

At midnight she heard a tapping on the door. She called faintly, 'Yes.'

Mr Travers opened it, stood there, a blanket over his shoulders. He closed the door behind him, leaning back against it, staring at her, hearing again that cracked and weary voice of his beloved captain saying, 'Love her, as she loves you. D'y hear?' That was all, nothing else. Was it true? It had to be true.

He stared at this woman, examining her thin white face, her split lips trembling with cold, her sunken eyes. 'I love you,' he said quite clearly. 'I love you. Please say you love me. He said you did. My heart's breaking, you see, for a good man's just died, and I can't grieve alone, and I must hold you, or I'll die too.' He stared at

211

her, remembering the feel of her as he helped her down the companionway, her eyes which had drunk in his words of winter, spring and summer, and the water which had rushed all around them so long ago but had been unable to tear their eyes from one another. 'I love you,' he whispered again. 'I shall always love you.'

She stared, his faint voice drumming in her head, grasping at the words which floated past, then back, swirling round and round now, as his eyes held hers, she was gathering them to her, clutching them, examining them, feeling the heat of their meaning, of their love, and slowly in this desperate cold she understood Captain Baines's last whispered words and silently said, Yes, I hear you, as she tried to lift her arm towards Harry Travers whose eyes never left hers as he crossed the tiny cabin to stand by her bed, and her joy gave her strength.

'At last,' she whispered. 'At last.'

He stooped lifting the blankets, laying down beside her, holding her gently, pressing his face to hers, brushing her forehead with his lips, looking deep into her eyes.

'I love you,' she murmured. 'And I loved that wonderful old man almost as much as my own father.' Now they held one another as though they would never let go, their tears mingling. She brushed his hair away from his forehead. He brushed hers away from her cheek. The moisture turned to frost on the pillow. He pulled a blanket over their heads. For a while it seemed warmer.

He murmured, 'We have as long as the winter lasts, Irene.'

She kissed his forehead, his cheeks, his eyes, his lips, all salty cold and never had anything been as sweet and as pure. 'I know.'

For a long time they just lay together, and then he stirred, kissed her eyes and said gently, 'We can't stay here together, like this. You are the owner. I am the leader of the men now. It can't be.'

She whispered, 'I know.'

'But it's too cold for you to stay alone,' Harry's voice seemed stronger, more powerful. 'You'll come and sleep with us. You need body warmth. We've been talking and all agree. We'll take what bedding you have – it's a question of survival, my love.'

She smiled at him, ran her fingers round his mouth, traced every line on his face. 'For such a long time I've merely survived. Now, until the thaw, I shall live.'

She lay that night between Harry Travers and Mr Justine and the sounds of the hull, and the rattling of the rigging and the howl of the wind were as sweet as any lullaby, and though the grief still remained, beside it was contentment, and a soaring joy.

The pattern was repeated night after night as the weeks progressed and more and more they found fleeting moments to cling together, just being as though one, but never knowing one another's bodies, for now was not the time. There never would be a time, for she was Mrs Prior. But for both of them it was enough that their souls had met and mingled. That, for now, every second, waking or sleeping, they knew the other was near, that the truth was known between them, and that love would endure, no matter what.

Day after day it seemed that frost and ice had never been more beautiful, that the sun had never been as bright, that the past which they conjured up as they checked the stations on the ship had never been as vivid, that their laughter had never been as profound, that their exhaustion never as manageable.

And how could it be that they never noticed how beautiful the wardroom was as they sat and talked with the officers over the meagre rations, she one end as owner, he the other as temporary captain of the *Wendham*?

213

How could it be that they had not realized how effortless it could be to care for the men? How could it be that they had not known how glorious it would be to lie together for a few precious minutes every evening on her berth and speak of their love, but never of their future?

Day after glorious day, as the temperature continued to plummet, she tended those that were ill, whilst he allocated supplies and instructed his officers, and daily they grew in one another's estimation, and in the estimation of the crew who agreed that never did an owner like Jack Prior deserve such a wife or captain.

By mid-March the current began tugging, and the ice began breaking up, and as they entered the third week of the month she knew the winter was over, and there was no longer any need for bodily warmth and despair tore at her, and so that night she lay awake in the officers' cabin, feeling him against her, evading sleep, storing away heaven, knowing it would have to last a lifetime.

Harry too lay awake, his breath lifting her hair. As dawn broke, he moved, kissed her hair and the nape of her neck. She pressed back against him and he wanted to hold her, love her, know her, sink his mouth onto hers, himself onto and in her. She reached out, touched his hand, then lay still again.

As morning progressed they stood at the waist, staring across at the water gnawing away at the edge of the ice, feeling the warmer wind lifting their hair. 'It's time,' Harry said.

'I know.' They nodded to one another, and that night Irene returned to her cabin, thanking Sinclair as he placed the bedding on her berth, following him with her eyes as he left the room. She looked at Harry as he stood in the entrance, longing to say, Stay. Knowing he would not, could not. He opened the door, longing to hear her call but knowing it was impossible, for she was Mrs Prior.

Neither slept for they could not cast aside the sense of emptiness and loss, until they grasped the fact that their love was immutable, was always with them, would be with them beyond the grave, and in that there was peace, an amazing peace. 'It's enough,' Harry told himself in the captain's cabin.

'It's enough,' Irene murmured as at last she slept.

They half believed it.

At last, the ice released its grip, splitting apart, the sun glinting on the wet surface of the ice pack as it did so. Before they sailed, Mr Travers, as acting captain, said prayers over the shrouded bodies of Captain Baines, and the other fifteen crewmen who had died during the long hard winter, committing them to the deep, and Irene's regrets were such that she felt she would never recover.

Throughout the return voyage she, Mr Travers and Sinclair seldom strayed from one another, staring towards the Davis Straits, talking of the man they had loved, the months they had shared. Never talking of the man they hated, the man who hadn't come, never voicing the thought that was in all their heads; is he dead? Please say he's dead, crushed, frozen, gone from our lives, giving us freedom, letting us live. Letting me take Harry to Wendham.

At the entrance to the Straits their plea was denied, for there, lying hove to, was the *Cachalot*. It was at this point that Mr Travers turned to her, and said, 'Never will I stop loving you.'

'Nor I you.'

The *Cachalot* was closer, so much closer. She said, 'Now God help us both to bear this.'

Mr Travers blindly made for the quarterdeck. Jack Prior would have offloaded in Dundee in the long months they had been marooned. They could not offload in New Bedford as they had hoped. They were trapped. He and Irene were trapped, by convention, by every breath that Jack Prior drew and now rage fought with despair and the peace evaporated.

CHAPTER ELEVEN

Irene stood again on the hated *Cachalot*'s quarterdeck staring down the companionway. She turned, lifted her head to scan the horizon, seeing the icebergs drifting in the distance, then the mast of Harry's boat alongside, waiting with Sinclair amongst the crew. 'Shout and I'll come. I'll protect you. Shout and I'll kill him,' Harry had said when the message came, barring her way from the transom until she had touched his face. 'The winter's over,' she'd murmured.

She ducked down the companionway steps, forcing herself on. She would not show fear but would enter Jack Prior's transom cabin with her head erect, just as any master's wife, upon answering his summons, then she'd return to the *Wendham*, to Harry, to her sanctuary – for that was enough.

She stopped as a great swirling ache caught her. She could not go on. She must. Another step, another. Now she was outside the door.

She drew a deep breath, feeling the wallowing of the ship, hearing the creaks and groans but nothing from inside the cabin. She read again Jack's note. *Please attend me in the transom cabin.*

Please, he'd said please. Did he want her back? Oh God. Sinclair had said, as he joined them in the cabin, 'At least he hasn't found out about the necklace or he'd be raging.' She and Harry had looked at one another, surprise pushing aside their misery. They'd forgotten the necklace.

She knocked. 'Come,' he called.

She entered. He was lolling back on the sofa, one

arm along its arm, the other along the back, one leg crooked up on the cushions, the other stretched out. She stopped just short of his foot. His boot gleamed in spite of the salt and damp.

His hair was still so thick, his bulk so great, the hairs on his tapping fingers so coarse and his eyes still so unfathomable, so dead and black. Somehow she'd almost forgotten what he looked like but not how much she hated him. No, never that.

He said, 'We're going on to the Azores, where the *Wendham*'ll be fitted up with a try-works and any damage repaired.'

She found her voice, 'Azores?' How could they flee from the Azores?

He shrugged, still tapping, still sprawling. 'There's civil war in America. I'm not taking my fleet into any of their ports. Don't want them taken and sunk to create a blockade for southern ports. No, I don't want that, do I, Mrs Prior?'

She stared. War? How . . . ? What . . . ? She grappled with the shock, then there was a pause, like the calmness of the eye of the storm, then her heart surged like the huge waves they had once endured. War! Even better. He'd have to put into a British port with the *Wendham*'s stinking blubber and baleen, as the Priors had done before in time of war. Once there she could escape, reach Wendham. Harry could come. Damn any scandal. Damn it to hell.

He said, 'England's hungry for baleen, Dundee's still after the oil. I'm sending your baleen there.' Her heart surged higher still. He continued, 'We'll render down the blubber in my try-works. In a couple of years the war'll be over and I'll take back the load to New Bedford. War makes money for people. Those people'll want oil and baleen and they'll have the money to pay good prices. I'll be able to buy one of them mansions in New Bedford.'

Her heart plummeted. She watched the tapping

finger, whilst he continued to stare at her. She could contain herself no longer and blurted out, 'Why not Britain, now?'

The tapping stopped and she cursed herself for the fool she was as he laughed that laugh, leaning back, roaring it to the ceiling, then slapping his knee. 'Why not indeed, Mrs Prior.' He straightened as he stared into her eyes and now she saw they were vibrant with hate and rage and flinched.

He put his hands behind his head as he said softly, 'Well, let me tell you why. It's because there is another whaler waiting for us in the Azores, ordered on my way to Dundee. A whaler – the *Island Queen* – with an auxiliary bought with a loan against the insurance money.'

She stared, 'You were so sure we'd die?'

He laughed again. 'I hoped Mrs Prior, I most sincerely hoped but it was the wrong ship that went, for it should have been yours that was crushed and sunk, with you in it.'

She stared at him for he was only repeating what she had hoped for him. Dear God, what had she become? He put his arms down, running one along the arm of the sofa, resting the other along the back. He said, 'Nothing to say to me?'

She murmured, 'Captain Baines is dead.'

He nodded. 'I know, Osborne told me that when he returned from taking you my summons. Never fear, my dear wife, I'll recover my debt from his lay, now I know it'll not be taken by the shipwright.' He slipped his hand down behind the sofa cushion and brought up the necklace.

He laughed again and she could not move, she could barely breathe. He hurled it at her. It struck her breast and fell to the floor. He said, 'You came in here, you took the key, you took the jewellery. Let me just correct that. You s-t-o-l-e,' he spelt the word out, 'the jewellery. Had you forgotten that everything you have is mine?'

His voice was deep, slow, level. His face was still, his eyes were alive. Sparkling.

She backed now, feeling for the door, wanting to call out for Harry. But no, she mustn't. He must be safe. She stopped, held out her hands, 'Forgive me, Jack. I didn't want to die. Baines was an old fool, twittering on about ice. That convict, and that Sinclair were laughing. I didn't want to die with them. You wouldn't have me back on your ship. I begged, didn't I?'

He was rising from the sofa. He was coming towards her. She put up her hands. He said, 'Still the same spoilt Irene, the Irene who thinks of no-one but herself. You crossed me.' He dropped his voice to a whisper as he reached for her, and now his eyes were dancing, and his face was working, and as exultant as when he plunged the lance into the whale.

His hand closed on her hair. 'You crossed me,' he hissed.

That night she lay on her bunk in the *Wendham*'s aft-cabin, cold from the water she had sluiced again and again over her body. The floor was still wet with it. She saw her dress, the one that Jack had ripped. She staggered to it, sank to the floor, soaking up the seawater, rubbing, rubbing at the boards. She knocked over the bowl and the jug. It broke. She picked up the pieces and hurled them at the walls. She tore up the dress, ripping it into smaller and smaller pieces.

Harry knocked on the door. 'Irene, Irene.'

She called, 'Leave me. Leave me.'

Harry Travers didn't leave. He stood outside listening, and all he could hear was Irene saying again and again, 'I hate him. I hate him.' He couldn't rid himself of the sight of her as she had been lowered by chair into the boat, her eyes wild, her face bruised, her cloak wrapped tightly around her, her movements stiff and awkward.

He'd yelled for the crew to row like madmen back to

the *Wendham*, but his eyes had not left her once, and hers had not left the horizon. Sinclair had moved to smooth back her hair beneath the cape. She'd knocked his hand away, 'He could be watching.'

'It's dark. He can't see. For the love of God, Irene. I'll kill him,' Harry had said.

'There's a moon,' she replied. 'You'll do nothing, Mr Travers. The winter is over.'

They'd reached the *Wendham*. Irene spoke. 'The chair,' she'd panted. 'I need the chair.'

Harry had moved to help. 'No,' she whispered. 'Don't help. He could be looking.'

He'd watched helplessly as she stumbled into the chair.

Once off the quarterdeck and descending the companionway he'd taken hold of Irene, gently. She'd leaned against him, the cape still clutched around her. He'd lifted her, carried her towards the captain's cabin. 'No,' she'd gasped. 'My own room. Please, my own room.'

'This should be yours.'

She'd closed her eyes, leaned on his shoulder for a moment, sinking into the comfort of the body which had warmed her in the cold. 'My own room, where we lay together. You are now captain. That is *your* cabin. It is a fitting punishment to have a convict wielding power over a wife who stole a necklace.' Her laugh was gentle for at least she'd kept him safe.

Now Harry Travers leaned his forehead on the door and called again, 'Irene. Please, let someone help you.' For her cape had fallen open as he'd put her to the ground in the aft-cabin, revealing her ripped dress. She'd looked at him. 'He has a right. He is my husband. He owns me.' She'd closed the door, then called for water. He'd shouted, 'Let me kill him.'

'No, I will get away, that's all. His kind don't die without dragging everyone down. No, do you hear? I won't have you at risk and what is more, I won't be as he is, and neither will you.'

He knocked again now. 'Let someone help.'

She didn't answer him, but just kept repeating, 'I hate him.'

They reached the Azores and it was almost two months before they left, with all damage repaired and all cargo sold to a returning blubber boat. 'You'll stay aboard and you'll hide yourself from my sight,' Jack Prior had instructed her on the *Wendham*'s arrival.

She'd lain on her bunk, trying to wipe away the memory of him, the taste of his mouth, the feel of his body, his fists, and the sight of his face as he lunged. She'd invoked Wendham House, but not Harry, for he and his love didn't belong in her sordid world.

Eventually she rose and wrote in her journal of her plans for the garden, and the house, and talked to Harry, sitting opposite him in the wardroom, making him promise to do nothing, for death was not the answer. There was no answer. They both knew that.

As the Azores faded from sight she could still not forget the taste of Jack's mouth and it drove all wish for food from her, all sleep, all energy though she made herself struggle to concentrate on the officers' plans to give a percentage from their own lay to Mrs Baines, and to their plans to give a percentage to Irene using a false crew member's name.

In the evenings she sat in the transom cabin with Mr Travers, as she had done with Captain Baines, and he read the paper as Captain Baines had done, for he felt it brought her peace, and it did, somehow it did.

They voyaged to Cape Verde and still Irene could not bear to eat, and her breasts became tender and increasingly she could not throw out of her mind Mrs Meldrew's words on the time of the month to avoid marital duties until one evening, when the *Wendham* was running before heavy seas and Harry Travers was on deck, she checked back through her journal, reading slowly, not wanting to see the proof, not wanting to make the calculations, slamming the book shut, hunching over, pushing it away. As though from a distance she heard the orders for furling the sails, raising the storm sail and wondered how the world could go on existing whilst this *thing* was inside, this thing that was forced there by *him*.

Sinclair knocked. 'Douse the lamp, wind's rising.' She did so, and sat in the dark kneading her stomach, sweat-drenched and panic-stricken. She rose, rushing up on deck, welcoming the violence of the elements against her.

Mr Justine called, 'Get below, ma'am. You'll catch your death.' Rain poured down his startled young face. He glanced back at Harry in the hurricane cabin for support. She retreated, pacing the cabin in the darkness, letting the jerk and slide of the ship take her, throw her to the ground, tumble her across the floor, thinking, all the time thinking, pushing back the rising panic, the great waves which threatened to drown her.

Violent activity, that was what Mrs Meldrew had said.

All night she tumbled with the storm, but in the morning she was tired, bruised and that was all.

She drank tea in the wardroom. 'You fell?' Mr Travers asked, staring at the bruise on her forehead.

'The squall caught me unawares, Mr Travers,' she said quietly.

Forgive me, he wanted to say. I would have kept the sea like glass if I could. Instead he murmured, 'Caught a few others too, I'm afraid. They're in the fo'c's'le and in need of a bit of patching up.'

She ministered to them then paced the quarterdeck, watching the crew at their tasks, wanting to scrub the decks with them, wanting to climb the rigging and then fall, wanting to feel the pain that meant her body was her own again, free of Jack Prior's taint.

With each day she grew more desperate, and in her cabin she jumped from her bunk when Mr Travers was on deck, relishing the jolt. She drank salt water, wanting the retching to strain her, but still *it* clung to its darkness as it had been doing for the last three and a half months.

She wouldn't sleep, for exhaustion was bad for expectant mothers, or so her mother had always said. Instead she paced her cabin, shoeless so as not to alert Harry, so as not to hear his voice at her door, for what would he say? Would he stop her? For he was a good man, not wicked like her.

In the evening in the transom cabin she sewed, dragging the pieces of damaged sail onto her knee, making jackets for the men, forcing the needle through several layers, straining, always straining.

In August Harry, unable to bear it any longer, said, 'Do you have to work like this?'

She threw down the jacket and stormed across to him, 'You sew then, instead of reading that stupid newspaper.' She snatched the newspaper from him and tore it into strips, throwing it at his feet, rushing from the room, running up the companionway onto the quarterdeck, where she paced backwards and forwards, longing for a storm which would hurl her against a stanchion, longing for a whale they could flense, one that would make the deck greasy, unstable.

Mr Travers stared at the pieces of newspaper, hearing the weakness of her voice, hating Jack Prior for the fear he induced in his wife, hating her for not letting him kill the brute, hating himself for not doing something. He rose, and rushed up the companionway.

She heard him come to the quarterdeck, felt him grip her arm, turn her about. 'You must rest.' His face was close to hers. 'I know it's difficult, being in this position.'

She stared at him. How could he know?

He went on, 'But the *Cachalot* won't be there for ever. I know he said we mustn't run before him and so be out of sight, but when we've some oil and baleen in the hold I'll run before the next storm to the nearest put-down point. I'll sell the oil. You must go home. I can't stand to see you so desperate. Somehow I'll stop him following. Somehow I'll come and find you. Somehow we'll be together.'

She stared at him, studying his eyes, his hair which still flopped across his forehead, his high cheek-bones, his fine lips. I can only go if I rid myself of my burden, she said silently, for this child is a Prior. This child will take my freedom from me. This child will make me a prisoner to duty. It will dictate that I stay.

She turned from him and stared out to sea. For once this thing was born *it* would have no life as the child of a runaway wife, a wife living with or without her lover. None of them would have a life, always fleeing, always ostracized until the day Jack found them, as he had found his mother, and then he would take sole custody as was his right and mould this child to his likeness. Yes, her duty would dictate that she stayed, to prevent this. Oh God, Harry. I'm the person you made me.

The sea was building as the wind rose, and with it her desperation.

Still it clung on, and more – moved within her – so each day now she summoned up its father's brutality, its father's hatred, and that kept her strong, pushed aside her disgust at herself, her guilt and she paced, jumped, forced sleep from her and despaired.

When they sighted a whale and the call went up, 'Bl-o-o-w,' she begged to go out in the first mate, Mr Morden's, boat, on the aft-oar.

Mr Travers shook his head, 'Of course not.'

She'd stared at him. 'If you have any sense of love for me at all you will let me go.'

'Why?' he begged, standing on the quarterdeck, his eyes scanning the crews piling into the boats, then coming back to her, then off out to sea again. 'Why?'

'Because of Jack,' she shouted, flinging her arm towards the *Cachalot*. 'I just want to. I want to feel strong again. I want him to see he hasn't beaten me.'

Mr Travers stared at her, then again shook his head.

She waited while they caught the whale, towed it back, and then the flensing began. She slipped on the greased decks, she hauled on the windlass, she minced and now she couldn't see for the tears that were streaming down her cheeks for there was no pain. 'No pain,' she muttered. 'No pain.'

She rushed to the windlass again and hauled on the handle, pushing a crewman aside as he tried to take her place. 'No pain,' she grunted. 'No pain.' Her hair flew about wildly, her voice became louder and louder. Harry Travers saw her at last from the quarterdeck. He shouted at Sinclair and pointed, then left the deck himself, running down the steps, shouting, 'Irene, are you mad? What are you doing?'

There were hands tearing at her now. She fought them. They came again out of the stench, the smoke, the glare of the furnace. She slipped and fell on the grease, and forced herself to her knees, hitting out at the hands, and the voices, and the faces that were grease-smeared, blood-smeared. 'No pain,' she shrieked. 'I have no pain.'

Then she sank to the deck as Sinclair and Mr Travers reached her. 'I have no pain,' she whispered, and at last Harry Travers understood.

Harry helped her to the captain's cabin, washing her, insisting that she use his cabin from now on. 'You need the comfort,' he said.

He positioned Sinclair by her bedside until the flensing was completed. With the dawn he sent Sinclair for rest, and handed her coffee, smiling gently, hiding his rage at Jack, his longing for this child to have been his, his envy, his burning gut-wrenching envy, and his fear.

She stared at him as she cradled the mug in her hand, forcing down the nausea which still threatened whenever she faced nourishment of any sort. She said, 'I will not house or nurture anything that comes from Jack Prior.'

Harry Travers stared down at the coverlet, unable to look any longer at her drawn face against which her auburn hair looked too strident, too rich. He said, 'You must stop all this. You could kill yourself and that I will not allow.'

She heard his fear and said quietly, 'I have every right to decide whether this thing lives or dies. It's his. It must die. I'll jump from the mizzen-mast if I have to, to free myself of it.'

He took her coffee, placed it on the locker beside the bed, then clasped her hand, which felt as delicate as a bird. 'You could kill yourself, never mind the child, and I'll not let you die, Irene Wendham. You've come too far to die. You will not die whilst I live.'

He was holding her hand in both of his, summoning up anything, everything that would make her stop. 'Think, Irene. This child could be a soul mate, someone to love, someone to belong to.'

She shook her head, she would not think, she would not feel. 'It's Jack's. I want nothing of his.'

Harry Travers reached out and smoothed her hair away from her face. 'Who had auburn hair? Was it your mother?'

Startled, she withdrew her hand and smoothed the sheet. What had her mother to do with this? She searched the room, seeing the photographs of Captain and Mrs Baines, and the two children who must be twenty-one and nineteen now. Was Emily a seamstress like her mother? She lay back, feeling so tired.

Harry persisted, 'Was your mother's hair as red as yours?'

She stared at him. 'Paler.'

He said, 'They must have dreamed of an heir and

227

when you were born they must have been so delighted. They must have played in their minds with the image of you caring for Wendham House and the estate, and passing it to their grandchild, then their great-grandchild, and so on, through the ages. This child is part of them too, you know, just as it is part of you. Child, Irene. Not a *thing*, not an *it*.'

She sat up. 'Get out,' she shouted. 'Get out, get out.'

He just sat there, reaching for her hands, holding them, fighting for her, forcing back the desperation, wanting to hold her to him. He said, 'We'll pretend the child is ours. I'll care for you both, for ever. For ever Irene. This child is your mother's grandchild, Wendham's heir. I'll drop you at an island. You'll go home, somehow we'll find you the money. Barratt will give up Wendham at the sight of a child. You can find that lawyer, reveal the illegal nature of the signing of the lease as we've always said you could. This child could be a daughter with auburn hair, and eyes as blue as yours and your mother's. Irene, you have a duty to this child, to yourself. You won't be alone. As long as you live you'll have me. And you must live, Irene.'

'Get out,' she repeated, pulling her hands from him. 'Get out.' Her face was as savage as her voice. 'I don't want to hear about my duty. Don't you think I have been thinking of that? Don't you think I know what letting this child live will mean?'

The next morning she came into the wardroom for breakfast. Mr Travers and his officers scrambled to their feet, their chairs scraping the floor. She motioned them to sit, and when they did so she remained standing. She drew herself up and said, 'I must apologize for my strange behaviour. You see, I'm with child, conceived aboard the *Cachalot*. Women can be strange sometimes when they are in an interesting condition.'

The men looked down at their plates, but before they did so she saw the pity in their eyes. She struggled on, her voice shaking, her eyes holding Harry Travers's, 'I would be so grateful if you would keep this a secret. I want to remain here, on board, for the birth. I need to be amongst friends. Then, of course, plans must be made. What I mean is,' and now her voice was a whisper, 'I do not wish my husband to know of my situation, I don't wish to go back to the *Cachalot* for my confinement.'

Harry Travers's joy was replaced by concern. He said, 'Would you join me on deck, ma'am?'

Together they climbed the companionway, then stood at the starboard side of the quarterdeck. 'You don't have to stay on board. I've told you, I will arrange your escape. At Cape Verde there'll be a return ship, many more will be going to England now, instead of America, with the war on.'

She felt the wind blowing her hair, felt her dress pulling against her swelling belly. This morning as the *child* moved, she had imagined her mother, had heard Harry's voice again, cutting through to the core of her, to the core he had created.

She smiled gently, pushing down the sorrow. 'No, I must stay with you, and my friends, as long as possible, and besides, I can't envisage having this child in some strange ship's cabin, or some lonely port. After the birth, then, of course, there are plans to make. My dear, beloved Harry.'

She saw the concern fade from his eyes, to be replaced by contentment, by hope and that was almost worse than everything that had gone before.

Day by day she grew stronger as the fleet cruised, taking on supplies where they could. She ate fruit, walked the deck, rested.

By the sixth month the sickness had gone and wrapped in her cloak she would drink in the sun and the wind, thinking of nothing, making herself think of nothing.

They rounded the Cape, and the ships put into Cape Town for more supplies. Again she stayed on board below decks because, thankfully, that was the order that came from Jack Prior.

Once at sea again their routine resumed and in the evenings Harry rustled his newspaper and planned for the life they would live together, strong in the face of scandal, responsible for this child who might have been sown by Jack, but was Irene's, only Irene's.

As Irene knitted she listened and felt the movement of the baby and pretended that there was no tomorrow.

By December they were cruising the southern hemisphere, catching and flensing whales and her body was cumbersome with her child, so she remained below or in the shelter of the hurricane cabin, hidden from the *Cachalot*'s view. In the evening Sinclair brought a chair to the quarterdeck and she would sit breathing in the sounds of the ship, the sight of her friends – Harry standing alongside the helmsman – Sinclair distributing coffee or tea, Mr Justine in the waist, Mr Morden by the boats, cherishing each image, for they must last a lifetime.

On the morning of Christmas Day her labour began and in the afternoon the crew sang carols in the waist and Sinclair opened the cabin door so that she could hear as the pain ripped through her. She clenched the sheet and groaned. Sinclair rushed across and bathed her head. He called out to Mr Morden, the first officer, who was standing outside, 'Another one. Come in, cain't do this on me own.'

Mr Morden hurried to the side of the bed, checking his pocket watch.

'That was a long one,' he murmured.

Sinclair shouted, 'What does that mean?'

'Guess it means we're getting somewhere,' Mr Morden said, running his hand through his hair, his face screwed up in concentration.

Sinclair dipped his cloth into the bowl and dabbed Irene's forehead again. 'What d'you mean, you guess? You're the one whose missus has had three kids.'

Mr Morden shrugged his shoulders and looked helpless. 'I was downstairs, boiling water.'

'Then go and boil some goddamn more, and tell the crew to sing up,' Sinclair yelled.

Irene eased herself up on the pillows, and took the cloth from Sinclair. 'Don't drown me,' she said weakly, laughing. 'I've seen a birth. It won't be long now. I keep telling you, don't worry. I'll go through the procedure again.' Another pain was coming, rearing, tightening. She threshed.

Sinclair said, 'What can I do?'

'Get Harry,' she whispered as the pain came in great waves. 'Get Harry.'

Harry came and held her hand, and talked and bathed her face, just enough, and her shoulders, and he wanted to weep with love and anguish.

Instead he smiled and talked of the soft sea breezes and the tides of the ocean, and the kelp that surrounded Tristan da Cunha. 'No,' she shouted. 'No.' For Jack Prior had spoken to her in that way in the glasshouse, and her husband had no place in this room. Here it must just be Harry, and herself, for a little while longer.

All evening her labour continued and now the crew were silent, lolling about the deck, talking of the Arctic, and how she had come with them, eaten blubber, sung carols, suffered, nursed them.

In the cabin the wicks were turned up in the oil lamps which swung in the swell. Harry was here. Of course he was. He'd been through all the other nightmares with her. He had made plans which could never be carried out. He had kept her warm in the ice. He had rustled his paper. And she had not told him that this was the end.

Another pain, and another, and within half an hour the baby was born.

Harry Travers said softly, 'You have a son, Irene.'

Through her exhaustion she heard the baby cry, and closed her eyes, saying, 'Does he have red hair?'

Harry and Sinclair looked at one another, and then at the child which was the image, even though he was only a few seconds old, of Jack Prior.

Harry said, 'It's dark hair, that's all I can tell, but he's perfect, and he's yours, ours. Remember that. And he's your parents' grandchild, he will love Wendham House.'

Harry wrapped the child in linen, and carried him to her. She took her son in her arms, and together they looked at his tiny hands, his soft skin. He stirred and she was suffused with love.

Harry sat in the hurricane cabin as the dawn rose on Boxing Day, staring across at the *Cachalot*, despairing, knowing the truth of what he'd done at last, for as Irene had held her son in her arms she had told him that she could not flee, that all the plans he had made were fine, but they were of no use to her, to them.

She had explained that she must remain with Jack Prior because, under the law, her husband would have custody of the child in any separation, and it is a custody he would insist on for a child would be his property. He would not rest until it was restored to him.

Harry had raged, unable to accept it. She'd said, 'I repeat. There is no haven from Jack Prior. We'd never be able to run far enough, or hide well enough. Even if we did it would be no life for the child for we would be ostracized, and he would be condemned to a life of shame. No, you made me the woman I am. I have duties. I must stay with Jack Prior, I must stand between my child and Jack's influence and cruelty. Just forgive me. Please, please forgive me.'

It was this plea, as the sun grew fierce, that tore at him, for it was he who should have pleaded for forgiveness, he who should have . . . 'Have what?' he ground out. 'What the hell could I do about anything. What the hell can she do?'

PART TWO

Tristan da Cunha, September 1862

CHAPTER TWELVE

Jack sat opposite Irene in the stifling cabin and threw Bernard up into the air, catching him, throwing him again, catching him, waving him about. The child, now nine months old, screamed with fear. Irene clenched her hands which were swollen and sore from deck scrubbing, forcing herself to smile as Jack settled Bernard on his knee.

He put his brandy glass to her son's mouth and forced some down his throat. The baby retched, coughed, backed away, screamed again. Jack glared at her. 'Goddammit, what's the matter with him? A taste'll do him good. And just you listen here, I'm having no namby-pamby British gentleman for a son. He'll learn to be a New Bedford whaling master or I'll know who's to blame.'

Again she sat quite still instead of wrenching Bernard to safety because over these last long nine months since she had arrived back on board she had trained herself to become a passive, accepting wife in the face of his taunts. To do otherwise brought down his wrath, not just on her, but on her son.

Instead, with increasing desperation, she had planned their escape for she had quickly realized that her presence would be no protection for her son, nor a guard against her husband's influence.

She continued to smile as Jack sank his brandy, belched, licked his lips, poured more, and now the smile was from the heart for at last here, at anchor, wallowing in the kelp-heavy sea of Tristan da Cunha, an opportunity had been placed in her lap. An opportunity she had grasped with both hands and that would enable her and Bernard to escape from Jack whilst remaining within the nominal edifice of her marriage.

More than that, as the years passed and Bernard became of age, her scheme should enable her and Bernard to return to English society and to Wendham House from a position of wealth and status and so ensure his future. About Harry she dared not dream.

'Take him,' Jack was thrusting the child at her.

Bernard buried his face against her breast, sobbing quietly, clinging to her with hot little hands, his hair drenched with sweat. She didn't look down at her child, she had learned not to, but surreptitiously she tightened her grasp, rocking slightly. Reassured, he calmed.

Jack tapped the table, eyed his glass. 'Yes,' he growled. 'He'll be a Prior, and he'll run an increased fleet, if those damned bloodsucker middlemen back home don't take all my goddamn profit.'

She kept her voice steady, unconcerned, as she made her first move. 'But as Jenkins, the *Bridgenorth*'s captain, said at cards last night – there don't have to be middlemen. Wasn't he talking of feeding his baleen into his own workshop, and on top of that, securing a uniform contract and making a killing from the Civil War? A wonderful scheme, but I suppose you can't steal another man's idea. How did he say he'd go about it? You sent me from the room.'

She watched him carefully as he poured more brandy. Watched as he picked up the glass and swirled the amber liquid round, seeing him struggle to remember just how Jenkins had said he *would* go about it, knowing that it would be a fruitless task for though there had indeed been talk of middlemen and uniform factories, it had been fleeting and without direction.

There would be direction tonight though. Indeed there would.

He picked up the glass, threw the drink down his throat and glared at her. 'Get out, put the kid to bed and make sure Sinclair has more brandy ready for the game tonight.'

Just before Mr Travers, and the *Island Queen* captain, Mr Danvers, came aboard that evening she slipped into the galley and whispered to Sinclair, 'Is Harry all set?'

Sinclair darted a look around, grinned and nodded. She retired to the sleeping cabin to wait, leaning back against the door, looking at her sleeping child. Please God, let it work.

In the depths of the evening Harry Travers sat at the table in the *Cachalot*'s wardroom watching Jack Prior scoop his poker winnings into a pile. Cigar smoke was thick in the room, Captain Danvers was sweating, Captain Smythe from the *Bounty Maid*, anchored alongside and bound for home tomorrow, sighed and said, 'You'll accept a promissory note?'

Jack Prior nodded, fingering the pack of cards. Captain Smythe wrote on a piece of paper and sighed again, handing it over, saying, 'No New Bedford mansion for me this trip.'

The others laughed, Harry loudest of all, for this man, God bless him, had given him the opening he'd been groping for all evening. He sat back in his chair, hooking his thumb in his watch pocket, thinking of Irene and the message they'd passed via Sinclair, who'd been transferred to the *Cachalot* at Jack Prior's insistence, saying that it gave him pleasure to humiliate a whaleman by assigning him as nursemaid to the captain's son.

Harry smiled slightly. Little did the bastard know how it eased all their hearts.

Jack leaned forward. 'Find it funny d'ya, Captain Travers, for a man to hand over his money? Didn't see ya laughing none when you did the same with your promissory note set against your lay.'

Harry sharpened his mind, though his expression didn't change. 'No, not at all, Captain Prior. I was just thinking that I'm not going to be satisfied with a mansion in New Bedford, I've set my sights on New York. It's where I'll found the Travers dynasty.'

Smythe barked out a laugh, 'You'll settle for a slum along with the other immigrants, you mean?'

Danvers was lighting up his pipe, Jack drew on his cigar. Harry sighed, 'No, that's not what I mean. At the end of this trip I'm going to take my lay and I'm going to make this crazy war work for me, just like it's going to work for lots of others if the talk on the other whalers is anything to go by. Somehow I'm going to set me up a workshop, making uniforms. I'll get me a government contract, make my fortune, and found a dynasty. I'm going to be like a duke would be in England. I'm going to have a position to hand on to my son.'

All the men laughed except Jack Prior, who stared. Then Danvers groaned, 'You're crazy. New York society is tighter than the English. You'll not blast your way through their barriers on wealth alone, unless it's real huge wealth.'

'Who's to say I won't?'

Jack Prior said nothing, he just looked as Danvers slapped his hand down on the table. 'I'm to say you won't. Unless it's huge wealth you'll need a New York society daughter or maybe a duke's daughter, fresh out of England. Someone with breeding, see. Happen to know a few, d'ya?' Again they all laughed, even Jack this time.

Harry tightened his lips, his voice, 'OK. Then I'll do what the *Bridgenorth*'s captain's going to do – feed my own workshop with my own baleen – once I get my own whaler of course. I'll set up a workshop for that, *and* make uniforms. Two-pronged attack scooping up real huge wealth. Just hope the war lasts long enough.'

Smythe laughed. Jack Prior cut across, wanting

answers, wanting some ideas, the thought of a Prior dynasty becoming more appealing by the minute. 'Going to split yourself in two are you? Who's going to run it while you're out getting your next batch of baleen?'

Bless your greedy, stupid, cunning mind, Jack Prior, Travers sang out silently then leaned forward. The light from the gently swaying oil lamp fell on all their faces. He appeared to think, then said, 'I'll marry an immigrant. She can pretend she's quality, start making friends amongst the high flown whilst she runs it, which'll answer Captain Danvers's point about society. Because she's my wife I'll be able to trust her. You can't trust anybody but family. And because she's my wife, I won't have to pay her.'

Smythe accepted a cigar from Jack, rolled it between his fingers, held it to his ear, laughing. Harry Travers almost writhed with impatience. Come on, someone, take me to task on that, for Sinclair, Irene and he had been frantically asking questions of the Americans in port about New York society. Come on, someone, or I don't know how I can bring up the rest.

Smythe lit his cigar, looking over the flame, sucking, then puffing the smoke across the table as he said, 'New York society would love that, I *don't* think. Their women don't work, any more than the British and rest assured they'd run a check on your missus. They'd know she wasn't the real goods. Anyway, she'd more'n likely run off with the cash. Give it up boy.'

Harry Travers frowned, forcing himself not to come up with the arguments too quickly, making himself look as though he was groping for a way forward, making sure he didn't show his pure joy.

He said at last, sounding uncertain, harassed, angry, 'I won't give it up. I can't afford to because the war's given me a chance that won't come again. It's given us all a chance.' He looked as though he was struggling with his thoughts. 'But you're right, what I really need

241

is a wife of quality, and someone who can run a business while looking as though she isn't, and someone who won't run off.' He paused, then looked inspired. 'So I'd get her pregnant. Once she had a child she'd never leave or she'd lose it to me. I'd make sure she couldn't fiddle me either because I'd . . . I'd . . .' Again he paused, staring at the ceiling.

Prior ground out, 'Because you'd what?'

Travers stared around wildly, then slapped the table triumphantly. 'Because I'd set up a paid front man, a lawyer or someone, who not only understood figures but kept a check on everything. Hey, I've another idea. If he was there, everyone would think he was running things so I'd be solving two problems in one.' He sat back, grinning. 'There. That's what I'd do, then I'd swan back from my trips, after she'd done all the work, and take the credit, and be the swell in my Fifth Avenue mansion.'

There was a silence. Danvers and Smythe exchanged a look and raised their eyebrows. Danvers said, over the laughter which was beginning to seep from the men, 'What you're looking for is a miracle.' The laughter was now a torrent.

Jack Prior just sat and stared at Harry Travers, and all the time he felt the fury rising for how dare this Britisher talk of making a fortune out of Jack Prior's nation while it was at war, how dare he talk of making uniforms, using baleen, how dare any of the whalemen in this darned port? If anyone did it would be a Prior and now he knew just how to do it, and he laughed that loud harsh laugh. The men looked at him.

He shook his head at Harry Travers, and shouted, spittle bursting from his mouth, 'You're a fool. The war is not nearly over. By the time you have your lay others will have got in first, and you'll still be working for me, d'ya hear?' He was jabbing the table. He shouted again, 'D'ya see? You're mine, you'll always be mine because you're a convict, a bound man, and if you step one foot off my ship and head for New York I'll blow your name sky high. I'll get you shipped back to England quicker than you can sneeze. Now get back to your ships, the damn lot of you. The game's over.'

He stretched his legs out as they left, knowing that for him the game was just beginning and that the Wendham woman was going to be working her fingers to the bone any day now to build up a home that he'd come and swan around in, one that would be big and grand enough for him, and his son. Big enough for the Prior dynasty.

Harry nodded to Irene as she stood in the shadows, stopping, pretending to adjust his boot. 'You were right,' he whispered. 'His eyes lit up at the thought of his wife working so he can swan in and take the credit. He'll take the bait, I'm sure. Be careful, Irene, for the rest of your life, be careful.'

He stood up, and they looked at one another and every minute of everything they had shared was in that look, and each knew it would have to last a lifetime. She reached out, drawing him into the blackness. 'Hold me,' she breathed. His arms came round her, holding her tight, tighter. His lips brushed her hair, breathing in the scent of her. She lifted her face to his. His kiss was tender and neither could bear the thought of what was to come. 'I love you,' he said against her mouth. 'I shall love you for ever.'

'When I'm at Wendham . . .'

He nodded but it was so far away, so uncertain, so impossible, such a dream. In her eyes he saw that too.

He turned to go. She snatched him back, burying her head against his neck. 'No, no, I can't bear it.'

'Irene Wendham can bear anything.' His voice was as broken as hers, then he was gone, striding across the deck, over the side, down the rope into the boat, and he didn't look back even once as Mr Justine headed for the *Wendham*.

Godspeed, my love, he said to himself. Be safe. As the boat beat across the waves he buried his head in his hands.

Irene made her way unsteadily to the quarterdeck, not watching as he left her, fighting back the tears, wondering how she could live from now on without the knowledge that he was there, within sight on the *Wendham*.

It was July 1863 and a steaming hot day in Lower Manhattan and Irene's clothes clung to her sweat-drenched body as she stood in the almost deserted workshop set amongst the slums, staring at the three broken sewing machines, the hand cutter, and the empty benches where workers should have been.

Through the broken windows came the stench of poverty and the sound of it – the shouts, the yells, the drunken laughter. She turned on Mr Palance, Jack's front man for Prior's Clothing Workshop. 'This is a disgrace. My husband bought a thriving clothing business.'

He shrugged, 'He got what he wanted, a quick and cheap buy. The owner took off for Canada when he thought the war might come here. How was I to know that his apprentices and workers would get out too?'

She stared at him, coldly, 'It's your job to know, Mr Palance. You are our front man, a known New Bedford businessman with contacts in New York, or so Jack said.'

The tall spare grey-haired man stared at her with his watery eyes, the stench of last night's whisky oozing from his skin and breath. He said, 'I guess I'm Mr Prior's front man, 'cos I certainly ain't yours, so forget the "our". You don't exist, do ya, ain't that the story? I'm in control, or that's how I understand it, and yes, I'm known.'

She held his stare, then gazed around the large high-ceilinged room again. 'You are the front man. I run it,' she corrected him. 'As I understand it, you are in thrall to my husband. Does he not have knowledge of some liaison with a woman that your wife wouldn't care for? So you will do as you are told.'

Mr Palance glared at her, she didn't flinch. She was merciless because this was her son's future, this was survival, and this man was a rogue – Jack's man – and, if this factory was anything to go by, a cheat.

He looked away first, his mouth a thin slit and said, his lips barely moving, 'I sign cheques, I do the accounts. You run this workshop, that's all. Jack Prior trusts me with the money. He trusts you only to get the most out of this heap, though how you, with no experience, will do that, God knows.' He added, his tone disparaging, 'Tells me you're after position and wealth and you'll do anything to get it.'

She stared at him, longing to strike the expression from his face, but somehow she kept her tone even as she said, 'I have someone with experience, a Parisian seamstress, Mr Palance, an old, old friend, a widow of a wonderful whaling captain, and we require band knives which will cut through wedges of material. We need up-to-date machines, we need good workers if we're to fulfil the previous owners' uniform contract.' She stopped, doubt striking her. 'We do still have the uniform order?'

'You ain't going to get band cutters, or new machines, but you can have all the workers you want, and for a pittance. Immigrants are still pouring in, so fast you wouldn't know there was a war on.'

She drew off her gloves, they were wringing wet. She repeated, 'We do still have the uniform contract?'

'Kind of lapsed when Levin went.'

Irene stuttered, 'And you kind of forgot to tell us. You're a fool Mr Palance, a cheat and a fool.'

He glared, and tapped his cane once on the floor. 'Mrs Prior, don't you go round calling me names. You ain't in no position.'

She walked into the centre of the room. A thick coating of dust lay on everything. No-one had been here for weeks. She drew in a deep breath, slowly she calmed, her mind racing, but then on the air came the smell of smoke, mingling with the stench.

'Is there a fire?' She was alarmed.

He laughed, 'There's always fires, like there's always cholera and yellow fever.'

'We're insured, of course.'

'Cain't say we are. Mr Prior said nothing to me about no insurance.'

'Then we're unprotected, Mr Palance. We could lose everything.'

He shrugged. 'Not a lot to lose.'

She stared back round the room until Palance grew restless, then she started for the door. 'I need to think, Mr Palance. I damn well need to think. You are to be in New York for a few days yet?' He nodded. She said, 'I have the name of your hotel. I will contact you there.'

She walked back to the rooming house that edged against the Bowery, pushing through the men, women and children who milled in the streets hawking their wares, or standing hopelessly. Sometimes a child laughed, but only sometimes.

They were the poor who had been chased from their countries by poverty or fear, or the poor who had been chased from the swamps of the area of Central Park where they had squatted until it began to be cleared five years ago. The poor who now found themselves living in shacks erected along the Hudson, or with another family in a room in the slum tenements.

Above her prostitutes lolled from windows, a rat ran across the garbage-strewn street and she thought of how Jack would laugh, then rage, for he had come into the sleeping cabin long after the poker players had left, dragging her out of what he imagined was sleep, shaking her as he told her of his plan for her, throwing her to the bed and turning to his son, picking him up.

246

'It's a dynasty we'll have. You'll go with your mother. She'll work for you for she'll not run off and bring scandal onto *your* head. She's a selfish greedy bitch and she'll get what I care to throw to her, like her father did to me, like the British to the Priors.'

It had taken until June to return to New Bedford, keeping a lookout all the while for Southern warships as they had always done, but more so as they approached the harbour. The *Cachalot* was alone and would meet up with the *Wendham* and the *Island Queen* in the Japan Grounds.

Irene's footsteps faltered now as a man brushed past her shouting at her in some strange tongue. She warded him away with her arm, standing quite still, thinking of the *Wendham*, where Harry and Sinclair were together again, but without her, and for a moment she had to lean against the crumbling wall of a tenement.

But soon she was nudged along by the stream of humanity and as she turned towards the lodging house her footsteps quickened, and she stepped out past a young couple scanning the houses for vacant rooms whilst a black man carried their bags.

Her rooming house was one of many in a faded and crumbling terrace which provided meals in a communal dining room, and never smelt of anything but stale washing. She climbed the stoop, nodding to the landlady in the high gloomy hall, before hurrying up the stairs, turning the key in the lock, standing in the doorway as Bernard tottered towards her, his arms reaching out, 'Mama.'

She held him, kissed his soft cheeks, stroked his fine black hair, and coaxed a smile from him that took the look of Jack away. 'How has he been, Antoinette?' she asked, smiling at Mrs Baines who sat on the sofa, wearing smart mourning, sewing ruffles on a deep-green dress she had insisted she make for Irene, saying that they would both feel better taking on a factory if they were proud of their image.

247

Together they had designed it in New Bedford where Irene had stayed while Jack closeted himself with Palance, issuing instructions and leaving for sea again within two days. It had only taken half an hour for Antoinette Baines to agree to join her in New York, nodding excitedly in her small house overlooking the harbour, telling Irene that her daughter Emily was already there, working as a machinist in another clothing workshop.

She listened closely to Irene's plans to build up a workshop in New York while Jack Prior still sailed the seas. Ultimately she would enter New York society Irene had explained, before finally taking her son to Wendham when he came of age. 'I have to keep him from Jack's influence, you see,' she had ended.

Antoinette had seen, oh yes, she had seen.

Antoinette now said, 'He has been almost an angel.' They laughed together. 'Almost.' The laughter continued. She held up the bodice. 'See, just two ruffles as you insisted and you were right, though with fashion dictating that the hoops are so much smaller I fear it might affect our profits once we extend into corsets and crinolines.'

Irene sat down opposite Antoinette Baines, settling Bernard on her knee before she said, 'We'll use less baleen though so costs will be down. It will all balance out, I'm sure. It must.' She felt suddenly tired.

Antoinette saw and asked, her eyes wary, her accent suddenly sharper, her plump face momentarily drawn, 'There is no problem with the factory? That Jack, he has not done something dreadful?' She held the material tightly.

Irene forced a laugh. 'No, no, not really, and careful, don't rip the gown.'

Antoinette put the bodice to one side, and placed her needle in the sewing basket, looking all the time at Irene with her large brown eyes. 'So, why the sadness, why the tiredness? I insist you tell me. A problem must be shared by us both.'

Irene told her of the empty workshop, the broken machines, not of Harry so far away, ending with, 'So, you have no workers to train in corsetry, in uniform making, in anything. I asked you to come here knowing I needed you, thinking I had a future to offer you in return for all that Captain Baines gave me.' She lifted her hands, then dropped them. 'It appears I was wrong.'

Mrs Baines shook her head. 'Tell Palance to get the contract back, or find us another one.'

Irene stared at the motheaten rug, the fireplace, the peeling wallpaper. 'I have, but first we need equipment, stock, and then workers.'

Antoinette came to her, sitting beside her. 'You have a warehouse full of baleen, out there are thousands of workers who just need training. Somehow we must get the equipment. We can start with the corsets, leave the uniforms for now.'

Irene snapped, 'I've just told you, I have no money for cloth or machines and I have only enough capital to house us in this disgusting rooming house for a month, not a dollar more or less. That way my dear, generous husband felt we would "put our backs into it" as he said. I've thought of raising a loan against the baleen, but then my name would be on the documents, and who will deal with a woman anyway? Palance would not co-operate, for Jack has not verified it.'

Antoinette said quietly, 'I have a little, a very little.'

Irene took her hand. 'Oh I'm sorry, I shouldn't have spoken as I did. No, that remains yours. You have Emily and Frank to think of.'

'Frank has no need of it where he works on the farm, and Emily is well paid in her workshop. They have no need, I say, and this is *our* business. You insisted on that, a *moral* partnership you said, nothing on paper because of Jack Prior. If you insist on sharing with me whatever *you* can get from it, why should I not contribute?'

Irene refused. 'You have already lost enough because of the Priors.'

The next morning she had changed her mind after a night spent at the window staring out over a city simmering in stench-ridden heat, thinking as Harry had always told her to do, and for a moment there, while the stars shone high above, she had smelt brine, the smoke of the cressets, felt the lurch of the ship and allowed herself to reach deep within her and touch the love which had not abated but grown, deepened and somehow sustained her, until the pain of the missing drenched her, as it always did.

But then she'd paused as she sat by the window, shaking herself free of memory as each night she told herself she must, retracing her thoughts, remembering the smell of the smoke again, seeking for the glimmer that had come to her.

It came and she'd sat bolt upright, thinking of the Arctic cold, the *Queen of the Isles* crushed and splintered by the ice, thinking of the *Island Queen* with its auxiliary engine – bought with insurance money – and now her mind was racing for she knew what she could do, and she had barely been able to wait until dawn to wake Antoinette in the next room, and request the money after all, saying, 'For insurance. It is essential.'

She visited an insurance broker, requesting quotes in the name of Palance, taking them to Mr Palance in his hotel, her veil over her face since unaccompanied ladies should not venture onto the streets alone, never mind entering hotels.

She insisted that he take out the insurance premium that she had chosen, saying, when he demurred, 'Mrs Baines has provided the money. What happens if there is a fire and I tell my husband that you were negligent?'

He called in at the rooming house later that day, his handkerchief to his nose, telling them that he had been unable to complete the procedure until a report on the premises was to hand. 'They will be sending an assessor to inspect the workshop, and the baleen, and the "working" machines,' he sneered triumphantly. 'None of which is there. So what kinda trick are you pulling, Mrs Prior?'

Irene stood at the table, her voice like ice as she replied, 'You are the one who deals in tricks, Mr Palance. Just what sort of noises have you been making to the insurers?'

He flushed and stormed out.

In the humidity of the early evening Irene and Mrs Baines hurried to the workshop, leaving Bernard in the care of the landlady. Irene had arranged for baleen to be delivered from the warehouse, and it was already there. Outside the door was Emily Baines, with a smile like her father's, and she had the bale of linen she had 'borrowed' from her workshop.

Once inside they dusted and swept, and oiled the machines, before swapping pieces at Emily's direction, inserting others she had brought from her machine until at last they had two that worked. For every minute of the time sweat poured down their faces, staining their clothes. 'What's it all about?' Emily asked at midnight.

'I don't know,' her mother said. 'But Irene says you'll have all this back tomorrow, and so you will.'

At two in the morning they returned to their respective lodgings, and Irene realized that she had barely noticed the effluvia from the sewers, and the manure from the horses and pigs, and the human urine in the alleys, and it was because this time the cheating was hers, not Jack's. Her spirit was uneasy, a growing guilt was gnawing at her.

Neither woman spoke as they climbed the stairs on legs which had no more energy, Mrs Baines going to her room, Irene to hers, waking the landlady as she slept in the chair by the open window, then falling onto the bed, knowing no more until the clash of the breakfast bell at seven.

She and Antoinette were at the workshop again at ten in the morning. Bernard was with them, for the landlady had said, 'I ain't no nurse.'

Irene slipped out into the street, and paid a girl a dollar to come and mind him in the office, and another to use a broom in the workshop whilst she and Mrs Baines worked on paper patterns. Irene checked the clock. Ten o'clock. The assessor would be here any minute.

He came. Mrs Baines let him in, saying, 'I'm the machinist. I've set the workers on. They're starting next week. This one started today. Not much English, but experienced.' Irene bent lower over the design for not even an insurance assessor must see Mrs Prior's face as she toiled over a machine. Mrs Baines added, 'We're expecting a uniform contract.'

All the time the assessor was walking around, humming. He stopped at a machine. Irene and Antoinette froze, then relaxed. It was a working model. He moved the drive belt, glanced around once more, then said to Mrs Baines on his way out, 'The owner, Mr Prior, should look again at that Palance. Troublemaker, he is, tall-story merchant. There's no problem here.'

That evening, when the baleen had been returned to the warehouse and the linen and the machine pieces to Emily's workshop, Irene returned to the workshop alone. She unlocked the building, shoved two tables together stacking paper beneath. She dusted her hands, memorizing the room in her mind.

Tonight she would return and fire it. No, not tonight it would be too suspicious. On Sunday, in the evening, when there were fewer people at work around them. When no-one could be hurt.

That night she stared down at Bernard as he slept in his truckle bed, trying to push aside her guilt. It was all she could do, if they were to survive. 'But surviving has made me no better than Jack is,' she whispered.

The next day she and Antoinette took Bernard out, taking turns to carry him as they walked along Fifth Avenue, gazing at the fine houses which lined it, safe in the knowledge that they were unobserved by the society inhabitants who had left for the summer season in Saratoga where they would be sheltering in the shade of verandas and basking in the breeze from the sea.

Every second Irene expected Antoinette to ask her why they had rushed to insure, but she did not. Instead she said, as they stood and stared at Central Park, where work still continued in spite of the war, 'One day it will be beautiful and you will be in one of the houses they say will be built where now there is open space.' Antoinette pointed further along Fifth Avenue. 'Then, in due time, you and your son will go home to Wendham House.'

'Yes,' Irene agreed, but deep down she realized that even her home had lost its power in the face of her love for Harry Travers.

Bernard strained towards the house, his arm stretched out. 'Mama,' he said. This time it was at him that she looked, and her resolve grew strong again. Irene Wendham could do anything, and she must, for Harry had given her the chance.

As they returned to the poorer areas the streets grew more crowded, and they were buffeted and nudged. Irene wanted to shut her eyes, close her ears.

She said to Antoinette, 'Does it ever become quiet would you think? Sundays will be quiet, won't they? Deep in the night it will be quiet?'

Antoinette gripped her arm. 'Careful,' she said. Irene had almost walked into a crowd outside the draft offices. 'Wait,' Antoinette said, and forced her way through to the front. Irene stared at the faces around her, the sunken eyes, the old thin men with stubbled chins, the worn women with shawls on their heads. They would all be in their rooms at night, wouldn't they? The raucous cries, the drunken singing that woke her every night would not be near the workshop? Please don't let them be near the workshop.

Antoinette was returning, her bonnet knocked askew, holding her black skirts to her. 'It's a notice about the lottery that's just been drawn for the draft. There'll soon be more widows, like me.' Her face was pale and strained. 'I thank God my son is on his farm and out of it.'

The evening meal, taken in the small humid dining room was subdued, and the other boarders talked quietly as the thrust and counter-thrust of the opposing armies were discussed, and the ever growing casualty lists decried.

'Those damn profiteers are happy with it, though. They'll not celebrate when it's over,' tutted a travelling shoe salesman.

'Maybe they will,' Alan, the journalist without a job said. 'War changes things. Industry's already more powerful, the rail system's better which helps distribution. It'll be rich pickings for some.'

Irene remembered Barratt, his voice as he talked of distribution, and for a moment her world stood still, and she could almost smell honeysuckle, but it was overlaid with the sound of the sea, the image of brown hair and eyes full of love. Bernard banged his spoon on his bowl. Everyone laughed. The travelling shoe salesman said, 'Lucky little chap. It'll all be over before he knows anything about it.'

She saw them looking curiously at her.

'Going back to England soon, are ya, Mrs Williams?' the travelling salesman asked.

She smiled carefully, her pseudonym still sounding strange, but knowing the masquerade was essential in case society attempted one day to trace her life since arriving in America, 'One day.' The salesman smiled broadly.

Again she slept little, going over in her mind the route she would take, the fire she would start. Please let there be no wind, let no-one be hurt. But guilt kept surging and repeatedly she told herself that she had no other option. It could so easily go up in smoke at any time. It should always have been insured. It was her duty. She had to do it. Or the business would fail, her son would have no future, and that must be her priority, nothing else.

She turned over, pushing the scent of brine away, hauling back the present.

But perhaps it wouldn't fail. Perhaps she could somehow persuade a dealer to lend on the baleen and so repair all the hand machines. Steam machines would have to wait. She could buy up remnants to make the corsets, and somehow convince the government she was capable of fulfilling Levin's orders, asking for an advance on the money.

She sat up now, resting her head on her knees. But then they'd have to draw baleen from another source, pay a middleman for it, and then Jack would beat her if he found out, and what if the government wouldn't give them an advance? What if . . . ? What if . . . ?

On and on it went, chasing around in her head, just as the noise from the streets was, noise which seemed louder than ever tonight. Why didn't people sleep? Why? Why? Didn't they know . . . ? She ran her hands over her eyes, praying for rest but it didn't come.

Dawn came though, but still there was no peace for her, and her head pounded until at last she could think no more. She dragged on her dress, her shoes, and lifted Bernard from his bed. He smelt of sleep. She held him, loved him, kissed him and he was so soft and warm. She rubbed her cheek on his hair. Yes, he must be her priority. Anything for him, but still her thoughts twisted and turned, and now it was Harry's face she saw; his goodness, his honesty, his love, his opinion of her. Until at last she was defeated and whispered into Bernard's hair, 'I'm sorry, my darling, I can't, even for you, I can't.'

With the words, the pounding in her head ceased, and in its place was a sort of peace, but it was a peace driven by anxiety because she did not know how to go forward. Bernard wriggled, his hands reached for her hair, grasped it. It was copper-coloured against his small plump hands. She kissed each finger, trying to think, trying to plan but she was so tired, and her head was pounding again, and it made the noise from the street seem louder even.

But then she saw that the noise was drowning out Bernard's laughter, and for the first time she realized that it *was* too loud, and ugly, and angry.

She hurried him to the window. Down below men and women were talking and shouting, spilling across the street, tens upon tens of them. She didn't understand. She was trying to lift the sash window when Antoinette threw open her door, running to her side, staring down. 'Mother of God, what is it?'

The men were moving off, walking, then running, their angry shouts reaching them. Irene thrust Bernard into Antoinette's arms, and lifting the window, leaned out. More men were collecting, setting up separate groups, flowing between them. They were milling, shouting, their faces wild with rage, clubs and knives in their hands.

Irene ducked back inside. 'Keep away from the window,' she shouted, running out of the door and down the stairs.

The landlady was easing open the front door. Irene stood with her.

'What is it?' she panted as part of the mob ran past, brandishing their knives and clubs. Some had guns.

They watched as they stormed into the factory at the end of the street, forcing people out, firing it. They heard the shouts, the screams, the noise of the fire, of the breaking windows. They smelt the smoke.

The landlady clutched Irene's arm. 'What if they come here? What if . . . ?'

Irene pulled from her grasp, lifting her skirts and pounding up the stairs, shouting, 'Out, out.' She banged on the shoe salesman's door, on Alan's, then tore into her own room, snatching Bernard from Antoinette, who stood, wild-eyed. 'I smell smoke,' Antoinette said.

Irene nodded. 'They've fired the factory, we've got to get out in case they fire the houses. Out into the yard, quick.'

Antoinette stared. 'They would not do that, not deliberately.'

Irene screamed, 'Just get out. People will do anything if they're desperate, believe me. Just damn well believe me.' She bit off her words as Bernard began to cry. She scooped up anything of value while Mrs Baines rushed to her room and did the same.

They rushed down the stairs, out into the back yard, and all the time Irene was filled with a scything shame for these men were doing what she would have done – but why?

The shoe salesman came hopping down the steps, one shoe off, to join them. 'Goddammit, hooligans. Crazy fools.' All around they could hear the screams, the shouts. They could smell the smoke, hear the fire bells. On it went all day, and into the night and they could still see the glow of the flames against the night sky.

Only Alan slipped out, his pad and pencil at the ready, eager to get a story.

'Why? Why?' the others just kept repeating, their heads pounding, their hearts too.

They did not return to their room even to sleep, and whilst the hours merged their eyes grew sore from the smoke, and fear increased at the sound of an explosion, then another.

'It's the Confederates. They've reached us,' the shoe salesman kept on crying, and nobody knew if it was true.

Alan slipped back, his eyes alive with excitement, his note pad almost full. He shouted at them from the back door, 'They're rioting because of the draft.'

The shoe salesman sulked, patting his chest, wiping his face with a handkerchief as he said, 'Well, it could have been the enemy.'

On Monday the landlady and Irene slipped out for food, dodging the rioters, joining up with other women who hurried through the streets, looking left and right.

'It's the draft.'

'They're rioting because of the draft.'

'They ain't gonna be told to fight. They'll only go if they feel like it.'

'They'll not fight to free niggers who'll only come up here and take their jobs.'

'That's right, some of them striking Irish longshoremen were drafted. They ain't no way gonna fight for the niggers who've already come in as strike breakers and taken their jobs.'

'They ain't gonna fight when the nobs in them fancy houses on Fifth buy substitutes if their boy's drawn.'

They crowded into the boarded-up store and bought provisions from the tearful storekeeper, who kept repeating, 'They're looting everything. Nothing's safe.' They left by the back door because there was noise now at the front. Panic lent them speed as they tore back to the lodging house yard.

Troops were ordered in from harbour posts and citizens joined up with the police to protect their city. Stores and banks were closed, all transport stopped. The rioters cut the telegraph lines to the police stations, railroad tracks were ripped up. Factories and workshops were emptied and sacked, some were burned.

The rampaging thousands beat and kicked police and soldiers. A colonel was battered to death and hung from

258

a lamppost. Blacks were hunted, killed and burned on bonfires. The Irish were attacked. Drunken men, women and children destroyed a tavern on Fifth Avenue, and headed for the Coloured Orphan Asylum.

The police took all the children they could find to the precinct station and the mob stole what it could and fired what it couldn't. Firemen rescued a group of children from them. On and on it went, or so the journalist told them when he crept back into the lodging house to sleep for a few hours.

Irene and Antoinette stared from their window and wondered what they were doing here, and Antoinette longed for the clean air of New Bedford, and worried about Emily, as did Irene who also longed for Harry and the trade winds and both Wendhams, and blamed herself for bringing them here.

On Saturday morning, when the acrid smell of burning still hung on the air but the worst was over, they walked through the streets, bemused, appalled, unbelieving and shocked at how quickly something like this could just burst out around them. Irene clutched Bernard as she and Antoinette skirted round debris on their way to Emily's rooming house, feeling weak with relief to see it standing and unmarked, but then wondering if Emily had been trapped inside the workshop. They pounded on the front door, almost screaming at the landlady when she answered, 'Where's Emily?'

'Gone to work, got bored and was more'n ready to go back,' the woman said, her arms folded, her face red and tired.

Irene and Antoinette looked at one another and laughed, stumbling back down the steps, laughing until they reached the end of the street, unable to stop, and it was relief, sheer relief, and amazement at the resilience of youth. 'Bored?' they kept repeating. 'Bored?'

At the store they fell silent, their bellies aching from

259

their laughter, their throat and eyes sore from the smoke. They waited outside while the storekeeper prized away the last of the shutters, and now they were rocking with tiredness as they read the reports of the riots in the *Tribune* that the storekeeper was handing out, and wondered how they could ever have been so insensitive as to laugh when over a thousand people had been killed, and property losses were expected to reach millions of dollars.

But as Irene began to turn the page Antoinette gripped her arm. 'No, read that again.' Antoinette's finger was stabbing the last paragraph. '*Property losses*. Don't you see – *property losses*. Could we be this lucky? Could they have fired our workshop? I even thought of doing it myself, I felt so desperate.'

Irene stared at her, latching onto Antoinette's confession. 'You too?' she whispered.

Antoinette looked startled, 'You also?'

Irene said, 'I was going to, on Sunday night, but I couldn't, not even for Bernard.'

The two stared at one another, and then together they hurried down the streets, ignoring the heat and smell of the charred wood heaped all about them. Bernard coughed in Irene's arms. On and on they went, running now, until at last they came to the workshop and there it was, a charred ruin.

CHAPTER THIRTEEN

Irene stood at one end of the workshop in January 1866. She held a mourning dress against her. Yes, they had made the right choice back in 1864 to set two girls on this line, whilst the rest produced the uniforms, and corsets and crinolines. Lincoln's assassination last April, a few weeks after the end of the war, had given a boost to business, of course, just when the uniform contract was drawing to a close, but it was one boost that she, Antoinette and Emily, who had joined them as foreman, wished had never happened.

She placed the dress back on its hanger, looking over the twenty pristine machines which were linked to a central shaft providing steam power. In due course this would be replaced by gas. There was the cutter's table, with the new band cutters. As well as the twenty machinists she had basters, pressers, fellers and cutters. The room would take more but she and Antoinette were determined that the principles of Prior's Clothing Workshop, now housed north of Greenwich Avenue, would be maintained.

Yes, *principles*. Irene perched herself on the edge of a table and enjoyed the sound of the word, because, just as the draft riots had alerted the dignitaries to the powder keg in their slums, and galvanized that class into a flurry of good works and soup kitchens, so she and Antoinette had pledged that no worker of theirs, whatever colour or creed, would be exploited, starved or humiliated, neither would they want for medical care when necessary, so each Prior worker had money put into a fund with her insurers, to realize at sixty.

261

'Damned do-gooder,' Palance had sniffed.

'Not at all,' she had replied, 'for now they will stay with me, and not be tempted away.'

Lint from the twilled cotton of the corsets hung in the air. She rubbed her hands together against the cold. She saw her breath in the air. It must be late for the furnace to have died down so far. She checked the clock. Seven p.m. She should return to the brownstone they had leased south of Greenwich Avenue. Indeed, she shouldn't even be here at all, for what if she was seen? But how could she settle whilst Antoinette and Emily did their rounds of the stores?

Had they had any success with their examples of morning and afternoon tea dresses, the workshop's first foray into non-mourning clothes? Had they managed to interest anyone, promising they could be run up swiftly and cheaply? Had they? Had they?

Lord, how she hoped so, because last week they had heard there would be no peacetime contract for uniforms. It had gone instead to a firm enmeshed in the Tammany Ring, that group of politicians led by Tweed who controlled New York, and looked kindly only on those who resorted to bribery.

She itched to be out with Antoinette and Emily too, but no, society was here for the winter season and she must not be seen in any such role, even by storekeepers who might one day serve her.

She drifted into her office, the office she officially visited on workers' welfare matters, the equivalent of good works. But in fact it was here that she and Antoinette discussed problems of manufacture that couldn't wait for the evening, or urgent correspondence, or problems with design sketches she had been working on since breakfast back at the house.

Should they have diversified sooner? She shrugged. Perhaps, but they'd been so busy they hadn't had time to think, let alone plan properly.

Irene pulled the designs towards her, scanning

through them. It was fortunate that even mourning had to be fashionable because the switch to normal wear would be painless for the workers. She eyed the dressmakers' models in the corner, weighing up the heavy boning stitched down the bodice seams, the sleeves set narrowly into tight fitting shoulders, a perfume sachet for each armpit, one in stark matt-black bombazine the other in crêpe, for deepest mourning did not permit shiny material. Beyond it, through the glass window, the workshop was clearly visible.

So many rolls of black, heliotrope or grey material. In the furthest room was the baleen and the linen for the corsets and small crinolines. How wonderful it would be to have deep rich vibrant colours to work on for a change. Would it happen? It had to.

She looked again at the clock, bringing her notebook out of her reticule, checking the list of outlets against the samples. Would they remember to visit the hotels along Fifth Avenue too and try to persuade them into allowing a glass showcase to be set up in the lobby?

For a moment she paused, tension building.

She flicked to the back of the book and examined for the hundredth time the capital balance of the business – for she kept her own set of figures to check against Palance's. No, it hadn't grown since Jack had left yesterday, after three drunken months. She eased her shoulders and winced. Damn him. Not only had he taken his fists to her yet again before he left but more importantly he had taken their hard won profits to pay off his gambling debts before he had returned to sea.

'All gone. It has all gone,' she murmured.

She threw the book to the desk. It scattered the designs. She rubbed the back of her neck. If only those Confederate gunships had found Jack Prior's fleet instead of those thirty or more whalers that it had torched. If only it had found him and shot him through the heart. But then she stopped. No, for then other good men would have been captured or killed.

She sat back. Harry.

She looked again at the mourning dress, heard again Jack's laugh as he had strode in here to survey his kingdom. 'War brings a darned rich harvest,' he had crowed. 'Forty whalers sunk by the Union to blockade Charleston harbour, and thirty or more torched by Confederate gunships. Richer pickings for me out there now there's less competition, so you'd better darn well keep up your end.'

She dragged herself back to the present. She knew she must, but could she?

Again she rubbed her neck. She was tired. She should go home but how could she disguise the worry on her face, how could she pretend to Martha that all was well?

Martha, who had arrived from England last week, and flown into her arms at the docks in New York, sobbing her delight at the ticket Irene had sent. Martha who had sworn that her former charge had not changed, though Irene knew that there were lines on Irene Prior's face and fresh bruises on her body that Irene Wendham would never have dreamed of.

Martha had brought a letter from Barratt promising that, for a considerable sum to be negotiated in due course, he would relinquish the lease on Bernard's coming of age, for Jack Prior had already offered him a further twenty-one-year term on the termination of his present lease in 1877. He had added that this would remain confidential. On that Irene's joy had been unconfined, for Martha was here, and in theory her future was safe.

She picked up the notebook, stared at the figures again. But then this.

Irene locked the workshop, and sat back in the modest hired brown coupé. 'Drive down Fifth Avenue before heading for the Court please, driver,' she instructed.

He looked at her strangely for it was well out of her way home to go via Fifth but she ignored him. When they arrived he clipclopped down streets piled high either side with cleared snow.

Once on Fifth Avenue she peered out at the florists where ferns, forced lilac and roses stood in vases behind their glass windows. She loved to see them for they brought Wendham back. In the summer there were no flowers here, the heat was too great.

She stared at the mansions between Washington Square and Madison Square with their carved façades and ornate metals of the brownstone houses. Brownstones which were far grander than hers, which were here, not in a court alongside waiters, and writers and those who were not in society.

She stared from the department stores to the *haute couture* salons, which is where Antoinette's inclination really lay. But now was not the time. Society used *haute couture* and her connection to Antoinette could be exposed and her plans wrecked.

She clenched her hands into fists, seeing the empty bank book again, seeing Antoinette's face when she had shown it to her. 'I hate him,' Antoinette had ground out.

'Do you hate me too, for bringing you here?' Irene had asked.

'I could never hate you,' Antoinette had said, but her voice was cold, distant, enraged. She had not spoken of it again, not spoken at all, sweeping from the brownstone with Emily, her face set.

As they passed people who were entering carriages driven by horses with burnished harnesses she shrank back in her seat, for Irene Prior must not be seen. She glanced at the liveried grooms who sat clothed to perfection. One day she would ride in such carriages, alongside such people. One day she and Antoinette would realize their dreams. One day she would make good what Jack Prior had just done. One day, would she and Harry? Here she stopped.

She called loudly, 'Back home now, driver.'

*   *   *

As she alighted from the coupé in Wandle Court the cold dug into her more deeply. She looked up at the narrow deep brownstone clenched in the middle of a terrace of eight in front of which an ailanthus tree spread its branches over the sidewalk. She hurried up the stoop, ignoring her pain. There was darkness from the basement apartment where Antoinette and Emily lived. So they were not home yet.

In the entrance hall the gaslight flickered on the green flock wallpaper as the maid took her cape and hat. She hurried on up the stairs into the drawing room, throwing her gloves onto the dark mahogany table on which were scattered pages of designs, swatches of material, and behind which was a sewing machine. She opened her arms, smiling as Bernard ran to her, lifting him up, kissing him, then looking beyond to Martha.

Martha, who was worth any number of beatings she had wanted to scream at Jack the night Martha arrived, hissing at him as his fists landed that a family retainer would raise his prestige, and that of his son once they were established in society. He had stayed his fist then and stormed off into the night.

'Hallo, my darling,' Martha said, rising, putting her embroidery away, coming to her, drawing her to the fire, which blazed in the tiled fireplace. 'Delph,' the landlord had pointed out proudly.

She rubbed Irene's hands and instructed the maid, who had followed Irene up, to bring milk. 'Thank you, Cynthia,' Irene said to the young girl.

'Pa's really gone?' asked Bernard, his lower lip jutting. 'He has to go out too much when he's here. He works too hard. It ain't fair.'

Irene smiled gently at her son. 'He'll be back again in four years, my darling. Perhaps your father's day won't be so full by then.' Praying that it would be, even if it was only to the gambling tables he went, for then her son, who physically resembled a Prior with every

266

day that passed, would remain the pleasant child he had been until his father had arrived.

Martha turned him towards Irene. 'You go and sit on your mother's knee, gently now, and tell her of your day, whilst I go with Cynthia to the kitchen for the milk. Gently, I said.'

Gently? Irene stared at Martha as Bernard trotted towards her, his black hair shining even in the dull yellow gaslight. Gently?

Martha merely looked at her, then said quietly, as Bernard stared into the flames, 'Remember, we sensed the true nature of that man even though you did not, and I recognize pain when I see it, and besides, I talked to Antoinette.' Her tone was defiant now.

Irene burst out laughing. 'When haven't you found out all you want to, you old witch?' She held out her hand and Martha came and rubbed it again, and it was as though she was rubbing away all the cares of her life.

Within half an hour Bernard was asleep in bed, and Irene had dined with Martha before instructing Cynthia to keep Antoinette and Emily's meal warm for their return.

At 8.15 p.m. Martha sat opposite Irene before the fire, and there was only the sound of clicking knitting needles, the crackle of the wood as it burned, the ticking of the grandfather clock and Irene's thoughts skated from Wendham as a child when they had roasted chestnuts before just such a fire, to Antoinette whose eyes had been so guarded, so cold and she could not settle. Just as she reached for the poker she heard pounding feet on the stairs, a breathless shout, 'Irene, Irene!'

Startled, Martha dropped her knitting whilst Irene sprang for the door but before she could reach it, it was flung open by Antoinette. 'What's wrong?' Irene cried, peering past her friend onto the landing.

Antoinette snatched a look behind her, dragging Irene back into the room, her eyes alive, her smile warm. Irene smiled with relief, 'Thank goodness, I thought you were angry with me. I thought . . .'

Antoinette shook her. 'Be quiet. Nothing's wrong. Everything's right. He's right behind us. I brought him here. A society gentleman, Irene. It will help build up the money again. It is what we need. Just say I was selling on Emily's behalf. Say I'm your seamstress. I told him Emily ran a workshop. *Haute couture*, Irene. At last.'

Irene caught hold of her friend. 'What? Sakes alive, what?'

Antoinette stuttered, 'This man . . .'

There was a light tap at the door and Cynthia entered, announcing, 'Mr Alexander Moran, Mrs Prior.' A man wearing a frock coat entered uncertainly, standing just within the doorway, carrying a cane and top hat. His face was thin, his pale blue eyes tired, his fair moustache neatly clipped, as were his side whiskers. He was about Irene's age.

His eyes swept the room, taking in the crackling fire, the plumped cushions on the sofa, the woven rugs, taking in Irene and Antoinette. He bowed, hesitated. Irene rallied, her eyes darting from Antoinette to Mr Moran. She said, 'Good evening, I do not believe I have the pleasure of your acquaintance. Perhaps you are lost?'

He flushed, backed, stopped, swept his hand around the room, saying helplessly, 'I must have taken leave of my senses to come unannounced and without introduction. Forgive me. I was hasty. I overheard this woman, I mean this lady, in a department store. She was discussing her merchandise with the manager. I had the temerity to approach her, liking her designs, stating my desire that she should create a gown for my wife. She bade me come. On impulse I did, feeling this was an artisan's area but now I am outraged at myself.

It is unforgivable, an intrusion. My wife would be appalled.'

Antoinette pinched Irene's arm as he continued to back from the room.

Emily was behind him in the doorway, anxiously mouthing, 'Stop him. It's too late. He's seen you, heard your name. Mother wouldn't listen. She doesn't realize what she's done.'

Irene stepped forward, wrenching herself free of Antoinette, wanting to slap her, forcing herself to laugh lightly, holding out her hand, 'I am Mrs Irene Prior, daughter of the late Sir Bartholomew Wendham, of Somerset, England, the eminent botanist. I have temporarily settled in this area whilst on our world tour. Indeed it is not fashionable but I find the chaotic quilt pattern of the streets more reminiscent of England than the grid style of the more prestigious areas such as Fifth Avenue – you must forgive my eccentricity, a touch of homesickness.' Her words had tumbled from her at great speed but now she could think of nothing further to say over the simmering rage, the bursting panic.

Mr Moran was tugging his hand free of his glove, approaching her, bowing over her hand, 'I'm charmed, madame, to make your acquaintance.'

Irene withdrew her hand. Had this gentleman, a member of New York society felt her trembling? Had her explanation been sufficient?

She gestured to the sofa, introducing him to Martha, who made her excuses and left. Irene pointed to the painting of Wendham House that Martha had brought with her and which now hung above the mantel, wanting his gaze away from the table and the dress designs and the advertisement proofs. 'Wendham House,' she indicated. 'Would you care to sit by the fire?'

She insisted he precede her to the sofa, saying, 'I find the cold intense after the mildness of our English climate.' All the while she was gesturing tersely and surreptitiously for Antoinette to take the proofs and designs from the room. She heard the door click shut and saw the table was clear but her mind was still in turmoil.

She sat opposite Mr Moran, struggling for composure, as he also appeared to be doing. She said, finding words at last, 'My personal seamstress will have been accompanying her daughter, that is all. Her daughter Emily joined us from a sojourn in New Bedford and pursues employment in a workshop. What my seamstress does in her free time is entirely her own business. Providing, of course, it is within the law.' She laughed lightly.

Mr Moran bowed his head as he sat awkwardly across from her. 'Yes, yes, I think I understand.' He put his hat on the cushion beside him as he declined Irene's offer of refreshment. 'No, thank you, Mrs Prior. I would not dream of intruding more than I have. As I say, I feel I've made a terrible mistake.'

Irene forced herself to laugh lightly again. 'But in what way? You wish my seamstress to create a gown for your wife, is that not so?'

Mr Moran looked at his hands, one of which was still gloved. He said, 'It sounds so bald, so impertinent, but I deemed her to be attached to a workshop, some commercial enterprise since she was . . . Since she was apparently attempting to interest the manager in her wares. But of course, she was not.' He looked up at her sharply.

'No, she was not. As I say, she was assisting her daughter, in her free time. In England we uphold the rights of the individual. Is that considered an eccentric folly here in a new country I had thought was open to all?' Irene raised her eyebrows, directing the anger she felt at Antoinette towards him.

Mr Moran shook his head, 'Oh dear, indeed not.' He was running his hand round his collar. Irene gestured to the fire screen. 'Please, adjust the screen to your requirements if you find the heat excessive.'

Mr Moran stopped fidgeting with his collar, and flushed again. 'No, the heat is quite delightful, it is just myself who is rather overheated. You see, my wife is to give a ball next week, her first of the season. I thought to surprise her with a new gown, but it was only a recent idea, one in fact which occurred to me as I saw your seamstress. I was taking shelter within the store from the harsh winds – just for a moment and I was extremely taken with the style, the nuance of her gown. You see,' now he leant forward, his voice quickening, 'I thought I would present my wife with it shortly before the ball. She had decided to wear one she wore last year.' His face shone with love, and then clouded, lines of strain appeared, he clenched his hands.

Irene blinked. To give a ball and wear a dress already seen was extraordinary. This man could not be society. He must be a parvenu, new money, and not a very rich one at that. He was obviously trying to force his way in, like her. She didn't know if she was relieved or disappointed.

He continued, 'As I say, I was taken by the design of your seamstress's gown, and that of her companion. Both so understated, so elegant, and I find yours even more so, if I may make so bold.' He stopped again and now stood up. 'Forgive me, this is just too irregular. I do not know what I am thinking of, to speak to you in this way, to force my way into your home. I must of course visit a couture salon.'

He bowed, began to leave.

Her heart went out to him, her anger at Antoinette fled, for hadn't Captain Baines's widow every right to feel aggrieved at the Priors who had taken her lay from her yet again, hadn't she every right to do what she could to recover it? 'No, wait. I'm sure Antoinette would be only too pleased to help, but you must ask her yourself, for I cannot accept on her behalf.'

271

She hurried to the door, knowing that Antoinette and Emily would be listening. She called Antoinette in, saying, 'Perhaps you should bring in your daughter, and if you are agreeable to the request this gentleman wishes to make, she may take notes. I have no objections whatsoever. Meanwhile I will leave you while your business is conducted.'

Now it was her turn to listen at the door, for he could still be dangerous to her.

Antoinette was careful, except when she blurted, 'But Mrs Prior designs . . .' She stopped. 'Mrs Prior has her own thoughts on her dresses and guides me towards her goal, therefore I will of course listen with great interest to your wife's ideas.'

It transpired that Mr Moran did not wish that his wife attend for fitting. 'It must be a complete surprise,' he insisted.

Antoinette suggested he brought along a fairly new gown of Mrs Moran's by lunch-time the next day. 'We will then create a wire model to size. You might care to bring the shoes Mrs Moran intends to wear at the ball so that we can match the colour of the material to the shoes.'

'I am most grateful.'

Antoinette said, her accent becoming more French with every moment, 'I would normally need at least two weeks. You say you need it in a week. Then it would have to be the day of the ball, sir.'

Mr Moran agreed.

Antoinette said, 'Emily, would you advise Mrs Prior that we are finished?'

Emily did so, shutting the door behind her, her face stunned with amazement, whispering, 'I had no idea she could be so determined. Oh la la!'

Irene laughed quietly, ruefully, 'Exactly.' She sobered, patted her hair, and entered.

Mr Moran bowed over her hand again. He said, 'I have found this interlude very refreshing. I have been

272

brought up for generations within New York society and this breach of etiquette would never have been permitted. A thousand thanks, to you, and your eccentricity. How British society must miss you while you travel.' His eyes were sparkling.

Irene stared at Antoinette as he left, not understanding anything Moran had just said, for if he had been brought up for generations within society he was clearly a patrician – old money – but his wife had been about to wear a dress which had been seen before, for her own ball? Nonsense. It was all nonsense.

Antoinette said, her voice hard again now, 'Through him we can bring in high-class custom, using me as a frontman. I *was* in *haute couture*. I *am* your partner. I *insist* we pursue this, and I have *every* right to insist for I have been stolen from again.'

The next day she asked Alan the journalist to find out about the Morans. His note came back saying that Moran was patrician, old money who had been ruined in the fires. He had been in insurance. His wife was a parvenu from a family rich from railroads. Alan ended his note. *That must mean Moran had to pay out on claims on the draft riots. He'd have considered it a debt of honour. I guess his wife's money must have gone for it too. Do you want me to confirm that?*

She didn't, for it was obvious it had, and she and Antoinette worked first on the design, and then created an exact model whilst Emily handled the factory and the orders which were pouring in from the stores they had visited.

Antoinette and Irene worked as though they were driven for neither could remove Moran's love for his wife from their heads and for now their differences appeared resolved.

On the third day Antoinette said, 'Though I still don't understand why they can afford a ball?' Her voice was

273

muffled from the pins she gripped between her teeth as they fitted the gown to the model.

'Perhaps it's a last throw. You know, trying to stay where they belong. Who knows. Poor devils. He was a good man. Chalk, please. We shouldn't charge, you know.'

Antoinette passed the chalk, shaking her head. 'I don't know. We are supposed to be business women and where will free work get us?' She paused, fiddling with a pin, then she said slowly, 'But on the other hand, of course, it could bring us more commissions from the ball guests. "Antoinette" will be in demand, though I agree you must not be seen to be involved.' Her voice was quickening, and there was an edge to it again. Irene looked up, on her guard.

Antoinette laughed and it was a high brittle sound. 'Yes, give it to them if it makes you feel any better. But there must be conditions.'

Irene struggled to her feet, her knees aching, striving to keep her voice calm, 'To get involved in *haute couture* is a risk. Do we need it? Won't we be spreading ourselves in too many directions?'

Antoinette stared up at her, dropping the hem, showering pins on the floor as she also stood, angry words spitting from her.

'I need it. *We* might not, but *I* do. Me, Antoinette Baines, the widow of the captain *your* husband killed, stole from, and still continues to do so, though you appear not to care.'

Irene stared in shock before the bitterness which spilled from this woman, but understanding it. Oh yes, how could she not, for it was how Jack Prior made her feel, made everyone feel.

Antoinette's face was flushed, drawn, tired, full of hate as she came right up close to Irene, shouting into her face, 'It's all gone, all that we have made these past years is gone. We have a loan from Palance, one *we* had to grovel for. Not Jack Prior, the great whaling captain. Now you, his wife, queries whether we need *haute couture*. We need everything, and anything. Do you hear me?'

Antoinette sank onto a chair, staring at the floor, her trembling fingers picking at the deep blue threads of Mrs Moran's gown which clung to her apron. 'Four years, Irene. Four years' work. I am fifty and I have worked until my fingers are sore and my knees creak and all because this man of yours steals my lay, not content with killing my husband.' Tears poured down her cheeks.

Irene came to her but Antoinette pushed her away. 'No, don't touch me. Don't you dare touch me. You talk with pity of Moran, but what of me, what of Emily toiling in the workshop? We work, all of us, but for what? Make the aristocrat pay, make him tell others of us. Don't talk to me of *haute couture* being dangerous. *Haute couture* is more money and that's what we need. Make him, d'you hear, for you have a debt of honour to me. Do you hear? A debt of honour.'

Irene went again to Antoinette, to be rebuffed as before.

'Leave me alone for I have work to do.' Antoinette went down on her knees again, but her tears were still falling, and she looked old and broken.

On the morning of the ball Mr Moran was admitted to the drawing room. When he saw Irene he was startled. 'Forgive me, I was expecting your seamstress.'

Irene gestured to the gown which was displayed over a modest crinoline on the dummy which replicated exactly Mrs Esther Moran's measurements. She and a silent Antoinette had had to unpick the seams the previous evening because the brocade of the bodice was stretched too tight, and while they worked Antoinette had said, her voice cold with rage, 'It is such a small thing we ask of him in exchange for a free gown. He is a drowning man. He will understand survival, he should

275

understand commerce. If he does not guarantee to promote us, then you must tell him he may not have the dress. He has no choice or his wife will have no new dress. It is too late to find another. His guarantee, remember, for that is what you owe the widow of Captain Baines.'

'But it is not a small thing for Moran or me,' Irene had whispered, for such blackmail would destroy her and Bernard's escape by casting her into ignominy in his eyes and that of society's, and destroy her own sense of honour. But then, why should she have escape or honour, when Antoinette only had grief?

Mr Moran was staring at the gown. He placed his hat in Irene's hands not taking his eyes from the shimmering creation, moving nearer, walking full circle round it. He turned to her. 'It is quite beautiful,' he said. Then, 'I don't know how I can thank your seamstress.'

She nodded, feeling cold, though the fire roared in the grate.

'I assume Antoinette will send her invoice?' He had turned back to the gown.

Irene walked to the fire, standing before it, her mouth dry. She said, 'There will be no invoice.' Her voice sounded parched and dry.

He came to her. 'But I have insufficient money on me. So an invoice, if you would so oblige. I can't thank you enough for allowing your seamstress time to work on this. Esther will be the talk of society. It will do her so much good. It will give her hope.'

She said, 'I will pack it for you in Antoinette's absence.'

She moved past him, holding her head erect, not looking at him, or she would weaken, looking only at the dress which she hated with a passion, and in which she no longer saw any beauty.

He followed her, took his hat from her. The clock chimed out on the landing. Eleven. She was needed in the workshop.

She took the box, undid the dress, folded it carefully, the tissue paper crackling, the dress rich and shimmering against the white. She closed the box, placed the already boxed shoes on top of it and held them, not handing them to him. He reached for them. Still she held them, and only now did she look at him, her heart pounding, her breathing shallow. He stood there, confused. Her mind was empty, her hands trembled. Still she held it. He repeated, 'Perhaps Antoinette will oblige me by sending an invoice.'

She could not blackmail. She could not, but she heard herself doing so. She said, 'There will be no charge. All Antoinette requires is a favour.'

He looked bemused. 'A favour?'

Her mouth was dry as she said, 'Antoinette would be grateful if you would undertake to tell those at your ball of the new *haute couture* salon that she will be opening on Broadway, or you may not take the dress.'

He stared at her. 'I beg your pardon.'

'I said that Antoinette would be grateful . . .'

He held up his hand, his face frigid with disdain. 'But a woman of your standing knows that I can make no such undertaking, certainly not at a ball. It smacks of commerce, of business. You also know that I cannot bow before a threat.'

Her mouth was still dry. 'You have no alternative, Mr Moran, for you have insufficient time to commission another.' She hated every word she was saying.

He stared, affronted and confused.

She repeated, 'You must tell them, or I will not hand over the ball gown, and your wife will have to wear last year's – something that both you and I know will not help your standing in your society, especially after your losses.'

He paled now, shock in his eyes, then rage, an appalling distressing rage. He turned from her, and strode to the door, spinning round as he reached it, his lips thin, his knuckles white as he gripped his hat.

'Mrs Prior, you have clearly made enquiries of me. I should have done the same, for I doubted your "world tour", suspecting instead your involvment in "clothing".' He nodded towards the boxes in her arms. 'However, I admired you for it, I did not condemn. Indeed, I hoped that you and my wife might be friends, I thought you a refreshing and delightful companion for a lovely woman. I see I was quite, quite wrong, for you are nothing more than a base and heartless bitch who dares to try to use our *losses*, our two successive stillbirths, to promote your business.

'Mrs Prior, I would rather die than take the gown. I would rather die than promote your wares, than have you step over the threshold of my door.'

Martha and Antoinette came running, when they heard Irene's frantic calls. Martha held her and listened, and could have wept for her charge. Antoinette sat, her mouth working, as Irene moaned, 'What have I done? What have I done to them? Oh, what have I said?'

Antoinette stared at her, appalled, and whispered, 'What have I become?'

Alex Moran stared at the package, barely taking in the contents, for Mrs Prior had pitched him back into the half-crazed world of loss and grief which he had struggled from so painfully over the last two months. He saw the gown and the shoes, and read the note. He threw it in the bin, not knowing what to believe, not caring. He sat staring out across the rooftops.

An hour later there was a knock on the door, and a messenger stood there. He held out two envelopes.

Alex took them, read them. One was from a woman called Martha and it enclosed a well-folded message from Alan Burchill, a journalist. The other was from Antoinette.

*   *   *

Harry urged the whale boat crew on, standing in the stern as Jacko, the harpooner, balanced at the prow, his arm drawn back. 'Get your backs into it,' Harry shouted.

The bowhead sounded. 'Damn and blast,' the harpooner roared above the turbulence of the sea, lowering his harpoon, easing his shoulders.

'Ship oars,' Harry ordered, searching the seas. Over to the west the *Cachalot* had all its boats out, and all the harpooners had struck. Of course they damn well had, for no-one else had been allowed near the pod until Jack Prior and his men had taken their fill.

Harry checked his boats. One had a line attached and was being dragged in the wake of a bull.

Jacko roared, 'East north east.'

Harry shaded his eyes. It was the bull. He yelled, 'Hoist sail.' It was hoisted, the wind took them, the boat surged through the rolling swell. He felt the wind, tasted the salt, fixed his eyes on the bull, on the line coiled in the well of the boat, on Jacko. Nearer and nearer.

Sinclair yelled from the aft-oar. 'Coming up starboard, Mr Travers. That bugger's coming up starboard.'

Harry swung round. Jack Prior's boat was cutting across their path, its sail full, Prior in the stern, his shirt billowing out, waving them back, goddammit.

Harry searched the seas behind, saw Jack's first whale being taken in tow by his second mate, who already had a cow.

'We won't give way, damnit,' he yelled to his crew.

Sinclair shouted up at him, clinging to the seat as the boat beat down again and again on the sea which was livelier now, as the wind increased, 'Harry, you know damn well we must.'

Spray soaked them, the prow crashed into a trough, out of it. Harry ran his hands through his hair, staring at Jack, then down at Sinclair. 'I hate him, I hate him,' he said, again and again, as Prior's boat drew nearer and nearer. 'I can't give way,' he repeated.

Jacko swung round. 'Another bull two points west, Mr Travers.' He pointed.

Harry turned. Yes, goddammit, and bigger too. 'Give way,' he roared, and trimmed the sail, taking the new heading, pulling away, but seeing the triumph on Jack Prior's face as he went.

He yelled to the crew, 'We'll get that bull, we'll tow it back so's he can feast his damn eyes on it.'

Sinclair laughed, relief and anger combining.

On they surged, closer and closer. They lowered the sail, took up oars. 'Get your backs into it,' Harry roared. 'I want him to see this. I want him jealous. I want him sick with envy, got it?'

Sinclair pulled at his trousers. 'Steady. Steady.'

But rage had been in Harry too long, loss had torn at him too much. He stared down at Sinclair. 'I want that whale. I want to tow it back past the bugger. I want its wash to wipe the smile from his damned face.'

Sinclair urged, 'Don't get careless, think of the bull, not Prior. Think, Harry, just think, goddammit.'

'Closer now, closer.' Harry wasn't listening, he was watching as Jacko stood bracing himself, his harpoon at the ready. The huge black bulk glistened, Harry's hand on the tiller was steady, the spray was bursting over them. The harpoon was thrown, the line spun out round the loggerhead, the whale sounded, dragged the boat, was taking all the line, the loggerhead was smoking. Sam threw water on it. They attached another, Jacko doubled back to the stern, Harry eased his way to the prow, looking back at Prior, who was glaring. On the whale drove. The line whipped out as the whale surged on.

Sinclair yelled, 'Harry, for God's sake, the line.' For the line was coiled badly and Harry stood with one foot within a snag. But he moved too late. The line tightened, gripped around his calf. Harry fell, was whipped towards the prow, the line tightening as the whale tore on. Tightening, slicing. The pain, the pain.

The fore-oarsman lunged, sliced the line with his knife. Harry fell back into the well of the boat, blood spraying, hearing nothing but screaming, feeling nothing but pain. It was his own scream, his own pain, and there was no light.

Sinclair yelled, 'Oh God, oh my God.' He scrambled towards his friend, holding him, as he writhed, as others did also. He ripped off his jacket, wrapped it round what had once been Harry's ankle, trying to staunch the flow of blood.

Jack Prior laughed, a gust of wind carried it across the sea but then it was gone, drowned again by Harry's screams.

CHAPTER FOURTEEN

By late spring the Penny Press advertisements had brought many orders and local stores were taking more and more of their lines. At last Irene and Antoinette had put behind them the memory of their actions, had accepted shared blame, shared shame, had promised that their friendship must never be threatened again. They had visited Alan and been told that his contact had made an error. It was Moran's father who had lost his money in the Great New York Fire of 1835.

'What can we do?' Antoinette had said to Irene, as they left the newspaper office the day after Moran had been, and Alan had told them. 'What can I say to you?' Antoinette said.

'That you're still my friend, still my partner, then I can go on,' Irene replied, hiding her despair, saving that for the long nights when she stared into the dark fearing she would never return with Bernard to her home, never save them both from Jack, never again see Harry.

During the next week Palance authorized the leasing of an extra workshop and argued that lower wages be instigated to make good the interest from the loan they had taken out to find the materials.

Irene refused, visiting him in his hotel, for what did it matter if she was seen here, or in the workshop, for Moran would have told society about the Prior woman, warning them against her, for by now he would have confirmed that his suspicions of her world tour were correct.

In the foyer, sitting opposite Palance at the small

table, she slammed her hand down, shouting at him, telling him that to lower wages would not be efficient, that quality would fall and that is what they were noted for, leaning forward, saying slowly and clearly, 'Try it, and then explain to Mr Prior when he returns in four years that you have single-handedly ruined his business. Try it, and experience the Jack Prior rage at first hand.'

'Such high wages are undermining our profits,' he hissed, spittle spraying the table.

'Rubbish. There would be no profits without the quality. Prices have increased one hundred per cent since the war, and we are one of the few to increase wages likewise. All around there are strikes, bad feeling, but we have had none of that.'

She slammed out of the hotel, taking the coupé back to the brownstone, storming up the stoop, running up the stairs into the drawing room, tearing off her gloves, shaking them at Martha who stood by the fireplace while Bernard painted on layers of newspaper at the rosewood desk.

'That Palance. He sits there with that pompous face on him telling me to cut my costs, when our quality of work has brought in treble the orders. Next he'll be insisting we bribe that Tweed and his crooked politicians at the town hall for some spurious advantage. Well, I'll run this as I see fit. Jack can't interfere, not yet anyway. Not for four years, and in the meantime I won't have my workers being hurt.'

Martha held out a note. 'This is for you. I had feared you would not return in time.' Her plump face was tense; half hopeful, half fearful.

Throwing her gloves on the table Irene took it. A note, but from whom? The handwriting meant nothing. She opened it. The words were written in a clear bold hand, but obviously in haste. Irene read aloud, 'Mrs Esther Moran wishes to thank Irene Prior for the gown and would be pleased if she would accompany her in her carriage at eleven prompt.'

Martha nodded, gripping her hands tightly together in front of her apron. 'She called near on an hour ago, in her carriage. Beautiful it is. Two horses with shiny coats. She was passing, she said. Most improper, she said. She should have left her card first. Oh Irene, I feared you'd not be back in time. She wrote this for me to give you. She wants to show you the sights.'

Irene felt as though she wasn't taking any air in, felt as though the room was reeling. Her hands were trembling too much for her to read it through again. She checked the clock. It was almost eleven now. The note fluttered from her hands. 'I won't go. I won't, Martha. I don't want to hear any more anger. I don't want to feel any more shame.' She felt behind her for the chair, and sat. 'No, I won't go. I've apologized in my note. I sent condolences. No. No.'

Martha tucked her chin down and glared. 'You'll go. You'll face her and you'll go. This is something you must do. She seems a nice sort of woman, fragile like, but with a spark in her I fancy, though it needs kindling. She looks – oh tired, and who can wonder after losing a babe, and one before that too. That's what you have to think of, that poor soul, nothing else. You are a Wendham.'

Irene shook her head, 'No, I won't.'

Martha raised her eyebrows. 'You'll go,' she insisted.

As the clock chimed eleven, the carriage drew up and Martha shooed her out of the door, still protesting. Irene walked out down the stoop, into a surprisingly warm day. Buds were forming on the ailanthus, shadows flickered on the ground, and she looked at these, not at the woman in the open carriage, who finally called, 'Good day, Mrs Prior.' Her voice was light and warm. Irene looked at her, seeing a frail fair woman who smiled at her approach. Her dress was of pale lemon, her shawl and parasol paler still, her hat the colour of her shawl.

The coachman opened the door, the springs gave as she climbed in and sat alongside Mrs Moran. Neither woman spoke until the coachman mounted his seat, flicked the reins, and the carriage drew away. Irene glanced up at the brownstone. Bernard was at the drawing-room window, waving. She smiled.

Mrs Moran drawled, her voice light and clear, 'He seems a fine boy.'

Irene answered, turning round to address her, 'Yes, he is.'

Mrs Moran stared at her and Irene would not turn away as those pale blue eyes, the exact colour of Mr Moran's, examined her. At last Mrs Moran reached out a gloved hand as the carriage approached Fifth Avenue, and lightly touched Irene's arm. 'I must thank you for that beautiful gown you allowed your dressmaker to create for me.'

The carriage was bowling along Broadway where spanking shops lined the thoroughfare. Esther drawled, 'Arthur, let's just slow down here, this isn't a race.' She was looking from one side of the road to the other. 'Seems to get busier every time I turn my back. I don't know, you get laid up for a while and what happens? The rich get richer, shopkeepers busier.'

Irene wasn't watching the shops, she was staring at Arthur's back, and now she said softly, 'I asked your husband for a commitment to recommend us. I was stupidly forward. I was misinformed about your loss. I offended your husband. I hurt him. It was unforgivable.'

Esther's gloved hand stayed perfectly still on her arm, then she squeezed and said quietly, in that clear drawl, 'Well, it seems that there's a veritable wave of apologies sweeping this fair city. See, I carry this note from my husband. It would have come sooner but I did not know until last week what had occurred. He is a pompous fool sometimes and is awful conscious of the position he is still allowed to hold within society – mainly because of his father's honourable actions – and was fearful of losing his place by hawking your wares, to put it kind of crudely. He was also distraught with grief. He called you by a foul name, incensed by what he saw as blackmail.' Her eyebrows were raised above a rueful smile as she handed a note to Irene.

Irene said, 'It was blackmail. The word was justified.'

Mrs Moran shook her head. 'What he called you is never justified, Mrs Prior.'

Irene read the words, stunned by the graciousness of Mrs Moran, embarrassed by her goodness. *Mrs Prior. Forgive me. What I said was inappropriate and unforgivable, and I hope that in the fullness of time you will allow yourself to forget.* Mrs Moran drawled, 'I guess "inappropriate" was in there somewhere, seems to be his favourite word for something he isn't too proud of?'

Irene laughed, and nodded.

Mrs Moran continued, 'Kinda wordy, but he's good through to his soul. Now, the thing is, is Mrs Jack Prior about to allow Mr Alexander Moran his breach of manners, and can we therefore get down to business?'

Irene stared at her. 'Is this all,' she waved her hand at Arthur, and at the note, 'because you wished Antoinette to make you another gown? You need merely have asked.'

They were slowly passing shop windows full of French laces, English woollens, *objets d'art*. Mrs Moran smiled at her, 'I know that, but perhaps I just chose to make your acquaintance?'

Again Irene stared.

'Gee those horses on Arthur.' The carriage increased in speed. Esther Moran said, 'Of course Broadway can't be compared to your Bond Street but wouldn't you say it was coming on?' Confused, Irene nodded.

At Washington Square Esther called, 'Just reign it all in, Arthur, we wish to enjoy the view.'

The horses ambled and Irene listened to the rattle of

the other carts and carriages, and saw other women with parasols smiling at Esther, but looking curiously at Irene. All the time there was the huff of their own horses, the light swish of the carriage springs, and now there was a burgeoning regret that these women would never smile at her, would never even know of her existence, would never facilitate her son's transference into English society.

She stared down at her tightly clasped hands, knowing that it was no-one's fault but her own for she could have rejected Antoinette's demands, but also knowing that they were perfectly justifiable, and that the friendship they had was more important.

Esther tapped her arm, indicating the half-built houses on the square. 'This is where those with money now build, though not us of course.' She coughed slightly, waving her hand towards a half-built mansion. 'All this building makes the city so dusty. Yes, we have moved to West Twenty-Eighth Street, but perhaps you knew of our change of address? Perhaps you have made enquiries again?'

Irene swung round defensively, but there was no guile in Mrs Moran's face, no sarcasm. Irene said, uncertainly, 'No, it is no longer important for me to know such things. Last time I merely asked a friend to discover . . .' She stopped. No, she would not explain, not any more, not to anyone.

Esther brooded. 'Well, that is kind of a shame, because it still should be important to you, you know. It's by no means out of the question that you'll be here, some day fairly soon, tucked up neatly into society, and your Antoinette safely in her own *haute couture* salon.' Irene swung round to her.

Esther laughed, 'Do look out at those houses, not at me. I'm nothing to aspire to, whereas they are. You see that grand one. It's the Guggenheims, they're "new" and over there the Astors. Back there the "old" Brevoorts, and the Schermerhorns. Commodore

Vanderbilt too. They were all at my ball, with noses twitching at my gown.'

'What do you mean, I could be there?'

Esther slanted her parasol, cutting off the sun. She brushed at her skirt and said, her voice a monotone, 'You sent condolences that Alex kept to himself until last week. You said things no-one else had said. You wrote words that gave me hope, that made me feel someone else had coped with loss.' Her voice broke.

Irene took her hand, pleading, 'Don't say any more. Please. I feel so deeply for you.'

Esther gripped her hand, staring at Irene with eyes full of tears. 'Then can we start again, can we be friends? I knew I would like you the moment I read the note. Alex said you were refreshing, and lordy, do I need to be refreshed.' There was a trace of spirit in her voice.

Irene flushed. 'I'm sorry, Mrs Moran. I do like you. I do sympathize with you, but why you presume that I wish to live on this street, be part of your society, I can't imagine.' Her voice was cool, detached, proud.

Esther Moran burst out laughing. 'I just love it!' she exclaimed. 'Now, if that chin way up in the air isn't refreshing I just don't know what is. Come now, Irene Prior, I don't presume, I know.'

'How?'

'Your Martha, and your Antoinette also, wrote on the day the gown was delivered. They love you deeply, they told Alexander that you acted against your better judgement, your instincts, your decency and kindness. They told him that you were willing to put aside all this to fulfil a debt of honour. We understand that. We applaud it. They also informed us of the dream.'

Esther smoothed back her chignon, adjusted her hat, sat back and her voice was firm now as she said, 'You will need help or you will not breach the barricades that the patricians are scurrying about frantically erecting, now that the war is over and so many deeply rich parvenus are squeezing into the ranks.' Her voice was ironic, her face exasperated. 'It's a tougher job to make that *squeeze* than it's ever been, and only a few make it. You, Mrs Prior, will not, for you do not have the purse. You might have had if you had "bought" wartime contracts, or chose to line the Tammany wallets, or paid unfair wages, or hadn't a husband's debts to settle.'

Irene said, 'How . . . ?'

Esther raised an eyebrow. 'You are not the only one who can make enquiries. Now, as for your position as the daughter of Sir Bartholomew Wendham – well, if you were a handsome young *man* with a British title, or the son of a title, mothers of daughters would welcome you with open arms, but you aren't. You're married to Jack Prior, who just has a few ships, fewer manners, and no social standing whatsoever. So you need my help. Hey, I ain't such a witch, am I?' She switched to an extreme drawl.

Irene laughed, feeling as buffeted as a ship in a storm.

'That's better,' Esther said, sighing with relief, leaning back, spinning her parasol. 'Well, as I said, down to business, and first things first. You're passably beautiful, you know that. That'll help. You have style, that's even more important and you have some breeding, but little money.'

Irene shook her head again. 'You mustn't do this. You are a parvenu. I could bring you down if you nominate me, and it is discovered that . . .' She stopped.

Esther nodded, 'Go on, don't keep me in suspense.'

Irene clasped her hands and told her the truth about her runaway marriage, her years on the whaler, her plan to leave Jack when Bernard came of age, her role in the workshop.

'That's what I wanted to hear, and they're all things we already know.'

Irene flushed. 'You . . .'

Esther put up her hand. 'Forgive us a little more. I just needed to know I could trust you to be honest, patronizing though that seems.'

The carriage had stopped, Arthur was leaning forward talking softly to the horses.

Irene was thinking only that her plan to leave Jack had been discovered. She said, full of dread, 'If your detective has discovered my future plans, then Jack could too.'

Esther calmed her. 'No, it was Martha and Antoinette who told me. Move on now, Arthur, let's see St Patrick's.'

'But why?' Irene asked.

'Because it's going to be a grand cathedral.'

Irene shook her head. 'No, why have you gone to these lengths, are going to these lengths to help me? It doesn't make sense.'

'Nothing does very much though, does it?' Esther's laugh was deeply ironic. 'My daddy made his money. I inherited. I married a patrician, but one with a whole lot of honour and no money; kind of convenient for him. I married out of love but I sometimes ponder Alex's motives.'

Irene protested, swept by bleakness, 'Oh, believe me, I know what it is to live with a man who has no love. You fill your husband's world. You are so very fortunate.'

'But you, my dear Irene Prior, have a son. So you, too, are fortunate.' Now the bleakness was in Esther. Both women were silent as they approached St Patrick's Cathedral and once abreast they barely looked at it.

Esther raised her head and said, 'We were discussing my reasons.' Again the irony was back. 'You see, my dear Irene, whilst you are working and fighting for your family and friends, I, who am already in society, spend my time fulfilling rituals, leaving my card, spending the summer in Saratoga, the winter in New York, a useless ornament who cannot even bear children.'

She held up her hand at Irene's protest. 'I am bored, almost to death. Around me my fellow sufferers adorn their husband's arm while growing stunted by constraints, taking hash or alcohol to save the smile from fading, the mask from slipping. You wear no mask. You are alive, you have suffered, you have plans. I want to be part of that, and continue to be part of it once you are "in". For that I have Alex's blessing, so long as we take care. So yes, you are right, I am convincing myself that he must love me deeply.' She smiled, but her eyes were serious. 'Can a parvenu and a daughter of a knight be friends?'

Irene felt the sun on her, saw the brightness of the day, felt laughter bubbling, but then she sobered. 'Yes, we can be friends, but I haven't the money yet to support a society lifestyle.'

Esther chided, 'There's no rush, and I need to check through friends in Washington that no official hint of the reality of your runaway marriage is in circulation. If it is, we shall have to see if there is a way round it. I will set wheels in motion before I leave for Saratoga. Now, one last thing. Is Antoinette's daughter reliable, and the journalist?'

Irene said firmly, 'I would trust them with my life.'

'That is precisely what you are doing, my dear, and ours too.'

Summer was hot, the stench was high, the days long and hard, but Martha took charge of Bernard, allowing Irene to work at her designs, and on publicity plans, including an advertisement in the *Herald Tribune* which brought a great response. The last hour before luncheon was put aside for drafting correspondence that Antoinette would sign as she had done from the start, or which would be forwarded to Palance, for nothing must bear evidence of Irene's involvement.

The afternoons were spent with Martha and Bernard, playing in the small garden, or seeking shade amongst the burgeoning trees of Central Park as they watched the earth-bearing carts, and heard the blasts which were creating outcroppings of rock. They shaded their eyes and watched as men worked to drain the bog rills, gathering them into lakes.

Sometimes Martha and Irene would throw the ball for Bernard to hit with his new baseball bat, or watch, smiling, as Bernard rolled his hoop with other children. Once they went to Barnum's Museum but Irene could not bear to see such distorted animals and humans on display.

They took a hired coupé to view the exotic shops on Broadway and then the new houses, admiring the red brick and white stone Greek revival styles, but loving the brownstones more.

They stared at the Opera House and Irene wondered if she would ever draw up beneath the porticoes confident of her place amongst her peers. They gazed at Delmonico's which was preparing to move from William Street uptown, which was more socially acceptable now that warehouses and stores were taking over the downtown area. Would she ever dance there?

On to Union Square, and past Grinnell's restaurant. Would she ever eat canvasback duck and drink champagne there? She would look at Martha, who always nodded, murmuring, 'Patience. Mrs Moran will let you know when she returns in October how she will proceed with her plans.'

At night she would lie motionless in the great heat wondering where Harry was, and whether he had received the letter she had sent while he was at New Bedford, rereading the letter he had sent her from there and which she stored with his others. Again and again she read the coded polite phrases, the reporting of business as her first letter to him had suggested in case they were intercepted. But though they were reports they had been written by a hand she loved, touched by a man whose image had not faded, any more than her love had faded. Could he tell that in her cold replies? Please, please, say he could tell that. 'Write again,' she murmured. 'Please, write again.'

*   *   *

During the summer they established a corsetry outlet in the resort of Saratoga. They doubled their distribution of gowns to department stores and emporiums within New York, and to other cities, using the ever improving railroad system, finding that those which had taken their mourning took more and more of their other lines.

They found outlets for lower quality cheaper dresses, and mourning weeds made out of Borada crêpe, selling them to markets and smaller shops. Palance had not raised the question of lower wages again, but had insisted that he invoice all the outlets direct, and that payment was received by him, direct. He passed on living expenses to Irene, and wages to Antoinette and Emily. They pooled the money and divided it equally. 'Partners,' they insisted.

Some hard-pressed small market stalls struck a deal with Antoinette and paid half in second-hand clothes, half to be paid for in the normal way and sent direct to Palance.

He protested. Antoinette and she drafted a letter that evening, which Antoinette signed, advising him that the small market traders were a good source of revenue, and that the second-hand clothes were then sold on to the many immigrants who were flooding into New York. It was a section of the market that was bringing in a considerable revenue.

This revenue would be passed to him at the end of each month, bringing a bigger profit to Prior's Clothing Workshops. *However*, Antoinette wrote, *if you prefer the second-hand clothes to be sent direct to your office, you need only ask*.

They heard nothing for a week, then he wrote to say that Jack Prior would be more than interested in the situation when he put in with his blubber and baleen in September, for he had gone to the Arctic first, or had he forgotten to mention that to Mrs Prior?

He had indeed forgotten, and though the news was like an earthquake they brushed the panic aside, and spent hour after hour preparing their own set of accounts from duplicate invoices and payment records of all transactions to date for Irene was convinced that Palance was dishonest, that the profits he would present to Jack would be lower than they should be and she must be able to defend herself, and her running of the business.

On the last day of August Irene woke suddenly. She lay there knowing something had startled her from sleep, but not knowing what. She relaxed as she heard the clock in the hall chiming midnight, turned over, drifted, but was dragged awake again and now she heard a knocking on the front door.

She dragged herself from her bed, pulling on her dressing gown, hurrying down the stairs, where Martha was lighting the oil lamp, holding it up, a rolling pin in her hand. 'Where on earth did you get that from?' Irene asked, as she drew back the bolts, calling through the door. 'Who is it?' The knocking stopped, but no-one answered.

'I've always slept with one under my pillow, and I dare say I always will.'

'Well, it's hardly a burglar. He'd come in through the window.'

Again there was a faint knocking, then nothing. Martha hissed, 'Well, what if it's that husband of yours, drunk? He hasn't answered, has he?'

Irene closed her eyes, dread drenching her. 'But it's not September,' she whispered. 'And if it was Jack he'd be pounding, not knocking.' Martha shrugged. 'You never know with that one and his tricks.'

Irene called again. There was no answer. She waited, then reached towards the last bolt, and pictured Jack waiting. She let her arm drop. But then she heard, 'Irene. Anyone.' Martha looked at her askance.

'Harry,' Irene called, tearing back the bolt, flinging open the door. Martha held up the lamp. Harry stood there, his portmanteaux at his feet, the lamplight on his face. She held out her hands. He took them. 'Irene,' he murmured.

'You came. But . . .'

He nodded. She felt the tremble in his hands, the heat of his skin, saw the brightness of his eyes, the flush on his cheeks, the deep lines dragging at his mouth. He staggered, leaned against the wall wincing. Irene pulled at him, 'Harry.' Her voice was almost a scream.

Martha was with them now. 'Come along then, into the kitchen with him. He's running a fever. Needs a good drink of water at the very least.'

She bustled ahead, as Harry pushed himself free of the wall, smiling at her. 'So, you managed to bring Martha over. You always promised you would just as soon as you possibly could. I'm proud of you, Irene Wendham.'

She reached up and touched his cheek, all her love in the touch. She withdrew her hand, but he snatched it back, closed his eyes and leaned into the feel of her, and for Harry nothing else existed, not the pain, the fever, the exhaustion. He was here, with her and she was as beautiful as ever. She said, 'You are so very hot.' She struggled to keep her voice calm, for Martha must not know. No-one must.

She took his weight, putting her arm around his waist, helping him along the passage saying, 'You really are very hot.' Meaning, I love you. What's wrong?

He tried not to limp, but the pain was too bad. He whispered, 'Well, that's hardly surprising. It is very hot.' But the Arctic had been cold, so cold, and she hadn't been there, lying next to him. He stopped, shook his head. No, that wasn't this trip. His mouth was dry, his leg on fire. He couldn't grasp his thoughts, only his feelings. He was here, with her, but only for a few hours, and now he felt tears spring to his eyes. He brushed his arm across his face.

Martha had lit the gaslights, and opened the window in the kitchen and was pouring cool water into a bowl. 'Take that jacket off and get sat down.' She pointed to one of the chairs at the deal table.

Irene eased him onto the seat, dragging off his jacket. 'You've hurt your leg.' Her voice was still cool, but how?

He nodded, grunting with pain. 'I lost my foot, two months ago. Got it caught in the line as it spun out after the whale. First mate tidied the leg. It's fine now. Really, just fine.'

Irene hugged his jacket, staring at him, trying to get her breath as he sat there, his head hanging down, his hand on the table. His shoulders were almost sharp beneath his shirt. His breathing was shallow. 'Tidied it,' she repeated faintly.

Captain Baines had tidied a crewman's leg. Even after the man was insensible from the brandy they had poured down his throat he screamed at the first bite of the saw.

She dropped his jacket to the floor, and held him to her, stroking his hair, wanting to speak but knowing that if she did the tears that were thick in her throat would fall. She bent and whispered, 'Oh no, oh no.'

She looked across at Martha who was ripping up rags, staring at her as she did so. 'He's my friend,' Irene whispered.

'I can see that.'

Harry was hotter still, his whole body trembled, but he pulled away for if he stayed against her, and felt her lips on his hair for a second longer, he would cling to her and say, I love you, I've missed you, let me stay for ever, and he mustn't do that. Not here, not now, not until Bernard was old and that was a lifetime away.

He closed his eyes, bit his lips or the words would come.

Instead he said, with a voice so faint he barely

296

recognized it, 'I'm here with a message from Jack Prior. That's the only reason I'm here.' He stopped, began again, panting, but broke off, a groan breaking from him as his leg seemed almost on the point of bursting. Irene said, 'Not now. Rest now.' So cool she sounded. So cool and clear.

He said, 'Prior said, "Go see someone who's putting your ideas into practice, you stinking convict." His note's in the jacket.' He was panting against the pain, which was rising again, higher and higher.

'Don't speak,' Irene knelt beside him.

He stared at her, and now his thoughts were fragmenting, floating, drifting. He bent forward, leaning his head down on the table. 'I'm tired,' he murmured. 'So tired.' He jerked awake, sat up. His hand was still against her cheek. 'Foot,' he said. 'I have to get my new foot. My foot's gone, you see. It's gone. Quite gone, like . . .' he trailed away. 'Like Prior. Gone to Dundee. Oil. Back soon, Irene. He's back soon, to take my whales, to laugh.'

Irene rose, standing back, but wanting to hold him, protect him, love him. She said, 'He won't laugh at you ever again. We'll get you well. You'll escape. We'll do it somehow, won't we, Martha?'

Martha had put a bowl of water on the table, and now held out a glass to Irene. 'Give the man this, or there'll be no-one escaping nowhere.'

Harry felt the glass against his lips, felt the cool water in his mouth, throat, and as he swallowed he plunged back to reality and knew he could never escape for Jack Prior would beat this woman senseless if he thought his other bound, powerless Britisher had fled the coop.

Between them they helped Harry up the stairs, then Martha sent Irene from the room whilst she stripped his clothes from him, coming out of the room with her lips compressed. 'We'll need a doctor to that stump, and we'll need one fast.'

297

Irene ran through the streets until she reached Dr Mendel, pounding on the door, standing back as the lights came on and a window was pushed up. Dr Mendel shouted, 'Vot is it?'

'It's an emergency. Please come. I live at Wandle Court.'

He came, his black bag banging on his leg as he ran, his jacket flying open. On up the stoop, past Cynthia the maid, who had been woken by the noise, up the stairs, into the bedroom, where Martha sat sponging Harry.

The doctor examined him, and Irene stared at his leg which had been amputated just below the knee. She stared as he lanced the swollen wound, and Harry's pain was her pain, his scream her scream. She stared though she could see nothing through the blur, as she held his hand.

She sat with him all night, bathing his white drawn face in the soft glow of the lamp when his temperature soared too high, and barely gave a thought to Jack Prior's message, but as Martha entered at dawn with a steaming cup of tea she reminded her and dug it from Harry's inner jacket pocket, handing it to Irene. 'Forewarned is forearmed,' she murmured grimly.

Irene looked at the savage handwriting scored deep into the paper and could not bear to touch anything that he had touched. She handed it back to Martha, who sat on the opposite side of the bed. 'Please read it, Martha.'

Martha did so, in a voice barely louder than a whisper, while Irene straightened Harry's sheet. 'He says, I forbid the secondhand exchange. Palance can't keep track of the money which I am sure is not accidental. I don't want you lining your own pockets. Neither do I want that Martha turning my boy into a milksop. See that she doesn't, or she goes. And where's my damn big house, my dynasty, my place alongside all the Vanderbilts, the Astors?'

Irene dipped a cloth into the water, wringing it until

her wrists ached. 'Keep him cool,' the doctor had ordered. 'It is the best vay to keep the fever down. Keep the vound clean, keep it dressed. That vill hurt, but it must be done.'

Damn Jack, damn him to hell. She wrung the cloth again.

Martha said, 'I will go, if it is best, and please don't wring that cloth any more, it isn't Jack Prior.'

Irene rested her hands on the edge of the bowl. 'You will not go. Trust me. And I have Palance sewn up so damn tight he'll be out on his neck. Jack needs me. He knows that. We're safe, for now, and I'm going to make quite sure that Harry is, and Sinclair too. This has gone on long enough.'

The doctor called daily, his face more and more anxious. 'Yes, he could die,' he confirmed as she asked the question that had been tormenting her.

Irene left the running of the business entirely to Antoinette, and the designs, and the publicity, though she worked on the accounts as she sat beside Harry because Palance would not win, it was she who would. Just as it was she who would send this man far from Jack's clutches if he survived. Her love demanded that.

But there was no 'if'. He must survive.

Each night she slept in the chair by Harry's bedside, though Martha protested.

Irene merely insisted, 'No, it must be me.'

When Bernard came to say goodnight he pulled at her clothes, 'Me, mummy. Me, not him.'

Each time she pulled him onto her knee and whispered, 'For now, it must be Mr Travers, then it will be you again.' She murmured stories in his ear of the coldness of the Arctic, the wildness of the seas off New Zealand, the flapping of the sails in a light breeze, until he slept, and then she handed him to Martha, for she must not leave Harry.

Throughout the night she dozed but woke at every

sound he made, and listened to his stumbling delirium, being his mother when he required it, being his brother, his father, longing to hear her name, longing to hear that he still loved her, as she endlessly whispered that she loved him.

She heard him stumble through the biblical passages which had taught him to read, heard him plead his case in the court, heard his moans as he was once again in the hulk. At last she heard, 'Irene, Irene. I love you. Be safe. Prior might . . . I love you. Oh God, I love you. But, but . . .'

She lifted his hand to her lips, bent to his, kissed him, whispered again, 'I too. I too love you. I always will.'

She called for water, bathed him, adoring his body, brushing aside Martha's protests. 'Don't be so stupid, woman. This man and I have slept side by side while ice lay an inch thick on the walls around us and the floor beneath us. This man and I have fought, and laughed and feared together. He has shared my nightmares, he has forced me to survive, and now I will do the same for him. He's my friend.'

She didn't even look as Martha left the room, she just gently dried him, sat beside his bed, held his hand, smoothed his hair, gathering their life together to her, remembering the hours on watch, the words of anger which had become words of friendship, remembering the nightmare of the flensing; the grease, the heat, the stench, the sharks.

Remembering the feel of the spermaceti in the tub, Arnie's lessons, the beach in New Zealand, the peace on the *Wendham*, the cold of the Arctic, the feel of this man's warmth, the love, the joy, the pain.

After ten days he slept without a sound, and in the morning, as Martha brought Irene her tea, he opened his eyes, stared up at the ceiling, then at the sash window through which the late summer light streamed, then at Martha. There was no recognition.

Then at Irene, and now he smiled, lifted a finger. She laid her hand on his, whispering, 'You're safe, my love.'

For the next week she allowed Martha to take over between the hours of two and four in the afternoon and resumed her time with Bernard, but she still kept the night-time vigil, though Martha tutted and said it wasn't seemly.

Irene just smiled. The life she, Harry and Sinclair had led could never be called seemly but there had never been anything truer and each night they talked of their love, of their lives, and though she never moved from the chair it was as though she was alongside him, merging into him, becoming one with him.

It was enough, they both said, their fingers entwined, and that was as it had to be until Wendham House, for this they also talked of, folding the secret up inside themselves with the dawn, and knew that they would never speak of it, or act on it, once he was better. For that was also as it had to be.

So night after night she turned the wick high on the lamp to see the light play on his hair, on his eyes, on his lips which talked such fine words of love, and so that he, too, could see the truth in her eyes as she told him she would die for him, that their love would sustain her, that she would somehow keep him safe, keep him with her, for he had refused to escape.

By the end of the third week there was colour in his cheeks, and his eyes were no longer sunken, and Martha and Irene helped him down the stairs and as they did so the clump from his false leg sounded very loud on the polished wood.

In the shade of the small yard they eased him into a chair and listened as he told them, 'The cooper made the leg but couldn't joint the ankle, and what a cussin' and swearing that went on, when he tried to force it into my boot. Couldn't do it. Had to cut the foot in half. Useful things, false feet.'

Dr Mendel examined the wooden contraption and the next day sent a colleague who took measurements and returned within the week with a jointed replacement.

Now Bernard stood with Irene and Martha under the same tree watching as Harry, supported by Dr Mendel, bore down on the wooden leg. Seeing him pale, Irene started forward. Dr Mendel waved her back. 'Sure, it vill hurt for a while until his stump adjusts to the tighter fit. He must endure.'

'Harry needs to be told nothing about endurance,' Irene snapped.

Dr Mendel lifted weary eyes to her, 'Perhaps, neither do you. You need some rest.'

Harry was standing unaided now, his face triumphant. 'Look,' called Bernard. 'Look, he's clever, he's standing.'

Martha sniffed, 'Lot of fuss over nothing.'

Harry looked up at her and laughed, shaking his head, and now Irene saw that Martha was weeping.

At the end of September Jack Prior drew up outside the brownstone in a carriage, his frock coat expensive and well fitted, his malacca cane pristine. Irene watched from the drawing-room window. She had received his cable ordering her to be at the house on his arrival. Harry had left for the factory with Antoinette, as he had done all week, though both had wanted to stay with her.

She checked for the hundredth time that the books were in order.

She heard Bernard rush from the school room, his governess calling, 'Bernard, come here, you have this reckoning to do.'

She heard Jack boom from the hallway, 'Well, what a great big man my boy is.'

She heard Bernard's squeal of delight, which grew

302

louder as they climbed the stairs, and all the time the tension within her rose.

The door burst open. Jack stood there, with Bernard on his arm.

Jack glared at her as he put the boy down. Bernard tugged at his father's frockcoat. 'Not now,' Jack shouted.

Bernard backed away, confused.

Irene said, 'Bernie, off you go and do your sums. You were trying to add two pods of whales together, weren't you? After Daddy's fleet had gathered them all together.' She smiled encouragingly at her son, and then Jack.

Bernard nodded, then ran from the room. Jack was watching her quizzically. 'Is that so?'

She nodded. 'A child needs to be proud of his father.'

Jack flung his hat onto the table. It hit the books. She said, before Jack could speak, 'I'm glad you're here. Palance is a cheat. I have the proof.' She gestured to the books and the invoices, rushing on, 'I asked all our outlets for a copy of their invoices and their payments. You will see that our debt is paid, complete with interest. We should be well in profit, but Palance keeps on about paying lower wages to make good our losses. If his figures are different to mine, I can assure you that somewhere he has a fat little bank account. I'm also sure that he's trying to divert our attention from his doings by complaining about the second-hand clothes. So ask *him* why we're not alongside the others on Fifth Avenue.'

She stopped to draw breath, seeing his eyes narrowing as he listened. She plunged on, 'That man is playing us for fools. He must be laughing up his sleeve. Yes, I've made contacts, but how much longer I can spin them out, without the money to back it up, I don't know and at this rate it'll be Palance sitting alongside the Vanderbilts, and throwing dollars around the gambling tables, but they'll be your dollars.'

She opened the books. He came and stood by her, too close. She forced herself not to flinch. She talked him through the figures, matching them to the invoices. He pushed her aside, bending low over the books. Then he straightened, tapping his leg with his cane. 'You've been busy. You got my message then?'

She had no need to force the anger into her voice as she said, 'Indeed I did, and I also received that convict in my house. He was ill so what else could I do as he was sent here by you? He's still staying in one of my bedrooms. He's even taken to going to the workshop, says he knows of every trick in the book when it comes to dealing with customers.' She walked to the window and stared out across the court. 'Not to be wondered at of course, given who he is. He's got to go. I find him offensive.'

She kept on staring out of the window. She heard the rustle of paper. Jack was peering at the books again. She heard his heavy breathing, heard the scrape of the chair, heard him grunt as he settled himself upon it, heard the pages turning. Now she looked and he was checking the figures minutely again and she at last saw the flush of his rage rising on his neck.

She said, 'The problem is he's our front man. If we discharge him he could blow us out of the water by hinting of my part in all of this, and who, anyway, could be the new front man? It would have to be someone we already have in our power, someone fearful of what we could reveal about them, someone we had just here.' Now she pressed her thumb into the palm of her hand.

Jack stared at her, and she could almost see the wheels turning in his head, but were they turning in the right direction? She wanted to say more, to berate Harry, pound out the message of the front man, but she did not.

Jack rose, shoving back the chair. It tipped and fell. He reached for his hat and the books, and laughed, that was all, and all the time he stared at her. Then left the room.

He came back late, standing at the entrance to the drawing room where Irene and Martha sat by the small fire, for though it was the end of the summer there was a chill in the air. He strode towards them, then stood looming over Irene. They could smell the alcohol. He reached down pulling Irene to her feet, sneering at Martha.

'You don't mind if I take my wife.'

Irene shuddered. Martha hurried from the room, her face turned from them, and Jack laughed as he flung Irene onto the sofa, his brandy breath all over her face, the stench of cheap perfume on his clothes. He pawed at her breast, cursing at her corset. 'Get upstairs,' he yelled, hurling her from the sofa.

Irene scrambled to her feet as Jack sagged back on the cushions, his mouth loose from the drink, and she relaxed. He was harmless, too drunk to lift his fist to her, too drunk for anything else. She said, 'What of Palance?'

Jack's head lolled, his lids were heavy. 'What of Palance?' she insisted. He jerked awake, and slurred at her, 'Palance has left us, gone on a long trip, but paid us what he owed us first. He'll keep his mouth shut, believe you me.'

'But our front man?' she persisted. 'What of a front man?' She had no difficulty in sounding agitated.

Jack laughed, then coughed, saliva dribbling down his chin, pointing to the brandy decanter. She poured him some. He snatched the glass from her. She stepped back and saw the cabin again where he had sat paralysed by fear before striking her.

He downed the brandy, his eyes cunning as he looked at her. 'You're getting smart, starting to second-guess me.'

She grew still. He said, 'You move out of the way

now. Well, I don't care. I'm too damn tired.' He slumped back, the glass slipping from his hand. It crashed to the floor. She said again, her voice shaking with relief, 'The front man?'

He jerked awake and laughed again. 'Well, if this ain't the best bit of all. It's going to be that ex-convict lording it over you. But you'll do the books, which my lawyer will check. Travers'll just do the work, just be up front 'cos he's here.' He squashed his thumb into his palm. 'If he steps out of line I'll return him to England and the cells. Good eh, Irene Wendham in harness to a convict, again.'

CHAPTER FIFTEEN

By November profits were pouring into the business. Harry had taken a room north of Greenwich Avenue to be close to the workshops, and Sinclair had joined him, sent to New York by Jack who felt him too old to be useful on board, so he might as well be useful ashore. Antoinette and Emily remained in the basement rooms of the brownstone, and never for Irene had there been such a wonderful autumn or 'fall', as Antoinette kept reminding her, tutting as she and Irene cut cloth and oversewed the seams.

'But why work so hard?' Harry said. 'Isn't it enough that you oversee the workshops, design and train me?'

'No, for I must become as expert as Antoinette for the couture work, when, or if, it comes.'

Irene bought herself a better Singer sewing machine and installed it in her bedroom, and whenever she was not designing dresses and gowns or playing with Bernard, she was pouring over the accounts with Harry and Antoinette at the drawing-room table, or talking over the latest publicity plans, seeing Harry fill out and the lines ease around his mouth, seeing her contentment mirrored in him and she barely noticed that Esther had not made contact, though the summer season at Saratoga had ended, and the winter season in New York had begun.

'I know everything will be all right,' she soothed Martha in the sitting room. 'I just know.'

Martha lifted the teapot and poured another cup for Harry, and said, 'Well, that's all right then. For you have the gift of second sight, I s'pose.'

Harry, Antoinette and Irene laughed, long and loud. Harry stretched out his leg. Irene said, 'Maybe I do. I just know, from now on everything will work. The bad times are over. It's how I felt when I reached the *Wendham*.'

Martha stared into the fire, 'The bad times came back.'

'Not for long, and not really, for I have my son, and had I fled to Wendham House before the Arctic he would not exist.'

She looked at Harry. 'The bad times are over, aren't they?'

He nodded, looking down at his cup.

Irene said to Martha, 'There, you see.'

'So he has second sight too?'

Harry stretched, flexing his leg. Irene noticed immediately, 'Does it hurt? It's not enflamed again?'

Harry smiled, 'It's just going to sleep.'

Bernard pulled at him, 'Let's play then. Wake it up because I want to go in the yard.'

They all laughed, Harry groaned. Martha took his cup as he pretended to struggle to his feet. Irene smiled. It was really the most wonderful autumn.

In the second week of November Esther's card was delivered by a liveried footman, and the next afternoon she called in her carriage, taking Irene along Broadway, smiling graciously at all the other carriages, hissing, 'Parvenus, incline your head,' or 'Old money, grovel.' Each time it became harder not to laugh.

But when they swung through Central Park Irene smiled even more broadly when Esther confirmed that her Washington contact had heard nothing untoward about Irene Wendham's marriage, merely that she had married a shipowner who had to sail suddenly, hence the haste.

'So romantic,' cooed Esther. 'But if only they knew. How hard your godfather must have worked, shame they died of cholera. Isn't that what Martha said? Yes, how romantic it all sounds.' Now her tone was sad.

Irene shrugged, 'It doesn't matter.'

Esther looked at her sharply. 'You seem different.'

Irene looked up at the sky, which was a deep blue. She breathed in the crisp air. 'We've chased off Palance. We have a new front man, a good man. He's my friend, one I thought I would never see again, one who shared my nightmares.'

Esther swung round, her face alarmed, 'He won't say anything about you and the business?'

Irene was astonished. 'Harry is a friend,' she repeated. 'We know everything there is to know about one another. He wants to escape from Jack too, and one day he will.'

Esther relaxed, then said, 'What about Palance? How will you keep him quiet?'

'Jack says he's gone on a long voyage and won't cause trouble. People usually do what Jack says.' Irene shrugged.

'Jack didn't hurt you while he was here?'

'A little, not much, no more than usual.' She thought of Jack who had left the house early and returned late reeking of cigar smoke, brandy and cheap perfume. He had never wanted her, merely beaten her, and somehow the blows were not as bad as the carnality.

Esther's voice was curious as she said, 'You're not frightened of him any more are you?'

Irene inclined her head at another carriage whilst Esther waved, and she thought about Esther's words. 'No, he can't touch me inside, not any more. Besides, he's not back for another four years, so I can afford to sound nonchalant, can't I?'

Esther smiled and settled herself back on the seat, her pale-blue hat casting a shadow over her face, her hands restless on her deeper-blue dress and cloak. The rich green of Irene's outfit complimented Esther's. Esther said, 'Whilst in Saratoga I made plans. What I intend to do is to ask you to the opera next week. It's where society goes to be seen, to mingle, to introduce new members, *not* to listen to the music.' She wagged her finger, and they laughed together. Esther continued, 'I'm going to take a gamble and ask the Old Dame to dine with us beforehand, relying on her fondness for Alex . . .'

Irene interrupted, 'Who's the Old Dame?'

'She who is God in society, and sits at the very pinnacle by dint of being from just about the oldest family society has known. If she comes it will mean the old money will take you to their bosoms. If she doesn't it'll mean that we go for the respectable parvenus, get their acceptance for you, and rise up with them. It will take longer, but be more exciting.'

Her eyes were sparkling, then she sobered. 'If the Old Dame refuses to dine it's no great problem, just as long as she acknowledges you in some way. For instance, if she visits our box at the opera then we need do no more. If she doesn't, as I say, it is a longer route, but more interesting.'

Again a carriage passed and over on the grass children ran, laughed, chased balls. Gentlemen were walking, swinging their canes, their shadows long, their coats buttoned. Esther mused, 'Alex's father sold off his house to pay off the Old Dame's insurance policy in the Great Fire. It was a gesture of honour. He then shot himself for he could not pay off the last of his debts. Since then she's protected Alex, accepted me, helped him get established in real estate, but she's got a nose that's just a bit too sharp. She hears and sees things others don't. She's, let's say, cautious.'

Irene nodded, unease stirring. 'Esther, I think we should forget this. It's not a game at all. You and Alex could get hurt.'

Esther grinned. 'I've told you before that I would use the summer to make sure it was a sound gamble, and I have done so. I'm not stupid but I want you to succeed.

So, you must come next week and you must come bearing a gown for me, and one for you, for I told you I had been planning and I made sure the talk in Saratoga was all of the cut on my ball gown, and the Parisian seamstress who might, or might not, be available to produce wonders for the ladies of society. I made special mention to those with daughters who are winging their way off to the season in England. There's nothing the parvenus like better than an English title, and nothing an English title likes better than money.'

She laughed, 'I thought this might be a second string to your bow. These poor little lambs to the slaughter have a need, you have the means.'

When Irene looked perplexed Esther tapped her with her fan. 'Buck up, think. You know the rules of English society. You can coach them.' Esther trailed off, deep in thought. A carriage passed. Irene jogged her. Esther started, saw the carriage, smiled until it had passed. 'That was the Old Dame. No, don't turn.'

Irene had a picture of an elderly woman with high cheek-bones, and deep dark eyes. She had been dressed in deepest mourning. Esther tapped her arm again. 'Now, also this week you have to find a house just off Fifth Avenue, for you'll not afford the lease for one actually on it. There's one in Twenty-Eighth Street, two doors from ours.'

One week later Irene walked to Esther and Alex Moran's house from the brownstone two doors down. Harry and Sinclair were now installed in the Wandle Court brownstone basement, insisting that Antoinette and Emily take the upper house, for none would move to Twenty-Eighth Street with her, though she had wanted to take a lease on yet a further brownstone. 'You can bring us the business. It's safer this way, fewer explanations, and cheaper,' Antoinette had said. 'She's right,' Harry had reiterated. 'You're the advance guard.' But how she missed them, though not Harry as much

311

as she'd feared, for he was always here, deep inside her, and he said the same of her.

She stepped into the brilliantly lit hall, hung with paintings, its black and white tiled floor modern and exciting. She allowed the maid to take her cape and then Esther called from above, 'Up here, don't wait. Come up and see the gown on me.'

The stairs curved round and were wider and more spacious than her house, for this was not a narrow deep brownstone, but a newer house built in the Grecian style. Up and up she hurried whilst Esther waited impatiently, calling, 'Hurry, hurry.' When she reached the top Esther pirouetted in her deep damask gown, looking radiant and well. She drew Irene close, kissing her cheek, stepping back, holding her hands, saying, 'My, don't we both just look wonderful?'

Irene laughed. 'I thought a deep turquoise would save me from being totally overshadowed by you.'

Alex called from the drawing room, 'Come along and show me. Esther would not allow herself to be seen until you arrived. Does she think she's a bride or something? Or are we in need of that much luck tonight?'

Esther pulled a face. 'Perhaps, but don't worry him. The Old Dame wouldn't show, he doesn't know I asked her.'

She pulled Irene along the landing, and into a spacious light high-ceilinged room. Alex stood by the fireplace in his evening suit, his white shirt and waistcoat startling against the black of his tails. He came to Irene, smiling gently, 'So we meet again, though tonight there will be no trace of mis-understanding.'

'Mr Moran.' Her voice was strained.

He squeezed her hand. 'I knew you two could be friends, and yes, you both look wonderful, and no, don't be afraid, all will be well.'

Those were the words that Harry had spoken when

312

he had brought round the gardenia she wore on her shoulder. She touched it.

They ate downstairs in a dining room panelled with dark oak. 'Wendham House also had panelling, but in both the dining room and the library,' she said, ignoring the flicker of the spermaceti candles on the sideboards, trying to ignore the image of Jack Prior at the dance, pushing him aside until the image faded.

'We'll have such fun. It's to be such a struggle, but we'll win.'

They ate oyster soup, boiled turkey, canvasback duck and Irene thought she would burst. She drank a little vintage wine, but only a little, for the smell of alcohol offended her and she thought of the champagne she had drunk when she signed the lease, and of the smell which oozed from Jack Prior's breath and pores.

Alex checked the time. 'Come along, my dears. I know one must not be early for the opera, but there is late, and there is very late.' He rang the bell-pull and asked the footman for their capes.

They walked out into the cold crisp air, he handed Esther into the covered brougham and then turned to Irene, whispering, 'Whatever the outcome of tonight, and whether it brings us down too, I want you to know that Esther's involvement with you has focused her mind away from her grief, and out of the ennui she had descended into, away from the dangers that can befall women of this set. For that I will always be grateful.'

Irene took his hand and entered the carriage, but now the tension was rising. She said to Esther, 'I have changed my mind. I will leave now. I can't risk your position for this.'

Esther put out her hand, 'You will not, and neither will we be brought down. You and I are too clever for that.' There was steel in her voice. She turned to her husband as he entered and sat beside her. 'Do you hear that, Alex Moran? I would do nothing to hurt you. I will keep you safe till the end of your days, and it warms me to hear you whisper to my friend such words.' She brought his gloved hand to her lips. She glanced at Irene, grinning now, 'These men, they don't know that when they whisper women's antennae bristle so that they hear every word.'

Irene turned from the sight of such mutual love, staring out at the falling snow, and the houses, the mansions, the half-built hotel, summoning her own beloved, and felt serene.

They joined the queue of broughams, landaus and coupés which were crawling to the portico of the Academy, descending at last onto the red carpet, walking towards the bright lights that Irene had looked at so longingly. 'Late indeed,' Esther tutted at Alex.

They hurried through the doors, into the glittering hall, straight on to the rear of the box, nodding at the liveried footman who held the door for them. In they went, to a muted darkness. After a moment their eyes adjusted and Irene heard a murmuring all around. On the stage, the opera had already begun.

They eased their way to the chairs at the front of the box and as they settled themselves Irene gazed round at the horseshoe of red and old boxes, down into the well of the auditorium, ahead to the stage where behind a row of footlights *La Traviata* was being staged. Alex handed her mother-of-pearl opera glasses. Irene directed them to the stage. Esther hissed, 'No-one watches the opera, use them for the audience.'

Irene lowered them. Throughout the auditorium people talked, waved, peered. 'Use your glasses,' Esther insisted.

Irene would not, for they reminded her of the telescope and Jack's face when he killed the whale, and this time the image would not dissipate even when Esther shook her arm, sweeping the audience with her glasses, and then the boxes. 'Most people are here,'

Esther breathed. 'And yes, there's Mrs Morgan. I knew I'd hooked her.'

Alex leaned across, 'Irene, are you feeling quite well?'

In the dark his face was as slender as Harry's, his cheek-bones as high, his eyes as kind, and now Jack's image left her. She laughed shakily, 'It's just rather strange to be here at last.'

She lifted her glasses and looked as Esther directed. Most of the boxes were full. The older women wore brocade, the younger tulle. Esther explained who was who as she waved to those in the box next to them, and to many others. All eyes appeared to be on Irene.

An old woman lifted her quizzing glasses, inclining her head to Esther and Alex as she did so, staring hard at Irene, until slowly she gave the merest nod. Irene did the same. Esther gripped her hand and hissed. 'That's the Old Dame, bless her damned old nose. She wouldn't come, but she hasn't snubbed you.'

Alex laughed slightly in obvious relief and slumped back in his chair, running his hand over his brilliantined hair. Esther touched his knee. 'I told you to trust me. I knew it would be all right.' But Irene noticed that her voice trembled and the knowledge of how much she owed this couple was reinforced.

Esther leaned forward to wave graciously at the occupants of a box almost opposite. 'We ain't there yet, but we're on the way.'

As the first act ended people were already rising from their chairs. Esther put her hand out to Irene. 'We'll stay sitting, and be ready to think real fast. Lucinda Morgan is coming. She's parvenu, money from food profiteering, fingers in the Tammany pie. Her gal is marrying an English something or other. I told her there was nothing you didn't know about the etiquette of the English houses, being part of English society yourself. I also told her there was nothing your seamstress couldn't make, told her she'd made your whole

315

trousseau, told her there were strict rules about what the English expected a bride to pack.'

Alex burst out laughing as he rose. 'For heaven's sake, draw breath woman while I go and suck in some healthy cigar smoke, leaving you two to weave your spells.'

He opened the door, standing back, saying as an older woman entered, 'Mrs Morgan, what a delight. Please come through for Esther has an acquaintance she wishes you to meet.'

He slipped out as the woman approached. Esther gestured to Alex's chair, 'Lucinda, I was so hoping you'd come. I'm just so thrilled that Irene Prior, of Somerset, England has been able to attend with us tonight. I first made her acquaintance when I did the grand tour. I find it wonderful news that she's to stay in New York for some years.'

The door opened again, and another woman entered, kissing Esther, peering at Irene, and another, and another. They were all introduced. Mrs Morgan said, her eyes suspicious, 'Your husband does not appear to be with you?'

Esther snapped out her fan, moving it rapidly, annoyance at the woman's directness obvious. Irene smiled calmly and said, 'My husband has links with whaling both directly and indirectly. He divides his time between the sea, Dundee and London where he deals in baleen and other commodities. We are in America because this is where he feels his heart lies – his grandfather left at the time of the War of Independence to build up his fleet in England. Mr Prior wishes his son to spend his formative years in this land and for that reason we have leased out Wendham Estate, which I inherited from my father, the botanist, Sir Bartholomew Wendham.'

Mrs Morgan leaned forward, the vulgar embroidered ruffles of her gown glittering, her eyes less sharp, her voice more accepting, 'London you say. Mr Morgan wondered why he had not had dealings with your husband.'

Esther's sparkling eyes met Irene's. One of the other women leaned forward, 'You look so wonderful tonight, Esther my dear. Your gown, it even surpasses that which you wore to your ball.'

Esther fanned herself gently now. 'Irene travels with her own seamstress. Well, I say her own, Antoinette is known to accept commissions from others though always her first priority is Mrs Prior, for her taste knows no equal.'

'But how could she create your ball gown if you have only just arrived in New York?' Mrs Morgan said softly, her eyes sharp again. 'Indeed I feel I've seen you somewhere.' Her eyes became vacant as she stared across the auditorium, searching her memory. Irene forced her hands not to tighten on her fan. Esther's smile faltered.

Mrs Morgan swung back to her. 'Ah, I remember. We passed you in Esther's carriage before the summer season. I remember your lemon gown so clearly, dear Esther.'

Irene maintained her smile, grappling with her thoughts. She said slowly, 'Goodness, so much has happened since then. Indeed, Esther, we did have a fleeting meeting did we not, recapturing our travels. It was, my dear Mrs Morgan, when my husband and I passed through New York so that Mr Prior could conclude a matter of business.'

Mrs Morgan cut in, 'But that was after the ball.'

Esther stared out across the theatre. Irene nodded, still managing to smile, still relieved that Mrs Morgan had not seen her at the workshop, or in the Bowery lodging house or anywhere else as irrecoverable. Her mind was racing. She laughed lightly and fluttered her fan, 'Indeed it was, what a remarkable memory, Mrs Morgan. Mr Moran had met my husband when he was discussing a baleen deal in New York. It was mentioned

317

then. I was at that time in New Bedford, with Antoinette. Mr Moran cabled his requirements.'

'But the fitting?'

Irene stared at the woman with exaggerated surprise, and her voice was cool and haughty as she answered, 'Antoinette is a miracle worker, measurements can be cabled, dressmakers' dummies created. But from what you say I presume you have not been to Europe, you have not experienced the expertise of Parisian salons?' Her tone was surprised, incredulous.

She waited. Mrs Morgan flushed, 'I haven't yet. One day I will.'

There was a frisson of reflected defensiveness from the other women, a muttering. Esther signalled a warning to Irene with her eyes. Irene continued to look cool and superior.

Mrs Morgan began to rise, but then a young voice from the back of the box said, 'Oh Mama, if we do not know that, what else do we not know? What will Edgar think of me? What will his family say?'

Mrs Morgan said nothing. She just inclined her head as the lights darkened and left, the other women trailing in her wake.

Esther stared after them, then shook her head at Irene, 'What on earth do you think you were doing? You've offended the woman, and she was the key to my plan.'

Irene turned, caught the scent of her gardenia. She said, her voice aloof and disdainful, 'I'm Irene Wendham of Wendham House. No parvenu should assume too much.'

Esther flushed. Irene laughed, and her voice was warm as she said, 'As you said to Alex, trust me, it was an act. That poor child will need every assistance to cope with her Edgar, so she must get it, and she will. That mother of hers would have had whatever suspicions were brewing inside that raw and ambitious mind of hers confirmed if we had wriggled.

Mrs Morgan is tough, a survivor – she must be to be where she is, and survivors can sniff fear because they have felt it, believe me. Believe me also that Mrs Morgan is fearful for her daughter. She loves her. I like that.'

During the second act there were curious looks from the other boxes, stares which slid from them before they could be acknowledged. Alex returned halfway through the act. Esther mouthed progress so far. He frowned.

It seemed to Irene that the soaring voices from the stage would never end, and her hands ached for they held the fan so tight. She made herself relax. She had told Esther to trust her.

Again those in boxes rose, again Irene and Esther remained seated, including Alex this time, his eyes on Esther's face. 'Will they come?' Esther whispered.

There was a tap on the door. It was Mrs Morgan and her daughter. Esther called, 'Wonderful, we were just saying how pretty Venetia was looking.'

'Indeed,' Irene said. 'She will grace whatever great family she joins. The Duke of?' she queried as Mrs Morgan took the seat that Alex hastily vacated.

Esther told her. Irene nodded. 'Of course. I haven't met him but Edgar I believe is a pleasant young man. He has a fondness for breeding horses, isn't that correct, Venetia?'

Venetia was standing beside her mother, beautiful in spite of her overly ornate white gown. Alex found her a chair. Venetia said, 'I met Edgar when he was over here, and yes, he did discuss horses rather a lot. But Mrs Prior, I ain't . . .'

Her mother frowned. Venetia corrected herself. 'I haven't been to England, yet. Is it very different?' The young girl's face was as worried and uncertain as her voice.

Irene smiled reassuringly. 'Not so very. People are the same inside wherever you go, don't you think? They all love, like, dislike. They all go to bed, need to sleep. It's just their rules that differ.'

Mrs Morgan leaned forward now, 'Your seamstress made your trousseau, so Esther was saying?'

More women were coming into the box.

Mrs Morgan said, flicking her fan open and shut, 'Perhaps your seamstress would be grateful to be offered a further commission.'

Irene looked shocked. 'Oh, Mrs Morgan, I think I must have given the wrong impression. My seamstress, as I said, works miracles but with her talent comes perhaps what you would call an eccentricity. She will only create by invitation, her own invitation. It is she, you see, who invites society to commission her. She who decides who is worthy of her talent.'

Esther gasped, and fluttered her fan. Mrs Morgan said, 'But that's . . . That's . . .'

'Unusual,' offered Irene.

Esther fluttered her fan even faster. Alex was standing by the door, his eyes watchful, his shoulders stiff. Irene looked at him and smiled, 'Mr Prior felt it would be a pleasant gesture if Antoinette created a gown for just such an occasion. I was able to advise Antoinette that here was a family worthy of her talents, here was a young woman of beauty, just as your Venetia is. As always she took my advice and issued her invitation.'

Esther turned away, and stared at the stage, her knuckles white as she gripped her fan. Alex left, shutting the door quietly behind him, unable to bear the tension.

Mrs Morgan stared at Irene, who calmly smiled at the other women, listening to them discuss their summer season in Saratoga, then talking of her own grand tour, and of her son who would be brought up to experience the mores of both English and American society. She ended, 'So important to feel confident when entering a new society, don't you think?'

The lights were darkening again. Mrs Morgan leaned

forward, 'May I leave my card tomorrow? I would so like to know you better.'

Irene smiled up at Venetia, remaining calm, but wanting to hurl her fan into the air, and hug Esther, for now she had at last begun the long road home.

CHAPTER SIXTEEN

It was October, 1870, and Irene was packing alongside Martha in the moonlit bedroom in Saratoga. 'It really would help if we lit the lamp,' Irene said again.

Martha shook her head firmly. 'The moths will come in, and there's enough light from the moon.' Every year since 1867 they had said the same things to one another. Irene waited for the inevitable. It came.

'Be glad to get back, I will,' Martha said. 'All this sitting about makes a body lazy. Not that you've done that much sitting, working away at them designs, and sewing them gowns. You've packed them, have you, ready for Antoinette to deliver when we get back to New York?'

Irene smiled gently and said as she always did, 'All packed.' Excitement was building. They were returning. She would deliver the orders and designs for the new fashion at 'Antoinette's', the salon they were running, though her own involvement was carefully shielded.

She had thought that the disappearance of the full crinoline would affect their profits, but the crinolette, the half crinoline which concentrated at the back had proved as popular as the skirt that was merely tied back from the underside forming almost a tail. Besides, the corsetry workshop was expanding its markets weekly it seemed.

Once the gowns were delivered she would talk to Harry who had taken a separate brownstone house off Fifth Avenue, more fitting for Jack Prior's associate, and the architect of his success. The man who was steering, with Irene's discreet help, a course through the financial disarray which had been left by the market crash of 1869 when half of Wall Street had lost everything. It was that that accounted for the missing faces this year in Saratoga.

Antoinette, however, preferred to remain at the Wandle Court house. 'It feels like home,' she had said to Irene.

She would meet him at Antoinette's and following an update of the firm's progress they would discuss tactics for the extension of the second-hand business Harry and she had set up, and for which they kept separate and secret books, for it was her 50 per cent share of this money which would finance the buying back of the Wendham lease. An action she felt was totally justifiable now that the British courts had passed an act entitling women to keep their own incomes.

Together she and Harry had decided that for their own peace of mind their future must be bought with money earned from a source that Jack Prior had rejected. Therefore neither of them could accuse themselves or be accused by him of stealing from the Prior business. To this end she poured the 50 per cent share of the *haute couture* into the Prior coffers, leaving Antoinette the other half.

Once business was concluded she would talk to him of the summer days in Saratoga, of the new and old money that visited, but which still did not include the Old Dame, and she would tell him of her fears that this arbiter of society had her suspicions, and could bring them down. She would tell him of the designs Esther had created for the fancy-dress balls which would be arranged in the winter season. She would tell him of the golden rod which grew in the flower beds, of the young girls who played croquet and chattered, of the races at which their fathers gambled.

He would tell her of his summer, the sights he had seen when he had travelled to other cities in the draining heat to open up new markets, of the evenings

323

with Alex at the club. He would tell her of Sinclair's progress as production controller. She would ask after his leg. Plead with him to leave the travelling until the fall and join them in Saratoga at weekends as Alex did.

They would look down on the tree in the yard. They would stand in silence for what need was there for words? They were on their way home.

'Can't wait,' said Martha, standing back from the trunk, her hands on her ample hips.

'I miss New York,' Irene agreed, her voice distant. She folded the last of her clothes, and dropped the lid of the trunk shut.

Martha called, 'Stop your day-dreaming and sit on this lid for me. If I do it, I'll squash it and everything in it. There's more and more of me every minute. Just too many lobster salads and no garden to potter in. I did a lot of that when Barratt took me back. I tried to keep it up for you, but then he turned it into them fancy shapes and it didn't seem to help the missing of you any more.'

Irene lay across the trunk while Martha buckled the straps. 'I'll get rid of those when I return. While I do it I will care for my people, I will show my handsome young man how to fulfil his duties, as my mother tried to show me. Most of all, I will remove him from his father's influence, once and for all.' She pushed herself upright and took Martha to the study, showing her the garden plans she had drawn up in her journal, and the plans for the drawing room which must in no way resemble the room that Jack Prior and she had danced in.

Martha looked at her. 'Bernard can share his life between the two of you. He is half-American and half-British. I hope he chooses the best of both those worlds to copy. I mean, I hope he imitates Mr Travers and Mr Moran, not his father. You know, my darling, I didn't think Jack'd come here. I thought this was one place free of the taint of him.' They stared out of the

324

window at the huge moon hung in the velvet sky, casting its glow across the sea.

He'd come all right, in September, pausing in New York only to check on the business. He'd come and stayed for a week, since his new steamships were not to be delivered to New Bedford until the end of September. He'd come and from the moment of his arrival he'd ridiculed Irene in front of Bernard, applauding when Bernard had said to his mother on the second day, 'Yes, you're a fool, a snivelling Britisher.'

'When is that devil going, and what damage will he do to us before he does?' Esther whispered to Irene as they watched Jack downing brandy after brandy at the dance held at the hotel on that second night. 'When he's ready,' Irene had replied, tense, almost unable to breathe as he talked to Mr Morgan, Mr Haynes, Alex and five others at the open doors which led to the veranda.

She had seen the Old Dame, her quizzing glass to her eyes, staring at Jack. The men were listening to him, nodding. Then they laughed, loud and long. Esther said, 'He's pulling it off, that devil is pulling it off.'

Jack came across the waxed floor to Irene, bowed to Esther, took Irene's hand. 'Dance with me, my dear,' he said, smiling, squeezing her hand, hurting her.

She returned his smile, for now the Old Dame's quizzing glass was on her as he swept her round the floor. It was a polka and he turned her, and turned her, flamboyantly, energetically, and now people were watching and still he smiled, and her lips ached as she returned it whilst all the time his grip was tightening, crushing her fingers, bringing exultation to his eyes. On and on the music went, round and round, until she thought she would faint with the pain he was inflicting.

The music ceased. Jack bowed over her hand, kissed it. Mrs Morgan caught her eye and her look was one of envy. The Old Dame lowered her quizzing glass, her look was unfathomable, but for a moment Irene thought a flicker of compassion crossed her features.

Then Alex was there, standing in front of Irene, requesting the next dance, asking Jack Prior for his permission. It was given, and Alex held her lightly. 'He's charming them,' he said. 'It's extraordinary but he's charming them. I had thought he would ruin it for you.' He gently led her to the rhythm of the dance, and she smiled again, though her hand was throbbing.

The next day her hand and fingers were too swollen to wear gloves, and so she stayed in her bedroom with the shades drawn, hearing Jack tell Esther she was unwell, hearing him later telling her son that his mother was a lazy good-for-nothing who had been brought up to sponge off people, sending Martha to the beach with the boy, and then coming to her room, taking her, laughing.

Jack left after only a week. 'Business,' he had said to Alex, leaning back on the veranda chair, smoking a cigar, calling to Martha, 'Get this child to bed, goddammit.' He'd not even looked at the boy who sat at his feet and gazed at him with such adoration. 'I've had enough of him now. He's too damn young to make good company, or is it just that you've made him a namby-pamby? Next time I'm back I'll put an end to that.'

In New York as the weather grew cold and November dawned Mrs Horatio Norden, the Old Dame, left her card at Irene's the afternoon of Esther's ball. When Esther heard she rushed over and danced Irene around the room, while Bernard laughed, calling, 'Aunt Esther, what if anyone saw you?'

Irene broke free of Esther, and danced with her son who was eight, and tall and dark, and no longer the rude boy he had become for that one week, then fell onto the sofa, dragging him with her, holding him close. 'I love you, Bernie,' she whispered. 'I have such things to show you when you are grown, and in the meantime you are going to love the school we've chosen for you.'

'I love you too but I don't want to go to sleep in a school.'

Esther pulled him to his feet, ruffling his hair. 'You will like it, believe me. It's where Uncle Alex's friend teaches, and it's near the house we rent on the Hudson sometimes. It won't be for a while and there'll be loads of boys, our nephew Timothy will be one. There'll be boats to take on the water. Think how pleased your father will be as you learn to sail.'

Irene closed her eyes in relief at Bernard's whoop of joy. Then looked over his head at Esther as Bernard asked, 'Father liked it too, did he?'

'I've written to him telling him all about it. He'll love it,' Irene said, knowing she had written it, and then put it into the bin, for she had decided after Saratoga that her son must not be available when her husband next arrived home.

'Enough of this,' Esther chided. 'We've decisions to make, gowns to try, shoes to check. By the way, Harry has at last agreed to come to the ball.'

Irene sat up. 'How did you manage that?'

Esther straightened Bernard's tie. 'Heaven knows, it's Alex's doing. Harry's my new project you see, my darling Irene. I've decided he's a waste as a bachelor and we must find him a wife. After all, Harry's quite a figure in the business community now, and inordinately well respected and liked, but such a social recluse, almost as reluctant as you. I swear you wouldn't budge out of the house if you didn't have to. I've told Alex he must nominate him for his club, and I believe that this evening he told him he must come, to talk business. Bit of a trick really. I've lots of eager girls lined up.'

That evening while the music ebbed and flowed in the Moran drawing room, which had been converted into a ballroom for the evening, Irene sat in the conservatory talking to Venetia and Edgar who were over in New York until after Christmas.

Venetia wore diamonds around her neck, and in her hair, but even they didn't match the shine in the young woman's eyes. So, thought Irene, she has found happiness with her young husband, her heir to a dukedom, and she was glad. Glad too, that the young woman's dress – of white and silver with swansdown around the neck – so became her. It had been made by Antoinette to Irene's design, though it was Esther and Irene who had sewn on the swansdown.

Irene smiled slightly as she listened to the girl tell of the hunting in Leicestershire. What would this young woman think if she knew that the fingers of her hostess, and the woman who held the Viennese fan – Irene shook it out and fluttered it – had actually helped to make her dress?

Edgar was speaking. Irene said, 'I'm so sorry, I was momentarily distracted.'

He said again, 'You must miss your home.'

'I do indeed.'

'You will return.'

'Of course.'

Venetia touched her husband's arm. 'It depends on Mr Prior's plans does it not, Mrs Prior?'

Again Irene fluttered her fan. 'Changes always have to be carefully planned.' Her voice was calm, but then she thought of Esther's new project; Harry.

Edgar moved to one side, reaching out and touching the towering fern that grew by the glass wall. Irene could see the ballroom now, and the dancers, drifting, swooping, turning.

Sitting directly opposite her, beneath the huge oil painting of London Bridge, was the Old Dame, who had waved Irene over to her chair when she had first arrived, and greeted her very publicly, holding her in conversation, her eyes kind, her voice firm, as she talked of the delights of Saratoga, enquiring if England possessed such tranquillity, listening carefully when Irene described Lyme Regis and Wendham.

As she had finished speaking the Old Dame had reached out, grasped her arm. 'My husband . . .' Then she stopped, lifted her quizzing glass as Morgan approached, and with him, Mrs Morgan. The Old Dame turned to them, 'You enjoyed Saratoga I assume, Mr Morgan?'

'It was as usual a welcome respite from the summer heat.' Mr Morgan bowed to Irene. 'Mrs Prior, your husband is on his travels again, I see. Two steamships and four with auxiliary engines. A good life, but a lonely one for you.'

Irene smiled. 'One must make sacrifices when one's husband is born into a shipping family.'

The Old Dame murmured, her voice hollow, 'Indeed one must, though sometimes things aren't as they seem.' Her gaze was empty as she stared at Irene but even a resurgence of the threat this woman posed to her future did not seem important tonight. Harry with a wife, and a life of his own. Surely not. Surely their love would endure?

The sound of Venetia's and Edgar's laughter snapped her to attention. As she looked up she saw Alex and Harry in conversation. He had arrived. Still Edgar talked. Would he never stop? She kept her eyes on Harry. He moved away with Alex. She began to rise, but then sat again, heedful of the rule that a woman may not rise and approach a man. Rather, she must sit and wait for him to approach her.

Venetia was saying, 'Don't you think, Mrs Prior?'

'Undoubtedly,' replied Irene, though she had no idea what she was agreeing to.

'There I told you, and who should know better than Mrs Prior? After all, he is her husband's associate.' Venetia pouted at her husband. Irene was quick to focus her attention now.

Edgar was laughing. 'Very well, I concede defeat. Though one would never know that he was a cripple, since there's barely a limp. Mark you, your mother says he has never danced to her certain knowledge, so he's obviously limited in his movements. I hear he was too weak to continue as a ship's captain. Must be sad to have one's manhood in doubt. He's never made an appearance, you know, at the balls, before tonight. Probably here for business. Never married, but who'd marry a cripple? Bet he leaves early. Pathetic, really.'

Irene began to rise, understanding Esther now, for it was these rumours she must have heard. She began to walk from Venetia and Edgar heedless of rules, for this man must not be mocked, he *was* loved, more than most mortals would ever be loved and she couldn't bear to hear him called pathetic, she couldn't bear it, d'you hear, she wanted to shout.

Alex turned, saw her, and hurried across, taking her hand. 'My dear, may I drag you from your friends,' walking her away quickly, saying beneath his breath, 'before you break a rule on this of all nights, right in front of the Old Dame, just when she's talking of persuading you to commission a gown from Antoinette's salon. I thought earlier in the evening that she suspected something. I overheard her comment to you.'

Irene said, her voice strained, 'Damn the Old Dame.' Harry was approaching her.

She watched only him as he walked with dignity, his face and body strong, handsome, everything a young woman would want. Everything any woman would want and it was as though she was seeing him with new eyes. What right had she to condemn him to so many years alone to suit her convenience? Every right. I love him, she answered herself. He loves me. He reached them and she smiled, though a terrible uncertainty was dragging at her.

She inclined her head, saying softly, 'Dance with me.'

Harry flushed. 'You know I never dance.'

She repeated, her voice urgent, 'Dance with me.'

His eyes said – I must not stand so close to you.

'Dance with me, Harry. Please.'

He looked from her to Alex, then back to her, shrugging, his eyes not meeting hers. 'I can't dance. So allow me to refuse.'

She said, her voice almost a whisper, 'I can't allow you to refuse.' For no-one must mock this man. No-one, and no-one else must have him. No-one. But what right had she to decide that? Every right. No, none.

The musicians began to play a Strauss Waltz. She held out her hands. 'You can dance, for you told me so. Dance with me, Harry,' she whispered.

He said, 'Irene, what's wrong? This is a wonderful night for you. The Old Dame has taken to you at last. What's happened to upset you?'

Irene shook her head. Who cared about the Old Dame? 'Dance with me.'

The candles were flickering, the mirrors reflected their glow. Now she saw the women talking in groups, the young ones eyeing Harry, and a greater rage swept her, tinged now with fear for to see him dance would reveal the strength and the grace of this man, but Harry Travers did not deserve to be mocked, although the proof of that to these absurd people might open avenues away from her. She looked at him, pleading in her eyes. He didn't understand.

Venetia and Edgar passed, inclined their heads. Harry at last bowed over Irene's hand. He led her to the floor along with the other couples.

Her gloved hand was in his gloved hand. His other on her waist. He dropped his gaze to the floor. She said, 'Look up, Harry.' Her voice was gentle. He looked into her eyes, his brow furrowed, for it was dangerous to do so, it was dangerous to be so close, to have her hand in his.

She smiled and whispered, 'It will be all right, Harry.' But her eyes were tormented and again he didn't understand, and wanted to drag her to him, never let her go, for this closeness was different to the sickbed,

331

to the Arctic, as they surely had both known it would be. For this is why he had never come before.

They began to move, and her eyes were still on his, and his feet glided with hers, and he breathed in her scent, felt the warmth of her hand through her glove, looked into eyes that were grey, beautiful and deep, and he no longer cared that his love must be in his eyes for anyone to see, for nothing could stop it, or the passion which was sweeping him, the desperate longing for her, every bit of her.

On and on they danced and it was as though she had never taken to the floor before, never danced with anyone other than this man, never drawn breath, or gazed at stars, only at him, into those hazel eyes which held hers and the closeness of him made her long for more, made her crave everything, made her mad for him.

The candles flickered, the flowers scented the room as before, but nothing was as it had been. For her mind was tracing the contours of his body as she had bathed it. It was as though the hand on her waist was burning through to her skin, as though the hand holding hers was on fire.

Their feet were in time, their breathing in tune, their eyes looking deep into one another until there were no flowers, no candles flickering, no music, no reality, nothing but the love they felt.

On and on they danced and could have wept when the music faded, and their arms had to fall, but not their eyes. No, not their eyes as they walked to the conservatory, past Mr and Mrs Morgan, who smiled and nodded, but whom neither saw. They walked on, past the fern, stopping finally, as though one body, staring out through the glass but seeing nothing of the deepening frost which whitened the shrubs, or the cold light of the moon, hearing nothing of the music, or the talk, or the scraping of the gold ballroom chairs.

Together they stood, their arms touching, aware only

of one another, aware that they had passed to another plane, into danger.

Three months later Irene walked with Esther along the path of cleared snow leading to the trees – trees which seemed to crouch beneath their burden of frozen snow. There was no wind, just an aching silence.

In the distance ahead of them Bernard was being pulled on the sledge by Alex. It was New Year's Day 1871 and Esther had sent for Irene and Bernard two days ago, insisting that they join them at Wideacre, the house they had rented on the Hudson, near to the school that Bernard would go to.

Martha had grumbled as she dragged out the trunks, packing blankets as well as warm clothes, saying that she would not budge from her room, for these big old houses were draughty just as Wendham had been. 'And there are never enough blankets, and far too many chilblains,' she had grizzled.

Esther said, as their feet crunched into the crisp snow, 'Is Martha still stuck like glue to that bedroom fire?'

Irene murmured, 'Yes.' What did she care?

'Was Christmas pleasant?' Esther persevered.

'Christmas was very pleasant thank you,' Irene said, her voice sounding unused, even to her.

Esther slipped her arm around Irene, walking in step. Her breath was visible as she said, 'He still hasn't come back?'

Irene said nothing, she just stared ahead, seeing but not seeing her son walking beside the sledge now as Alex pulled it up the slope, to stop just below the trees.

She stopped dead, stared at the crows rising from the wood. 'How can they fly when it's so cold? They froze in mid-flight in the Arctic. Our men froze. The rigging froze. He warmed me . . .' Her voice broke.

Esther held her.

Irene laid her head on her friend's shoulder. 'You

saw us, didn't you? I didn't imagine it. We danced, we stood together, then he was gone. He walked from me, Esther. He never looked back.'

'I know.' Esther held Irene. 'But luckily no-one else noticed.'

Irene pushed away from her, her eyes wild. 'I don't care about anyone else, Esther. How can I care about anything like that when I feel as though half of me's gone, when I feel torn and ripped apart? I can't sleep, I can't eat.' She stopped – continued, 'We were one. We've always been one. We always will be. But he just turned and left.'

She walked on, and now they could hear the sound of Bernard's laughter. Esther ran, caught up, linked arms, panting slightly as she said, 'Antoinette said he was sorting out distribution problems.'

'He's gone, and he was my friend.'

Now Esther pulled her to a stop, shouting at her, 'You stupid woman, he's the man you love.'

Irene nodded. 'He's my love, my friend, my past, my present. But he's gone, and I can hardly breathe without him.' She was raging, tears were streaming. 'I need him to help me get through my life. I need to see his face, to hear his voice. I can't stand it. I can't stand it.' She was rubbing her chest.

Esther held her face between her hands. 'Shh, shh.'

Alex turned, and Bernard stopped laughing. Esther called, 'It's all right, we're talking of the latest order.'

Bernard pulled at Alex. 'Come on, Uncle Alex, it's only business.'

Alex pulled the sledge up the rise again but he knew it wasn't only business, and before tea he telegraphed Harry at his hotel in Seaport, New York, insisting that he come to Wideacre the next morning, for there was too much pain coursing through both his friends.

*　　*　　*

At eleven the next morning Irene trudged through the snow, her head bent against the wind which blew from the west, bringing fresh snow with it. It stung her face. She lifted her head, opened her mouth, tasted the moist cold flakes, stopped, let them fall on her closed lids. Then she trudged on again, towards the woods, sinking up to her ankles with each step.

As she ploughed up the slope she pulled her scarf up and round her hair. Now she was in amongst the trees, and the wind was howling as it had howled in the Arctic. A branch creaked, snow fell. She ignored it, forging ahead, keeping to what she could see was the path.

'The old woodcutter's house is in the centre,' Alex had said, rustling the papers he was working on. 'It would help so much, Irene, if you could fetch my scarf. If Esther finds I've left her Christmas present in amongst a load of old logs I'll be hearing about it until the day I die.'

Snow was dusting down from the trees as the wind increased, then lulled. On she walked, the cold air hurt her lungs. The darkness was lightening as the trees thinned, and there, in the clearing was the house. She approached, and now she saw that smoke was rising from the chimney. She hesitated, then carried on, seeing another set of footprints, but what did it matter if the woodcutter was there?

She climbed the steps onto the small veranda, lifted her hand, and knocked lightly on the door. She waited, knocked again, more loudly. She heard footsteps, stepped back. The door opened. It was Harry. Harry.

He was drawn and tired. His eyes devoured her. Those beautiful eyes. They stood silently staring, and she heard the wind, felt the cold, saw his love. She reached out. Her glove was snow-covered. She traced his lips, leaving traces of moisture. 'I love you,' she whispered. 'I shouldn't have made you dance. But I did. It's too late now.'

He pulled her to him then, holding her fiercely, kissing her hair while around them the wind increased and brought fresh snow.

He stilled. She laid her head against his and clung to him. 'Harry, I love you,' she sobbed. 'You left. I can't bear that. Don't leave again. Promise me you won't leave.'

He bent to her mouth at last, kissing her, his lips so full and soft, and the shaft of passion which drove through her took the strength from her legs. He kissed her eyes, her cheeks, her hair, her neck, saying over and over, 'You're my life. I love you. You're my life.'

Still the wind blew and the snow gusted and they clung together, not relinquishing one another even when he backed into the room, kicking the door shut behind them, shutting out the cold, and the noise. An oil lamp lit the rustic room. A fire roared in the grate. He backed towards it. The heat burst on her. He brushed back her scarf from her head, her hair tumbled free. 'I love you,' he repeated.

There was no flinching from either of them for they knew that they were about to seal their love, to acknowledge that they were everything to one another, and for this there would be no dimming of the lamp, no turning from the glow of the fire, and neither was there, as passion surged, and their bodies fused.

For Irene there was no pain, only joy, tenderness, exploration into a world she hadn't known existed, and then there was peace as they lay naked together before the dying fire and she told him of her fears that he might not wish to wait for her, of her guilt that he had to, and he told her that he would wait for ever, that his love would endure for ever, that his own guilt was there because he could not take her and Bernard to safety, away from Jack.

'We will wait,' they said to one another as the cold

snapped in the air. 'We will wait until Wendham before we hold one another again. That will be our time.' For Harry would not risk discovery for her sake. 'Think of Jack,' he said.

CHAPTER SEVENTEEN

In July of 1871, in her house in Saratoga, Esther was delivered of a baby girl, and as she lay back against the snow-white pillows, she lifted her hand to Irene's cheek and said, 'You were right, you're always right, you said one day it would happen. Now we're both at peace.' The breeze wafted the light muslin curtains, the sound of Bernard's laughter drifted up from the garden to be swept aside by Harry and Alex's roars of pretended rage as he drenched them with water from his pail.

Later Harry came to Esther's bedroom with Alex and Bernard, putting his finger to his lips, mouthing to Bernard, 'Quiet now, Alexandra is sleeping.'

Bernard came to his mother, put his arm around her neck as she sat beside Esther's bed and peered into the cradle. The baby stirred and woke. Harry and Alex crept to Bernard's side. Harry reached down and laid his finger on the back of the tiny fisted hand. 'She's as small and as perfect as you were nine and a half years ago,' Harry said. 'No-one would believe how tall and strong you are now.'

Bernard glowed, Harry smiled across his head at Irene, and they knew that they were both remembering the small creaking captain's cabin. Yes, they were all at peace.

In the late summer of that same year, shortly before the season decamped for New York, word arrived of the Arctic whaling disaster in which over a thousand men and women and children evacuated thirty-two trapped whaleships rather than be held in the freezing wastes all winter. In heavy, overloaded boats they sailed, rowed and when the ice impeded them hauled the boats over its surface. For sixty miles they struggled until they reached the seven ships which had come as close as possible to rescue them.

As Mr Morgan read them the report in the *Tribune* she glanced at Harry, who was sitting with Alex and Mr Morgan round a cane table on the lawn. He met her gaze and both knew that the other was thinking that Jack Prior had not come for his fleet, all those years ago.

On the veranda, the women clustered in groups alongside Irene whilst their husbands rattled their newspapers in the full sun of the garden, tutting at the strain the lost thirty-two ships would put on the whaling industry, not to mention the insurers during this period of great financial instability that America was still experiencing.

Mrs Morgan's youngest daughter, Mary, said, 'You must be so relieved, Mrs Prior, that your wonderful husband is cruising the Tropics.'

Irene stared at the heat-faded sky. 'Oh yes, of course.'

Bernard, who was at the archery pad, with Tim, Alex's nephew, swung round. 'But he was once frozen in you know, Mary. He managed to escape, while Mr Travers stayed trapped. Father's wonderful, isn't he, Mother?'

Irene paused. What should she say to this boy? She called, 'Someday I will tell you all about it.'

The Old Dame who sat opposite suddenly leaned forward on her stick. 'Help me up, my dear Irene. Old bones become stiff if one sits too long.'

Irene hurried to her side and took the Old Dame's arm, feeling it thin and trembling. 'Walk with me a little,' the Old Dame murmured, her cane tapping on the veranda boards, reaching out for the rail, descending the steps onto the lawn, walking tentatively, nodding to the left where Bernard was lining up to his target, his back to the sea. 'Very like his father, isn't he?' It was statement.

Irene shook her head. 'In looks, perhaps. But underneath he's a Wendham.'

The Old Dame pursed her lips. 'He's obviously proud of his father?'

'Aren't most boys?' Irene said, her voice neutral.

'Difficult though, is it not?'

The Old Dame wore the black of mourning, as she always did. Irene said nothing, but every sense was alert.

The Old Dame pointed with her cane to the golden rod growing in the borders, her black lace cuffs hanging low on her mourning gloves. 'I made the error of speaking of my love for that flower in my husband's hearing, so he ordered that it should be uprooted.' She waved her cane in the direction of her fine 'cottage', her voice breaking slightly, 'You have the same brand of husband, one who hurts you even as he smiles and dances with you. As I say, it is difficult, for to leave them is impossible in our censorious society and to denigrate them to their children can be counterproductive. One simply has to hope that they will observe the truth as one lies trapped beneath their father's fists. Trapped, my dear, by love and duty towards one's children. Death is the only release.' Her voice was dry and steady as she nodded at Irene. 'Their death, one trusts. I now grow golden rod and my son is in *my* image, though a slightly less forbidding image. I hope you win your battle for his character. Try to let him see that the Prior position in society can only be laid at your feet, it may help.'

They reached the boundary of the garden, and stood at the hedge hearing the insects, and the sea beyond. Irene looked up at the swallows soaring on the wind, and the white clouds scudding the skies, amazement almost striking her dumb. At length, she said tentatively, 'I wondered why you were suddenly so kind. But

I have to warn you that I will leave when my son is of age. I will take him to his family seat and if that offends your social code then I offer my apologies in advance, and suggest that you cut me now.'

There was silence from the old woman at her side until Irene heard the unused sound of the Old Dame's laugh – rolling on and on, and now Mrs Horatio Norden banged her stick on the ground. 'Offend me? I will glory in it.'

In 1873 Harry entered into a discreet partnership with Alex, setting up property deals in the areas he visited for Prior's Clothing Workshops, setting aside his salary from that for the Wendham years.

Antoinette was eager to open another salon on Broadway in partnership with Irene, shaking her head as Irene put her hands on her hips and challenged her, with a mock frown. 'But what about retirement to New Bedford?'

'Not yet,' Antoinette said. 'I'm having far too much enjoyment.'

They were, all of them, and the gilded days were long and happy though Irene and Harry were true to their word and never knew one another's bodies again. Instead they basked in their inner peace. A peace which continued even when the market crashed further, and they had to fight to survive.

Somehow they all clung on, mainly through exports, though some friends did not, and so the year ground on, and in the evenings Irene painted word pictures of England for Bernard; of the land that was part of his heritage, of the family that had been hers, of the garden she had created, of their duties to their tenants which were the same as their duties to their workers.

'Is that why you won't cut their wages?' he asked.

'Yes. Even though we have reduced profits. Things will change, we need to keep the loyalty of our workers, their experience. And what's more, it is important to care about people.'

She explained how the growth of the business was achieved, the strategy behind it, and behind their entry into society. She also took him with her to the aid centres which she and Esther and others in society had set up in the slums and together with Tim, Esther's nephew, he helped.

As the year progressed and stability was again achieved within the business Harry showed him around the workshop, then he and Alex took the boy sailing in Saratoga, and to the races, and taught him to swim in the tumbling surf for he was a fine strong boy, seeming older than his eleven years. Once Harry took him and Timothy to Philadelphia during the Easter vacation.

But neither Irene nor anyone ever spoke of her whaling days, or her involvement in the workshop, because of the disgrace still attached to women who worked, and the danger a lack of discretion would bring to Bernard's future.

Twice Bernard said he would like to go to see Wendham, and yes perhaps he should try living in England for half his year and America for the other half when he became a man.

In January of 1874 Bernard, now just twelve, began at the school near the Hudson for Jack's fleet was due back shortly and Irene's equanimity faltered. Esther chewed her pencil as they worked on pattern designs in the room Alex had set aside for them in the house on Twenty-Eighth Street. 'He won't take the boy out of school, if that's what you are worried about. It's just not done and he's too eager about his position, and his dynasty. Our plan will work, believe me. His time with Bernard will be too limited for him to corrupt or influence him.'

Irene merely raised her eyebrows at Esther. 'These last four years have dulled your memory, my dear, but please God, let us hope that they have completed the formation of my son.'

Every day in the morning Irene, Antoinette and Esther surreptitiously designed gowns for the balls which were still held at the various mansions in spite of the difficult times. In the afternoons they received or visited, and at night they expressed their admiration for the latest gowns from Antoinette's salons, and there was never a hint of suspicion.

They designed clothes for those attending the junior patriarch dancing classes, to which one day Bernard would go, with his friends, one of whom was Mr Morgan's son. They designed for the afternoon levees at which those not admitted yet to the evening scene were observed, weighed, decided upon.

In the spring of 1874 Jack returned, striding into the brownstone on Twenty-Eighth Street, flinging down his hat, but keeping hold of the account books that he carried, shouting, 'I've been to the workshop. That damned convict is on his travels again. Well, let's see how much the pair of you have cheated me.'

He worked all afternoon on the books, then stared at her, 'You've learned well. I'd expected few profits, given the state of things.' He rose, walked towards her. 'But perhaps it has made you too pleased with yourself.' She felt the old fear, the old hate, and it seemed there was no light in the room from the late afternoon sun, no air to breathe as he reached for her, and dragged her upstairs, taking her, whilst she thought of nothing.

The next day he took the train to the school, bringing his son home, brushing aside her protests, yelling at her, 'I've a voyage to make. He'll come. I'll make the son I want, d'ya hear?'

She blocked his path to the drawing-room door. 'He's becoming the son you need. He's becoming the Prior who will understand business and society. He can learn about the sea later.'

343

He lifted his arm to strike her. 'He'll learn about it now, so it's in his blood, so it's second nature. He'll come to the Arctic with me while baleen's still on the up, and before the losses of the thirty-two whalers are made good. He'll come with me and see me take advantage of every last whale that fleet'll never harpoon again, and he'll see what real men do, and if that ain't good business, I don't know what is.'

All summer at Saratoga she waited. Harry came when he could, staying with Alex and Esther, having business meetings with Irene, wanting to take her in his arms and bring her comfort but saying, 'There is too much at stake. If we were discovered . . . No, we must do nothing to jeopardize your safety. Irene, I fear for you.'

'Knowing you are here is comfort enough. Knowing of our love is enough. I have no fear, and one day we'll be at Wendham.'

In August Barratt wrote to her, saying that he and Jack had agreed on a further lease, that he felt she should know, since her concurrence was no longer deemed necessary in the eyes of the law, and that he would await her proposal with interest in the fullness of time.

In October Bernard returned, pushing ahead of Jack, swaggering into the New York brownstone, his face ruddy, his language coarse, his tone contemptuous as she ran down the stairs, her arms outstretched. 'For God's sake, Mother, I'm not a child.' He pushed her aside. Behind him Jack laughed, then said, 'He'll be leaving with me on the next voyage.'

All evening she argued with Jack whilst Bernard remained in his room. Finally Jack seized his hat and stalked into the hall, calling for the carriage, yelling back at her, 'Very well, he stays at the school for now, but only 'cos I want him managing the business, instead of that damned convict, just as soon as he damn well can. Remember though he's a Prior and a whaler first and foremost, and I ain't having him forget that.'

When she entered Bernard's room to explain that he would stay at school he was standing on his bed, hurling darts at pictures of whales he had drawn. She stared, and saw his face exultant, his lips drawn back, death in his eyes.

'Bernard,' she shouted, rushing to him, wrenching the darts from his hand. One tore her skin. She tore the pictures down. Her blood smeared the wall.

'I won't have it,' she cried. 'Do you hear me? I won't have it. You will behave. You know better than this.'

'All I know is that I want to be with my father. He's a great man, a strong man, so I ain't having you damn well talk him out of it.' Bernard's face was ugly.

'You are a mere child. He's a man. He should not have taken you this time, he has agreed that the voyage must wait.' She clutched the torn pictures to her. The blood was seeping onto her pale-blue dress.

'You're boring, dull. I hate you. I hate this, no wonder he takes his fists to you,' he screamed. 'Why did we ever leave the sea? It's all your fault.'

The next morning she and Esther returned him to school. He refused to kiss her, jumping from the carriage without a backward glance, shouting at the porter who came from the old wooden school building which had once been a hunting lodge. 'Get my trunk to my room, you old fool.'

Irene called, 'Bernard, how dare you?'

'Go to hell.' He scuffed his way up the drive.

Esther stared after him, white, her hands balled into fists. 'He's Jack,' she whispered. 'After such a short trip he's already Jack.'

Irene leaned back against the leather of the seat, hearing the horses' hooves on the hard-packed earth of the track leading from the school. 'No, he's my son. This won't last. It must not last.'

In 1876 there was a second Arctic disaster. Many lives were lost and in New York the talk was all of this. Would

345

it also be the talk of the Hudson school? Irene wondered, fearfully. She and Esther visited him, watching as Bernard swaggered down the steps towards them, the image of his father. Irene said again, 'This won't last.'

The boys clambered into the carriage and Bernard barely spoke, leaving Timothy to tell his Aunt Esther and Irene of the boats they had sailed on the lake, the baseball they had played, the Greek they were learning, until Bernard cut through the strained conversation.

'What the hell good is Greek when there's a man's work to be done, when there's whales out there to be caught, a crew to control, to goddamn beat into submission?'

At the end of the fall semester Bernard glared at Irene when Harry Travers and Alex Moran brought him to her house from school. The two men unloaded his school trunks, their faces sombre and angry as he stormed from them into the house, pushing past his mother.

Harry called, 'Bernard, get back here.'

Alex added, 'That's no way to behave.'

Bernard came to the door, his face ugly, 'It's every way to behave. She's keeping me from my father, she's keeping me from the sea. She's making me stay in that poxy place with them other namby-pambys, just like father said. Well, I ain't going back. I ain't. I should be out there, chasing the whale, learning Prior ways like my father said until *she* talked him out of it.'

On Christmas Day, his fifteenth birthday, he was the same, throwing the baseball bat to one side, and the horse-riding equipment, muttering, 'The only present I want is to be away from here, and that damn school.'

Finally, on New Year's Day in Esther's drawing room, Irene talked, and Esther, and Martha too, of the advantages of continuing his education. 'Your father *did* agree after all, Bernard, and for a very good reason.

346

You see,' Irene explained yet again, 'his empire is being built up for you. He knows you need to have many skills to control it. Brute strength is not enough.'

Bernard glared at her. 'Strength, Mother, not brute strength. My father is not a brute unless he has to be, unless the victim deserves it.' His look was scathing.

Esther interrupted, 'It's an expression, not a criticism, Bernard.' Her voice was firmer than either Irene or Bernard had ever heard before. Bernard flushed, then flung himself from the room.

The next day they took him for the weekend to Wideacre, the house on the Hudson, and he stormed ahead of them as they walked in the snow towards the incline, refusing to drag the sledge as Alex requested.

His limbs were as gangly as a fifteen-year-old boy's should be. He kicked at the snow. Irene said hopelessly to Esther, 'He's a good boy really. He's confused, who wouldn't be? This is just part of growing up. I love him. I must help him.' She began to run to him. Alex held her back. 'Wait. Let him be on his own.'

Alexandra whimpered, holding up her arms to her mother, 'Carry me.' Laughing, Esther did so.

No-one spoke as they approached the bottom of the slope. Irene stopped and looked up at the wood, remembering the hut, feeling Harry's arms around her. He was in Maine. She wished he was with her. She wished he was Bernard's father. She wished . . . She shook her head.

Alex and Esther toiled on up the slope, Esther's fur hood lightly dusted with the powdery snow which had begun to fall. Irene touched the scarf she always wore here, for it was the one she had worn when Harry had come back, then hurried after them staring at Bernard who stood with his back to them his hands deep in his coat pockets. Still he kicked at the snow.

Alex and Esther ignored him, Irene too as she

reached them, her heaving chest raw in the cold air, her breath visible and rapid.

'Come on, darling,' Esther placed Alexandra on Alex's knees on the sled. 'There, your first sled ride.'

Alex clutched his daughter tightly. 'Push,' he shouted.

Esther and Irene shoved. Alex dug his heels into the snow, trying to walk the sled forward. Esther shrieked, 'You're too fat and heavy, no more port for you.'

He laughed back, 'How dare you?'

To the side of them Bernard turned round, staring at them. They pretended not to see. 'Push,' Alex ordered again.

Bernard called, 'Aunt Esther's right. I'll take Alexandra down.'

Alex swung round, though Esther and Irene forced themselves not to. Alex scrabbled to his feet, handing Alexandra to Bernard, holding the sled as they settled themselves, pushing it off, standing back with the women, watching as the sled gathered speed and Alexandra's laughter soared skywards, to be joined, as they fell off into the soft deep snow at the bottom, by Bernard's. The adults exchanged a look, and mutual relief was in their eyes.

They stayed on the slope until the snow fell more heavily, and then straggled back to the house, Bernard giving Alexandra a ride on his back until Alex took over, saying, 'Duty done for today. You're a fine boy.'

Bernard fell into step beside Irene, matching his strides to hers. She said, 'Alex is right. You are a fine boy.'

Bernard stared down at the snow. Flakes were falling faster now. Everything seemed so quiet. He said, his voice cracking as it had been doing for the past three months, 'Sometimes I don't know what I am, who I am.' He was looking at her now, in confusion.

She touched his arm hesitantly. 'I didn't know who I was either when I was growing up. One moment I

348

imagined I was a pirate on the ocean, standing on a branch of the apple tree, looking out for merchantmen. The next, there I was tending the sick with a halo round my head. Some moments I loved my parents, sometimes I hated them. You see, it takes time to find yourself. I think perhaps the best thing is to aspire to the best of those around you. The best, Bernard, never the worst.' Her voice was insistent. 'You're a fine boy, you are going to make a wonderful life for yourself. You will become a fine man and control the world your father and I, Antoinette and Harry, have built. It will be very much a man's task to take on so much.'

Bernard stood taller.

Irene wiped the snow flakes from her face, tasting them as she continued, 'Remember, too, that Wendham is part of that empire. Whaling, business and Wendham – all these are your heritage. I will take you there whenever you wish. Perhaps it should be soon, just for a visit. We are here to help you, and to love you. And we do, all of us. Your father, me, your friends.'

He stared around him, and then at her. 'I miss him, Mother. He makes the air move. He makes excitement out of nothing. He makes me feel alive.'

Her heart nearly failed her.

But July 1878 it was as though their reconciliation of that day had melted without trace under the barrage of letters Jack Prior sent to his son about the Arctic trip he had swept him away on in 1877. In that same year Irene wrote to Barratt and set up terms for her return after Bernard's sixteenth birthday, at which age he would be beyond custodial care. They would be free.

Again and again Irene had suggested that Bernard might like to visit England. Again and again he refused. December 1877, on his sixteenth birthday, she had given him money – for his trip to England that she told him she was arranging, so that he could explore the rest of his empire. Once there, it would be different, it must be different.

Bernard refused, 'Not now, I have better things to do.'

'What can I do?' she had asked Harry and Esther. 'Tie him up, force him?'

Now in Saratoga the sixteen-year-old boy flung himself on the sofa opposite Irene, his skin ruddy from sailing with his father to San Francisco, tired after his arrival only yesterday.

Irene sat across from him in the airy sitting room of the 'cottage' seeing Jack in the tapping of his fingers, the blank hardness of his eyes, the curl of his mouth, the thickening of his body, all gangliness gone.

'You returned overland, you say, all the way from San Francisco?' Martha asked from her chair by the fire, her hands like lightning as she knitted his jumper. 'I was knitting this for you. Don't know if it'll fit, seems you've grown.'

Bernard stared at her. 'Yes, I returned overland 'cos we've decided to run the fleet out of San Francisco now. New Bedford ain't worth the candle no more, but that damned convict needn't worry, for we'll ship his damn baleen overland.' His laugh was his father's.

Irene felt the dread and rage which had become so familiar sweep over her. She snapped, 'You should remember, Bernard Prior, that it was Mr Travers who earned the money which enables you to wear those clothes, to slump all over that sofa, to take railroad journeys whenever you please. Just as it is he who had brought you from the station, as it is he who was always there for you, as it is he who—'

He snatched his arm from the back of the sofa, leaned forward, stabbed his finger at her, 'He who is a lackey, a convict put here by my father to pretend to be someone he ain't. He's nothing. He can be ruined by us like that.' He clicked his fingers. 'You remember that. Just you remember that, for those my father builds

350

he can pull down, man or goddamned woman.' His stare was full of contempt, of warning.

He pushed himself up off the sofa and strode to the door.

She stared after him as Martha dropped her knitting, her mouth working. Irene's voice was strangled as she called, 'How dare you take that tone with me? You are my son, and you owe me respect. You have gone too far. You must not do this to yourself, or to me.'

He swung round, his hand on the door. 'You ain't got no right to respect, nor to nothing. Not as I see it.' He slammed the door, and left the house.

Martha whispered, 'He's so much worse, Irene. What can we do?'

That evening, as she paced the drawing room, Irene decided that she had to take her son to England, drag him screaming if she must, just as she should have done last Christmas. Was she mad? She hit her forehead with her hand. 'Why have I waited so long?' she cried out to her friends.

Esther sat with Martha, 'Because what else could you do, can you do? Jack's got to him, and I don't know the answer any more.' Her voice was quiet, distressed. 'Maybe there isn't one. Maybe you should give him up and get on with your own life? That's what you've got to decide.'

Irene swung round. 'He's sixteen. A mother doesn't give up on a boy that age. Would you with Alexandra?'

Esther looked at Martha and murmured, 'But Alexandra has Alex for a father, whilst Bernard has Jack. Go home, Irene. Leave him and go.'

'But would you leave her?' Irene demanded to know.

Esther was at last forced to shake her head. 'No. I love her.'

'Exactly, just as I love Bernard, and somehow I've failed him, somehow I must change that.'

Martha gazed at her hands. 'Maybe you should accept defeat. There's a time to walk away.'

Irene stared at her. 'There's never a time to walk away from your own child.'

She walked blindly from the room, her hands to her head. She stumbled out onto the veranda, leaning against the rail, feeling its heat from the day, remembering Bernard as a small boy; the smile that took the blankness from his eyes, his shrieks in the garden at Saratoga, his face as he took Alexandra on the sled, holding these images to her, pushing away any others, his early rudeness, his blank eyes, brushing aside the memory of his words, 'He makes the air move.'

'You're my son and I won't let that man destroy you, d'you hear?' she wept up at the night sky. 'D'you, Bernard? D'you hear, Jack? You've only had him for a few short years. I can reverse it. I know I can.'

The next afternoon a telegram reached Irene as she sat at her desk listening to the sound of Bernard's ball banging furiously again and again against the wall. The telegram was from Jack, demanding that his son join him in New Bedford where he would put in for him before taking course for Cape Verde.

She screwed it up. 'I won't let you have him, d'you hear?' she whispered, hurling it from her. It skidded across the floor.

Bernard's voice was harsh at the open window. 'Was that a cable you've just screwed up? Let me take a guess – from Father, is it?' He nodded to the ball of paper on the floor, his voice heavy with sarcasm. 'Yep, I'm pretty certain it was.'

She stared at him, rose, picked up the paper, smoothed it, handed it to him, staying by the window as he read it, saying, 'I don't want you to go, Bernard. I want you to see England. You said you would like to last year. You said you wanted to see Wendham. You talked of living there, for half your year. Come back with me.'

He was reading the cable, and when he had finished

he threw it up into the air, and caught it, his eyes blank as he stared at her, then he laughed. It was the same laugh as his father. She almost flinched. He said, his voice triumphant, 'He said he'd cable. I was looking out for the boy.' He stabbed his finger at her, 'He said you'd chuck it. It was a test, see. He's right, just like he always is.'

Irene shook her head, reaching out, pushing his finger away from her. 'I'm afraid of what he's doing to you. Perhaps I would have given it to you eventually but I . . . You are too young to go whaling. It's hard, and you've so much to learn here.' Desperation welled. 'For God's sake, you're half me. You're half me, Bernard.'

He stabbed his finger at her again, 'Be myself, you told me in the snow with your namby-pamby friends. God, you couldn't even push a damned sled down a slope between you. It had to be me who took the kid – a Prior. A Prior who ain't going to spend his life cooped up in an office while I could be out there hunting the whale with him. There ain't no man alive better'n him, and one day there'll be no man alive better'n me. No-one tougher, no-one more powerful.'

She shouted at him, 'Haven't you seen through him yet? Haven't you seen the man he is?'

'I sure have – he's the man who started this business, got it going, got you into society, built the Prior empire. This is the man who worked his bootstraps off, *worked*, mother, which is a word you don't know the meaning of.'

He stormed along the veranda, slamming open the door, stomping across the sitting room. She ran out into the passage, following him to his room, pulling at his shirt, making him stop, hauling him round, gripping his arms, her hair falling from its pins, desperation making her voice soar. 'You know nothing. You're not thinking. How could he build it up, he wasn't here. I've already told you how the business was built up but it was me, not your father. I've worked hard with Harry and Antoinette.'

Bernard laughed. 'Harry Travers, that convict who couldn't even get himself out of the ice, as my father did. D'you call drawing pictures of dresses work? How come you've all this time to be sitting on verandas laughing and giggling, if you're so damn busy?'

She shook him, enraged at his Prior arrogance, his Prior stupidity, shouting up at him, 'We sit there because that is work as well and how dare you criticize Harry Travers? Did you know that your father had an auxiliary engine whilst we were in the Arctic? Did he tell you that was how he forced his way out? How he could have forced his way back to a suitable point to try and help us, but he did not, and so we nearly died. All he did was gloat over the insurance.'

He stared at her. 'We, what d'you mean – we?'

Caution was gone as she raged on. 'Because I was there. Work, you dare to talk about work. I've scrubbed the decks of your father's stinking whalers. I've flensed, I've washed his damn clothes in urine, and I've nearly died, trapped in the ice, left by your father. Your wonderful father who stole my house. Your wonderful father who treats me as though I were dirt. Whose fists talk for him. Think, Bernard. Think. What sort of man beats his men, his wife? A weak man, a cowardly bully who cannot get obedience any other way. Is that the sort of bully you really want to become? If not, stop now, for you are on the way.'

He stared at her, horror in his eyes. She felt exhausted, distraught. She touched his cheek, 'I'm so sorry to tell you like this.'

He slapped her hand away, stepped closer, looming over her, staring down into her face, his lips barely moving as he hissed, 'He said you'd tell me this pack of lies. The first mate told me too and what's more he told me how you and that Travers had stolen his watch. But even they didn't think you'd shout it out like this, for God knows who to hear. You say you built this business up. You've just shown yourself to be the liar he said you were because no-one who'd really built anything up would jeopardize it by mouthing off about working.

'Goddamn, you want to bring us down, don't you? You want to get us cast out of our position just to hurt him as you've always tried to do. Well, I won't let you. You'd better just keep your damn mouth shut and never open it again or you'll answer to me.' He was shaking her, 'Keep your mouth shut, d'you understand?'

She tore from him, backing to the wall, 'This is nonsense.'

Bernard sneered, 'Ruin is all you know about, ruin and lies. A few drawings, that's all you've ever done. I've never seen you lift a finger in the workshop, never seen you in a store, but here you are screaming out, loud enough to make the Old Dame strike us off, about working, about scrubbing decks. Urine – have you no decency? Wasn't it enough that you flung yourself at Father in Somerset, swearing that you'd been bedded so that Father had to lease that house to buy off your godfather just to protect your honour? Is it any wonder he beats you?'

He was gone the next morning, and that week Harry and Alex instructed the lawyers to hurry up negotiations started a year ago with the British authorities which would allow the escaped convict, Harry Travers to return to England. Again they emphasized his willingness to serve out his term and/or to pay a fine. They also pleaded with Irene to leave now. She would not. 'He's my son. I must try again. He's worth more than the person he's become.'

Bernard returned in the fall of the next year, 1879, and while he lounged around the house, surly and disgruntled, barely speaking to his mother, Irene made Martha fight for him with her. 'It is not too late,' she ground out. 'He's my son. It can't be too late.'

She made Esther and Alex fight for him too, pleading with them, begging them.

Esther said, 'Get Harry to tell him the truth about the Arctic. Get Antoinette and Sinclair.' Irene refused. 'He'd think they were on my side. He wouldn't listen.'

Alex said, 'We'll hire a man to find some of the old crew.'

They did, but could not.

A week after his return Alex, Esther and Irene took him to Philadelphia and whilst there Alex offered him a role in his firm, travelling around the country, gaining valuable real estate experience to add to his skills as a businessman. He refused, saying, 'I ain't going to work anywhere but where my father tells me, you got that? And my father tells me I'm not to do anything. I'm to stay in New York and watch Travers work, 'cos that's what the convict's paid to do. But he's also supposed to make my mother's life a misery, along with that Sinclair, just by being here, and I can't see any of that happening. In fact, if you ask me he gets on a sight too well with all of you, especially her.' He flung his napkin on the table, pulled out the watch Jack had given him. 'Now, I've people to see.' He strode from the restaurant.

Alex stared at his plate. Esther at hers. Irene said, 'New York. At least he's to be in New York. It gives us more time.'

Esther murmured, still looking at her plate, 'He'll be eighteen in December and that is old enough to know better. But don't wait until then. Go, Irene. Just go.'

Irene shook her head. 'No, I can save him. I know I can. I must, for I've ruined him by staying.'

Alex slammed down his hand on the table, 'Jack's ruined him. Not you, for God's sake. You could do nothing other than what you have done. Go. It's not safe to stay.'

Irene stared at him. 'Harry is leaving soon anyway so they can't hurt him. But I can hurt my son if I don't show him that though duty and commitment might seem onerous there is fun and excitement to equal anything that a whaling voyage might involve. I can try to show him that beneath the excitement that stirs the air around his father is bestiality. I must stay because, despite what you say, I should somehow have stopped this.'

Back in New York, Harry sat opposite her in the workshop, holding her hand. 'Not you. It was never you. You had to stay. If you had gone Jack would have come after you, taken him back. If you had managed to escape what life would you have had? What life would your son have had? You made your decision way back. It was the right one.' He pressed her hand to his lips. 'It's up to Bernard now. Only he can change himself.'

'Hold me,' she said, and for only the second time he came to her and held and kissed her. She whispered against his mouth, 'It's my duty, and it's because I love him. Say you understand.'

Harry kissed her hair, looking through the glass window out over the deserted factory. Yes, he understood.

At the end of November Jack Prior sent a cable dismissing Harry Travers, for his son was the only front man he required, he said. It coincided with the conclusion of the negotiations for Harry Travers's return. By Christmas Harry was gone, straight into a British prison to serve his sentence of nine months, and after that to prepare for Irene's return.

In October 1880 Irene sat at one end of the dining-room table in the Twenty-Eighth Street brownstone watching her husband and her son at the other end shovelling food into their mouths. She stared down at her uneaten lamb, then around the room with its flock wallpaper, its oil paintings of ships, the oil painting of himself which Jack had commissioned and presented with a flourish to Bernard on his eighteenth birthday. Since that day he had stayed here, with them, while the ships were being refitted in San Francisco.

She looked again at the two men, her son – so dark, so tall. At Jack, with just the same dusting of grey at the temples that he had when she first danced with him. She touched her own hair, knowing it had faded, and was streaked with white as Harry's was. There was a burst of laughter from the two men. Jack slapped his hand on the table. She touched her glass, running her trembling finger round the rim.

She was leaving tonight. It was over, all over. Last week her son had struck her as she had pleaded with him to visit Martha who was dying at the Greenwich house, the place she had chosen to live since Jack Prior had returned to New York.

He'd turned away impatiently, 'She shouldn't be here anyway. We've no babies for her to look after. She's living off my father's money and never a good word to say about him. It's time she went, one way or another.'

'Bernard, please, for my sake.'

'You've done enough to us without boring us to death.'

'Bernard,' she'd shouted. He'd backhanded her across the face. Martha had died the next day, whilst Antoinette and she sat by her side. The same day that Jack Prior announced over the breakfast table that he had bought the lease of the Greenwich house and that Antoinette and Emily had to leave by the end of that week, and Irene was to 'Get that goddamn body out of my house by the next day.'

In the afternoon Bernard had announced to the workforce that the wages were to be cut. Emily had been sacked. Sinclair too.

Antoinette and Emily had sufficient money from the salons to start again and to buy another house on Greenwich Avenue.

Irene had arranged the funeral, but Bernard and Jack

would not attend. She had made her own mourning, carefully, painstakingly, working day and night until her eyes ached, for she couldn't cry. She couldn't eat. She couldn't sleep. All she could do was sew. She made Esther's too.

After the funeral she had read Harry's letter from Somerset – sent to Esther's – which confirmed that Barratt was gone. That his sentence was concluded. *So, we're both free. The sale of our second-hand business had given us enough capital to pay Barratt's price, put in hand the changes to the estate, and begin another commercial venture. We are no longer in anyone's power. I'm in the house. I'm waiting for you. Come soon, my love.*

Still she ran her finger round the glass.

Jack and Bernard thrust back their chairs, throwing their napkins on the table, not even looking at her as they left the room, Jack's hand on his son's shoulder and again they laughed. She stared after them, after the son she still loved, and would always love. One more try, just one more. She ran after them, 'Bernard.'

He stopped by the front door, not looking at her as he cursed and said, 'Why don't you just be quiet 'cos I'm going gambling and there's nothing you can do about it, so just sit at home and damn well weep, or sew.'

She watched the door slam shut.

She leaned forward in the carriage which Sinclair urged on through the streets, staring at the city which had grown and blossomed and thrived out of all recognition. He drew the horses to stop in Wandle Court. She hurried into the house, calling back softly over her shoulder, 'Wait, I won't be long. It's just the painting of Wendham House that I want, and some papers. Then we'll board the ship.' For Sinclair was sailing with her, though they were both registered under assumed names, just in case.

Sinclair looked at her and saw despair vying with relief. He said, 'I'll come and help you.'

She shook her head. 'No, stay with the horses. It'll be all right. None of it's heavy.'

She hurried up the stoop for the last time, opening the door, stepping into the hall, remembering Antoinette, Emily, hearing Martha, beloved Martha. Hearing, seeing and feeling Harry. Remembering Bernard.

She pulled the front door wide open so that the moonlight touched the pale-green flock wallpaper which Martha had chosen. The hall seemed larger than she remembered, the stairs wider. She walked to the left and into the dining room where she and Harry had done the books, where Bernard had sat with her at breakfast, with Martha buttering toast soldiers for him.

For a moment she closed her eyes but still she couldn't weep. Was there anything else she could do? She knew there was not . . . Harry had been right. Now it was up to Bernard.

'Go to Wendham,' Martha had urged as she died. 'Live your own life now. It's not before time, my dearest girl.'

She hurried up the stairs, leaving the front door open to light her way, seeing the boxes at the top. Boxes which Jack had ordered to be sent over from his den on the afternoon of Martha's death. On top of these he had flung the painting of Wendham. It was still there, and propped in the corner were three of his lances. 'We'll use bomb lances,' he'd told his son, 'but keep these for old times' sake.'

She stumbled against a box then felt her way along the dark landing and the closed drawing-room door, until she reached the stairs to the bedrooms. 'I will use this house,' he'd shouted at her on the day Martha died. 'It's where I will bring the women I need, those who give me what you never could – pleasure. You have a week to get it cleared.' Well, *he* could clear it now.

She climbed up the stairs to the top floor, entering the small room where Harry had lain – so ill, so thin. Long ago she'd put a barrier of old boxes between the bed and the desk to deter anyone who thought of entering. She touched the pillow, she stared round the room for the last time.

Her modest trunk was already on board together with her journals and the will she had made when she realized she had lost her son to Jack Prior. A copy remained with Esther, beloved Esther, and a copy of her journals in case the ship foundered. She was taking merely a few clothes which she would destroy on arrival for she wanted nothing else which might remind her of Jack Prior.

She'd bade farewell to Esther this afternoon. Esther had wept, clutching her until Alex had pulled her away, saying, 'We'll visit, and the Old Dame will too, flying over on her broomstick, you mark my words.' But there had been tears in his eyes, and they had been not only at her going but for the loss of her son. 'Be happy,' he'd said. 'It's you and Harry now. You've waited far too long already.'

She touched the pillow again. 'Harry,' she whispered. 'Oh, Harry.' Now she wept, and they were tears of release, and of farewell to her son.

Bernard sat next to his father in his carriage as it trundled through the streets. Would he win at poker tonight? He felt excitement rising. If he did, he could afford one of those women his father used. Jack passed him his brandy flask. He took a drink, handed it back. Jack wiped it on his sleeve, and slapped his son's knee. 'Kind of feel we might be about to make a great team. Time to get things straight, get rid of any damn fool principles.'

Bernard grinned, 'Does seem stupid to pay out those wages. I've cancelled the pensions too. I'll tell 'em at the start of the week. Bleed them dry, let 'em know who's boss, like you do. Hey, Father, talking of bleeding folks dry – I sure think we got a good deal for that second-hand clothes business we sold recently. Didn't even know we had one. I couldn't find a record of the company in our books though. Wendham Holdings. Some fiddle of yours, I s'pect.'

Jack looked up from his brandy which he had been about to raise to his lips. He stared at Bernard, 'We ain't got a second-hand business. What the hell you talking about?'

Bernard shrugged, 'Found the papers in the Greenwich house, up in that small bedroom, stuffed with rubbish it is, with this desk and a bed. I know it was a Prior business 'cos the bill of sale was signed by Travers and mother.'

Jack Prior froze with his brandy halfway to his lips. He said quietly, 'When?'

'Last November.'

'Where is it now?' Jack ground out, his voice full of fury, full of awareness.

'Still in that poky little drawer in the desk. I go through desks when I see them. You find all sorts of things. There's always a secret drawer. It was the day the women left. I took Mother's key since the women took theirs. Thought they might have left some pickings.'

In the bedroom Irene eased the switch, took out the bill of sale. Harry had left a copy in case there had been any queries. 'Keep it safe,' he'd said. Well, what could be safer than a house none of her family visited, even at the request of a dying woman?

Jack Prior yelled at the driver to make for the Court, but when he saw the carriage he said, 'No, carry on and head for the back entrance.' The carriage rumbled down the lane. Jack said to Bernard, 'I'm going in. You stay here. There have been some pickings, all right, but it's not us who've found them, it's your mother, and Travers.'

'But Father—'

'Shut your mouth,' his father snarled. 'This is man's work.'

He slipped from the carriage and into the yard through the back gate, creeping stealthily along the yard wall to the house, smashing a small window. He unlatched the door and kicked the glass to one side.

On the stairs Irene stopped. What was that? She listened. Nothing. She waited, hearing only her own breath. She continued to feel her way down from the top floor, reaching the landing which led past the drawing room to the head of the stairs. She felt her way along the walls and nearly fell into the drawing room. She regained her balance, laughing slightly, her heart pounding at the shock.

She worked her way along to the faint moonlight which reached the top of the stairs from the half-open front door. Then she stopped. Surely the drawing-room door had been closed when she felt her way along before, or she would have fallen into it then?

She looked down at the moon-bright hall and shrugged. What nonsense. Sinclair would have seen anyone coming in. She took the painting from the box, tucked it beneath her arm, put her hand on the banister, took her first step down the stairs.

'I guess you must be running off to Travers. I guess you stole the second-hand business from me and your son. I guess you crossed me, you double-dealing bitch. I kind of thought I'd warned you about doing that?'

She froze, unable to move, then slowly turned her head towards Jack Prior's voice which came from the darkness of the drawing-room doorway. He stepped out onto the landing where he remained an indistinct unfeatured figure in the darkness.

She couldn't move, couldn't speak. He took another step and now he was to the left of the boxes, three yards from her, and the moonlight gave him form and she saw his face distorted with hate. 'Nothing to say?'

His voice was cold, so cold. She backed against the wall, her eyes never leaving the great brooding figure. She inched her way down the next step, and the next.

He bellowed, 'Nothing?'

She flinched, her heart leapt, but then the suppression of years exploded and her own rage and anguish cast aside her fear. She shouted, 'Yes, I have something to say. You didn't want the second-hand business, so I started it up. I've bought back Wendham, the house you stole. I'm taking back my life, the life you tried to steal. I can't take my son, for you have taken him, destroyed him, just as you destroy everything.'

'I? Shouldn't it be we? You and damn Travers?' He raged, 'It was signed by both of you.'

'He had every right to set up the firm. You don't own him, and you don't own me any more. We've stolen nothing from you, and you know that. By your orders we stopped the second-hand clothes. We made sure we didn't make our money from anything that would compete with you.' Her throat felt dry now, and her anger was gone. All she could hear was the heavy sound of her own breathing.

She kept her eyes on him, making herself move, inching her way down. She flashed a look towards the front door. So far? Oh God, so far. She looked back at Jack Prior. He was moving out from the boxes and now the moonlight was on his face, and along with the hatred was exultation. He lifted his arm and she saw the lance he was holding.

'Sinclair,' she screamed. Her legs wouldn't move. Jack stepped forward, his arm went back, his body too. He twisted. She stirred at last, ran, down the stairs, hearing him shout, 'You crossed me, like my mother, like Palance.'

She heard that laugh. 'No. No,' she moaned. She was

at the bottom, running across the hall, arms out-stretched for the door. She heard his thrusting grunt. Too far, the door was too far. There, she was there. She stumbled. 'Harry,' she screamed but that was just before the lance struck.

Sinclair was in the garden at the back of the house when he thought he heard his name. He had been thirsty, had come into the kitchen for water while Irene was up in the small bedroom, then stepped into the garden, staring out into the shadows, remembering it as it had been. He hurried in, his feet crunching on a piece of glass. He saw the broken window for the first time. For God's sake, how had he missed it? He heard Harry's name being called, but no, not called – screamed.

He bounded through the kitchen, opening the door like the cat he could be, running silently down the passage, then stopped as he heard Jack Prior's voice from somewhere at the head of the stairs, out of sight above him. 'I didn't miss with my mother, or Palance either.' Sinclair heard his laugh, and flattened himself against the banister, inching his way forward, staring always upwards, but he couldn't see Prior.

He flashed a look back towards the kitchen, then into the dining room through the open door. Where the hell was she? What did Prior mean – he didn't miss with Palance either? He stood stock-still as he heard creaks from the landing above. Then inched forward again, peering towards the front door, leaning out to get a better angle of the area leading from the stairs to the door.

It was then that he saw her, the beautiful woman who had bathed his wounds, who had nursed him in his fever, who had taken him to the peace of the *Wendham*, who had brought him here.

He saw her there, on the tiles, her arms reaching for the door, moonlight playing on her wet red hair. Hair so wet. Hair too red. How could he see colour in the moonlight? He couldn't, he just knew because he could see the great gouge where . . . Oh God, oh God. Where part of her head should have been.

In the hall wall, just above the skirting boards, staining the pale-green flock wallpaper a lance quivered up to its hilt.

Oh God, oh God. He melted back against the wall, crept out into the garden, over the wall into the next garden, and the next, before slipping into the lane, seeing the carriage behind him, waiting.

He stayed in the shadow, walking, walking. His mind was a blank, no grief, no pain, just blank. Just like there'd been no colour. But there had been colour. In his mind there had been colour. Now the blankness faded, and he saw her, and the blood, and the lance, quivering. The blood. The scream, the goddamn scream. Now came the agony, and he ran, and ran, but it came with him. The colour, the agony, the scream.

PART THREE

Wandle Court, Greenwich Village, New York,
October 1995

CHAPTER EIGHTEEN

'You're not goddamn listening, Mother,' John Prior, Jack Prior's great-great-grandson roared, slamming his hand down on the polished mahogany table at which they were dining, glaring at Sarah Prior who sat at the opposite end of the table. The Chablis in the crystal goblets shuddered. His daughter Jane reached out, lifted her glass and drank, trying to drown the familiar misery.

She rested the rim of the glass against her lower lip, as her grandmother leaned back in her chair, her gold hoop earrings glinting in the candlelight, patting her silver necklaces with scarlet-tipped fingers, her dyed auburn hair rich in colour, and totally in keeping with this feisty lady. How could she not be afraid? Jane wondered with envy.

Her grandmother snapped, 'Don't behave in this fashion in my house. This isn't the Prior boardroom.'

Or one of your floozy's nests, Jane thought forcing herself to look at him; his black hair, his broad body which seemed to strain at the seams of the dark suit. Her mother sat opposite Jane, pale-skinned, faded, hair bottle blonde, divorced from the tension by her usual pre-dinner martinis.

She shifted her gaze to the bright ethnic rug hanging on the wall, the raw gutsy modern paintings. Did her grandmother paint in this style to spite her dead husband who had dictated what should and should not have a place in their home, and whose style had been severely conservative? Or was this the real Sarah Prior?

If so, Jane wondered, who was the real Jane Prior?

She sipped the Chablis. This morning her grandmother had asked if Chablis was her favourite. It had seemed enough that it was her father's. She looked at him and asked herself again – so what or who was she? A crazy girl with deep-brown hair, with the merest of red tints and grey eyes which didn't seem to come from her mother or her father. Maybe the hair was from Sarah Prior – it was difficult to say for hers had always been dyed.

Anyway here was Jane Prior with twenty years under her belt, a Prior child, a cuckoo in the nest – one who wanted to write the definitive novel, paint the definitive picture, do something that would make her be admired, just once, by these parents of hers. Better still, one who wanted to feel loved.

She drank again. The real Jane Prior? Hey, that was quite a question, but now her brother's voice, loud and rude, dragged her back to the table. 'You got to listen to him, Grandmother,' Rich said, turning his back to his mother who sat next to him, leaning towards Sarah Prior, his fingers tapping the table, his tone harsh.

Her father leaned forward in his chair, his shoulders hunched, nodding, 'Yes, Mother. This is more important than slapping paint on canvas, for Chrissake, or are you too senile to understand that?'

Jane slammed her glass down. 'Don't talk to Grandma like that.' Love for her grandmother giving her courage.

The Chablis slopped over the edge of the glass to pool on the polished surface. Jane repeated into the silence, 'Don't talk to Grandma like that.' This time there was a crack in her voice and her mouth was dry with fear. Yes, this was the real Jane Prior, frightened of her own shadow.

John Prior turned to her, his lips thin, his voice like ice, 'I guess you've had too much to drink, or maybe just taken leave of your senses, again.' His eyes were so dark, so dead. Had they always been? No, she remembered the years when she had been a kid. He'd swing her round on the sand outside their beach house. Why, he'd even laughed with her, swooping her high, then low, landing her onto that hot dry sand. Telling Rich he was too old to be swung, throwing a ball to his baseball bat instead, looking across at his wife and smiling.

I'm going to England tomorrow, Pop, she wanted to say. Be nice. Just be nice for tonight because grandmother and I sorted out the menu, and I chose things I knew you'd like.

She felt a hand on hers and dragged herself from her father's glare to her grandmother's thin blue-veined fingers, their heavy ethnic rings and her voice saying, 'Jane doll, I've been thinking. Salad is what you need for the flight, and no wine. It makes the jet lag worse and you must start the year well, make it a good time.'

'Mother,' John Prior ground out. 'I'm trying to talk goddamn business, not jet lag cures.'

She felt her grandmother's fingers tighten as Sarah Prior said, 'I've already told you, this is not your boardroom, this is my home.'

Rich glared at his grandmother, and then at her. John Prior was now standing, pounding the table with his fist.

'I know it's your home, for God's sake. That's why I'm asking you to mortgage it for the good of the family. Or at least mortgage part of it, the two top floor apartments and the basement.'

Her grandmother's grip increased as she replied, 'I've told you once, over the asparagus soup if I remember rightly, that I won't do that. The income from the flats keeps me independent.'

Was grandmother scared too? Is this why she gripped her hand too tight? Or was it rage, or was it both, like hers was? Her father seethed, 'I ask again, are you senile? Can you not see that being independent is a luxury you can no longer afford? Can you not see that

371

this house is Prior property, bought by the founder, and that you have no moral right to it?'

Her grandmother released her grip on Jane's hand, picked up her starched napkin and patted her mouth, before laying it down neatly by her half-eaten salmon. Lipstick smeared the linen. Sarah Prior's voice was calm and unafraid as she looked up at her son, 'Do sit down. I am not intimidated by word or gesture, and I consider I have every moral right to it, after years with your father. Besides the one decent thing he did in his life was to leave it to me. The fact that I told him I would run to the newspapers with evidence of his rather revolting affair with the hooker if he did not might have contributed to that course of action.' She looked pityingly at Monica Prior. 'Now, I think it's time that Jane told us about her plans after she arrives at Sussex University for her exchange year in England.'

No, this lady wasn't scared. How come? How had she learned that skill?

'Mother,' John roared, sitting down, bringing out a letter from his breast pocket, 'this is a letter from the bank. They won't put up for the real estate deal unless I inject a percentage, and we're too goddamn stretched after the 1994 hike in interest rates. It saw a twenty-three per cent fall in our assets – twenty-three per cent for God's sake. Prior Associates needs that real estate deal to keep up our image, to make a show of confidence.'

Sarah Prior beckoned to Josephine, the Filipino maid, who began to clear the salmon, and said, 'Ask one of your three colleagues in Prior Associates to put up some money.'

Rich interjected, 'How in hell can we do that after that damned Travers and his Wendham Holdings moved to buy their shares last year? We stopped them selling by talking hard and fast, making projections that included the acquisition of this real estate. It'd kill any confidence to go round with cap in hand to 'em now.

Damn it, they might offer their shares to Travers after all.'

John Prior interrupted, 'You're right, and this generation can't be the one to let those bastards take us over in any way, shape or form. Jack Prior'd turn in his grave.'

Sarah Prior thanked Josephine. 'Pavlova anyone?' Everyone shook their heads. Josephine brought coffee. 'Coffee, perhaps?' Sarah touched the silver coffee jug.

'Mother,' John Prior insisted. 'We need the money.'

'This is the only unencumbered property left in our family, and it will remain so, as long as I live. That is my final word, John. My dear, has it never occurred to you that one day this ridiculous feud could blow up in the faces of the Priors and you will need a bolt-hole? I've ensured that you and your family will always have that. Though vastly the more sensible thing to do would be to draw this whole unsavoury Travers-Prior thing to a close as that letter from Travers has suggested.'

John was alert, 'How'd you know about that?'

Monica Prior spoke now, her voice languid, distant, 'I told her.'

Rich turned to her, 'Well, you'd no damn right.'

Jane stood up, her fists clenched, 'Don't speak to Mom that way.'

Sarah Prior reached for her, 'Sit down, Janey. Sit down. I don't want you involved, not tonight of all nights.'

Jane slumped onto her chair. Her grandmother said, 'Now, this is Janey's farewell dinner. We ought to concern ourselves with her, not business.'

John Prior grunted, 'I'm past concerning myself with her. There was another demonstration last week.'

Rich guffawed, 'What was it this time? Some little old lady not wanting to leave her home which is blocking a road? Some big bogeyman wanting to take over a store, get it on its feet, make it efficient, sack a few time-wasters? Get real, get a job, do something other than be a pain.'

Anger was sweeping Jane like a forest fire, roaring free, and her voice was strangled as she said, 'I just want to stand up against people like you and your crass fascist friends, Rich. Why don't you just grab a sheet and go burn a cross on someone's lawn? When did you ever think about what's happening around you? When did you ever think of anything for yourself? You just parrot what the last person said.'

'Think? What d'you think I spend all day doing? Just thinking about how to make money for us, that's what. Money for you to go spend a useless year poring over books. What good's that to anyone?'

She sprang to her feet, 'I have to go. It's part of the course. Mom, tell him.'

'Oh get hysterical somewhere else.'

She sat down, and drank her coffee with shaking hands, staring at her mother who was sipping her drink, off in a world which didn't contain any of this. Jane clutched her cup tighter. Sure she demonstrated but she really cared about little old ladies. Was that so hard to understand? She sipped the coffee, draining it to the dregs.

Rich leaned forward, 'Going to see you standing up for gays and dykes next? See you're wearing the ribbon. But best not to bring your girlfriend home.'

She replaced her coffee cup carefully onto the saucer, then leaned forward herself, saying conspiratorially, because for one precious moment she felt no fear, 'Have you practised hard to be such an asshole, Rich? Has it taken every second of your twenty-six years?'

John Prior roared, 'Leave the room, Jane, and wait in the hall. You're not fit to be part of our family, you haven't even bothered to get out of your jeans, and that sweatshirt's a disgrace. You're nothing but a waste of time. Rich is right, what good're books? It's money down the tube, but no, you never think of that, just yourself. Now get out.'

Jane swung round to her grandmother, frustration, hurt and grief tearing at her. 'Tell him, Grandma. Tell him you said to come as I usually looked. You said you wanted to be able to think of me this way while I was gone.'

Sarah Prior smiled, her face scything into deep lines, her eyes full of love, 'I know, and your father knows too. He's just being obdurate. Go get some air, Janey. It's getting stale in here.'

Jane shot a look at her mother, wanting her to tell Rich to go take a jump, wanting her to tell her father what he already knew – that she couldn't do maths, had never been able to no matter how hard she'd tried, but her mother was running her fingers through her peroxided hair. Her dark roots were stark, her lids heavy over preoccupied eyes, her lips loose.

In the hall it was darker, cooler. She leaned back against the wooden panelling, holding herself, wanting to be gone, wanting to be in England but longing to stay, for maybe they'd forget her, maybe there'd be even less room in their lives when she returned.

Her grandmother came into the hall, shutting the door carefully behind her, spreading open her arms, holding Jane when she came to her. She felt those ringed hands stroking back her hair, and now she wept, and all the time her grandmother repeated, 'I'll miss you so very much. I love you, sweet girl. We all do.' Then she said, as the sobs subsided, 'Business just seems to get in the way for the Prior men.'

'I don't think even Mother loves me. They won't miss me. It's always been the same.'

'Shh. Think. Once it wasn't. Before your grandfather died your father had time, but once this darned feud becomes their responsibility it turns them into devils.'

'It's stupid, the whole thing's stupid and you're right,

375

they should get out of it. What's the lousy point?' Jane leaned back against the panelling, wiping her face with the back of her hand.

'Jack Prior made it a matter of honour that the Prior family would smash the Travers family, but you know all that.'

'But why won't they get out?' she repeated. 'Especially now they've had the letter.'

Her grandmother handed her a handkerchief. 'They won't believe him, they'll think there's some trick, you mark my words – and they want Wendham House. Above all else, they want the return of Wendham House because there's all that money waiting in trust for the Prior who manages to take it from the Travers. It would make my little house superfluous. It would make your father's world alive with riches. It would make him king of the heap, the victor. That's what drives them on and I loathe even the sound of Jack Prior's name for leaving such a bitter legacy.'

The cab drive back from Wandle Court was silent and, once at the apartment building on Central Park West, her father and brother strode ahead of them into the foyer, nodding curtly to Jake, the doorman. Behind them, still on the sidewalk, Jane reined back her pace to match the uneven clicketty-click of her mother's strapped heels, nodding to the doorman as he held open the door, 'How you doin', Jake?'

'OK, Miss Prior. Have a good trip, if I don't see you.'

'I will,' she said as she crossed the lobby, taking her mother's arm, seeing her father and brother enter the lift and press the button, still deep in conversation. The doors closed. The lift ascended. In the lobby the leather armchairs, one with the *New York Post* folded on it, were empty as they always were at this time of night. Who'd they expect? she thought, waiting for the elevator, watching the numbers light and fade. Damn

376

you, Father. Damn you for not waiting, for not having even a whisper of graciousness.

She stabbed at the button again and again. Her mother said languidly, 'Won't bring it any faster, honey. Use your time to breathe.'

'For God's sake, Mother, we'd be dead if we weren't breathing.'

'No, breathe deep. Like this, it keeps me sane, that and the colonics.'

Jane didn't turn to watch, for her eyes were fixed on the numbers lighting and fading as the lift returned. 'Sane, mother?' she whispered. 'You're sure about that are you?'

She saw her mother's reflection in the button panel, saw the head which drooped, the momentary sadness and she felt ashamed. 'You breathe all you want, Mother, if it helps.'

The doors opened. They entered, and as they rose the loud alcohol rich breathing of her mother was the only sound. Jane slipped her arm around the frail woman, who tensed as she always did when touched. 'I'll miss you, Mom.'

The lift stopped, the doors opened. Her mother pulled away from her, saying nothing. They walked separately along the carpeted corridor, through the open door of their apartment into the entrance hall, past the two mock Queen Anne chairs, into the living room.

The decanter was gone from the side table. Her mother said, 'I must . . .' She drifted off, weaving her way unsteadily between the white leather armchairs towards the corridor and her bedroom.

Jane walked to the picture window and stared out across Central Park, seeing the huge buildings of the lower city, seeing the sky which was illuminated by the lights of Manhattan. A city so full, so high, so alive. How could she be so lonely living here, amongst so many, amongst so much?

She turned and faced the room with its white

armchairs, its white deep-pile carpet, its glass tables, its minimalist decor all mortgaged to the hilt, glaring at the portrait of Jack Prior above the fireplace. Damn you too, but not as much as the Travers family. Not as much as those people who have dogged my family every year since that Prior woman stole from us, died, and ripped the heart out this family, leaving nothing but rage and bitterness.

The door to her father's den, which led into the living room, was open. She rooted in the cocktail cabinet and found white rum – what else would it be in this white world? It was half full.

She poured a shot into a glass, then another, and another, downing it in one. It felt hot and strong. She poured more, kicked off her sneakers and walked across the deep pile towards the study, standing in the half-open doorway, watching unnoticed as the two men pored over stapled papers, her father sitting at the desk, her brother perched on it.

She should have been a boy, then she would have been included, listened to. She sipped again, catching the words. Wendham Holdings. Wendham Holdings which was always there, always taking her father from her, making the memories of being swung on the beach fade. She rolled the rum around her mouth as her father read aloud from the papers.

'Murphy's report says that from his analysis of the Wendham finances the recession's reined them in, but according to the index they're still OK. So why've they shut up Wendham House? Could be the letter's not a blind, could be they *do* want to consolidate and be done with meddling in Prior contracts.' He tapped his teeth. 'Or maybe they're deliberately sending out the wrong messages – getting ready for the big one, for the hostile bid, shutting down all unnecessary outgoings, going for us from the flank. Jeez, I'd like to know what the hell's going on in Roderick Travers's mind.'

He tapped himself out a cigarette from the pack

beside the blotter. Rich flicked the gold desk lighter for him, then lit his own, leaning back, exhaling up into the air, saying, 'I say it's the precursor to a hostile bid and if so, we don't want to get caught sitting on our asses, thinking good thoughts.'

John Prior flung the report onto the desk. 'Yes, you're right. We've got to go in, hard and strong, and end it once and for all and when we do we've got to make sure we clean up on everything they own, especially Wendham House. Once we've got the trust money we're home and dry and can shore the Priors up for good and all.'

Jane swirled her rum around her glass. Business, always business. Trust fund, always the trust fund. She walked away from the den, down the passage to the painting of Wendham House which hung outside her mother's bedroom. She slumped against the wall, rolling the glass backwards and forwards across her mouth, feeling the stickiness. Wendham House – well, it was nothing great but it was everything. Absolutely everything.

She walked back into the living room, standing before the portrait of Jack Prior. 'Damn you, damn Wendham House, damn Travers,' she whispered, her words slurring. She poured more, drank deeply. Now her hands were sticky too. She looked back at the portrait.

OK, Jack Prior, so she stole from the business to set up back in England with her lover, Travers, abandoning her son. OK, so she died of a heart attack before she could go but why set up a trust fund that could only be accessed by the Prior who grabbed back Wendham House? A trust fund and a feud which steals our fathers from us, and husbands from their wives?

Jane squinted at the portrait. What should her father do? She sighed. Rich was right – he had to make the Travers give back what wasn't theirs, for what kind of a woman would leave her son, and then bequeath Wendham to her lover? What hurt must that son have

379

suffered? How cruel for a husband to then be accused of murder when the cause of death had been certified as a heart attack?

How dare Mrs Horatio Norden and Esther Moran speak out against them and roll them way back down the social register without a vestige of proof, just Travers lies whispered to them, or so her father had told her. Again Jane sipped, feeling queasy now, staring up at the portrait, into those hard eyes. But they weren't killer's eyes. The Priors couldn't be killers. Her father wouldn't fight for something, and his father before him, and his father too, if they thought Jack Prior was a killer.

She edged towards the den door again, leaning against the door jamb, seeing Rich lean across and stub out his cigarette, only to light another immediately, and one for his father and the smoke was still on her father's breath as he said, '. . . everywhere we go, they're there, bidding across us. Ever since the start of it all they've been there. Clothing – they took away our British markets. Coffee, tea, real estate. Wherever we turn they're in competition. They're close to ruining us. This generation of Priors is close to losing it all. We've got to do something but all we do is go round in circles, knowing what we want to achieve, but not how to do it.'

Jane stepped into the room. 'They've shut up the house, you say. Well, put in an offer under another name, that's all you have to do. They'll sell it if they don't know you're a Prior.' She could taste the rum, she could feel its warmth. She stood there looking at the two men. Her lips felt almost numb. 'It's so simple,' she said. 'So very simple.'

They swung round. Rich and her father raked her with eyes that were both so dark, both so like Jack Prior's. Her father almost spat the words, 'Get out of here and get to bed. If it's so simple d'you really think we wouldn't have thought of it? Of course we've tried, we're always trying, and always failing, so stop thinking you're God's gift to the business world and while you're in England do some work. That'd make a pleasant change.'

She turned on her heel, clutching the glass. He said, 'Put the glass down here. I'm not having another goddamn lush in the family. Your mother's more than enough.'

Now the room was beginning to spin. She swallowed, clenched her teeth, walked slowly and carefully to the desk, put the glass down, and left, hearing Rich's snort of laughter. 'Shut the door,' her father bellowed. She did, pressing her head against it, harder and harder, fighting down the fear, fighting down the need to say – Be sorry I'm going.

She heard her brother say to her father. 'Hey, did you read this, at the bottom of the report? They've put in for planning permission to start a theme park at Wendham House. Murphy says it must be to make the house self-sustaining.'

'Give me that.' There was silence, then her father said, his voice soft, and murderous, 'Peace they said they wanted? They're a load of charlatans because if this goes through then Wendham House is safe, whatever happens to Wendham Holdings . . . it'll be a separate company, and we'll never damn well get it, or the money. Jeez, what do we do now?'

She could hear her own breathing. She should move but nausea was rising. She closed her eyes, but the spinning made bile rise. She opened them, put her hands against the door, tried to push herself away from it, panting, hearing her father saying, 'OK, they'll need permission to do that, so we'll have to try and organize protests, get it stopped before it starts.'

She pushed again, and was upright. She steadied herself, focused on the passageway, headed for it, walking unsteadily, feeling the sweat breaking out, seeing her sneakers on the floor, stooping, almost falling, snatching at them, hugging them to her. 'You'll come with me,' she breathed. 'You'll come.'

She paused as the door to her mother's bedroom opened. Her mother stood there wavering in her pink satin robe, a martini glass in her hand. 'It's time those sneakers were put in the trashcan, dear. They smell.'

'Oh Mother,' whispered Jane, but her mother drifted towards the painting of Wendham House, raising her glass to it, saying, 'You tried to get away, and who can blame you if your life was like . . .' she trailed into silence, then peered round at Jane. 'They say that after her funeral Jack and his son, Bernard, disappeared for two months. They returned, more bitter than ever. No-one knew where they'd been. It was after that that the trust was set up and the feud began.'

She drank the martini dry, ran her finger around the inside of the glass, sucked it. Jane felt tears threaten. She came to her mother, and held her, and for once her mother let her do so. 'Mom, will you be all right? You'll see Grandma. She said she'd visit.'

Her mother dropped her glass to the carpet and clung to her daughter. 'I'm glad you're going, getting away. I'm glad. So glad but there'll be a hole in my life. A great big hole. Will I fall down it?'

Jane stroked her hair. 'No, we won't let you do that. I promise we won't let you do that.'

CHAPTER NINETEEN

Jane walked along the pebble beach beneath the grey October sky which seemed to sink down over Brighton. Screaming gulls wheeled above her, and beneath her feet pebbles clinked and their dust whitened her old sneakers as she walked.

She lowered her head into the wind, dragging her jacket around her, and headed for the steps, climbing them two at a time, then slowing, taking it easy, letting her throbbing head settle. Too much to drink again last night. Warm thick English beer, not like the cold, light, pale schooners of home.

She reached the pavement, rested for a moment against the railings, her back to the sea, staring up at the sky, then at Brighton's buildings, then at the cars which zoomed past. Where were they all going? The men home to their wives, the kids home to their parents?

They made her feel as much of an outsider as when she sat in her room on campus at the university, hearing the slamming and banging of doors all around, hearing the laughter, then the exaggerated groans as talk – such English talk – became work.

She hadn't worked, she'd just steadily drunk her way through the white rum she'd bought at Kennedy.

She ran her hands over her face. Her mouth tasted like the bottom of a bird's cage – was that what the guy at the party had said last night? The party held in the room below hers. They'd dragged her down, saying she'd stayed locked up long enough. 'Three weeks, and we still haven't had a chat,' the girl in leggings and a T-shirt had said.

What was her name? She stared up at the sky. Nope, she couldn't remember, but wished she could. Just as she wished she could sink into their lives, be one of them.

The boy hadn't stayed long. He'd smoked a cigarette and then said, 'An essay,' brushing her lips with his. 'See you,' she'd said to his retreating back.

She crossed the road and set off towards the main shopping area. Well, she hadn't seen him. She'd waited in all morning but he hadn't been back.

Now the loneliness hit her again. She wandered around The Lanes, which were so different to the sparkling shopping malls. Here there were no bright tiled floors, no covered walkways. Here there were no yellow cabs, no bagels, no Bloomingdale's, no twenty-four-hour shopping, no shadows cast by huge buildings. Here the town spread out, and out and out, and the suburbs too. Here the sky sank grey and damp.

She took the train to the university, checked her pigeon-hole for mail. None, of course. Her grandmother had written twice, her letters arriving on Thursdays and today was Friday, and still nothing from her parents. She stood still amongst the swarming students, hearing their British accents, hearing a French one, and German one, and over there, an American one. She peered, saw a clean-cut boy, heard his drawl. North Carolina?

She struggled in his direction, but he was gone when she reached the spot.

She unlocked her door, sat on her bed and fingered the books she'd bought second-hand from the bookstall. She stared at the files, the A4 paper, the word processor and printer she'd bought on the second day using her charge card. 'Why didn't they tell us everything had to be typed?' she'd asked. The others around her had nodded. That girl, the one whose name she couldn't remember, had shrugged. 'Character forming, so my dad would say, but then he'd sit down and talk me through it. I'll give him a ring tonight. He'll help me sort it out long distance.'

Jane had turned away, the momentary comradeship spoilt by the thought of what her own father would say.

Of course, when she got the word processor it had to be set up. That's what the Britisher – what was *his* name – was supposed to do this morning. She'd rushed out and bought cookies, coffee, something to keep him with her for a while longer.

She heard her father's voice again, remembering more clearly with the miles between them what he had once been like. Surely he could be like that again. Surely he could smile at her, laugh with her, talk to her. If he did that to all of them her mother would stop drinking, her brother would be put in his place, they'd be a family again. He'd maybe say, 'Character forming, give me a call, let's sort it out.'

She stared down at the notes she'd written down last week. Maybe her father was right. Maybe it *was* a waste of time. What did words, black ink on white paper, have to do with anything? Maybe she should go home, see her mom who was staying at Wandle Court with her grandmother. Yes, maybe she should go back, stay put, never leave, for then they couldn't forget her.

At the party she'd told the Britisher of the view over Central Park. It'd made it seem closer. He'd looked at her. 'Rich but not famous,' he'd said, holding out a cigarette. She'd taken it. 'A joint?' she asked.

He'd shaken his head, affecting a drawl, 'I smoke straight, like I take whisky straight, but not my women. My women I take anyways.'

She'd laughed, inhaling, feeling it sear down her throat. She'd sunk the rough wine from a plastic cup which flexed as she drank.

But that was last night. Now, this morning she had a headache, a foul taste, and no way did she know how to work the Amstrad.

And her parents still hadn't rung, or answered her letters, and she still couldn't get rid of this dark fear that she'd been forgotten the minute she took off on the plane, and would be even more firmly forgotten at the end of her year here.

She picked up a ballpoint, opened Thomas Hardy's *Jude the Obscure*. There was a knock on the door. The girl from next door called through the door, 'Hi, it's Sylvie again. We're off to the pub. Why don't you come?'

She hesitated, half rose but then sank back. 'No, got to work.'

'Suit yourself.' The tone was annoyed. 'You left early last night. It was a shame.'

'Had a headache.'

'Better now?'

'Yeah. But look, I'm trying to work. OK?'

There was a pause. 'OK.'

She could almost hear the shrug in the girl's voice, and wondered why she hadn't gone. But she'd had enough of being an outsider for today. She was too tired, too awkward, and *he* might be there, the Britisher who had promised to come, but had not.

Instead she read her grandmother's last letter through again, smiling at the paint-smudged sheets, frowning at the ending as she had done the first time. *Put the family to one side. Make the most of this year. They think of you, I know they do. By the way, I've fixed your mother up with a shrink. She seems better. Not so many martinis and not so much talk of falling down holes. We all love you. Everyone loves you, they just don't write it.*

I'm kind of mad at you for being there, for seeing things I've always wanted to see, but your grandfather refused to visit England – this Prior hatred. And now, I'm too darn busy. Keep a journal, paint word pictures for me. I love you, truly madly deeply. Go see that film. Give you something to think about. Go see Wendham House. Take care, doll. Your grandmother

She wasn't sure if she was glad that her mother's hole was being patched. After all, its advent had almost heralded an admission of love.

The next morning, Saturday, she drove the hire car along the A303, putting her foot down, hitting sixty then seventy like everyone else, saying in her mind, Here you go, Rich. Sixty and you're stuck at a crawl in Manhattan. Eat your heart out.

She glanced down at the dash of the Astra where she'd stuck the list of place names and road numbers. She'd come via Salisbury, which was a place to see, or so the Britisher, Terry, had said when he'd come after all, yesterday evening, to set up her computer. He'd been kind, he'd set it up and then he'd kissed her, said he had to go, he was meeting the others. He'd grabbed her hand. 'Come on,' he'd said, then put on the drawl, 'live a little.'

She'd laughed and gone with him to the student union bar, and supped that warm beer, and listened to their talk, sitting next to Sylvie, who'd flicked her blond hair in her face every time she turned her head. She'd wanted to speak but nothing would come. This was their world, not hers. This was their language, not hers, for it *was* a different language.

As the bar grew louder Sylvie had turned, her face kind, speaking slowly and carefully, 'Head better? It must be very strange coming so far. We must seem so different after New York. There must be none of that buzz we hear about. Sorry Terry took so long coming to do the word processor. I was painting him. I'd like to paint you, all that deep brown hair, the red glint, those deep grey eyes, that pale skin.'

She'd found herself saying, 'Hey, I'm only American, not someone from another planet. I can follow you, you don't have to slow up like that.' Everyone laughed, looked at one another, relaxed. She sat back on her chair, accepted a cigarette from Terry, sucked in the nicotine, coughed. She said to Sylvie, 'My grandmother paints. Huge bold kind of ethnic things.'

Sylvie had turned right round to her then, putting up her hand to hush the others, making Jane tell her about her grandmother's work, gripping Jane's arm in her excitement, telling her in return about the palette knife she used in preference to a brush, the sketches she made anywhere and everywhere and as she talked Jane imagined her in Sarah Prior's warm vibrant home amongst the laughter that always lurked, the love.

Suddenly the darkness and fear loosened its icy grip, ebbed, and she sat back smiling amongst these students who were sipping frothy pints. All evening they talked, laughed, and other Americans came across to join them and she talked to Chris, the boy she had seen earlier, and she had guessed right, he was from North Carolina. There was Phil from Boston who was a Baptist and didn't drink, or not much, he'd told them as he sank his second pint of beer.

They'd all laughed, Jane too, and linked arms as they walked out of the bar and back towards their rooms and Sylvie had said to Jane, pulling at her arm, 'Hey, I meant it. You really must sit for me and I'll slap you onto canvas – well, I'll slap you onto board, can't afford canvas. Make a nice Christmas present for your parents. I could get it done in time.'

Suddenly the evening had soured. She said no. 'No,' she'd said again when Sylvie pushed it.

She was coming up close behind another car and they were approaching yet another roundabout. Why did this darn country have roundabouts? What sane place would have crazy circles in the middle of roads as well as driving on the left? She felt the tension and anger flare, just as it had done last night.

She eased up behind the truck, which slipped through a gap in the traffic. Her shoulders felt rigid, her hands stiff. She changed gear, crawled forwards, stopped, straining to guess right, straining to judge the speed of those cars sweeping around the great grass mound which had trees planted. Why did the British have to make a garden out of everything?

God, she'd hardly ever driven a geared car. There was a gap. She slipped the clutch as she pulled away, her hands sweating. She'd done it, and now as she roared along the dual carriageway again she laughed to herself, relief making her sing, but then she stopped.

Why'd Sylvie pushed it? She came up close behind another car. Why'd she, Jane Prior, yelled, right there as they were climbing the stairs up to their room, 'Just leave me alone. We haven't all got parents who want stupid pictures of their kids on their walls.'

She checked the turn-off point she had written down on the paper, flushing at the memory, wondering if she'd ever feel safe, if she'd ever do the right thing, ever fit in, anywhere.

That's why she'd hired the car, packed a rucksack and driven away to Somerset for the weekend. Why not go and see the place that was driving her family mad? Why not? She could kick and scream and curse at it, then maybe it would crumble into dust and the feud along with it. Some hope.

She found Wendham village after leaving the A303 and threading her way down narrow winding lanes. Cars had overspilled from the pub car-park onto the verges either side of the road. There were bikes propped up against the hamstone walls of The Rose and Crown.

She continued to drive slowly along the road, noting old cottages on the left. They were so old, so cramped. Everywhere was so cramped. There was a left hand turning down to a post office. Cottages lined either side. She parked in front of one which had, *Polite notice. Please do not park*. Did they mean police? Couldn't the British spell?

She locked up and tucked the keys into her bumbag before hiking back up the road to the pub. By the steps there were some discarded placards. *Ban the Park* was emblazoned across them. Some in red, some in green. The paint had run. She stopped, shook her head. Well, guess what? Dad and Rich had had time to organize a protest, but not write to her.

The pub was crowded and smoky. She forced herself between a group wearing torn jeans, stained sweatshirts and their hair in dreadlocks. Another was comprised of girls wearing Laura Ashley dresses and body warmers, and whose hair was shiny and long. Some wore head-bands.

She squeezed through to the bar, standing next to an old man perched on a stool. He smiled at her and called to the man washing up glasses further along, behind the bar, 'Come on, Keith, customer, leave them suds and get serving. If this goes on you'll have to put your hand in your pocket and pay someone to help – or give 'em a couple of pints.' He had very few teeth, and needed a shave.

The publican, his round face red with exertion, finished drying the glasses, grinning at Jane, then at the old man. 'Well, it won't be you, Saul. You'd drink me dry. Now, what can I get you, miss?'

He flung the tea towel over his shoulder. She saw the sign for Dry Blackthorn cider and nodded towards it, her mind still on the placards.

'Pint or a half?' Keith asked, smiling.

'Half please,' she decided.

The publican poured it. She paid. He gave her change. She sipped. It was cool and dry, it was wonderful, a burst of sunshine on a grey day. All around there was laughter, loud voices, quiet ones. She leaned across the bar and asked the publican, who was wiping more glasses dry and putting them on the overhead shelf. 'Where's Wendham House from here?'

He peered suspiciously over his glasses at her, his smile evaporating. 'You another of them loonies, are you?' He nodded to the crowds of people.

Saul cackled, 'Be fair, Keith, it's upped your takings.'

Keith put more glasses on the shelf, his shirt straining over his paunch as he did so. 'Aye, and if that lot with the hair and the big mouths and the bicycles propped up against my pub had any sense they'd realize that's what the theme park'll do – to the whole village an' all. This lot are just a load of damn townies shoving their noses in where they're not wanted.' A young protester reached over Jane to put his empty beer glass on the bar, saying, 'I don't know how you can defend it. There'll be damn great seal pools, a café, adventure playground. It'll spoil the environment. Planning permission's got to be stopped, and we'll do it.'

'Aw, come on Ted, save it for outside the gates,' another voice called. The boy withdrew his arm, patted Jane on the shoulder. 'You coming with us, then?'

She shrugged, wanting to stay and listen, wanting to glean all that she could.

The old man tamped his pipe, then rubbed the stubble on his chin. Horse brasses glinted on the dark beam behind him. The pub was quietening as the protesters straggled out.

The publican looked after them and shook his head, pulling himself a pint of beer until the froth overflowed the glass. 'We need the Travers family back playing their part in the village. We've missed 'em, that we have. T'ain't been the same having them weekending, and now they've shut it completely it's sort of killed the spirit of the place. I bet them stupid young fools like that lot waggling them damn great banners about didn't even bother to come to the meeting young Hal Travers called in the village hall backalong. Oh no, they don't want to hear anything good, once they've made their minds up to have a day off work and make a load of noise.'

The old man nodded, sucking on his pipe. 'Aye, 'tis the only way to get the village thriving again. It'll give our kids work now the glove factory's closed.'

Another man came to the bar. 'Oh, not that old chestnut, Saul. Factory's been closed long since, and they can get work in Westlands. The café'll take some of your trade too, Keith.'

'Oh no, it won't. I've young Hal's word on that. He'll do teas, he might do snacks, but he isn't going for a licence.'

The old man, Saul, nodded. 'Sid, you don't know what you're talking about. If we have work on the doorstep our young'll stay and we won't get incomers pushing up the value of property.'

Sid said, 'Don't know why they just don't sell the house and estate and be done with it. They had another offer for it, or so's I heard.'

The publican picked up Jane's empty glass. 'Finished, have you, miss?'

She nodded, smiling her thanks, moving away from the bar, hearing the old man say, 'That'll be the damned Yanks. Always they offer, always the Travers refuse. Too much history there to ever let it go and they love it too much anyway. That young Hal just belongs there. Not many youngsters who'd make do in the gatehouse when they could have that big house in London.'

The publican raised his eyes at Jane as she stopped and walked back. She said, 'What Yanks? What's the story?'

Keith groaned and said, 'We'll be here for ever now, old Saul loves to tell this, he does.'

Jane shook her head, smiling, struggling to keep urgency out of her voice, needing to know what these people thought of the Priors, needing to know what was being said in the enemies' territory. 'What damned Yanks? Maybe I know them. After all, the US is huge, but not that huge.'

Saul was holding his beer up to the light. 'Bit cloudy isn't it, Keith?'

'There's nought wrong with that, and you're not getting a free refill so get on with it.'

Yes, just get on with it, she wanted to shout.

Saul cackled, 'Worth a try. Just like them Priors keep thinking, I 'spect. My old great-gran always said it started when that Irene died.' The old man took a sip, savoured and swallowed. 'Like I says. Bit cloudy in the taste too.'

Keith laughed, 'You get as boring as the story. I should get on out while you can, miss.'

Instead Jane asked, 'What started?' as though she knew nothing.

Saul rested his arm on the bar, and smiled knowingly at her. 'Prior and his boy came over, you know, and tried to force Irene Wendham's fancy man out but it'd been willed to him, right and proper. But, oh what an upset there was when, me old gran says, the village heard she'd died, poor wronged girl. He had a black heart, that Jack Prior, and his descendants after him.

'My old gran thought they was having her back, where she belonged, so did that young Travers, but she never came. Prior saw to that. He was good to the village, though, was that Harry Travers. Got the factory built back in the village, just as Irene wanted. Damn Yanks. Had 'em in the war. Over-sexed, over here . . . Should never have come, none of them.'

'Ah, shut up, Saul, for pity's sake. You're being rude to the young lady. She's just said she's American,' the publican said.

Jane urged, 'But . . .'

The publican cut in, 'Shouldn't bother with any more questions just now. Once you get him on the war it's hopeless, and I'm sorry he sounded off. He's a good 'un really.' Jane nodded and strode towards the door, pulling it open, wanting to stay and defend herself, her family, her country, put these people straight about the truth, because all that Saul had said was the same old lies she had heard before.

And they were lies, they must be, for Jack Prior wouldn't have opened a trust, wouldn't have spent so long righting a wrong if it had been based on a lie. I mean, how could you defend a woman leaving her son? How could you? she wanted to shout. How could you defend a woman who left such a legacy, who destroys each male Prior, and therefore his children in turn?

She hurried out after the protesters, going past the road that turned left into the village, her bumbag clumping against her body, her hair falling into her eyes. She was panting as she reached them and fell in step beside a girl in a paisley skirt and shawl, and a boy in a camouflage jacket.

They looked sideways at her. She made herself grin, 'Good day for it.'

The girl's answering smile was wide as she glanced at the sky. 'Blue skies always make me feel better. D'you find our weather grey, coming from America?'

What did she care what colour the sky was? She didn't bother to answer, but asked, 'How much do you get for doing this?' Nodding at the protesters who were gathering outside a pair of high wrought-iron gates beyond which wound a neglected and overgrown gravel drive. As they approached she saw there was a small gatehouse with diamond-paned mullioned windows.

The girl flushed. 'Nothing. We do it because we care. These people have so much, and want so much more. It's indecent, it's wrong. They have no principles, no morals. It's rape of the countryside for a quick profit. Typical.'

Jane looked intently at her, 'Typical – of the Travers?'

'And their kind.'

Now Jane smiled for at last she had heard a condemnation of the Travers from an independent witness, and suddenly she felt strong, driven and determined and wanted to proclaim herself a Prior, but bit back the words, for now was not the time.

As they reached the gates the boy jerked his head towards a section of the group who stood smoking and chanting, 'Ban the park', 'Stop this now'. He said,

'They're the ones that have been paid. They were talking to the reporters earlier on, pushing themselves forward, shoving us aside. They don't care nothing about the park, they just care about the cash going in their back pockets.'

She shook her head at the cigarette the boy offered, trying to think, trying to clear her head. She stared up the drive, and knew what it was she wanted.

'Can't see the house from here,' Ted, the protester who had reached over her in the pub, said. 'It's supposed to be beautiful.'

She stood staring up the drive, nodded. 'It is,' she murmured.

Ted looked at her. 'You've been here?'

She shook her head. 'Not yet,' she said quietly. 'Not yet.'

She walked back the way she had come, her mind made up, searching for a gap, any gap. There was one in the hawthorn hedge which grew behind the oaks. She glanced around, checking that she was out of sight of the protesters, then eased through, feeling the thorns snag her jacket, forcing herself on until she was clear of the hedge.

She set off through the wood, hearing the crack of twigs beneath her feet. It was dark here beneath the beeches, and the ground was springy from the fallen leaves, moss grew on the trunks. Above her more leaves fluttered from wide spreading branches. She made mental notes of the word pictures she would paint her grandmother.

She passed the centre of the copse where a fallen tree lay. She skirted it, heading onwards, not knowing if it was the right direction, feeling the tightness of anticipation mingling with the kindling of a vindicated anger towards the Travers.

There was growing brightness beyond the trees. She was almost running now, round the huge trunks, ducking beneath low-hanging branches, and then out, into the open. She stopped, staring at Wendham House.

There it was at last, come to life, though there weren't flowers in the garden, there was only mown grass. To the left was a walled garden which hadn't been shown, and a glasshouse. She focused on the house again, and no, she was wrong, it hadn't come to life. It looked dead because its windows were shuttered, and they looked like her father's eyes, and it was the Travers who had done it to both.

Well, perhaps she was the one to bring them alive for she, Jane Prior, was standing on Prior property, laying claim to it, knowing – really knowing now – that this belonged to them.

Her breath was white in the chill. Clouds scudded behind it. She headed for the house, unable to take her eyes from it, drinking it in, appreciating its beauty as only an owner could.

She skirted the lawn, staying in the long grass and the shadows of the apple trees whose branches bowed to the ground. Apples were composting amongst the grass, squelching beneath her feet. She barely noticed for she was here, at Wendham.

She alone of all the Priors, except Jack and his son, had come. She was the one who was standing here, and would return. If only she could make it theirs, return it to her father. She'd be loved then, for ever.

She climbed the steps to the terrace, staring at the house, walking across the overgrown slabs, smelling a sweet aroma as she did so. She crouched down, rubbed her hand amongst the herbs, breathed in the scent. It was as though it was familiar, as though she knew it, as though . . . She brushed the soft green plants back from the hamstone slab. 'You shouldn't be theirs,' she breathed up at the house. 'You should be ours. We'll love you. We'll let you live again. We'll keep you tidy.'

She rose, looked back down the garden, imagining her father waving to her from the centre of the lawn, her mother sitting beneath a sunshade, drinking coffee, that was all, coffee. She'd not need martinis, because there'd be no harshness. There'd be no need. At long last there'd be no need.

She walked towards the bow windows which were shuttered on the inside.

She hurried round the corner, peering in through every window she came to, until at last she was at the back. A door hung open. She slipped in through a scullery, past a green-stained earthenware sink, into a kitchen with a huge oblong table standing on flagstones. There was a dust-covered range. Stained copper pans hung from the ceiling. An incongruous gas cooker stood in one corner. Cold beat up from the flagstones. It was dark with the shutters at the window.

She opened the door and edged along the passage, pushing through another door into a wide panelled hall from which rose a sweeping staircase. Panels, like these, were in the Wandle Court hall. Had Irene been trying to copy Wendham House?

Through another door to the right, into another panelled room with a billiard table half covered by dust sheets. There were book shelves, more panels. Jane ran her hand along them, seeing the dust transferring to her fingers. There were no panels in the Wandle Court dining room. Irene was one of those people who never finished a job.

She'd write to her grandmother and tell her how much more in keeping it would be to have panels put on the dining room walls as well. Perhaps Claude, the interior designer who lived in the upstairs apartment, could do it for her.

Dust sheets covered all the other furniture. Daylight streamed in narrow slits from the gaps in the shutters. She moved out across the hall, into the living room.

She stood stock-still gazing down the long length of it, ignoring the covered furniture, ignoring the walls panelled to a height of about four feet, ignoring the dust that lay thickly on the ceiling coving, ignoring the motes that teemed in the light which sliced in above the hinges of the shutters, just staring, and being, and loving, and understanding absolutely Jack Prior's devastation at its loss. Endorsing his drive to bring this back to its rightful owner.

She walked the length of the room, and stood in the bow of the window, staring back down. Yes, this is ours. She turned, eased up the bar of the shutter, swinging it free of the latch, pulling it back. Light flooded in.

Again she stared down the room, moved by its beauty, moved by something which pulled at her. She lifted her hands to her face, smelling the herbs and for a moment she felt a great peace, a falling away of anger, of loss, of fear. For a moment it was as though she'd come home, as though she'd been here before, as though . . .

But then an outraged voice roused her, 'What are you doing here? This is private property.'

She started. A young man stood in the far doorway, his hands on the belt of his dark-brown cords, his thin face flushed with anger, his brown hair falling onto his forehead. He said again, 'This is private property. Now go on, clear off, go back to your friends with their placards. I've just about had enough of you all.' He stepped to one side, pointing to the hall.

She walked towards him, her sneakers squeaking on the wooden floor and leaving an imprint in the dust. She reached him, turned and pointed to her footprints, then looking square into his hazel eyes, which were sunk deep with tiredness, 'You should be ashamed to leave it in this state. You don't care, not really.' She unzipped her bumbag, took out two pound coins, took hold of his hand and slapped the money into it, saying, 'Look, I'm paying you for an early look. Put it towards your theme park costs, and I hope it chokes you.'

She stalked away from him, down the passage, hearing him behind her. On she walked, through the kitchen, through the scullery and into brightness. The sky was still blue. He was still behind. She swung round the corner of the house onto the terrace and still he dogged her footsteps, like a shadow.

She swung round, her voice full of anger as she spat, 'You don't deserve a place like this. It should be a home. You should have honeysuckle climbing the house, you should cut back these herbs, prune the apple trees, not slam up theme parks. You don't deserve it. None of you deserve it.'

She started to cross the terrace, and heard him run up behind her, felt him catch her arm and pull her round. His cheeks were flushed with anger, his lips tight with rage as he answered, 'There is honeysuckle, see. It's autumn, it's dying back. So much you know, Miss America.'

He took hold of her hand and slapped the two pounds into it, closing her fingers over it. 'There, put this towards your bus fare back to wherever you came from, and get your facts right before you hang around my gates again. But before you go, just for the record . . .' He dragged her to the steps, pointing to a spot to the left of the woods. 'Another fact. Down there's a valley and that's where the theme park will be. It won't be seen or heard. It's not going to be a fairground though it will have animals. It'll have nature walks, and yes, an adventure playground, but why shouldn't kids have fun? And if you'd damn well come to the meeting in the village you'd have seen the plans and heard me speak.'

He let go of her arm, his eyes narrow as he glared at her. 'I'm sick of it, all the lies, all the fuss, and all you people standing outside my gate spouting nonsense to whoever'll listen, especially if it's the newspapers, when I'm running myself ragged trying to keep Wendham, trying to restore the glasshouse, plodding on slowly while I wait for the theme park to get going. That's what'll bring in the money to complete and maintain the restoration – why can't you all understand that? Now go back to the others and tell them again – or is it just that they can't understand words of more than one syllable?'

She shrugged and slammed down the steps. 'You should sell it as it is. Let someone with money do it up, then there'd be no need for any of this.'

He laughed bitterly and said, as though to himself, as he stood at the top of the steps, 'I'm getting awful tired of you Americans sticking their noses into Travers business.' He stopped, stared at her, then started down the steps, suspicion in his voice, 'Just who the hell are you? What's your name?'

She stood her ground, her mind racing. God, he mustn't know. She shouted, 'I'm a student at Sussex Uni. My tutor heard about the protest, he's into conservation. "Go and make notes," he said. "It'd be something to write about." I'm majoring back there in journalism, and he was right.' She looked up at Wendham again and said nothing for a moment, then murmured, 'It's a tragedy. It's the most beautiful house I've ever seen.' There was no hint of a lie in her voice.

He had reached her and was scanning her face. 'But who are you?'

She kept her face impassive, and shrugged as she said, 'Jane Essex, from Vermont. Why, you going to deport me?'

He stared at her, brushed back his hair, shook his head and turned from her, murmuring, 'It gets lonely. You start to see Reds under the bed, isn't that what happened over in your neck of the woods? Go on, clear off, write your piece but don't forget balance. Or will it sell more copies to slag off the decadent land-owner?'

He was walking back across the lawn. She looked from him to the house, her mind working. She shouted, 'Balance you say? OK, say you get the planning permission, but what I can't see is how you're going to get it up and running when it looks as though you haven't two dimes to rub together. I mean, you can't have or it wouldn't be in this state in the first place.'

His face was thoughtful as he turned to look at her, then he said, 'I'll get the planning permission then find a backer. So put that in your piece – maybe it'll help entice one.'

'A backer?' she asked, her hand shading her eyes, watching as he picked at the dry earth in the urn at the foot of the steps. He shrugged, 'You're right, my family hasn't any money to spare. Wendham's got to be self-supporting. It's got to be, or I think the worst will happen and we'll have to sell.' His voice suddenly became tired. 'It's all become too much of a strain on Pa.' He wiped his hands on his trousers, turning from her again, his shoulders slumped, then he stopped. 'You can find your way out?' There was no anger any more.

'Oh yes,' she called, setting off. 'I can find my way.'

She turned, he was watching her. He lifted his hand and even when she entered the copse, he was still watching. Suspicious Mr Travers? she thought. Well, you should be. Then she slowed. What if he checked whether there was a Prior daughter? What if he got a photograph? She hurried on. So what? She wasn't coming back until it was hers.

She drove back to Brighton that night, although she'd intended to make a weekend of it. She fed pound coins into the house pay phone just inside the door, not daring to call collect to her home in case her father refused the call.

When he answered, she said, her hand around the mouthpiece, her mouth close to it, not wanting to be heard by anyone in the house, 'Father, I've news of Wendham House,' not bothering with preamble, wanting him to listen, not bark.

There was a pause. He said, 'And?' That was all. But she wouldn't be upset, because soon everything would be all right again, the Priors would be as families should be.

She said, 'The protest is working. They're outside the gates.'

'And?' his voice was dry. 'Or d'you really think I'd pay good money into something that wouldn't work?'

She swallowed, seeing his eyes. She said, 'I talked to the Travers boy. He let slip that after he gets permission he's still got to get a backer for the theme park, or his father will sell.'

There was a longer pause, then her father said 'You talked to one of them? Good God, girl, are you . . . ?' Then he stopped. 'He said what?'

She repeated herself, all confidence gone, feeling foolish, exposed, knowing this would make no difference, knowing that nothing ever would. 'He didn't know who I was. Just thought I was a trespasser. I gave him a false name.'

He said, 'Well, damn me. You've done well.' His voice was as it was when he talked to Rich. She held the receiver with both hands, looking out across the campus, feeling a half-fearful, half-hopeful joy. She wanted to say, Have I? Will everything be all right now?

He said, 'Keep with it. Let us know what's happening. Now, I'm thinking off the top of my head, so bear with me. Could be we could come in with the money as a backer under an assumed name. I'll sound out the trustees of the Wendham House Trust, see if they'll advance a loan under the circumstances. Otherwise I'll try your grandmother again.' He paused, murmured, 'Just let me think a moment. Second thoughts. Give me your number. I'll ring you straight back.'

She waited, and Sylvie passed her, her rucksack hanging off one shoulder. She grinned at Jane. The phone rang. Jane lifted the receiver, and waved at Sylvie then hunched over the phone again as her father said, 'OK here's what we'll do. I'll have checks made on the theme park "set-up" because if it's somehow allied to

402

Wendham Holdings it could make the backers share-
holders. If we're the backers we'd have what I've always
wanted, a toehold onto the Travers board. If it's a
separate company there's nothing lost, because ownership of the house will release the trust money, and we'll
make a hostile bid they can't fight off.' His voice was
quickening. 'I'll keep on with the protest because if
permission is refused then we'll come in and buy
anyway.'

He paused again. Then spoke, and now there was real
excitement in his voice. 'God almighty, we've got them,
any which way, we've got them. D'you hear that Rich?'
His voice faded and she could picture him turning to
her brother and the joy fled, then grew strong again as
he said to her, 'Swell, didn't know you had it in you,
Janey. I'll phone. Give us your fraternity number again.'

She did so. He repeated it. She said, 'It's the most
beautiful house, Dad. It'll be like coming home, we'll
be a real family . . .' There was a click, the line was
dead, humming in her ears. She shut her eyes, clenching her teeth, swallowing, but then Sylvie called from
across the pathway.

'Come on, come and join us.'

She did, wanting to dance along the pathway because
he had actually called her Janey, as he had done all
those years ago.

He phoned the next day. Sylvie stood nearby, breathless, mouthing, 'Pub?' She nodded as she listened to
her father. Sylvie put up her thumb and left. Her father
was saying, 'Damn trust won't wear a loan, neither will
your grandmother, even for you. So I'm calling off my
protesters. I've a tame journalist who'll put something
in about it being good for the area. Protests'll die in
time. Planning permission's got to be given, because
then that kid'll find a backer somehow, and when he
does, we'll divert them, scupper their interest in him,
and it'll cost us very little but will sure leave him high

403

and dry. He'll have to sell then. Your job is to stay with it, and find out who they are when he manages to get someone on side. Keep in touch now.'

'I need proof that I'm Jane Essex if I'm to go back. Please get someone to write to me and post it from Vermont. You could do it.'

'I'll arrange it.' Again the line went dead. He'd said, 'Keep in touch now.' He'd said, 'I'll arrange it.' He'd meant he'd do it himself, hadn't he?

CHAPTER TWENTY

The following weekend, the first in November, Jane returned to Wendham. She parked in the Rose and Crown car-park, for there were fewer cars this time, and fewer bikes and placards propped against the wall.

In the pub a fire burned in the inglenook, and a tortoiseshell cat sat on the carver chair nearest to it, almost indistinguishable from the orange and brown patchwork cushion. She approached the bar, smiling.

There was no recognition in Keith's eyes as he poured her a half-pint of Dry Blackthorn cider, but when she said, 'It was good to talk last weekend, and I see the protesters have slimmed down their numbers,' he looked more closely. 'Oh, you're old Saul's audience. You've forgiven him then, for being rude about Yanks?' She laughed and nodded.

He rested both hands on the bar, smiling. 'You're safe today. He'll not come until half-past midday. His old woman rules him like a sergeant-major.'

Jane slipped up onto a stool, bringing the full glass carefully to her lips. 'It's a real good drink. Different to Manhattan's. Slower, gentler, like the difference between New York City and Brighton, where I'm at uni.' She was straining to find the right things to say, straining to make these people open up, give her something that might help her get to know the Travers boy.

'That where you're from, is it?' the barman said, his stomach straining over his belt. 'My girl went there for three months after her degree. She's off backpacking in Australia now. Can't see her settling down in dozy old Somerset after all that. Can't see her settling nowhere.'

Jane held her glass in both hands, looking around the pub. The girl in the Laura Ashley dress was sitting beneath the window, her face pinched, her nose red. She murmured absently, 'Couldn't get much better'n here, I reckon.'

She slipped across to the girl, 'You still here?'

The girl looked up, sneezed, groped for her handkerchief. The boy with her, a different one to last time, handed her one. The girl said, her voice full of cold, 'Yes, the paid ones have gone. It's an honest protest now.'

Jane liked the sound of that. Yes, an honest protest against a dishonest family. The door opened, a waft of cold air scythed through the warmth, the fire belched smoke. Keith called, 'Shut the door, Saul, for the love of Mike. You're early. You been a good boy then?'

Saul waved his walking stick, his gnarled hand bare of gloves. 'You'm cut out your cheek, young Keith, and get that beer on the bar.'

Jane smiled, joined him at the bar. 'I kind of liked our talk last weekend, Saul. Made me want to see more of the village – get to know more about it.'

Saul rested his walking stick against his stool and picked up his pint with one easy movement. 'There y'are, Keith. Takes a foreigner to see me worth. Prophet's got no honour in his own home, missy.'

Keith groaned, winked at Jane. 'You don't know what you've done.'

Oh, but she did. Indeed she did. The next half hour was spent priming the old man, hearing of the Travers family. Of the young 'un, Hal, who loved the big house so much that he'd come down and camp in the grounds, 'cos it's only been used at weekends for the past twenty years. How he'd got the gatehouse warm and dry at last and set it up as a studio, and lived there full time now. How the old 'un Roderick had a heart attack recently and had enough of big business, of the feud. How he'd tried to take over them damned Americans last year in a bid to end it all. But was now preparing to fight off one from them, for them devils refused his olive branch.

'Nothing but trouble, them Yanks – right from the start, begging your pardon miss, as you're one. But these Priors is a special sort of nastiness.'

As Jane listened she sipped her cider, swallowing her urge to say, Only because they've had to be. Now was not the time. It wasn't the time to dig for the past either, but she couldn't help it, she wanted to know what lies had been told, what hatred had been stirred. She said, 'Nastiness? Sounds kinda extreme?'

Saul shook his head, his face sombre. 'Didn't I tell you last Saturday?'

She nodded. 'You sure did – a bit. But tell me more.'

He smiled, looking up at the ceiling as he gathered his thoughts, then fixed his rheumy eyes on her. 'Sinclair came over, told Travers of the murder. Nearly killed poor old Travers it did. Then that Black Jack Prior, Irene's husband, he came over with his boy. Went for Travers, reckon they meant to kill him, as well as get Wendham back, but Travers had Irene's will to show them. She'd bequeathed it to him. Sinclair helped to fight them off. The staff too, one rang the fire bell. The village came. Sent them devils packing. Sent them packing again when Jack and Bernard came on back that night and tried to burn it down. The Travers've kept a watch ever since. Even today they's looking over their shoulder, fighting off them buggers, for Irene's sake. I still feel it's for her sake – a sort of thing of faith. Can't think they'd ever sell, let 'em have it. That's why the theme park's got to work.'

Anger was washing through Jane in great waves at the flip repetition of these lies. Murder, destruction. God, it made her family out to be monsters, and therefore her too. This was crazy. She gripped the glass, forcing her voice to remain calm as she said, 'So

407

why'd they take such a shine to Travers? He wasn't a Wendham.'

Saul picked up his walking stick, and stroked the cat, which had woken, and was rubbing its back against the leg of his stool. 'She wants her beer too, Keith,' he cackled.

Keith snorted. 'She'll have her milk and like it, and don't you go putting that ashtray down with any of yours in it.' He shook his head at Jane. 'Old devil he is.'

Jane forced a smile in return. She said again, 'So, why? He was a convict after all.'

Saul stared down at the cat, then at her, his eyes sharp suddenly. 'How'd you know he was a convict?'

She met his eyes, smiling, though inwardly cursing herself. She said, 'One of the protesters said last weekend.'

Saul continued to stare, then shrugged, and tipped a bit of his beer into the large clean ashtray. Jane put it on the floor for the cat, dripping a little on her jeans. The cat was lapping before she was sitting on her stool again. Saul relaxed and said, 'Convict he might have been, but he was good, and he was kind, and my, how he loved our Irene – who trusted him good and proper, according to Martha, who'd write home to my great-gran's mother. No time for that Black Jack though. Brute he was, a real brute.'

Keith joined in now, 'Travers built up a good family, started the glove factory, looked after our houses. The family still do, even though the big house is shut. They even let us buy them if we want. We've got to keep 'em here, somehow. Most of us realized that when we had the fête in the grounds as usual this year and there was the house, all shut up. Young Hal's doing his best, slogging away all hours of the day and night to renovate it, but it'll be a slow job, and no job at all if the theme park doesn't happen. You seen the glasshouse have you, Saul? Coming on a treat. Just hope it's not wasted effort.'

Jane couldn't finish her cider, it would stick in her throat, and neither did she want to listen to any more of this, the landlord had given her what she needed. She didn't know how she managed the smile as she slipped down from the stool, but she did, saying, 'Great stuff. I'll have a look round the village now. Something to write home about. See you.'

She waved to the girl protester, then swept from the bar to stand outside, aching with rage. She glared at the oaks across the road. Well, when Wendham was hers they'd have to beg for their fête.

She hiked along to the gap, but saplings had been laid across it, barring her way. She hoisted the small rucksack she had taken from her car higher on the shoulder, and waved as she passed the protesters squatting outside the wrought-iron gates, their placards propped up between their knees.

'Joining us?' one shouted, his striped muffler almost covering his mouth.

'Not today. Exploring England, this is called. Seeing the natives at play.' She slapped her rucksack.

'Damned Yanks,' a girl with an earring through her nose shouted.

'Get a life,' Jane drawled, not bothering to turn and look.

On she went. Beech trees grew both sides of the road now, their branches meeting. Fifty yards past the gates she found her way through another gap, then worked her way back to the gatehouse. She tapped quietly on the door, then peered through the diamond panes into the living room.

A clothes horse draped with shirts, pants and socks stood before a slow-burning stove. An easel was propped in the corner, newspapers were scattered on the old oak table. She knocked again. No answer.

She set off towards the house, keeping behind the rhododendrons which edged and sprawled onto the gravel drive, not wanting the protesters to see or hear her. It was cold in the shade and she hurried, scanning the woods for Hal, wanting to see him first, call a greeting, get close, get information.

She rounded the bend, and there was the house with a porticoed door opening onto the turning circle. At the top end of the drive, near to the house, was the glasshouse, and beyond that was the walled garden. Hal Travers was nowhere in sight. She cupped her hands and called, 'Hi there. Anyone at home?'

Rooks rose in a flurry from the trees, and then there was the sound of a door shutting. Hal Travers appeared from the direction of the glasshouse rubbing his hands on a cloth. He wore faded jeans and a faded red tartan shirt open at the neck, his sleeves were rolled up, his arms muscular. She called again, 'Hi there.'

He saw her and she saw the surprise on his face, then the annoyance. She hurried across the drive, the gravel crunching beneath her feet. 'Hi, remember me, last week's trespasser? I was rude, out of order. I've come to make amends. I hear you're working on the glasshouse – sounds neat. I want to help, and give some balance to what I'm writing. What you're doing sounds a pretty good idea.'

She stopped a foot from him. He was about six inches taller than her and more tired than she remembered. His brown hair curled on his frayed collar. He shoved the cloth in his pocket, and hooked his thumbs in his leather belt. 'Come again?' he said, his voice flat and cold.

'I want to help. I've brought tea from uni, bought cookies and pasties from the store. Thought it seemed too big a job to tackle on your own. I barged in, I'm sorry. I owe you.'

He shook his head, folding his arms. 'You don't owe me anything. Is this a trick? You going to do some sort of exposé on an English family ruining a beautiful

410

estate? Come off it. D'you think I was born yesterday? I think you'd better leave.'

She dragged her long brown hair back and stood her ground. She had to. 'I said I'm sorry, and I don't say that unless I am. It's a great house, a real beauty, but it's sad. It needs some help – just like you do if you're going to get it right. Sure, I brought my camera but not to do an exposé, just to record its stages. It's only for a college project, not for publication. Publication would be nice, though, but I'd get your say-so first. I'll put that in writing, if you like. Come on, my labour in exchange for an A grade? It'd help us both.'

He stared at her. 'Jane Essex, you said?'

He'd remembered.

She nodded, dragging out the letter which had arrived yesterday, sent from Vermont, addressed to Jane Essex. She showed him the envelope. Her father had written it himself, and there was a letter inside, which he had written too. His first to her, ever. Only half a page, and about the weather, and the traffic, but a letter, one she had read again and again, one in which he had called her Janey.

She said, 'Look, I remember you said you had some hang-up about some Americans. Well, I'll go away if you like. I mean, if this is something you feel you got to do on your own, well, I can get a hold of that. But hey, I been thinking about what you said about balance. You're right. It's the first rule unless you're writing crap, and I'm not into that. I'm going to be good, the best.' She was warming to it, living this new role which had materialized during the week. She hitched her ruck-sack. 'It's just that the idea's got its claws in me, won't go away. I mean, just take a look around – what wouldn't I give to cover this house coming into its own again.'

He was still staring at the envelope, tapping it against his thumbnail. She said, reaching inside her jacket, 'I'll find something else, maybe you need an ID card. What've you got in this place, the crown jewels? Or maybe you think I'm going to blow it up? Check the rucksack. It's food, not semtex.'

He looked from her to the house, then he threw back his head and laughed and suddenly his face was alive.

She grinned, then laughed, withdrew her hand, the sweat breaking out on her back for she had nothing else with Jane Essex on it. He reached for her rucksack, sliding it off her shoulder, testing its weight. 'Feels as though there's enough food in there to act as a password. Sorry I seem paranoid. It's just been a tough few months, a tough few years.' He fell silent, then laughed again, quietly this time, his eyes alive as he looked at her. 'What you'll give, Miss Jane Essex, is your back, and your hands, and your weight behind a shovel. Let's see how it goes.'

She felt faint with relief, rubbing her forehead, then jamming her hands in her pockets. He said, 'Yes, we'll see how it goes – but just today for starters. OK?'

He grinned, turned, walked back towards the glasshouse, taking a worn path along its side, brushing past azaleas. She ran after him, reaching him, matching her stride to his. 'This is great,' she said, striving to keep the insistence from her voice. 'This is really great.'

They were at the door of the glasshouse. He entered. She watched from the doorway as he dragged an orange box across the damaged red-brick herringbone floor, and then folded a worn anorak on top of a terracotta rhubarb-forcer. Behind him was an old packing case on top of which lay a tub of putty, a chisel, paintbrushes and sandpaper. He turned to her, pointing to the rhubarb-forcer. 'Take a seat and let's start with the tea.'

They drank it, ate the pasties and the cookies, all without speaking. As he screwed the stopper back into the flask she asked, 'Can I take a photograph of this glasshouse?' He stood up, brushing off the crumbs. A bird fluttered in through a broken pane, then back out of the skylight. 'He'll be back for the crumbs,' Hal said. 'Yes, you can take your photograph, and then get to it.'

He reached for a piece of sandpaper and threw it at her. She caught it. He grinned and said, 'Let's hope your sanding's better than your tea.'

'Goddamn Brit,' she laughed, yanking her camera out of the side pocket of her rucksack.

'That's what all the girls say,' he replied, pointing to an area of woodwork. 'See what you can do with that, and one word about broken fingernails and you're out, back through that gap quicker than old Saul to a pint.'

She took her photograph and they worked all afternoon, both saying little, for Jane was guarding every move, every word, whilst Hal was thinking of her rich brown hair with its deep red sheen, her pale skin, her eyes, so deep and grey, and her smile which didn't quite reach her eyes, and he wondered why. But hell, if she wanted to mess about here, if she wanted to do well at her work, why not? It was another pair of hands.

When the light faded she walked with him back down the drive, and the protesters saw them, catcalled to her. 'Traitor. That's no native, that's a spoiler.'

She waved. He shrugged. 'They'll get tired of it, but I should have taken you another way.'

She shook her head. 'Let them jeer. One day . . .' She stopped. He said, 'Yes?'

She began again, 'One day they'll change their minds, when Wendham comes into its own.'

He led the way to the gatehouse, unlocking the door, saying as he did so, 'You really do like the house, don't you?' His voice was curious.

He flicked on the light, went to the wood burner, dragging the clothes horse away. His pants fell off. He blushed and replaced them.

'It's gone out,' she said.

'Always does, but I'll get it going in two ticks.'

He thrust paper and kindling onto the bed of ash and struck a match. She smelt the sulphur. He repeated, as he shut the doors, pushed open the vent, 'You really do like the house?'

'It's beautiful. It's going to be lovely.' This time, when she smiled it lit her eyes, flickered, died. She hitched the rucksack higher on her shoulder.

Hal said, staring at her, 'Then you must come again. It's good to build, to restore. It heals.' This time he wasn't just thinking of her as an extra pair of hands, but as someone who had worked hard today with never a complaint, someone whose notes he had read and approved, liking her style, liking her perception and commitment to detail, someone whose smile had at last reached her eyes, someone who had gained in some way he didn't understand. Someone who was very beautiful, who had somehow made the air seem warm and soft.

She kept the smile going, even as she was thinking, What does he mean by heal? Is he crazy or something?

He cooked for her, burgers, frozen peas, chips cooked in vegetable oil. She carried the plates into the living room, holding them with the tea towel, putting them down onto folded newspaper. He said, 'Next year I'll have the kitchen garden sorted out. None of this frozen stuff. It'll be runner beans, peas, spinach.' He pointed to the chair, and returned to the kitchen, calling, 'Tomato sauce?'

'Excuse me?' she queried as she sat down.

He came back through, brandishing the bottle. 'Ketchup,' she declared.

He handed it to her with a laugh. 'Another world, another language.'

She smiled, 'Yes, I've found that. It's all so different. I didn't think it would be. So much smaller, so much greyer, older. So much history.' She thought of Irene Prior leaving her son, cheating him, hurting him. God, how he must have hurt.

He saw the smile die in her eyes and it bothered him.

They ate, and now the room was warm. 'Tell me about

your world?' he ventured once the meal was finished and the kettle was on the gas hob in the kitchen.

'What can I say?' she shrugged. 'My folks are in Vermont. Vermont is mountains, ankle-deep leaves in the fall, bonfires and fog in the valleys, snow. I'm at Columbia University, New York City. It's fun. New York has been re-invented under Mayor Giuliani. Crime is down, graffiti is less, the streets are cleaner, Bloomingdale's is great.' She leaned her elbows on the table, her eyes on the ketchup bottle.

'Your folks?' he queried.

'Just like other folks,' she countered. Her face was guarded, her eyes wary and now he felt he knew why the smile died. Something was wrong there, something to do with 'the folks'. Poor kid, maybe they were too busy for her, or maybe he was being paranoid again – she was probably just homesick.

The kettle was whistling. He hurried to the kitchen, calling back, 'Sit yourself down near the stove, I'll bring this through. Tea or coffee?'

'Coffee,' she called, settling on the sofa. 'I guess a slug of caffeine'd be a great idea. *And miles to go before I sleep.* D'you know that poem?'

'Robert Frost,' he called back.

'I love him,' she said. 'I studied him at Columbia. Maybe we'll do him at Sussex some time during the year.'

'Black or white?'

'Black, no sugar.'

He carried in two steaming mugs. She took one, cupped it between her hands. The stove was exuding heat. He closed the vent with a poker, looked at the empty space beside her, then sat in the chair opposite. 'You could have been reading him today, not sandpapering a glasshouse.' He kept his voice light. 'Thank you. I liked your writing.'

She shrugged, 'I like the idea of what you're doing. Tell me more, in detail.'

There was a genuine interest in her tone, a curiosity in her eyes. He smiled, 'On or off the record?'

'Off. Just between you and me. Or is it secret? I don't *need* to know. I just kind of want to.'

He rose, shrugging. 'No, none of it's a secret. I'm just edgy because of the protests, because of . . . but these were in the village hall for anyone to see.' He dragged the plans over from a card table beneath the window, set them on the worn rug at her feet, kneeling as he traced his outline for the garden.

'Joseph Barratt, who leased it over from Irene Wendham, landscaped the garden in the geometric style. He was new money, a city gent who was "into" the latest fashion. Then he changed his mind, grassed over the flower beds, installed a croquet lawn, ignored the kitchen garden, let it go to seed.' He was stabbing the plans with his pencil, his voice quickening and rising in anger. 'He knew that the Wendhams had spent years creating it but he didn't care about educating by example, about seeing beauty in the absence of any pretentious plan, about letting flowers tell their story to the heart.'

He broke off, laughing at himself, 'Excuse me, I just get so damn angry. Poor old Travers did his best, got it back as close as he could, took cuttings from the villagers who, in their turn, had taken seeds and cuttings from the Wendhams. In the spring, I'm going to do the same. I'm going to put back Irene's flowers. I'm going to grow leeks, and lettuce as she did. I'm keeping the faith you see. She loved this place. I think she died for it, and Harry.'

Jane drank her coffee. Serve her damn well right, she thought, for where was her son in all this, and again her eyes became guarded. Hal Travers saw. He said, 'We're a long way from Vermont. You must miss it. You're homesick aren't you, or is it something more? Talk about it, if it helps.'

She stared at him, seeing the kindness in his face,

416

hearing it in his voice. She was surprised, nonplussed. Eventually she shrugged, 'Yes, it is a long way. I guess everyone gets homesick, and thanks, but there's nothing to talk about.' Her voice was embarrassed because this was the enemy, a Travers. The Travers weren't kind, they were liars and thieves. They were to be kept at arm's length.

He flushed, looked down at the plans. She wanted to reach out, to say thanks anyway but she couldn't, not to a Travers. Instead she said, 'What about the house? What will you do to that?'

He shifted the plans, finding the one he wanted, looking at it, not at her. 'I'm bringing it back to Irene's day, starting with the kitchen. When the theme park is built . . .'

'When?' she cut in. 'Has permission been given?' Her voice was eager, curt.

He looked up at her, smiling at the light in her eyes. '*If* I should say.'

'Oh.'

'Yes, oh. But it will be. It must be.' He drew his knee up, rested on it, staring at the stove.

What do you expect to see in that? she thought. It's not a crystal ball and anger at Irene and all of them nudged her. 'The kitchen,' she prompted.

He sighed and stared down at the plan, then traced the outline of the kitchen, showing her the positioning of the large elm table. She said, 'But it's already there. I crept past it the other day.'

He smiled, 'Oh yes, Jane Essex, the trespasser.'

She grinned, but thought, Oh no, the owner, the rightful owner and Irene Wendham can turn in her grave all she likes because she's caused more than enough damage.

He saw the grin, saw the flatness of her eyes, and touched her knee. 'I'm sorry. I didn't mean to bring that up. Yes, the table's there, but it needs stripping. I can start that right away. I'm getting traditional

417

relief-patterned basins, white inside and clotted cream out. That'll have to wait. So will the heavy knives and herb cutters, though I've a few already. I'll find more in antique shops. Brass containers and so on too. I'm doing up the pastry room. There's still the original provision cupboard, and the marble slab. There are drawers for rolling pins, but no rolling pins.'

'So?' she queried, leaning over, her coffee finished and forgotten in her hand.

'I'll turn them myself.'

She stared at him, looked at his hands, then at the easel in the corner. 'Can you?'

'I'll learn.'

She shrugged. 'Just like that?'

'If you want something badly enough you can usually make it happen.'

She leaned forward, her elbows on her knees looking at the flames flickering dimly behind the smoked glass of the stove. He was right. If only he knew how right.

He reached for a log, opened the stove, tossed it in. The flames flickered for a moment on his high cheek-bones. He reached for another log and said, 'Once I've set up the kitchen I'll open it to the folks who come to the theme park. They can see their cream teas being made. They can buy the bowls . . .'

'The rolling pins too,' she chipped in.

'Exactly,' he grinned. 'In no time at all it'll all be as it was in poor Irene's time.'

She sank back against the sofa. 'Has it ever occurred to you guys that there's no evidence? All these bleeding hearts over Irene Wendham could be a waste of time. It's only legend. If I was writing it up I'd want more than hearsay.' She saw him looking at her, a query in his eyes. She hurried to reassure him, 'But there's no point in anyone writing it up in this day and age. Who'd be interested?'

He threw on the last of the logs, clicked shut the door and dusted his hands, settling back on his knees, rolling up the plans. Over the crackling of the stove and the paper he said, 'It wouldn't matter if it was published. The Travers have nothing to fear from the truth. You see, there's evidence of the fire that's talked about, right here at Wendham House. I'll show you one day, if you ever come back.'

She said, 'And the murder, what evidence for that?' She struggled to keep her voice cool, but she could hear its crispness.

He turned to her, 'Old Saul's been spouting again, has he?'

Was there suspicion in his tone? In his eyes? No, they were curious, that was all. He laughed gently. 'Oh, he loves Wendham almost as much as I do. Almost.'

She rose, flicking back her hair, checking her watch, not referring to the murder again, there would be other times. 'I got to go. I've a long way to drive.'

He leapt to his feet. 'God, what am I thinking of – it's eight thirty already and Brighton's a hell of a thrash. We should have eaten earlier.' He was rubbing the back of his neck. 'Look, you have my bed. I'll kip on the sofa, and you can go back in the daylight, even do a bit of sanding before you go. Yes, then you can stay for the Guy Fawkes bonfire down in the Home Field. I'm to set off the fireworks, and I'll let you light the rockets.' He grinned at her.

She reached for her rucksack. 'No, not even the rockets'll tempt me. The ride's no problem – it'll be a breeze. I've an essay to write.'

She walked to the door, wanting to stay, never wanting to leave *her* house. But she mustn't seem too eager. He reached past her, opened it, walked with her to the gate which was devoid of protesters now that the dew was down and the cold more intense. There was a mustiness in the air from the fallen leaves, and somewhere a bonfire was smoking.

He walked her down the road to the pub. Lights and laughter seeped from the opened windows. She unlocked her car. He held open the door, the smell of chips was still on his clothes. She eased the rucksack over to the passenger seat. He said, 'You're sure you'll be all right?'

She nodded. It was cloudy. There were no stars. She stood. Her face was in shade. He kissed her lightly, on the lips. 'Thank you,' he said against them, before pulling back. He took the keys from the door, threw them up, caught them. Handed them to her. 'You're welcome,' she said, slipping into the car, pulling the door shut, wiping the condensation off the window, wanting to wipe the kiss from her mouth, backing out.

He shouted at her, 'If you want to, you can come again.'

On Sunday, to her surprise, she worked on Hardy, making notes, underscoring the text, an excitement in her, an energy, though she threw her notes on Wendham in a drawer. By five her neck and wrist ached. She returned the car to the rental company in Brighton and walked along the front, breathing in the ozone, remembering the bonfire, the smell of chips on his clothes. Yes, she'd be back next weekend, to work on *her* house.

CHAPTER TWENTY-ONE

The next weekend she hired the car as usual, but collected it on Friday night, parking it on campus, having a quick drink with Terry, but only one, for she wanted to be up early and on the road.

At Wendham she parked in the pub car-park as usual and strode in light drizzle towards the gates, but before she reached the protesters she saw that the saplings had been removed from the gap in the hedge.

She hurried through the copse, across the lawn, up the terrace, across it, the scent of the herbs rising as she disturbed them. Round to the glasshouse, seeing movement through the condensation, tapping on the glass, pulling open the door at the opposite end to last time, entering.

Hal Travers was perched on a stepladder, wearing a different tartan shirt over a T-shirt this time. He grinned down at her. 'You're late.'

'Quit the insults. So what do I do today?'

She dug her camera out and took a photograph of progress so far, though made sure Hal Travers was not in the shot. She wanted none of that family recorded on any film of hers.

They worked in the glasshouse all morning, but by lunch-time the drizzle had stopped. Hal called her to the packing case, and presented her with sandwiches wrapped in foil. She shook her head. 'They're yours.'

He pointed to another foil pack. 'Those are mine.'

He was perched on another rhubarb-forcer, un-screwing a flask. 'Coffee this time,' he murmured. 'You only drank half your tea, so maybe, as a Yank, you like coffee best.'

He poured and held out the mug. She took it, looked at the black coffee. 'You knew I was coming?'

'I hoped,' he said, pouring his own.

'You remembered I like black coffee?'

'It's not hard.' He drank, not adding that he thought it might make her feel more at home, that it might soothe her.

She drank. No it wasn't hard. Of course it wasn't hard. Anyone could remember that. She ate her sandwiches. The bread was moist, the ham salty.

In the afternoon, after she had taken a photograph of the garden from the terrace, they started digging out the footings for a hamstone path which would lead from the bottom of the terrace steps round to the left, following the course of the wide beds.

'I'll plant camomile and creeping thyme between the gaps, following the planting pattern of the terrace,' he panted as, beside her, he thrust the spade down into the earth again.

So that's what the herbs were. The gardening gloves he had given her to wear were too big. She rested her spade and pulled on them.

He said, 'Irene's father planned the terrace and planted the herbs. Sometimes he'd dance his wife out onto the terrace in the soft summer evening and Irene would watch and swear that one day she would dance in this way with the man she loved, or so her journal said.' He heaved the spadeful of earth into the wheelbarrow. 'Never did, of course.'

He dug again. She took up her spade, thrust it into the earth, levering it down with her foot, straining to lift the earth out, throwing it into her wheelbarrow. Jane Prior would though, she'd dance on it, pound out the music, whoop up her world. She straightened, eased her back, caught the gleam of light on his hair and remembered the coffee, and confusion was edging into her life.

He said, 'Yep, you're right. Time for a break.' He drew off his gloves, threw them onto the wheelbarrow, took hers and did the same. He brought out two cans of Pepsi from the rucksack hanging on the wheelbarrow handle, pulling the widget of one. She heard the hiss of air, felt the warmth of his hand as he passed it to her. She drank, raising her head to the sky, feeling the cold wind.

There was the hiss of his can. She didn't look, she just kept staring at the sky.

'Come with me,' he said. She turned to him now. He was drinking, his throat was moving, his eyes were shaded by his lashes. He walked ahead of her across the lawn. She followed, up the steps to the terrace, her Pepsi cold in her hand. He led her round to the kitchen door, and then further. Here there were scorch marks and crumbled brick. He pointed his can at it. 'Jack Prior's stamp. The evidence. Every generation's kept it like this – it keeps us on our toes.'

She stared, reached out, touched it. The memory of coffee fled, the feel of his warm hand against hers too. She touched the wall again. This is your proof? she wanted to say. *This is your proof?* she wanted to scream. Anyone could have done that. Anyone. You, your father, your father's father. Anyone. And for years you've fought us on the basis of this, and the confusion fled and she wondered how there could ever have been any.

They finished their Pepsi, standing there, and she looked only at the wall as she crushed her can, wishing it was the Travers, all of them. He took it from her, and she wanted to recoil as he touched her. She watched as he threw it into a dustbin before they walked back to the path. Her shoulders ached, her hands were sore as she took up her spade again. She examined her blisters, reached for her gloves. He put up his hand, grasped hers, ran his finger gently over the blisters. She let him, but wanted to slap him away. 'We've done enough for the day,' he said, taking her gloves from her, heaving both spades into the wheelbarrow. 'Come on.'

He made her sit in the glasshouse whilst he put away the tools in the potting shed, then leaned against the doorframe, rubbing the back of his neck, looking at her. 'You need better gloves. The thing is . . . What I mean is . . . Are you coming again? Are you going back tonight? You can have my bed. I'll kip on the sofa.'

She looked down at the fingers, the one that had touched that wall and smiled. Too right she'd come again. Too right she'd build up Wendham House and take it from these people. And it would be easy now that she had his trust, for that was what the look on his face meant. That was what she'd phone and tell her father. That was what would make them all love her. She looked up at him and her smile was wide and full.

He saw the light in her eyes, the joy, and it was as though the sun had come out, as though the air had moved around him, and now he knew why he had not slept all week, why the plans had not drawn him as they usually did, why he had always seemed to be waiting.

She drawled, 'I guess it seems a bit crazy to keep coming and going. Yeah, I'd like to stay, but the sofa'd be great for me.'

He shook his head. 'No, I couldn't let you do that.' His gaze was still on her.

'Then I'd better go back.'

She saw the shadow cross his face. She waited. No way must she seem too keen. No way was she going to be obliged to a Travers, one who had remembered how she took her coffee and then taken her to see an old scorch mark.

'Then have the sofa.'

They drove in his old Morris Minor to a garden centre which had late Saturday opening. He insisted that he buy her gloves. 'It's work you're doing for me, after all,' he said.

'And myself,' she replied, then added. 'I'm getting the project out of it.'

Returning through Wendham village he drew to a stop by the church, reached across and opened her door, saying, 'I thought you might like to see Harry Travers's grave, and Sinclair's.'

'Why not?' she said, wanting to spew out all the reasons why not.

They strolled up the gravel path which was free of weeds but spotted by soggy confetti. Along here were new graves, their stones uniform and unweathered. Yews edged the churchyard, beyond which ploughed fields stretched as far as the eye could see. She said, 'The drive at Wendham is such a mess. We should have bought weedkiller at the store.'

He shook his head. 'We'll hoe. I try not to use chemicals. I try to keep to the old ways.'

She asked, as they left the path, 'Any news on the planning permission?'

He touched her arm to guide her to the far corner of the plot and now the stones were adventurous, old. Some tilted, all moss- and lichen-covered. 'No, no news,' he said, shaking his head. His hand still touched her arm. A Travers hand. She suffered it.

He was pointing ahead now. 'There's Sinclair. He died before Harry. Irene's death affected him almost as much as Harry. She'd done a lot for him. He'd done a lot for her.'

She approached the grave, standing before it. She stared, reading aloud from the stone. 'Sinclair, a dear friend, loved by us all. OK, but how'd you know Irene loved him? Are you telling me you have a through line to the other side?' She kept her tone light, though she wanted to yell at him for projecting this vision of a sainted Irene.

Hal had moved along now. 'Here's Harry. No, I've no

through line and I'm not a mind-reader but perhaps Irene was and knew what was going to happen to her because she kept journals. That's how I know she planned the path we're working on now. And we've letters, Harry's diary too. It tells us his thoughts, their experiences, his life afterwards. It was Sinclair who saw . . .' He stopped. 'Oh, what does it matter now? What matters is today, and the future.'

He started to walk back towards the car. She ran after him. 'Anyway how come if Travers loved her so much, you're here?' She made herself add, 'Mind you, I'm kind of glad you are.'

He swung round, a smile lighting his face. 'You are?'

'Sure,' she said, sauntering up to him, digging her hands into her Levi pockets. 'How could a girl get to bust a gut digging in hard clay soil without you?'

He laughed, and it rang out across the churchyard. 'You're wonderful,' he said. 'You're bloody wonderful Jane Essex.' He was still laughing as he came to her, though he didn't touch her. Thank God he didn't touch her. He just walked alongside.

She asked sharply, 'So why're you here, if Harry Travers loved his Irene so much? Didn't waste much time getting over her, did he? Though he still held on to her property?'

They were back on the gravel and the confetti, crunching along it. Harry saw her face, saw the bleakness in her eyes, heard the anger, and knew without doubt now that this was a girl who was bruised. Had her father betrayed her mother? It would make sense. He ached to hold her but merely said, 'He married Emily Baines who had worked in Irene's workshops, the ones on which the Prior wealth was based. She and her mother came to him when Irene was killed. They nursed him for he was prostrate with grief. Emily loved him, always had done apparently. She convinced him, and so did Esther, Irene's New York friend, that

426

the way he could best serve Irene's memory was to somehow go on. He did so, setting himself the task of restoring Wendham according to the plans in her journal. It was a labour of love. He concentrated on the garden, for that is what she had spoken of most.'

They reached the lych-gate. Hal ushered her through first. 'He wrote that as he worked he could hear her voice, feel the touch of her hand on his, feel her love all around; he achieved a sense of peace. He knew she was here, with him. That their love transcended even death. Emily stayed. He grew to care for her, though never with the adoration that she felt for him. They married. In his diary he writes of a sense of obligation to her, a respect for her, a need within himself to create a child, a line, who would defend Wendham from the Priors when he was gone. Emily bore him a son and Harry died when the boy was fourteen but lived long enough to instil a love for Wendham, a determination to thwart the efforts that the Priors were already making to ruin the clothing and the glove business that Harry had begun.'

They bought fish and chips from Yeovil and whilst Hal showered she put them on plates in the oven, and dried her shampooed hair by the wood burner, sketching out her own plans for the house, noting down the cream and beige tones she would use to draw light into every room, the rugs she would scatter across the polished floors, for there would be no thick carpets as there were in her parents' apartment.

When her hair was dry, Hal was dressed. She dished up the fish and chips whilst he laid the table. He poured white wine he had kept cool outside the front door. They ate, talking of the hard core they would trundle across from the back of the vegetable garden to the path, of the sand he would order in the week, of the hamstone which had been heaped for years behind the orchard.

She made the coffee whilst he threw logs on the fire. She stared at the milk, did he take it? She couldn't remember and had to call through and ask. 'Yes please,' he answered, 'but no sugar.'

As she poured it she couldn't forget that when the positions were reversed he had remembered. So what the hell, she thought angrily. So what the hell.

She carried two mugs into the living room, jerking to a stop when she saw him looking at her sketches. The coffee slopped, scalding her fingers. He leapt to his feet, took the mugs, rushed her into the kitchen, held her fingers under the tap, ran cold water until the stinging had stopped.

As he bent over her fingers, drying them on the frayed towel he said, 'I don't know, you come here to help and what do you get, blisters on your palms, and scalded fingers. Hope it hasn't put you off?'

She saw that his hair was still damp, the curls clinging together like tails. She said, 'It hasn't put me off.' She waited. Would he now comment on her sketches? He did, leading her back to the sofa, putting her coffee on a table he drew up, lifting them from the pile. 'I like these. They're better than Irene's ideas. You really are interested, aren't you?'

She relaxed, lifted up her coffee, smiling at him over the mug, and his heart turned over at the warmth in her eyes, and he could still feel her hands in his, could still smell her shampooed hair as he had dried her fingers, fingers he had wanted to kiss.

That night she slept on the sofa and she feared that Hal Travers would come to her in the night, sit on the sofa, play with her hair, seek out her lips, then her body. Get close, her father had said. But there was close, and there was close. Then she shrugged. What did it matter? She could close her eyes and think of something else as she usually did, and then he might lie asleep beside her, and for a moment it would bring her the warmth of human contact.

In his bed Hal Travers tossed and turned, aching for this girl who had taken over his thoughts and dreams, loving her, wanting to care for her, to keep her safe, to make her smile always reach her eyes.

November passed and at the weekends she took photographs, made notes which he still read, though not because he no longer trusted her, he told her, but because it gave him pleasure. When it was fine they worked on the path, and when it was not they worked in the glasshouse, and their days achieved a pattern, and their nights too, though now Jane slept on his bed, bringing a sleeping bag with her, not wanting to smell him on the sheets, not wanting to rest where he had rested. Harry took the sofa, sleeping well because she was in his house, on his bed, safe, and the smile was reaching her eyes more often.

During the week she worked and drank with Terry in the pub, and let him use her body, for her father was abrupt again when she rang, shouting at her each week, 'Well why haven't you got any news of the planning permission? We need it to be passed. We need to know the backers.' Each time she whispered, 'I'm doing my best.'

'Do better. Come on, you know you can, Janey. I know you can.'

Janey, Janey. It was that she clung to because she was Jane Prior, not Jane Essex, and she knew that soon she would have her family back. At last she would have it back.

On the second weekend in December, when frost whitened the verges of Wendham, she parked the car as usual in the car-park but Keith called from an upstairs window, 'Message from young Hal. He says to take it in through the gates.'

She pulled her scarf tighter around her neck. 'The gates?' she yelled back.

'Aye, see for yourself.'

She drove along, and there were the gates flung open and no protesters in sight. Were they up at the house? She drove in, stopped just inside, hooted, looking at the front door of the gatehouse. Hal came out, toast in his hand, beckoning her in. 'Just leave the car,' he shouted. 'We're celebrating.'

She shut off the engine and dragged her rucksack from the passenger seat, slamming shut the door, looking at him, hardly daring to breathe, hardly daring to ask, but she did, 'Well, is it granted?'

She walked round the car, her eyes on his face. He nodded, a broad smile breaking out. She threw her rucksack up in the air, and ran to him, whooping, 'We've won, we've won.'

He clasped her, lifted her from her feet, whirled her round. 'You bet we have, Jane Essex. You just bet we have.'

She didn't mind him touching her, not today. Oh no, not today.

All day they worked but she finished early, driving to buy champagne from Safeways to celebrate, and to collect change from the girl at the till which she fed into the public phone at the entrance, leaving a message on her father's answering machine, saying, 'We've won, the Priors have won. Planning permission's been granted. Now I'll find out the backer.'

The next weekend the university term ended. The following weekend she had arranged to meet some of the other Americans in London at the flat of a friend of one of the boys in Earl's Court. It was here that they'd all spend Christmas rather than fly home.

She drove to Wendham Friday evening, asking the moment she arrived if he'd found a backer. He had not.

She worked with Hal all Saturday, on the kitchen now for the cold was bitter and here at least they could feed the range with coal and wood whilst polishing the brass they had brought down from the attic. At the end of the day her hands were black, her nails ingrained.

In the evening she soaked in the bath realizing for the first time just how tired she was after the term's work, the manual work, everything. She lay back, letting her hands float, her eyes drift, taking in the curtains she had hung at the window, her toothbrush, her mirror. She was going to be here all week. She squeezed the sponge over her breasts. All week at *her* Wendham and for a moment her tiredness lifted.

During the days they worked. In the evenings they talked, they read, or she studied whilst he sketched her and she allowed herself to be Jane Essex, to sink into the lie, because it made the charade easier. By the end of the week he had begun painting her on canvas and the smell of oil paint was strong in the air. They could have gone down the road to the pub but somehow they never did. Instead she bought a small Christmas tree from the garden centre mid-week, and Hal stood it in a bucket.

Together they bought decorations and white lights. 'Not coloured,' she insisted. He raised his eyebrows as people thrust passed them in Woolworths. 'Still sticking with the white and beige,' he said.

'You'd better believe it.'

Together they decorated it that evening and the scent of pine filled the small room. There were Christmas cards coming with every post. She had brought ones given to her by university friends, those sent by her Columbia friends, and from those she still saw from the beach house days. He insisted that they join his on the mantelpiece, or on the ribbons they strung down the walls.

Just before she had left Brighton her grandmother's present had arrived, and one from her mother, the card attached by Sellotape was written in a strong hand, her Christmas card had included a note; *I'm so much better.*

431

I'm even painting. I will write properly after the festivities.
Remember to breathe. Imagine that white liquid flowing
through you. Your father is sending you his own Christmas
present. He says this year's a special year.

On Thursday flowers were delivered to her. They
were waiting on the doorstep in their cellophane wrap
when they clumped down the drive from the glasshouse
where they'd be clearing out the last of the rubbish now
that they'd finished the staging.

She picked them up, turning over the envelope
eagerly. It was addressed to Jane Essex. It would be
from her father. He always sent her flowers but these
would be different, for he'd said this was a special year.
That's what he'd said, a special year. But 1996 would
be better. Hal stood at the door, looking back at her.
She called, 'You go on in.'

She waited until he had entered, turning the card over
and over, imagining his words, his love, his laugh,
picturing them here, her mother, father, Rich, and
herself, happy, united. She'd lead them through the
house. Her father would look at her, whirl her round,
say to Rich, 'Look and learn from this girl.' Slowly she
lifted the flap, removed the card and read, *John Prior.*
It had been sent by her father's secretary, and was one
of a long list her father would have given the woman,
as he always did. As he damn well always did. It wasn't
special at all. Not at all.

Her rage and pain were as jagged as the pieces of
the card she was tearing into bits. She let them flutter
to the floor, then ground them into the dirt. And he'd
said John Prior. He'd named himself. He could have
exposed her. 'How could you?' she whispered. 'How
could you do this to me?' And hurled the flowers across
the drive, but it wasn't only the risk he had taken which
scored her so deeply – that was nothing besides what
else he had done.

She walked into the kitchen, stopping dead as she
smelt the coffee Hal was brewing. It would be served

black. A Travers had remembered. Her father never had. But now she felt very tired as she stared at Hal Travers. So what the hell, neither the remembering or the forgetting meant either were any different. She thought of the charred wall, such stupid proof. The talk in the village, the lies. Yes, this man and her father were both liars, users. But she was too, and now her mind was whirling, darkening, and they were all dragging her down, all pulling at her.

Hal looked up at her. She was so still, so pale. 'Where are the flowers?' he asked, alarmed. 'Who were they from? What did they say? Why . . .' She just stared, thrusting him aside as he came to her, rushing through to the bedroom, rolling up her sleeping bag, stuffing her clothes into her rucksack, lifting it onto her shoulder, barging back, but Hal was in the living room. He grabbed her.

'Out of my way,' she shouted. 'I'm going to London. I was going on Sunday anyway. I'm tired. It's Christmas soon for God's sake and all I'm doing is working my butt into the ground, and for what, for who?'

He still held her. 'You're not going like this. You'll have an accident. You're not going, d'you hear?'

She fought him, fought the tears that were coming, falling, blurring everything. He pulled her against him. His jumper was prickly on her cheek. She felt him take the rucksack from her shoulder. She let the sleeping bag slip to the floor and now the sobs were choking her and a Travers was rocking her, and it was wrong that he should. His arms were strong around her, his voice gentle, his breath warm on her neck, and it couldn't be so.

She clung to him, raised her mouth to his, feeling his lips open over hers. She gripped his neck, wanting him to take the pain away, wanting his body to take it away. What did it matter if he was a Travers? He was a body, wasn't he?

Hal cradled her face, her mouth was urgent, her

433

fingers were at his belt. Passion swept him, love burned, his breathing quickened, he ran his hands over her body, pulling her to him, wanting her. God, how he wanted her. He kissed her cheeks and they were still wet with tears, more were falling. He drew away, staring at her face, so pale, so tired. Still the tears were falling.

He took her in his arms again, but gently now. 'Please,' she said, her lips seeking his.

'Shh,' he murmured, stroking her hair, wiping her face with his fingers. 'This isn't the time.'

For what felt like hours he held her until she was all cried out, and then he carried her through to the bedroom, stripped her clothes from her, and now she tensed because, for a moment she had believed him, she had believed there could be comfort without use, without payment.

He dug in his drawers and brought out pyjamas, handing them to her, standing with his back to her while she put them on, saying, 'Don't laugh, I wore these at boarding school. They made me less homesick because my mother had bought them. I thought they smelt of her.' He walked to the door, took his dressing gown from the hook. 'Put this on, stay in that bed. The radiator's quite warm. I'll bring you supper, then you must sleep.'

She ate an omelette, perching the tray on her knees, whilst he ate in the living room. He brought her chocolate and a steaming mug for himself. He stood at the window gazing out into the night and said, 'Tomorrow we'll go into town. We'll have a Christmas lunch with all the trimmings. We'll shop till we drop.'

She watched his reflection in the glass. Was he coming to her now?

He turned, came across, took her mug, kissed her hair. 'Now go to sleep.'

She watched him leave the room, watched the door

close quietly. She undid his robe. It smelt of him. She shrugged out of it, sank onto the pillows. They were all right, they smelt of soap powder, not Hal Travers. The pyjamas too. She slept, and in the morning she woke and found she was clutching the robe.

CHAPTER TWENTY-TWO

It was Christmas Eve and Roderick Travers insisted that they take a taxi down to Oxford Street. 'We have an American guest and so she must see the British in all their gory detail.' He winked at Jane. His wife, Annette, laughed.

Hal groaned, 'Did I prepare you properly for all this, Jane?' He was holding up her coat, whilst his father did the same for his mother. Annette's turquoise dress was expensive and chic. Jane's was from Yeovil's Denners, a creamy silk which almost matched her skin.

Jane smiled as they stood in the pale blue hall of the Eaton Terrace house. No, nothing in her life had prepared her for this. She was a Prior, and the Priors hated the Travers so why was she here? She still didn't really know, though the darkness had lifted and the whirling in her head was gone. All that was left was a great tiredness and a confusion.

A confusion which had been present since Hal had woken her the morning after her father had sent her the flowers. He had brought a mug of tea. He had taken her to Yeovil. They had listened to carols played by the Salvation Army band on the corner outside the Burger King.

They had eaten turkey in Littlewoods. They had shopped till they dropped, or at least until they could stand the piped carols in the stores no longer. She had bought a book from Ottakers, and one from The Yeovil Bookshop. Then he had brought her home to the gatehouse and they had wrapped their gifts before

the fire, though he had taken the book he had bought
her into the bedroom to wrap, whilst she wrapped the
gardening gloves she had bought for him.

'Who sent the flowers?' he had asked again. 'Your
lover?'

She'd laughed. 'No, my father, or his secretary.'

She didn't know why she'd told him. He'd reached
out and stroked her hair. Separate presents from her
parents. Separate lives with her in the middle. It was
as he'd thought – poor kid, poor dear lost Jane.

That evening his parents had rung. He had asked if
he may bring an American friend for Christmas. Jane
had shaken her head. 'No,' she mouthed. 'No.'

He merely smiled, then nodded. 'Thanks, Mum,
Christmas Eve then.'

On Monday she'd sent the gifts to her friends at
Earl's Court, then bought more for Hal's parents.
They'd worked all week, and while they worked they
sang carols until their throats were sore, and still she
hadn't been able to push the confusion away.

She'd rung her father who had said, 'Swell. Just what
we want. Find out all you can, Janey.'

'Dad,' she'd said. 'You're sure about everything?
You're sure they've lied all these years?'

'No doubt. No doubt at all, Janey. They've run us
ragged right from the start,' he'd replied.

'But the fire I wrote you about?'

'Forget it. Crazy lies. We got someone in there to
check it out years ago. The carbon dating didn't check
out, believe me. These are clever, cunning people who
know how to cheat and lie with a smile on their
goddamn faces. Come on, Janey, you're doing swell.
Don't let them trick you. We'll make a businesswoman
out of you yet.'

She said, 'Dad, why did you get your secretary to
send flowers?'

'I knew you liked them. Knew it would please you –
besides I'm so damn busy, you know what it's like, and

I wanted you to have something from me.' He'd rung off.

She'd replaced the receiver.

The front door bell rang. Mr Travers opened the door. It was the taxi. They hurried to it, the men sitting on the dicky seats, Annette Travers laughing as they settled themselves. Annette turned to Jane. 'I do so like to have the men at my feet, don't you my dear?'

Jane drawled, 'Right on.'

Hal smiled, searching her face, seeing the uncertainty still there, not understanding it, but feeling it was better than the bleakness and despair, and again he cursed this girl's father for hurting her, for sending her flowers when she had hoped for something more personal, and he didn't think he would ever forget Jane's voice as she told him this.

They crawled with the rest of the traffic down Oxford Street, then slipped into a small bistro. 'We always come here on Christmas Eve,' Annette said, smiling at Angelo, the head waiter.

'Then we always go to the Evans for their party. We really must stop being such creatures of habit, darling,' Mr Travers said to his wife as they followed Angelo through the restaurant. The red candles set in wine bottles on the tables flickered as they passed, making the decorations hanging from the ceiling seem almost alive.

His wife was serious as they sat. She reached out for his hand. 'No,' she said softly. 'Let us be creatures of habit, let us live for years, let us come here, let us go to the Evans. Let me not have to do it alone. Let that gallant heart of yours keep beating.'

Mr Travers lifted her hand and kissed it. 'It'll do its best.'

Annette said, 'Too right it will.' She turned to Jane. 'Is that right? Is that what you'd say?'

Jane was unable to smile in the face of such love, in the face of such kindness to her, for she shouldn't be

438

here. She should leave, and never return. Now. Get up. She didn't. She said, 'If you were Australian. But it sounds great anyway.' They laughed. Go on, leave now. She didn't. She was too tired. Where would she go? Earl's Court. Go on, leave now. She didn't know why she couldn't.

They chose their meal. They toasted Hal's absent brother, who was travelling in Australia. They toasted Hal's backers.

Jane almost spilt her wine. She looked up at him. Now she knew why. Yes, this was why. 'A backer, you've a backer.' Her voice was urgent, sharp.

His father smiled. 'You said you had a helper in this lass. You've an apostle more like. It sounds as though it's as much a matter of life and death for her as it is for you.'

Hal reached out and touched her hand. 'No backer. We're toasting the hope of a backer. A couple of firms approached Dad yesterday. We'll just have to wait and see.'

She stared at him, disappointment drenching her. He hadn't told her. He'd known since yesterday but he hadn't told her. She clenched her napkin on her lap. Her father was right. They tricked with smiles on their faces. What was the matter with her?

Hal saw her disappointment but couldn't understand it. He said quickly, 'Dad only told me as we left the taxi.'

She drank her wine. Who was lying? Who wasn't? Her mind was whirling. She wanted to go home. Anywhere, as long as it was away from here. She drank again.

At the party Hal stayed by her side, introducing her as his friend, his hand light on her arm. She couldn't summon up dislike of his touch. A girl in a close-fitting black dress came through the bunched guests, grabbing him, hugging and kissing him, square on the lips. She ruffled his hair. 'Hi, gorgeous. I've missed you. Has he been a good boy while I've been away? He's so good at keeping little girls warm,' she said as she turned to Jane, her hand still on Hal's shoulder, her nails red and too long.

Jane smiled, 'Yes, well, I've sure kept him warm.' She turned on her heel and cut through the group to their left, for now dislike had sliced through her, a sharp, roaring dislike of the hand that had been on her arm, of the man who had brought her here. God, such a hate sliced through her, such a hate it hurt.

Hal called, 'Jane.' She slipped through and round groups, out into the hall. There were more people there, clustered in ones and twos. Mr and Mrs Travers were with another older woman. Mrs Travers beckoned, 'Jane, over here. Do let me introduce you to Hal's godmother.'

Jane saw the front door. She wanted to leave. Find Earl's Court. Camp on the doorstep until her friends returned from whatever party they were at. Mrs Travers had detached herself from her husband, and forced her way through to cut off Jane's retreat.

'Come along, my dear.' Firmly she took her hand, almost dragging her back to Mr Travers, whispering just before they arrived, 'Don't take any notice of that ghastly girl with the nails. She will cling to young men so. Hal can't bear it.' She nodded to the left. There was a hatch through which Jane could see Hal, and the girl. Hal was removing her hand, his face white with anger. Jane stared.

His mother said, following her gaze, 'Oh yes, he can fight. But only when he feels it's worth it.'

Mr Travers said, 'Now, Jane m'dear, do talk to Mrs Williams. She's a star of her poetry group and I was telling her of your degree course. She despairs of me for my knowledge runs to accounts and business, hardly food for the soul. It's something I should have liked to do, perhaps something I still can – who knows? I shall be back in a moment. I need a cigar and Sid Evans is a reformed smoker, and zealous in the extreme. We all have to slink to the garden if we need to puff.'

Annette warned him, 'One cigar only.' She turned to Jane and Mrs Williams. 'A special Christmas treat.' But Jane barely listened. She followed Mr Travers with her eyes, his words echoing, his tone with her, so warm, so approving, so envious of literature, whilst her father had said, 'We'll make a businesswoman out of you yet.' Whilst he had said, 'They'll lie with a smile on their face.'

'Jane, dear,' Mrs Travers was saying. Jane turned back. Mrs Williams was peering at her. 'Wonderful. Now, perhaps *you* will be able to explain to Annette why a perfectly bloodthirsty passage can sound beautiful. It's the rhythm, isn't it? But what rhythm?'

A waiter poured more wine into their glasses. Annette was waiting for her answer, interested and attentive, her soft blue eyes kind. Jane felt awkward and clumsy, for she was not allowed to speak up at her parents' gatherings. She said, 'It's the meter. Iambic trimeter I think . . .' She trailed off. Annette smiled, 'Go on.'

Jane continued, 'Well, if you think of Klytemnestra's speech in *The Agamemnon* there's a music to it which just, kind of, tolls. Sure, the speeches are bloodthirsty, but they ache with pain too, and it's that meter that draws the tears from you, not just the content.'

Mrs Williams breathed, 'So true, so very true.'

Annette was smiling proudly at Jane. She leaned forward and kissed her cheek, staying close for a moment, saying, 'Yes, Hal has found someone well worth fighting for.'

Don't say that, Jane wanted to scream at her. Just don't say anything else. I can't think straight any more.

They arrived back at midnight. Annette and Roderick Travers went straight to bed, but Hal and Jane sat on the rug before the fire in the gracious living room, and now he told her of the backers. 'Two London firms who probably have more money than sense,' he joked.

She pushed off her shoes, staring into the embers. 'Who are they?' she forced herself to ask, not wanting to know. Not yet, not now, but why? The sooner she knew the sooner it would be over. Because she'd have to hug the knowledge to her all Christmas, knowing but unable to tell the Priors. Yes, that was why, you stupid fool, she told herself savagely.

'I don't know, I didn't ask. Crazy I suppose. I just wanted to have a break,' he said, resting his chin on his knees, reaching for her hand, holding it to his lips, kissing each finger, and then the palm, then burying his face in her hair. She let herself be Jane Essex and sank into the relief she felt.

She let him hold her, kiss her gently, let him raise her to her feet, hold her once more.

'One day,' he whispered, 'I want to love you. I want to hold you and love you. But first I want you to feel safe with me.' He led her from the room, and kissed her once more outside her bedroom door, leaving her to enter alone.

'Safe?' she whispered to his back. 'Safe, what's safe? I've never felt safe in my life and I doubt I ever will, and I don't know what's happening to me.'

On New Year's Eve the Travers took her with them to a party. During the day they'd insisted she rang her home, Annette brushing aside her protests. 'I know very well if it was a daughter of mine I'd want to wish her all the love in the world and give best wishes for the New Year coming up, and I'm sure your parents will want to do the same. Indeed my dear, I do so wish you'd passed on our number so that they could have rung you before.'

Hal saw Jane's eyes, the wariness, the bleakness. He said, 'Mother, they'll have rung Earl's Court.'

Hal led her into the study, kissed her forehead and

left her. She dialled, standing by the desk, unable to sit while she spoke to her father. Rich answered the phone. She said, 'Hi, Rich. It's Jane.'

'Well, I guess it is,' his voice was curt.

'Get Father for me.'

Her father came to the phone. 'You got news.'

'Happy New Year, Father,' she said.

There was a pause, he had covered the mouthpiece and was talking to Rich, saying, 'Hold the cab, this won't take long.' Now he said to her, 'And to you, Janey. Hope 1996 is a good one, for us all, but I guess that depends on what you've been finding out. Is it useful?'

She said quietly, 'They've a list of possible backers. Two are interested. I don't know who.'

'Well find out, and ring me when you know.'

'How's Mother?'

'They tried to ring that Earl's Court number. They said you weren't there, so where the hell are you?'

She said, 'With other friends. Goodbye, Father.'

She put the receiver down, pressing it until her knuckles went white, swallowing, feeling her eyes fill, feeling tossed about on a raging sea. She pressed her hand to her mouth. She took deep breaths, gulping them in, picturing a white stream flowing through her. Nothing worked. She thought instead of Wendham, imagining the scent of the camomile and thyme, the honeysuckle as it would be, and peace came.

She took her hand from her mouth, breathing easily now, seeing a glass cabinet on the wall ahead of her. In it were some old books. She approached, tried the door. It was locked. She peered at the spines. *Diary. H. Travers* said one. *Journal. Irene Prior* said three others. Next to the cabinet was a portrait. Underneath it said Harry Travers. She stared, for Harry Travers could have been Hal.

At the party in Hammersmith the music was loud, some of the laughter raucous. There were young people in a garden room and they were dancing. Hal dragged her there, putting his arms around her, dancing to Eric Clapton, but the girl with red nails came up again. She grinned at Jane, and tapped Hal on the shoulder. He lifted his head from Jane's hair but before he could speak Jane said, 'Happy New Year, and good night.'

The girl melted into the crowd, Jane laid her head back on his shoulder. It was shaking. She lifted up her head and stared up at him. He was laughing silently. She grinned, 'A girl's got to learn to take a hint.' He kissed her, full on the mouth. 'You're wonderful, Jane Essex,' he shouted.

Yes, she was Jane Essex tonight.

At ten a buffet was served and the young people mingled with the parents. Hal and Jane found Annette and Roderick and took their plates into the conservatory, finding a table, eating caviar, sausages on sticks, smoked salmon, anything and everything. Roderick said, wiping his mouth, 'Good old Sonny, he's a splendid trencherman. None of this newfangled rice and pasta.'

Annette said dryly, 'Just lots of coronaries.'

A middle-aged couple joined them, drawing up chairs, and talking to Annette and Hal. Jane passed mineral water to Roderick. He topped up his glass, but poured white wine for her. She said, 'I saw some diaries in the study while I was phoning home. They looked interesting.'

Roderick sipped his mineral water. 'One day I must show them to you, but they're a bit like those Greek tragedies that Dolly Williams has been going on about ever since you put her right at the party. Too damn sad, though whether they're using Iambic trimeter, I couldn't tell you. Poor Irene. Tricked out of her home, and never to know real happiness again.' He stared into his glass, then up at her. 'You know, you have a look of her about you. She had grey eyes but her hair was red, a glorious red.'

She said, 'After all these years I've never seen a picture of her.'

'Years?'

She said quickly, 'Months. I meant months, just seems like years slogging away at Wendham.' She grimaced, hardly daring to look at Roderick. Had she recovered the situation?

Roderick Travers smiled, 'It's meant a great deal to Hal to have you there. He loves that place, and I just wish I wasn't so financially strapped. I can't bear to think that he won't make a go of it. Can't bear to think of it leaving the family, of letting old Harry down, and Irene. Can't bear to think of letting it go to rack and ruin either though.' His face was sad and suddenly old, confused.

The man who had joined them leaned forward, and now Jane realized that those at the table were listening to the conversation. 'Perhaps it's time to let the business go instead?'

Roderick shook his head. 'I've thought of that, Stanley, but it'd be selfish. We employ so many and employee loyalty is always something we've considered important. If we handed them over we'd be repaying our people very badly. No, we've got to get the backer. Got to make Wendham self-sufficient. It's the only way.'

Jane didn't want to hear this. She didn't want to know how much Hal loved it, how much thought Roderick had put into it. How he could not betray his workers. She doubted if her father knew any of his employees by name. She clung to the fact that her father had checked out the fire. That he was right. That murder had never been proved, though the Travers had not hesitated to hurl the accusation. That Irene had left her son. Yes, she mustn't be tricked by the smiles, by the kindness.

Annette was undoing her necklace. It was a locket which she opened and handed it to Jane. 'You do have a look of her, but I think it's because you are both of a

445

similar age,' she said softly, no suspicion whatever in her voice. The locket was silver and light in Jane's hands as she looked at the delicate woman with pale skin, grey eyes and red hair.

Jane said, as Hal craned over her shoulder, 'My mother's grandparents were Irish. Perhaps Irene's were too. Her eyes are much paler than mine.'

She snapped shut the locket and handed it back.

Stanley asked, 'Tricked? What did you mean just now when you said Irene was tricked?'

Roderick shook his head. 'I'm so sorry, I should not have spoken openly of it. I'm afraid I was indiscreet. It concerns a matter best not spoken of. It is not to be bandied about. Bit unfair when the other parties are not here to defend themselves.'

Jane pushed away her plate of food uneaten. She suddenly had no appetite. She rose, 'I'm so sorry, I will have to leave. I have just such a headache. Please, Hal, stay.'

He wouldn't. He brought her back to the apartment, escorted her to her room, made her promise to call if she had need of him. She stood at the window, trying to summon up anger at him for returning with her. If he had not, perhaps she could have seen the diaries, perhaps the journals if she had located the key.

But as she turned back into the room she knew that she would not have looked at them, for suddenly she was doubting the Priors, deep down she was doubting them and how could that be? Trust was on their side. Her father had checked the fire. He said he had. He wouldn't lie. He wouldn't hound a man like Roderick into another heart attack if he wasn't sure. No, of course he wouldn't. Even he wouldn't.

She sank onto the bed. Even *he* wouldn't? For the first time she stopped and really thought about her family, and compared them to the Travers who would not discuss another family's shame, and she shrank from what she thought she saw.

No, she was just tired. No, John Prior was a business-man. No, he wouldn't lie. He wouldn't continue a feud unless he had a reason. Of course he wouldn't, but it was a question, not a statement. And at last she acknowledged where her eyes came from and the discovery only tore her apart even more.

CHAPTER TWENTY-THREE

Jane worked hard during the first week of the new term for she couldn't rid herself of the image of the diary, the journals, the discretion of the Travers, the shape of Hal's face, the sound of his voice, and her foolish doubt about her father, about the Priors. And she couldn't stop looking in the mirror.

She had returned to Brighton immediately after New Year, not to Wendham, saying to Hal that she was too busy, not asking the backers' names either. Not phoning her father. She had just worked hard and long in her university room and it gave her some respite.

It wasn't until the end of the week that she agreed to join Terry at the pub, and Sylvie too. The air was thick with smoke, and all around were young people with eager eyes, fast talk and their bursts of laughter, outbreaks of sarcasm, heated discussions were good, and normal, a relief. But somehow, even here, Wendham kept breaking through in wisps of bonfire smoke, of camomile, that scent which she loved, which she had felt she remembered. Somehow Hal was here in that boy's cheek-bones, in that one's hazel eyes. In that one's laugh.

She drank her beer, half listening to her friends, half examining her nails which for once were clear of the residue of earth.

'You disappearing off this weekend, as usual?' Terry asked, flicking the beer mat on the edge of the table.

She shook her head, brushing back her hair, 'No.'

'Why's that then?'

'Just want a break.' She shrugged. Yes, she wanted a break, wanted to think, wanted to recapture the hunger to succeed, to be free of this dull ache within her.

'What d'you do there, at this place? Are they relatives?'

'Sort of,' she replied. 'I'm just helping to do it up.'

Terry flipped the mat in the air and caught it. 'Maybe we should come and help, get a carload together?'

No, she didn't want that. She didn't want questions, didn't want exposure. She didn't want intruders in her world. She didn't know what she wanted. She said, 'No need. They're private people, keep to themselves.'

'Well, why aren't you going this weekend then? It's not as though you need a break – you had one over Christmas?'

She drank her beer, 'Give it a rest, will you.'

Terry raised his eyebrows at Sylvie, who grimaced then leaned back in her chair, 'So how's the course, Terry?'

'Not bad. Not good. The law is the law you know. Property is property. Just be glad you're born now, you two, whilst we men grieve that we were.'

Sylvie said, 'What are you going on about?'

Terry balanced the beer mat on his finger. 'Well, we know that Jane is restoring a house back to its 1850 state. Back then, when women married the husband took over the lot.'

The mat slid from his finger, into a pool of beer. He rescued it, waving it about, a few drops of beer fell to the table. Jane reached across and gripped his arm. 'What would happen if a woman died and bequeathed her house and land to her lover?'

Terry covered her hand with his. 'Ooh, I didn't know you cared.'

'Come on, Terry, what would happen?' Her voice was urgent.

He said, 'Well, it couldn't happen, because – as I've

just more or less said – common law laid down the unity of husband and wife, with the convenient result that the husband acquired all his wife's property on marriage, and in effect her rights to the land. Quite right too. Ouch!'

Sylvie had slapped him.

He grinned, rubbed his head. 'OK, it's tough I know, but really the fairer sex didn't have a leg to stand on. I say "management" because there wasn't land ownership as we now know it. Back then it was still quite feudal. One dealt in rights to the land, because practically all land was owned by the crown, and bestowed, or leased, on down to the lowliest tenant farmer. But to answer your question – it was only after 1882 that she had the right to bequeath *anything*, before that a wife couldn't make a valid will unless her husband joined her in the action. He'd hardly be likely to agree to the lover inheriting. No, it was bound to go to the legitimate heir. You know, land and its ownership is very—'

'Never mind all that theory, stick to the point, can't you? You're saying definitely that a wife could not have left her property and land rights to her lover in 1880?'

'Pretty sure.'

She sat back, a great disappointment wrenching at her, a great looming ache. She rose slowly, knowing what she had to do. 'I've got to go,' she whispered, knocking over her drink but not noticing.

She left, walked to the phone box, clinked in money, dialling. 'Hal,' she asked. 'Any news of the backers?'

'I'm so glad to hear you,' he said quietly. 'I'm just so glad. I was worried, thought I'd done something to upset you. I wanted to come and see you, but thought no – don't push it.'

'Any news of the backers?' she repeated, ignoring his voice, the echoes it evoked.

'Still just those initial two.'

'Who are they?'

450

'I'll tell you when you get here. You are coming aren't you?' he repeated.

'Who are they?' she shouted, suddenly alight with rage, with a great dark agonizing rage.

There was silence. Then he said, 'Why do you want to know?'

'Because I care,' she said quietly, holding the receiver so tightly that her arm ached. But then the money ran out. The phone burred. She replaced the receiver and stared at her reflection in the glass, not noticing her eyes, just hating him, hating Roderick and his even, reasonable voice talking to her of Prior tricks, making her doubt her family, making her love them, wooing her whilst all the time her father had been right. It *was* the Travers who had tricked the Priors out of their inheritance, out of Wendham. It was the Travers who had ruined the Priors' lives, were still ruining them behind their smiles, making her reject them – almost.

For Irene had died in 1880. She couldn't bequeath anything. Damn them, damn Terry for telling her, damn her for asking, and the pain was far worse than anything she'd ever known. Damn Hal. Damn him. 'I almost believed in you,' she whispered, and now knew what her mother meant about a big black hole.

She rang her father collect the next morning, after a sleepless night. 'Father, I'm getting the names of the backers on the shortlist tomorrow.' Her voice was a monotone.

'Great.'

'Father, before you go, they really do have no right to Wendham. Irene died before 1882.'

'D'you think I don't know that? Course they have no right, that's what all this is about.'

She ran her fingers through her hair. 'No, I mean we could take it to law. Let's just bring a case. It'd be quicker, easier, less messy. Just the threat of it would cave them in. Let's not have any more to do with them direct.'

There was a silence. She could hear him breathing. He said, 'We'll do it this way. It's safer, more in our control. Get the names.'

She protested, 'But Father . . .'

'Do as I damn well say. This ain't going to law, you got that. It'd cost a fortune, and I haven't got a fortune. The Travers have seen to that. Now go to it, Janey.'

Again the phone burred.

She rubbed her forehead with the receiver. 'It would be better,' she repeated into the burr, 'if we didn't have to see any of them again.'

She drove down the next morning, her eyes sore and tired, a headache brewing but her father was right – the Travers had seen to it that they had no fortune. Just remember that. Remember it all. She swept into the drive, drove straight past the gatehouse on up to the house, drawing up in front of the porticoed door, jamming on the brakes. Gravel shot from beneath the tyres. She got out, stepped back and gazed at the house, hanging on to the image.

Hal came round from the terrace, hurrying towards her, his hair dishevelled and even longer.

'I hoped you'd come. God, I've missed you.' His face was drawn and tired, but she didn't want to look at him, wouldn't look at him.

She let him take her in his arms. She let him kiss her, and hold her, but then she said, 'I can't stay.' She stepped back, knowing she had to make herself meet his eyes, knowing she had to smile. She did so. 'I'll have to be back by tonight. I've just so much work.'

She ducked into the car, dragged out her rucksack, hauling it up on her shoulder. He reached out to take it, his hands brushed hers. She snapped, 'No, I can manage.'

His face closed, he walked ahead of her. 'I'm laying the last of the hamstone today.' She could hear the hurt

452

in his voice but ignored it, summoning up instead all the knowledge she now had, all the pain.

'I'll work in the kitchen then,' she said to his retreating back.

He looked at her and smiled. It didn't hide his hurt. 'You see, Hal, I'd prefer to do something lighter today. I'm tired.' Her voice was soft, soothing, but it was only because she had to get the name of the backers. Yes, that was why.

He brought wood into Wendham's kitchen and started the range and she wouldn't look at the way his hair curled over his collar, wouldn't look at the lines which dug deep to either side of his mouth, or the dark patches beneath his eyes, or the tiredness which dragged at his shoulders. He was a Travers, a cheat. He had made her doubt her heritage. He had no right to be here, just as none of them had a right.

He leaned back against the range, looking at her working on the copper pans at the table. In some lights her hair had the same gleam. He said, 'I've missed you.'

She said, laying down the soft rag, pushing aside the copper kettle, 'Tell me what trick Jack Prior used. Tell me.' It was a demand.

'Why?' he ran his hand through his hair.

She said, her voice quiet, 'Because I want to know. I'm good enough to work here, but not good enough to know the story behind it. It's kind of like I'm an outsider and you and your family are putting up walls against all comers. As though I'm nobody, and you're lords of the damn manor.'

He stared at her, and now he shouted, 'Oh come on, that's ridiculous. For God's sake—' Then he stopped, saw her recoil, took control of himself and said gently, 'Look, I'm sorry, really sorry if we hurt you. We weren't trying to keep you out.'

Shut up. Shut up. Don't say sorry. Don't be so nice. Shout again. Don't lie. Why does everyone lie, you, me, everyone? She picked up the cloth and picked at an edge.

Hal cleared his throat. 'It's just that there's some things we feel shouldn't be bandied about, something that can hurt others. They may be our enemies but that doesn't mean we make public accusations.'

Only those that drag the Priors down the social register, she wanted to shout but said nothing, she just waited.

He dug his hands into his jeans. 'OK. Jack Prior married Irene Wendham. Her godfather and Martha, her nanny, knew he was a liar and a cheat. The profits from the whaling trip were suspect, and the "lay", the wages for the crew, were suspect. His treatment of the men was, to say the least, brutal. Nonetheless she married him. They leased the house to Barratt for what she thought would be four years. She concurred and signed. It was, in fact, for twenty-one years. He proceeded to take everything of hers, plus her dignity and her love, for she did love him. He threw it back in her face. He corrupted her son. He killed her.'

She looked around the great room, her outrage at this myth they had created as violent as the flames that were roaring in the range. She put her hands on her lap, clenched them, said calmly, 'It doesn't make sense. This paragon of virtue died, and Travers inherited this. But that wasn't possible. It wasn't hers to bequeath.'

Hal closed the vent on the range, and moved to sit opposite her, tracing his finger down the grain of the table. Up and down, up and down. 'Harry and Irene made it possible,' he said at last. 'Shortly before 1880 Harry came back to England to serve his time – for he was an escaped convict. Before he did so he had arranged for investigators to trace the lawyer who had brought the lease for Irene to sign all those years before. They found him. He confirmed in writing that she was drunk, unable to read, her signature is a mere scribble. He confirmed his conversations with Jack

Prior and Jack's clear intention to mislead his wife. Harry obtained Barratt's copy of the document. He also obtained a report written by Irene's godfather which laid down in black and white the warning he had given Irene at the boarding house. Harry persuaded Barratt to pass into his keeping all Irene's correspondence to him over the relinquishing of the lease. It makes heartbreaking reading.' He rubbed the back of his neck, staring at the ceiling.

He continued, 'He also set in train an investigation into the death of Jack Prior's mother, and the disappearance of a man called Palance.'

Jane looked at the cloth in her hand, not at him.

He continued, 'When Irene was murdered—'

She interrupted, 'How?'

'In the Wandle Court brownstone, by a lance thrown by Jack, a lance which sliced through her skull, coming to rest in the wall, staining the pale-green flock wallpaper.'

'Such detail?' she murmured. 'How?'

'Sinclair was there just afterwards.'

'Afterwards? So he didn't see it.'

'He saw the lance, and her body.' Hal pushed his chair back, ran his hands through his hair. 'Harry and Irene had spoken of the undeniable legality of Jack's right to Wendham by dint of outliving her. She couldn't bear the thought of Jack Prior in her Somerset world.'

'Even though it would deny her son his birthright?'

'She felt certain Jack would destroy Wendham, and leave the village and the tenants to rot. She had crossed him you see, so there would *be* no birthright. When Jack first came over he was seen off. Then he tried to burn the place. Harry and he had a secret meeting where two lawyers were present. Harry showed him the accumulated evidence of his "misdeeds", shall we say, for reports were coming in that Palance, who was supposed to have taken passage on a ship, wasn't listed on any. He had just disappeared, taking no possessions.

There was no money taken from his bank, no message was ever sent to his wife or mistress, or to his office.'

'He could have found another floozy. Men do, you know.'

'Yes, he could have. But he disappeared on the day Jack Prior called, just as Jack Prior's mother disappeared on the day her son found her.' Hal held up his hand. 'Let me go on. Harry told Jack he was perfectly prepared to take the dispute to law, when all the Prior grievances could be aired. Jack Prior knew that if that happened all his machinations, his cruelty, his further misdeeds, or should we say murders, might become public. The Priors would be totally ruined, both in England and, more importantly, in New York, rather than merely damaged by rumour, as they were. A rumour that was started not by the Travers but by Esther Moran, Irene's friend, and a Mrs Norden.'

'There was no proof that he murdered Palance and his mother.'

'No, but maybe some could have been found. Either way, he backed off and agreed before a lawyer to confirm Travers's right to Wendham. So Harry had, he thought, saved Wendham, and Irene would be at peace.

'But Jack set up a trust that would ensure that one day Wendham would be bought back, and those Irene loved, living in the place she loved, were never again able to feel safe from the threat of eviction, never safe from the Priors. Jack Prior was into the business of destruction, Jane, nothing more, nothing less.'

She stared at him and saw Harry Travers's portrait. This self-satisfied man was a replica of the originator of all this nonsense and as quick and silver-tongued. For the one fact in all this was that there was no green flock wallpaper in the Wandle Court hallway, there was instead some of the oldest panelling in New York.

She sat staring at the table. She'd wanted proof she now realized. Proof that Hal was in the right. There was none.

'Who are the backers?' she asked gently, feeling nothing, just operating as her father would have wished. 'The backers that are going to make Wendham House safe for you all?'

'Bertrams,' he said. 'We sign the contract next week.'

She left for Brighton early, on the pretext of black ice. Hal watched the tail lights of her car grow smaller and smaller. He wanted to run after her, call her back, hold her, for something had died in her today. It was the love he had thought he saw blooming through the uncertainty that had appeared over Christmas.

She rang her father the moment she returned and, over his whoop of triumph, she said, still feeling nothing, 'We will renovate Wendham House, won't we? It's so beautiful, it deserves to be lived in properly.'

'You can have any damn thing you want.'

'Just the house,' she said. Then, 'What will you do?'

'I'll offer Bertrams a much bigger project in the States, and the carrot of many more, with conditions. I'll do the same for the other main backer.'

'What projects?'

'I'll find some. Money's no object now, for this'll finally break open the Wendham trust and there's eighty million in it. Couldn't even draw on the interest, you see. It's all been ploughed back into the trust.

She replaced the phone, his pleasure echoing in her head, but her footsteps were heavy as she walked into the hall and climbed the stairs and once in her room she pulled out her plans for Wendham, then thrust them aside. She pulled out her notes on the progress she and Hal had made but couldn't bear to read them, looked at the photographs and put them down. She went to the window and gazed out on the buildings opposite, then she pulled an almost empty bottle of white rum out of her cupboard, filled a glass and gulped it down. Nothing. There was nothing inside her.

She hurled the glass at the wall. It smashed. Dribbles

of rum dampened the plaster. 'You deserved it, Hal. All of you deserved it,' she croaked, for she was crying as though she'd never stop, but still she felt nothing.

At the end of the week, one of the girls in Jane's house answered the phone in the lobby. 'No, no-one of that name here.' She paused, then said, 'OK, I'll try.'

She called up the stairs. 'Any Jane Essex here?'

Jane came from her room, clattering hurriedly down the stairs. 'I'll take it.'

The girl, Sally Wentworth, looked at her strangely.

Jane waited until she'd gone to her room, then said, 'Jane here.' It had to be Hal, only he would call her Essex.

'It's me,' he said, his voice little more than a whisper.

'I told you not to phone unless it was an emergency.' Her voice was calm, a monotone.

'It is an emergency. Bertrams have withdrawn. It is an emergency. The others aren't interested.' She could tell that he was crying. She felt nothing. 'I've got exams. I can't come.'

He said, 'I need you. I love you.'

'I'm busy,' she whispered, and replaced the receiver. She returned to her room and opened the new bottle of rum, sat on the bed and drank, and drank until she couldn't hear him in her head any more.

The next morning her head throbbed, she felt sick and Hal was in her head, his face, his voice, and so was the click of the phone. She drank again the next evening, and the next, but still he was there. When she slept she dreamed of walking down the Wendham path, and he was waiting at the end, or leaning on the range, or sanding the glasshouse. He was there, always he was there.

At the end of the week the phone rang for her at midday. Sylvie took it, expecting Terry. She called instead, 'Jane, for you.'

She sat at her desk and didn't move. 'Tell him I'm

458

out, gone back to America, whatever goddamn thing comes to mind.'

'Jane, it's your father.'

She walked to the door, and down the stairs, taking the phone. 'Hi,' she said, that was all. Her voice flat.

He said, 'Sorry, pick another prize. Can't oblige with Wendham House. Now our offer's been accepted on the house – which I've made through a subsidiary company of course – the second clause of the trust has been revealed. The residue of the trust money is only transferable on the destruction of the house. Goddamn it, we'll have to get contractors in to do it, but now we can sell it as a prime sight.'

She took a taxi to the seafront, walking down the steps onto the beach, leaving her coat undone, letting the freezing wind slice into her, hearing the crunch of the pebbles, hearing the crunch of the gravel, hearing Hal, hearing Roderick. She put her hands to her ears, shaking her head. But no, they were still there.

She walked down to the water, watching the foam of the surf, hearing the gulls, the waves, the gravel, Hal's voice. Seeing the scorch marks. But they'd been dated much later. Hearing Hal's voice.

She stared up at the grey sky, the low clouds. Destruction. Destruction. All this time, all this effort on destruction. The Priors were bent on destruction. Had they always been? Was it all true? Oh God.

The gulls were crying, swooping, the surf was sweeping in, dragging the stones, clattering and tumbling back into the depths.

Who were the Priors? Who was she? What was she? What kind of a person had she become? She felt as though it was her the surf was drawing back into the sea, that she was drowning, gasping for breath. 'Who am I? What the hell am I?' she whispered.

*   *   *

That evening she called her grandmother at Wandle Court from the phone booth, not the house, using the phone cards she had bought. 'Darling,' her grandmother said, 'how wonderful. Your mother isn't back from Hawaii yet, I'm afraid. Another therapeutic visit, but she really is sticking to the straight and narrow. No martinis whatsoever.'

Jane said, 'Grandma, when was the panelling put into the hall?'

Her grandmother paused. 'Janey doll, what a strange question. Talking of martinis . . .'

'Just listen, Grandmother. When was the panelling put up in your hall?'

'Well, I can't rightly say. I'd have to find out, somehow.'

'OK, I'll ring you, or you can ring the house.'

Her grandmother said, 'I'll ring the house the moment I know. Janey, are you OK?'

'Probably,' Jane said.

She used one of her remaining phone cards to call Hal at the gatehouse. An answering machine clocked in. She heard his voice, distant, rehearsed. Him, but not him. After the tone she said, 'It's me. I gave my father your backer's name. My father is John Prior. I am Jane Prior. Forgive me. They're going to destroy the house. Don't finalize the sale.'

She then used the remaining cards to contact the private investigators her mother used to track John Prior's women. She instructed them to view the death certificate of Irene Wendham, and then trace the doctor's family.

That night she didn't sleep, she didn't drink, she didn't read. Instead she planned.

She took the train to London in the morning, looked up the address of Bertrams. She wore a short straight black skirt, smart green jacket, black tights and heels. She asked to see the director handling the Prior account.

'Who may I say is asking?' the receptionist asked.

'Jane Prior.'

The director's secretary took her up in the elevator to a thickly carpeted floor. She was ushered into a spacious office with glass and chrome furniture. The desk was huge, and behind it sat a grey-haired man who came to meet her, his dark-grey suit immaculately pressed.

The secretary brought coffee while they sat either side of his desk and discussed the coldness of early February, the pier at Brighton, the attractiveness of The Lanes.

The secretary left. The man stirred his coffee, looking at Jane. 'But I'm sure you've not come to discuss the weather. Perhaps you are here on your father's behalf?'

'On behalf of his actions,' Jane said. She replaced her cup and saucer on his desk.

The man sank back in his black leather swivel chair, his eyes wary.

She said, 'You should not be seduced by his promises. Instead you should back the Wendham House theme park, not the Prior schemes. Please, it's important.'

He stirred, steepled his hands. The swivel chair rocked. Behind him the venetian blinds glistened. His eyes were cold, remote now, fixed on her face, not the console he was reaching for. He pressed a button, his eyes still on hers, his voice like ice as he said, 'Show Miss Prior out. Our meeting is concluded. Call my car. I'm already late for my next meeting.' He stood, walked to the door. 'It's been interesting, Miss Prior. I shall inform your father of our meeting. I'm sure that he, too, will be interested.'

In the gatehouse Hal stared at the canvas on the easel. The smell of oil paint was thick in the room. He put down his brush. It was finished. Jane Prior stared out

461

at him, her jeans grubby from digging, his scarf around her neck just as she had worn it, her hand on a pile of books, the window behind. Her eyes were blank, her smile glacial.

He picked up the kitchen knife which lay on the palette, weighed it in his hand, then dug the point into the canvas, ripping from corner to corner, then again, and again. He let the knife fall to the carpet, then sat before the stove as he had sat every night since she had said with such finality, 'I'm busy.'

CHAPTER TWENTY-FOUR

Her father phoned her the next day. 'What the hell are you playing at going to Bertrams?' he roared.

She said, 'You can't destroy it. It's too beautiful.'

He said, 'So's money. Don't be so goddamn weak.'

She replaced the receiver, cutting him off. She didn't care, not any more. He rang again immediately. She said, 'I've work to do. I need to think. You get on with your life. I'll get on with mine.'

'Jane. When you've goddamn stopped sulking you get back on this phone and apologize, and no more meddling. No more visits to Bertrams.'

'There won't be.' And no more Janey, ever. She knew that now. Fool that she'd been.

Again she replaced the receiver, and returned to her room. She sat at her desk and slowly tore up the sketches she had made of Irene Wendham's house, reached down and took out the notebook and tore up the pages she had written, and which Hal had read. No, she wouldn't approach Bertrams again. There was no point.

The next day her grandmother rang at seven a.m. Sylvie groaned, as she called up the stairs, 'Get 'em to phone later. I was asleep.'

Jane picked up the receiver which Sylvie had left dangling. Her grandmother said, 'About the panelling. I had my friend upstairs take a look, you know, the interior designer. He said it could have been put up in the 1880s, but checked in case there was anything about it in his notes on brownstones. He uses the history of the brownstones for some of his lectures, you see.'

'Grandma, please.' Jane made no attempt to keep the urgency from her voice.

'OK, doll. Seems he couldn't date it properly, and couldn't find anything else on it. But, he said it's always struck him as strange that it was put up in the hall and not in the dining room or up the stairs. He wondered if it was used to hide damp, or something.'

Irene said quickly, 'Thank you, Grandma. Don't tell anyone I'm asking these questions. Does your friend know it was me?'

'No. And I won't, but why?'

'Soon, I'll tell you soon.'

She put her hand on the phone rest. At Wendham she too had thought it strange that the Wandle Court dining room had no panelling. Was there damp – or was it something else? She phoned Hal at the gatehouse and reached the answering machine.

She booked a car for the day, ordered a cab, made a flask of tea, picked up her gardening gloves, stuffed them into her rucksack together with a change of clothes. There was a hammering on the house door. Sylvie opened it and called, 'Now it's a damned taxi. Can't a girl get any sleep around here?'

Jane pounded down the stairs and out to the cab. She collected the car and drove, slowing only for the built-up areas, welcoming the wide spaces of the Somerset countryside, and suddenly Hal's voice was in her head and she was crying, pain was clenching. She put her foot down, faster, faster. She turned off the A303, almost losing the car on the bend. She slowed, dragged her arm across her eyes. Breathed deeply, but the tears still came.

On into Wendham, skidding to a halt before the closed gates. A huge chain locked them shut. She screeched to a stop, jumped from the car. 'Hal,' she called. There were lights on in the gatehouse and smoke from the chimney. She shook the gates, the chain rattled, 'Hal.'

Nothing. She ran off down the road, searching the hedge for the gap. It was all boarded up. She tried to push the saplings back. They'd been wedged too firmly. She ran back to the gate, shook it again, crying out, 'Hal Travers. I won't move until you come, d'you hear me? I won't move, I tell you.'

She rested her forehead on the cold metal, then heard him say from the corner of the gatehouse, 'You've told me enough, I think.'

He was so pale, even thinner, even more drawn. She was crying again, 'Let me in. Let me talk to you. Did you get my message? He's going to destroy Wendham, your house, and I don't know what to do.'

'You've done enough.' He turned from her, starting back to the house.

'Hal,' she screamed, shaking the gate.

He turned. 'I won't let you in. You will not step one foot onto Irene Wendham's property until it is owned by you, do you hear?' Rage and torment were in his face and voice.

'He's going to destroy it,' she almost whispered.

He smiled bleakly. 'He can't destroy it. There's a conservation order on it.'

'That won't stop him. Guard it, don't sell it to him. Do anything.'

He still smiled that smile as he shrugged. 'My father won't renege on his word. He's said he'll sell it to the firm we now know to be Jack Prior's, father of Jane Prior, so he will. His word is his bond, you see. In a way I admire him for it. You know where you are with honourable people.'

She brushed aside his contempt, running along her side of the gate, getting as close to him as possible, clutching the bars. 'I tell you, a conservation order won't stop the Priors. They'll buy it, and then they'll fire it. You must guard it.'

He just stared at her, then turned on his heel and walked to the door of the gatehouse.

She called 'I love you, Hal. I just didn't know I did.'

He didn't even slow in his stride as he entered and shut the door behind him.

She drove to Yeovil, rushed into Bath Travel, booked a flight from Heathrow to New York, then drove straight on to Heathrow.

She took a cab to Greenwich Village, not really noticing the roar of New York, the towering blocks, the slicing shadows, the chaos, making a stop along the way. She pulled the bell. Her grandmother opened the door. 'Janey, doll.' Her arms were round Jane, pulling her in. Her earrings were jangling, her gold and silver chains glinting. 'Janey, doll. What the hell is going on? Your father's raging like a bull, you're making strange phone calls.'

Jane wanted to stay in the comfort of her arms for ever but there was no time. She had called her father from the airport, and she needed to hurry. She said to her grandmother, 'I've got to do this. I've got to do it now, before I get frightened, before I start to think.'

She was offloading her rucksack, squatting on the floor as she undid the buckles, peering up at her grandmother through her hair which had fallen over her face. 'It'll repair. I know it will.'

The door was still open, the cold of the New York winter blasted in.

Her grandmother looked puzzled. 'What will repair, Janey?'

Jane pulled out the jemmy she had bought at the hardware store.

'Janey?' Her grandmother looked incredulous.

'Please, Grandma. I need to know if he murdered her.'

Her grandmother shook her head, not understanding. Jane took hold of her hand. 'I need to know, and I need Father to know, so I have to take the panelling off. There was pale-green flock paper when he threw the lance and killed her. Sinclair said. I have to know if it's true.'

Her grandmother's skin was smooth and dry. Her rings dug into the palm of Jane's hand as the gnarled fingers squeezed hers. 'It's Wendham House?' Sarah Prior asked, her face suddenly still, a dawning realization in her eyes. She put her hand to her throat, suddenly looking old. 'I don't think I want to know what's behind the panelling do I, but I must, mustn't I?' Her voice was tremulous.

Jane nodded. 'We all must. Father's coming. I phoned from the airport. I didn't say why. I just said to come. He needs to see, but I don't want him to stop me.'

Her grandmother stepped back, her voice brisk, determined, 'Go to it. I'll leave you to tell me the whole of it when this is over.'

Jane looked up at the stairs. Hal said Prior had been there when he'd thrown the lance. She guessed the angle, and stuck the jemmy into the top of the panelling nearest the door, facing the stairs. She used her weight to lever the first panel free. There was a ripping sound, it splintered. She used the jemmy on it again and there was a crash as it hit the tiled floor. The wall was smooth behind. She jemmied off the next, and the next, and then the last facing the stairs. They were all smooth. There was no flock wallpaper, no stain. She was shaking as she dropped the jemmy.

She turned to her grandmother, her hands spread wide in her despair. She wailed 'I don't know what to believe. I don't know what the truth is.'

Her grandmother was looking at the wall from the dining-room doorway. 'A lance you say? Come here, Janey.' She pointed to the wall. 'See the way the light strikes that.'

Jane squinted and there was an indentation low down on the wall where the panelling had been. They hurried across and ran their hands over it, then over the rest of the wall. 'And look,' the grandmother said. At the bottom, near the skirting boards there was a tiny remnant of pale-green flock wallpaper.

They heard the slam of a car door, then feet pounding up the stoop. The door swung back. Her father and Rich burst in, their coats open. They saw the panelling all over the floor, saw the jemmy.

'What the hell?' her father roared.

Standing with her grandmother beside her, she told him of the lance, she showed him the indentation. 'You need treatment,' he snarled. 'You put a plane fare on my charge card, order me to be here, then rip my mother's house apart. Goddamn, you're as brainless as your mother.'

Jane shook her head, 'Mother isn't brainless. She's been scrambled by you. Well, I've used her detectives, the ones that keep tabs on you and your women, to trace the family of the doctor who signed the death certificate. I've taken off the panelling because Jack Prior's lance was hurled through Irene Prior's head, to hit the wall here.' She fingered the indentation. 'I'm going to get someone to analyse this, to prove it to you. It's all got to stop. All of it.'

'You'll be in a home first.' Her father was close, looming over her. 'It's a lie, the murder is a lie.'

She didn't back away from him, she just stared up into his face. 'You're sure of that? You're sure that this Jack Prior, the one who didn't dare to take back Wendham legally, the one who set up a legacy geared for destruction, is an honourable and just man? Are you a just man, Father? Is there really an analysis of the fire at Wendham?'

He flushed.

She could see the answer in his eyes. 'It's us who need therapy, Father. It's the Priors.'

By the time the analysis report came through Jane was back in England. Her grandmother sent it to her. The tests had proved positive. There were traces of blood,

468

deep gouges into the brickwork. She sent a copy to her father, telling him that if the Wendham House sale proceeded she would reveal the contents of the report. If, on withdrawal of the Priors from the house sale, Wendham House was subsequently destroyed by fire or any other means, she would then publicize the report. If the schemes that he was putting together with Bertrams went ahead, the same would happen.

He rang, screaming and shouting, asking her how she thought he could afford to go through with Bertrams without the trust money anyway, and ended by roaring, 'You've set us up, left us exposed because there's a son, isn't there, and he'll have us. You just wait, he'll have us. Well, you're out of my life, d'you hear? Right out of it.'

She'd asked the question that wouldn't leave her alone, 'Did you know, Father? Did you know all along, just as you knew why a court case was out of the question, just as you knew there'd been no carbon dating, did—' But he hung up long before she'd finished the question, and she knew it was one that would never be answered.

The private detectives had found nothing on the doctor's family, but it didn't matter any more. None of the Prior–Travers feud mattered to her. It was all over. But at the start of May she had realized that it wasn't quite all over. Mr Roderick Travers should see the report. She sent it to him. There was an impersonal letter of acknowledgement, that was all.

All through May she worked long into the night because it kept Hal's voice from her mind, his eyes, his hands, his laugh. She also studied because for the first time it mattered that her results should be good. In August she would begin her final year at Columbia, paid for by Sarah Prior and by what work she could get herself, and there she would also study hard, because now she was on her own, except for her grandmother.

For her mother had returned to John, refusing to speak to Jane, for Jane had told him of the private detectives.

By the beginning of June the grief and the shock were more subdued. She could eat, sleep a little, even think effectively, without the panic of despair, without the panic of knowing that she was a Prior, and not safe to be around decent people.

It was only in fleeting dreams that she saw Wendham House, smelt the mists, the camomile, saw the flowers of spring, the flower beds they had planned and which she would never see. In every dream Hal stood, waiting for her at the end of the path. Was his future safe? She had no way of knowing, no right to that information.

She took the exams, and drank champagne with Terry and Sylvie on the beach, lying back on a towel, feeling the sun on her face, the pebbles beneath her, listening to her friends make their plans, listening to Terry mooning over the girl he had met last night, trying to give him the courage to ring her. 'But she's so important,' he whined. 'If you know what I mean.'

Jane knew what he meant.

'OK, so what about you?' Sylvie asked lying face down, her head turned to Jane, her voice muffled because of her posture.

'I'll get a life,' she said, and there was calmness in her now. 'Yes, I'll get a life. I'll find a job. I'm going to become a journalist.'

'What about a man in your life?'

'No, no men.' She was a Prior, she wasn't safe.

They took the train back, carrying their towels, their hands still sticky from the sea, their faces stinging from the sun. They left Terry by the phone, fumbling with the change they had heaped into his hand, calling, 'Go on, ring her. You can't say you will and then wimp out.'

Sylvie put her arm round Jane. 'You'll let me paint you before you fly out. You must.'

A voice from the landing above said, 'I tried that once.'

Jane stared. Sylvie left her without a word. She began to climb the stairs. Hal. Oh Hal. He was tanned, filled out, less drawn. He stared at her, his eyes cold, empty.

Jane unlocked her door, passing too close to him. He carried a parcel under his arm. She entered, he followed.

'I don't want to see you,' she said, going to the window, staring out. 'Go away.'

He thumped the parcel on the table. 'Not until you've read these. I want you to read about love. I want you to know what has made you and I the people we are. I want you to understand your past, and let go of it.'

She watched Terry come out, and cross the car-park, watched the foliage on the trees quiver in the breeze, the clouds float by behind them. 'I have let go,' she said. 'Be happy that the Priors are out of your life. But please, just tell me before you leave – are Bertrams backing the theme park?'

'I'm not leaving until you've read them, and I am telling you nothing until you read them.'

She turned. He was leaning against the door, his hands behind him. He didn't smile. Neither did she. She touched the parcel, sat down on the chair, unwrapped the brown paper. Inside were Irene's journals, and Harry's diary.

She read all afternoon. He poured her coffee – black – from the flask he had brought. She didn't lift her head, just sipped from the plastic mug and fought with the sea, wept as Irene wept, and even when she did not. She froze with her, toiled with her, ached with her, sewed with her, despaired for her when she wrote her final entry; *Tomorrow I leave for my beloved Harry and Wendham. My heart is breaking for I am not taking my son. I have failed him, and his grandparents, and myself.*

She pushed the journals back, and brought forward Harry's diary, reading of his convict days, his whaling, his love for Irene, his joys, his despairs. She examined Irene's letters to Barratt, the lawyer's disposition, the lease. She folded them carefully, laid them on top of the books, parcelled them back up. Stood up by the window again.

She said, 'I already believed you. I didn't need to see these.'

'Yes you did. To understand yourself.'

Still looking out of the window she said, 'I'm a Prior, what else do I need to understand? I hate well, I use people well. I destroy well.'

He shouted, 'You're a Wendham too. You're part of Irene. You have her eyes, you have her soul. I know you have her soul.'

Jane breathed on the glass, blurring out the world. 'I've been too long a Prior.'

Hal came to the table, picked up the books. 'We have a backer.'

'Good.' He was too close. She turned further from him. He touched her arm and it was as though she had received a blow to the heart.

'You can't leave the country without seeing Wendham again.'

'I can. What's more, I will.'

His hand was still on her arm. 'After all you've put us through, you have no right to go without making some sort of peace.'

She hit his hand away, and cried, 'I've made my peace with you. I've given you back Wendham, haven't I? That should be enough.'

He shouted, 'Well it damn well isn't.'

The route was still so familiar. She felt she could drive it with her eyes shut, but on this journey Hal drove and she kept drinking in the scenery, imprinting it on her mind, for it would have to last a lifetime.

As they drew near to their turn-off point on the A303 she said, 'Will you take over Wendham Holdings?'

He shook his head, his eyes on the road, his hand moving to the indicator stalk, flicking it down, turning off the road towards Wendham. 'Dad had another heart attack.'

Alarm snatched at her. 'Is he . . . ?'

'No, he's not dead, just even more eager to be out of it. He's selling to a large public company who will suck it in as though it had never been, but he has done his best for his people, and given a good package to those who want out now. He's offered the coffee and tea business to the Priors, as recompense for Wendham.' He flashed a look at her, before staring ahead. 'All this has given us time to think and I think we understand now that the Travers do not have an absolute right to Wendham. In the early days we also dealt in trickery.'

'For constructive reasons, for protection. There's a difference,' Jane insisted. Then asked 'Did my father take the tea and coffee?'

Harry laughed as they drove through Wendham. 'Nearly bit our hands off.'

He stopped at the gatehouse, leaned across her to open the door. 'Go on, then.' He nodded up the drive.

There were rhododendrons still in bloom, but the weeds were gone. She walked alone up to the house, round the corner of the glasshouse. Inside were seedlings. She reached out and touched the wooden frame, ran her hand along the glass.

She opened the door, and forced herself to go inside. It smelt of moist peat. The panes had been replaced, the wood was sparkling white. She went on through, out into the sun, and now her hands were clenched into fists because the garden they had planned and talked of was in full bloom.

Perennial geraniums splashed their dark blue and their pink in clumps. Lavender reared from the beds, catnip splayed over the path. Bees were busy, the roses arched high and fragrant. Which villagers had he gathered these cuttings from? She had no right to ask.

She walked along the path, Hal's path. She looked up, but he wasn't at the end, waiting for her. He'd not be waiting for her ever again. He'd brought her here because she hadn't yet done enough to make her peace. He needed to see her suffer. Well, she could understand that.

She turned, gazed at the house, forcing herself to look, bracing herself to cope. She saw Hal come out through the open bow windows onto the terrace. He stood at the top of the steps. 'Come on, come up here and see what you almost destroyed.' His voice was empty, his eyes too.

She did, crossing the lawn, unable to use the path, his path, their path, climbing up the steps to him. He said, 'Follow me.' She did, across the terrace. The camomile and creeping thyme had been tended, controlled, but the scent was just as sweet. Honeysuckle bloomed against the wall. He disappeared through the glass doors of the sitting room.

She stopped. 'No,' she called. 'I can't come in. I can't bear to do that. I'm a Prior, remember.' Her voice was harsh. It broke. 'I can't,' she whispered.

He called from inside. 'Come in, you have to. Then you can get on with the rest of your life.'

She entered, and sunlight shone brightly on the polished floors. Rugs were scattered. The walls and sofa were cream, the drapes and chairs beige, just as she had planned. She stood rooted. Hal leaned against the fireplace above which was an enlarged copy of the miniature of Irene Wendham.

'OK,' she said, her voice breaking, her throat hurting from the repressed tears. 'OK. So I nearly destroyed you. Well, now you've done the same to me, so we're quits. I'm never going to be able to get this place out of my mind, and wherever I go, whatever I do, from now on this room'll be here. That garden'll always be here. You'll always be here.'

'One more thing,' Hal pointed at the wall to her left. She saw another portrait. It was of her, in an overlarge sweater, at the table in the gatehouse, the window behind her. Her hair was brown with a reddish tinge, her eyes slightly darker than Irene's and full of warmth and love, and laughter, as Irene's were. She stared back at him.

Hal said, 'You nearly destroyed Wendham but only nearly. You pulled back and then you did as Irene did. Cast your mind back to the journals. She thought, planned, turned it around. So did you, but at a terrible cost to yourself. I brought you here to see that portrait, to see the woman you really are, the woman I love more than Wendham itself. Just as Irene loved Harry more than Wendham, more than life. And as he loved her.'

He was walking towards her. He stood close, reached for her hands. 'This is the only room I've worked on and from now on the theme park must take priority, for the backers are eager for me to get on. While I've my head stuck in those plans this house will stay as it is, unless I get some help. There'll be the grounds to mow for the fête, the bedrooms for the two point four children.

'I had in mind a Yank with taste, and a face like the girl up there, and a great capacity for love. She'd need to be a Wendham, of course. And she needs to write it up as she goes.'

His arms were gentle as he pulled her to him, his lips tender as he kissed her. 'I love you. I've always loved you,' he murmured. 'I always will, and I won't be without you, not for one day more.'

She clung to him, holding him, never wanting to let him go, for even one second, because at last she was home, at last she felt safe, at last it was over, at last she felt loved. 'I love you, Hal Travers,' she whispered. 'I love you and I'll never leave Wendham again.'

THE END

A DISTANT DREAM
by Margaret Graham

It is 1920 and Caithleen Healy, as beautiful and spirited as her Irish homeland, dreams of fighting back against the Black and Tans, and of avenging her mother's brutal death. Unsure how best to serve Ireland's cause, Caithleen turns to her childhood sweetheart, Mick O'Brian, who shows her the way: she must strike up a friendship with an English Auxiliary and distract him from the work of the Volunteers. But the young soldier Caithleen must betray is a decent man. Ben Williams believes her tender words, and all too soon Caithleen finds herself believing them too.

Determined to escape the Troubles, Ben leaves Ireland and heads for Australia. And soon Caithleen follows him, fleeing her home to help save Mick O'Brian's life. But her hopes for a happy future are shortlived, for both Mick and Ben, each believing himself to have been betrayed by her, abandon Caithleen.

In the dust and heat of the Australian gold mines, Caithleen becomes Kate, turning her back on Ireland and forging a new life for herself. Yet the echoes of past treachery resound still. For as the years go by, and Kate begins to prosper, the figure of Mick O'Brian, as embittered and impulsive as ever, returns to make her pay once more the price of betrayal.

'Margaret Graham has a sure and delicate touch'
Good Housekeeping

A Bantam Paperback
0 553 40818 6

GRAND AFFAIR
by Charlotte Bingham

Unaware of the misery that surrounded her birth, for the first four years of her life all Ottilie Cartaret knows is love. And when her mother, Ma O'Flaherty, moves her family to what she believes will be rural bliss in St Elcombe in Cornwall, their fortunes seem set fair.

Tragedy strikes when Ma dies and young Ottilie soon finds herself in unfamiliar surroundings. Adopted by the Cartarets, the wealthy couple who run the Grand Hotel, she grows up pampered and spoilt, not only by her adoptive parents but by all the visitors – with the exception of their mysterious annual guest, nicknamed 'Blue Lady', with whom Ottilie is unknowingly and inextricably linked.

But as times change, and the regulars to the now-decaying hotel die off, the Cartarets find they are unable to adapt to modern ways. Only Ottilie has the means to save the Grand, even though she may sacrifice too much of herself before learning once again the power of love.

A Bantam Paperback
0 553 50500 9

KITTY AND HER BOYS
by June Francis

Washing the linen, shopping, cooking, swapping stories with the guests . . . the rigours and dramas of life at the Arcadia Hotel in Liverpool's Mount Pleasant leave widow and proprietress Kitty Ryan no time for romance. Except in the shape of the occasional Ginger Rogers and Fred Astaire musical.

Then along comes John 'big fella' Mcleod, bringing with him the joyful sound of wedding bells. As Kitty nears forty, she even dares to hope for one last chance of a baby daughter to join her family of three boys, and to lighten the Depression years.

But in taking a second stab at happiness, Kitty Ryan seems to tempt Providence and finds she has invited unseen complications to the doorstep of the Arcadia. As Hitler grows too big for his boots and 'Peace in our time' becomes an empty refrain, she watches her brood splintering under the strain of living as 'step relations'. And unless she can reunite her menfolk, the future looks set to be that of a family at war in a world at war.

A Bantam Paperback
0 553 50429 0

GONE TOMORROW
by Jane Gurney

Louella Ramsay knows that it is better to have loved and lost than never to have loved at all. And as England recovers from the Great War, she embraces her new role as 'Widow Ramsay', and establishes a successful fashion label to go with it. Yet despite her success Louella holds bitter memories and her pursuit of a twenty-year vendetta provides the fatal link between two very different worlds: a family farm in Hampshire, and a squalid home in Bethnal Green.

At Welcome Farm, nothing has changed since the turn of the century, and oil lamps still light the way to bed. Family life is treasured – until the eighteen-year-old daughter of the household, Harriet Griffin, makes the mistake of swapping a kiss for a secret. At one stroke the past is lost for ever and, with Europe on the brink of new bloodshed, Harriet seems destined to search for happiness far beyond the familiar wheatfields of her idyllic childhood home.

A Bantam Paperback
0 553 40408 3

A SELECTION OF FINE NOVELS
AVAILABLE FROM BANTAM BOOKS

50329 4	**DANGER ZONES**	*Sally Beauman*	£5.99
40727 9	**LOVERS AND LIARS**	*Sally Beauman*	£5.99
40803 8	**SACRED AND PROFANE**	*Marcelle Bernstein*	£5.99
40497 0	**CHANGE OF HEART**	*Charlotte Bingham*	£5.99
40890 9	**DEBUTANTES**	*Charlotte Bingham*	£5.99
50500 9	**GRAND AFFAIR**	*Charlotte Bingham*	£5.99
40496 2	**NANNY**	*Charlotte Bingham*	£5.99
40895 X	**THE NIGHTINGALE SINGS**	*Charlotte Bingham*	£5.99
17635 8	**TO HEAR A NIGHTINGALE**	*Charlotte Bingham*	£5.99
40072 X	**MAGGIE JORDAN**	*Emma Blair*	£4.99
40298 6	**SCARLET RIBBONS**	*Emma Blair*	£4.99
40615 9	**PASSIONATE TIMES**	*Emma Blair*	£4.99
40614 0	**THE DAFFODIL SEA**	*Emma Blair*	£4.99
40373 7	**THE SWEETEST THING**	*Emma Blair*	£4.99
40973 5	**A CRACK IN FOREVER**	*Jeannie Brewer*	£5.99
40996 4	**GOING HOME TO LIVERPOOL**	*June Francis*	£4.99
40820 8	**LILY'S WAR**	*June Francis*	£4.99
50429 0	**KITTY AND HER BOYS**	*June Francis*	£5.99
40818 6	**A DISTANT DREAM**	*Margaret Graham*	£5.99
40408 3	**GONE TOMORROW**	*Jane Gurney*	£5.99
40730 9	**LOVERS**	*Judith Krantz*	£5.99
40731 7	**SPRING COLLECTION**	*Judith Krantz*	£5.99
40947 6	**FOREIGN AFFAIRS**	*Patricia Scanlan*	£4.99
40945 X	**FINISHING TOUCHES**	*Patricia Scanlan*	£5.99
40942 5	**PROMISES, PROMISES**	*Patricia Scanlan*	£5.99
40483 0	**SINS OF THE MOTHER**	*Arabella Seymour*	£4.99